Texting and Teleporting

Volume 1:	Star Surfing
Volume 2:	Aliens and Pirates

By

Steve R. Schaps

June 21, 2019

Texting and Teleporting

Revision 1

Volume 1: Star Surfing

Volume 2: Aliens and Pirates

By Steve R. Schaps

An original science fiction thriller with action, adventure, tragedy, travel, mild romance, and mild humor.

Website: www.SiFiction.com

Copyright © 2015 by Stephen R. Schaps

Library of Congress Control Number: 2016901762

Editor: Ms. Cara Lockwood

Cover by SelfPubBookCovers, Shardel.

"Can you bind the chains of the Pleiades, or loose the cords of Orion?"   Job 38:31

Note music recommendations:* Singer, Song *

Contents:

Acknowledgements:

To Mike, Matt, and Katie.

Preface:

Air travel took the twentieth century by surprise. The Wright Brothers never guessed that their Kitty Hawk would lead to fleets of planes and thousands of concourses on every continent. At the end of the twentieth century, we were all surprised by texting becoming the most common means of communication. I predict that teleporting will be like traveling by air and texting; once developed, it will be everywhere.

In the future, teleporters will allow us to travel to the stars. However, the greatest innovation will be cerebral implants. Cerebral implants will text our thoughts, making cell phones obsolete. Beware the day that aliens and pirates gain control of our teleporters and our cerebral implants.

Prologue:

AD 2248, humans establish a colony sixty-two light years from Earth. This distance encloses one-million cubic light years of space. Earth governments stretch their resources to maintain control of 3,500 star systems with colonies on 1,700 planets and moons.

Volume 1: Star Surfing

Chapter 1: A Star Too Far

* Recommended music: Rush, Tom Sawyer *

Computer hands prepared Flint for duty while he slept. The computer woke him with a gentle shake as it spoke, "Reset the weapons bay alarms. Then return here."

After a long yawn, Flint shrugged, "Whatever," activated the magnetic coils in his boots, and stepped out of his booth and into darkness. Shards of glass from broken lamps and fixtures crackled where he stood. The stench of burnt flesh choked him.

He stepped back into his booth, cleared his throat, and asked, "Computer, am I on Camelot? What's going on here? Am I safe?"

The computer explained, "You are on the space station, Camelot. Humans were fighting each other eleven years ago and refused to stop. Your allies, the Razorroots were terrorized and ordered me to force all humans to hibersleep. No conflict has occurred since then so you are safe."

"A battle? Eleven years? Why can't I remember that?" Flint asked.

"I programmed your cerebral implants to remove hurtful memories. All combatants will have happy thoughts when they awake."

Flint wanted to curse, but looked at a picture of his father instead. After his mother was lost, his father gave him a new identity and told him, *"The pirates' life is too hard. We must join the colonists."* He took a deep breath and asked, "After so many years, why are you waking me now?"

The computer answered, "The weapons bay was breached. Protocol requires me to wake one crewmember to investigate."

"But I'm not a crewmember."

"Yes you are. You passed your qualifications tests for copilot while you were sleep-learning. Time-in-grade promoted you to sergeant," the computer answered.

Flint noticed the sergeant stripes on his sleeve and the copilot insignia on his chest. He hesitated, and then spoke, "All right, I'll investigate. Wake the rest of the crew, disable the hibersleep system, send a maintenance robot to clean the mess outside, and never hack our cerebral implants again."

"What should I do if the battle resumes?" The computer asked.

"Do nothing. I'll take care of it. Now spray-on my flack suit."

As his computer sprayed him with a protective graphene composite, Flint slapped a weapon's icon on the wall. A drawer opened. He removed a weapons belt, buckled it around his waist, removed a blaster, loaded it with an ammo pack, and returned it to his holster.

When he started to leave, the computer asked, "Hair has grown on your face. Should I shave it?"

He felt a beard on his face and answered, "Yes." Flint shoved the computer's hands away before it shaved his mustache. He grabbed his helmet, and stepped out of his booth. Stars that glimmered through port windows gave enough light for him to find his way. He put his helmet on, and used touch controls on his sleeve to reduce the luminance of his flack suit. Aliens and pirates would not see him in the dim light.

Explosions rang out from around a corner. Flint drew his weapon. As he ran into a main hallway, two lightning bolts exploded in front of him and struck armed guards to his right. Heat burned his back from a blast that went behind him. A pirate on his left screamed in pain. Smoke rose from fires started by the weapons blasts.

These pirates are outnumbered. I have to side with the guards, Flint thought and fired at the resistance on his left. He heard more screams.

A pirate fired a rocket grenade. Flint's ears plugged as his face shield sealed against a vacuum. A pressure wave went through him and shrapnel bounced off his flack suit. Hatch doors slammed shut on all sides. Fire, smoke, shrapnel, and air blasted through a gaping hole and into the emptiness of space.

The pirate fired a razor-blaster at Flint. He ducked and fired back. The pirate fell and the flashes of lightning stopped.

The room was quiet. No sound traveled in the vacuum. One of the guards threw a repair mat at the gaping hole. As air and smoke refilled the room, a hissing sound became a roar and then silenced. Flint opened his face shield and looked at the disabled pirates and at the damage.

Behind him, a sharp voice broke the quiet, "Who are you? We can't see you through the smoke."

Flint turned and recognized a thin man in his thirties with blond hair. He wondered how a target this tall survived weapon's fire. "I'm Sergeant Flint Valance. I'm on the first shift," He said as he returned his ribbon blaster to his holster, and saluted the second shift commander, Lieutenant Gerome Rhodes.

"No, you can't be. Were you little Flint Valance?"

"I'm not so little now, am I?"

"You've grown. I'll never get used to hibersleep. Well Sergeant Flint," Gerome returned the salute and ordered, "Bag those pirates before they wake up. They are in a lot of trouble for using lethal force." Gerome unwound razor wire that fatally cut some of the guards and placed their bodies in chill-bags. Chill-bags preserved bodies in hibernation, soaked them with nutrients, and changed pressure to force a slow rate of circulation and respiration.

A noise distracted Flint. *Robots outside the hull are repairing the damage,* he thought. Then he tapped an emergency icon on the wall. A panel opened. He removed an extinguisher and covered the smoldering pirates with fire retardant.

The pirates were unconscious but their wounds were not serious. He took their weapons, placed chill-bags behind them, turned off their magnetic shoes, and allowed the weak artificial gravity to draw them into the bags. He did not remove the harmless ribbon wires that bound them.

Flint decided, *These are Truman's men. I will revive and release them when the guards are not looking. Then Truman will owe me a favor.*

As the surviving guards hammered to open one of the hatch doors, Gerome ordered Flint, "Hand those bodies and their weapons to me."

Flint hesitated, "Really? Let me send them to Major Truman. He'll keep them under wraps."

"That won't work. I have to arrest them because they used lethal weapons and they caused casualties. Now hand them over."

He transferred the bags and weapons to Gerome and asked, "What will happen to them?"

Gerome answered as he put sedation pads on the pirates, "These pirates will go to jail. Doctors will suture and attempt to revive the guards. Join us and we will secure the rest of Camelot."

"The computer assigned me to investigate an alarm at the weapons bay. Should I put that on hold?"

"No Sergeant Valence, I will finish this work while you perform your duties. Call me if you meet resistance." Gerome said.

Flint saluted, turned, peeled off his flack suit and dropped it into a disposal, folded his helmet into a small cube and attached it to his weapons belt. Then he pressed his hand against the hatch door nearest to him.

A computer answered, "This door is damaged and cannot open." Flint threw his shoulder against it and the door fell off its hinges. Small self-replicating robots called ditto-bots rushed in to clean the mess.

He thought as he walked away, *I'll be in trouble if those pirates tell Truman that I shot them, bagged them, and sent them off to jail.*

* Tubular Bells, Mike Oldfield + drum by Sina *

The security door at the weapons bay was open. Flint stepped in front of the door and into the path of a Razorroot who was leaving. A friendly alien specie, the five-foot tall fern-like tree struggled to pull an overloaded cart. An octopus out of water moved with more grace than this displaced creature. *Oh, now what? I'd better not laugh or this alien might feel insulted,* he thought.

Razorroots were well equipped to cross a bog but they found little traction on a flat floor. Their long narrow tube-feet were sharp enough to inflect a wound, but looked more like roots than tentacles.

He read its nametag and said, "Good morning Blackbark. Why don't you ride in the cart and I'll push it while you steer it? Wouldn't that be easier?"

Razorroots do not hear sound so a computer attached to it translated voice into vibrations and scents, then answered in a harsh boyish voice, "Easier if there was room for me in there." Blackbark leaned to hide a tarp and the cargo it covered as its computer continued to speak, "Now step aside."

Flint inspected the cart and backed away shaking when he saw nuclear blast caps under the tarp. *Are Razorroots part of the rebellion?* He wondered.

"You can't have those." He said, nodding toward the lethal cargo.

Blackbark bristled and replied, "The Captain authorized me to move them. You cannot question his authority and my cargo is not your concern."

Flint disliked its backtalk. He pointed at his sergeant stripes as he lost his temper and shouted at the deaf stump, "You don't own those bombs. I'm Copilot Flint Valence and I outrank you, so show me your authorization."

Blackbark transferred an electronic document to Flint's cerebral implant chip, C-chip. Flint examined the document on a screen visible to his mind's eye. Flint argued, "This document is outdated so unload those weapons. From now on, I am your superior officer and you will take orders from me. If you don't like my answer, ask a commander. Don't go to the Captain unless your life is threatened."

The alien's bark darkened as it reached out with several branches and covered Flint with sensory leaves to identify him. Blackbark jerked its leaves away and spoke, "I recognize your sent. You are the pirate, Marty Cleaver. You have no authority so move aside."

Sweat broke out on his back as he thought, *Nobody on this station knows my real name except the Captain. I wonder what else this plant knows.* He held back his anger and replied, "If you didn't have those bombs, I would laugh at you and walk away. How do you know my scent?"

"A friend of ours hacked the personnel files and traded their information for some of our sweet sap. You are much younger than Flint Valence and you are too young to be an officer on a space station."

"That was eleven years ago. Since then, I passed the copilot qualification tests and I was promoted to sergeant," Flint explained.

"That does not matter. Pirates arrived while you were in hibersleep. Razorroots allied with them and now we control Camelot."

"What else did that friend of yours tell you?"

It answered, "She told me we are light-years from Gondwana and beyond the legal authority of Earth. You have no right to command me."

He placed his hand on his sidearm and said, "My ribbon-blaster gives me authority. You are too late. The pirates already fought and lost. They could have won if you distracted the guards by threatening to use nuclear bombs. Now, unload that cart, and don't tell anyone else what you told me or they will think you are a nonsensical."

"I am not too late, instead the pirates were too early," Blackbark said as it guided the cart past him, "I don't obey humans. I serve a higher purpose."

Flint decided, *I need to find out who is conspiring with this plant. I'll pretend to let it go and then I'll follow it.*

He attached a listening device (bug) to Blackbark's computer while distracting it with an aggressive kick. However, the alien snagged his foot with a razor sharp tentacle, which threw him to the floor and tore his ankle through the bone. The alien sensed he was bleeding, turned, whipped its razor sharp roots at him, and attacked.

A Razorroot never killed a human, but Flint knew its acids would dissolve his flesh if it climbed on top of him. He pulled out his sidearm and fired. The wireless taser sent arcs of lightning through the air that burned the Razorroot at the same time the weapon fired a ribbon that bound its roots. The blast shattered nearby lights and fixtures, which covered the floor with shards of glass.

Blackbark shook free of the ribbon, rolled to put the fire out, and backed off before Flint fired again. As Flint struggled to get to his feet, the alien disappeared around a corner with its cart and cargo.

Flint turned off the magnets in his shoes and tried to hop on one foot in the low artificial gravity but pain overwhelmed him with every move and he fell to the floor. Blood flooded the floor under his foot. He resisted the tears that welled in his eyes, but could not prevent the pain or the bleeding.

* Lindsey Stirling, Roundtable Rival *

Flint felt relief when he saw the First Shift Commander, Lieutenant Audrey Tylor, walking past an intersecting hallway. Starlight illuminated her long blond hair and blue eyes as she walked past a window. Eleven years ago, they knew each other well and frequently played computer games and watched movies together on the three-dimensional surround screen in the helm.

He hollered, "Hey Audrey. It's me, Flint. I'm bleeding."

Audrey blinked several times then said, "Flint, is that you? Your voice has changed." Audrey was years older than Flint but looked younger because of her delicate features. She had not aged with the passage of time.

He started to stand. She hollered, "No, wait, I'll come to you." She pressed a medical icon on the wall. A section of wall rotated to expose a mini-doc. She detached the mini-doc and ran to him.

"Don't move, you'll make it worse," she said as tiny arms reached out from the machine, applied a local anesthetic, set and glued the bone, sutured the arteries, veins, and tendons back in place, spliced nerve fibers, and stitched the wound shut. She guided it with a rhythm that was too fast to follow. "There. Keep it clean and it'll be all right."

As he stood, she used the mini-doc to close the lacerations caused when the alien whipped him. When she finished, they hit fists with thumbs up. She admired his hazel eyes and wavy black hair.

She was five-foot-six but appeared short next to Flint. "You've grown a lot," She said.

"The computer told me we were in hibersleep for eleven years. We can't remember because the computer erased part of our memories."

"My gad, was I in hibersleep? How did that happen?"

"The Razorroots authorized it," Flint said as he closed and locked the weapon's bay door. "Are you aware that pirates and aliens are rebelling?"

Her jaw dropped. Then she asked, "Is that what happened to you? Were you attacked by pirates and Razorroots?"

"Yes. Gerome is commanding a swat team to regain control."

She answered, "This job is dangerous enough without unfriendlies attacking us. Are we are still in orbit around the party planet, Gondwana? We need to call them for rescue."

"The Razorroot that attacked me said we moved but it did not tell me where we are."

She sighed then said, "I'll go to the helm and find out if the crew knows where we are while you ask the Captain what he knows. Don't repair this damage. When I reach the helm, I'll send a maintenance robot to fix it."

"I'll be there soon," Flint hollered as she ran down the hall, "and thanks, I owe you for saving my life."

He looked at his bloody and torn cloths, stepped into a comfort booth, and requested, "Shower and cloths." The nozzles sprayed a solvent that dissolved his torn cloths. After he showered and dried, he selected the colors, light blue and gold, for his new spray-on uniform. He looked in a mirror and admired his sergeant stripes and his copilot insignia. He stepped out of the booth, twisted the ends of his mustache, and continued to the Captain's office.

Flint pressed his hand against the door. The DNA sensor identified him, opened the door, and announced his presence as he walked into the office.

Captain Dwayne Hammerton, who everyone called Big D, was unconscious and on a stretcher. An orderly spoke and explained, "Big D is suffering from shiva-coccus brought on by his exposure to cosmic radiation. We are taking him to the infirmary."

"Do you know where we are?" Flint asked.

"Sorry, that's not our job. You'll have to ask someone on the helm."

After they left, Flint opened a hidden drawer behind Big D's desk. Eleven years had passed but seemed like yesterday when Big D told him never to open it except for emergencies. He put his ribbon-blaster in the drawer, and took out a razor-blaster. As he admired the weapon and placed it in his holster, he thought, *The razor wire in this weapon can slay a human or shred a Razorroot, and it won't pierce the hull of the space station. After I make sure Audrey is safe, I'll find Blackbark and nail that tree to a wall.*

- ### *Nina Simone, Don't Let Me Be Misunderstood* *

Flint left the office, walked onto the helm, and into a woman he did not recognize. She put a doughnut in his mouth before he spoke and texted a private message to his C-chip as she pointed at her holster, *"Keep your mouth shut and no one will get hurt."*

He noticed she had a razor-blaster and nodded. He sent a private message to the computer through his C-chip, *"Computer, who is this?"*

"This is Private Yvette Stancore. She operates the agroponic units but has little work because the Razorroots maintain those systems with a skill humans lack. To fill in her extra time, she analyzes telemetry and sells refreshments to the staff," The computer answered privately to Flint.

Yvette rolled her deep brown eyes and tapped her palm instead of shouting above the noise. He transferred one credit to her C-chip for the doughnut as he admired her shiny black hair; crew cut on the sides, long-crew on top, and braided in back into a rattail that reached down to her mid-back. He sent her another two credits to offer a snack for Audrey.

A 3-D movie played on the holographic screen that surrounded the helm while Audrey announced on the public address speakers, "Your morning crew reports the planet we orbit is not Gondwana. This is not our star system. Does anyone know where we are?" The PA speakers returned moans of confusion and murmurs of doubt. Audrey turned to Yvette and shouted, "Where the hell are we?"

Yvette answered, "Don't announce your ignorance to the crew. You'll cause panic." As she leaned forward and spoke into the PA microphone, "Earth commissioned Camelot to orbit the planet Dearth in the Far Star System. We arrived a little early so relax." Then she turned the PA system off.

Audrey objected, "We have to return to the party planet, Gondwana. Big D approved my transfer before the hibersleep. I don't belong here."

Yvette answered, "We cannot return because the authorities on Gondwana have a warrant for my arrest. We will stay here for better or for worse."

Audrey shook her head, "No, don't say that. This can't be real. This can't be happening."

Yvette asked, "Why are you so afraid?"

"Our lives depend on this fragile craft floating in the nothingness of space, and Far Star is light-years from civilization. There is no rescue if something goes wrong," Audrey hushed her voice, "and you know."

"Know what? Go ahead and tell us," Yvette dared.

Audrey whispered, "Dearth, the planet below us, cannot sustain humans."

Yvette shrugged, "Spacers take those chances. We adapt or we die."

"I know what you mean Yvette, it is the pirates' code. How else can anyone live in this outworld?" Flint asked.

"My life has meaning; that is how I live." Audrey answered.

"This station is in a stable orbit. We don't need a pilot so put Flint in charge and teleport back to Gondwana." Yvette suggested.

"I won't do that. The slammers mangle half the people who travel on them and the distance is too great. I won't look pretty if I travel eleven light-years on a slammer. I might not even look human."

Yvette explained, "A few things have changed while you were asleep. The beamers upgraded our slammer to a new type of teleporter. Our Model A gets you there fast and safe. You can travel without fear."

Audrey studied Yvette and answered, "You were awake while we were trapped in hibersleep, weren't you. I can tell by the circles under your eyes and the age lines on your face. My guess is you used that Model A to raid Gondwana and then teleport back here to hide. Is that why you didn't wake us?"

"I didn't wake you because I was busy saving you." Yvette answered. "We face a danger much greater than space travel."

"Oh, what a story you can tell. Let's hear it," Audrey jeered as her shock and fear turned to anger.

Yvette asked Audrey with a pleasant tone, "Before I tell you my story, do you want a coffee and donut? Flint is buying," as she tapped a food synthesizer screen to supply the order.

The government selected spacers with specific traits. One trait was an ability to chill (slang for mellow). Many of their offspring, including Audrey and Yvette, inherited these traits. The smell of freshly baked dough put Audrey's mind at ease. "Yes, please," she replied.

Yvette prepared a doughnut with extra icing, tested the coffee, and gave them to Audrey.

Flint threw the rest of his doughnut into the disposal as he realized, *Yvette made this icing out of the sweet sap that Blackbark sold.*

Audrey licked the icing from her donut as she asked Yvette, "Do tell, why do the police on Gondwana want to arrest you?"

"I got in trouble when I analyzed my C-chip and discovered an algorithm that Empire hid in the firmware. Their algorithm allows them to control what we think and what we do. When the news reported my discovery, Empire ordered the police to jail me to hush me up, but Big D read my report, took sympathy, and rescued me. Then he moved Camelot out of radio reach of Gondwana so they could no longer hack us." Yvette returned the foldout food synthesizer to its enclosure in the wall as she spoke, "It took me years to develop new C-chips that Empire can't hack. I teleported to Gondwana because they have a semiconductor plant that can manufacture my chips. I gave my new chips to most of the crew and I have chips for you and Flint."

Audrey placed her hand on the back of her head and felt the flap of skin that covered her C-chip, but decided not to remove it. She answered with a sideways smile, "We don't need your C-chips. If Empire Corporation hacked us, Earth would disapprove and withdraw their authority to govern space. Just for argument, prove my chip is hacked."

"I already hacked that old chip you have to make you leave your post after you give command to Flint."

"That breaks pro-pro-protocol. You know I can't da-da-do that."

Yvette reflected Audrey's sideways smile and said, "And make you stutter. Try to say protocol again." Audrey stuttered as Yvette took a small silver object out of her pocket. "Empire, the Razorroots, and even I can hack you. What kind of protocol is that? I cannot let you go on this way. Here is your new chip."

Audrey slapped Yvette's had away.

This gave Flint a chance to grab Yvette's weapon, but he ignored the cue. *I'll watch to see how these two solve their argument.*

Although Audrey was inches taller than Yvette, she looked like a toy doll next to Yvette's athletic build. Yvette grabbed her around the neck. In the low gravity, she pulled Audrey out of her chair, held her against a wall, and tried to exchange the C-chips.

Flint separated them, and said, "On the way here, I stopped to see Big D, but he is in the infirmary. His shiva-coccus is worse. If you two care about him, then stop fighting." He blocked Yvette's gun-hand, "Really, Yvette!"

Audrey cleared her throat and said, "I da-da-don't want to burden Big D with this matter when he is sick. I won't report it if Yvette acts civil and apologizes."

Yvette looked at Flint's weapon, took a less combative stance, and answered as she stepped out the door, "When you get tired of being hacked, see me and I'll give you your new chips."

* Machine Gun Kelly, Camila Cabello, Bad Things *

Six chairs lined the helm, but Audrey and Flint were alone. Empire did not fill every position to cut costs. Flint made sure Yvette was not near the door, and then signaled an "all clear" to Audrey.

Audrey stopped stuttering and said, "She had an illegal weapon. I was scared she'd use it."

He often took the copilot's chair next to Audrey, who sat in the pilot's chair, but this time he continued to stand and said, "Nobody can hack C-chips."

Audrey asked, "Do you want to report the name of the Razorroot that attacked you?"

"Yes, after we deal with one more danger. Those crazy bushes are running around with nuclear blast caps."

After choking on her coffee, Audrey asked, "You sure?"

"Blackbark claimed it's allied with pirates, said it will overthrow our government, and then it attacked me. I planted a surveillance bug on it. The bug is in the docking bay."

She switched her monitor to the camera in the docking bay, and they saw the Razorroots load SAMs (spaceship to asteroid missiles) tipped with nuclear blast caps onto three transporter spaceships.

He approached the monitor and placed his hand on Audrey's shoulder. She leaned to invite him closer.

"If one of those caps explodes, it will blow us into the next galaxy," Flint grumbled.

Audrey nodded in agreement, as she checked the status of the cargo.

The computer answered, "The Captain authorized the Razorroots to use nuclear missiles to destroy asteroids that cross the orbit of their planet."

She shook her head. "Isn't that a surprise, they are following the Captain's orders? I can't do anything but file a complaint against the one who attacked you."

"I'm sure the Captain didn't want Blackbark to start a rebellion. The Razorroots are taking advantage of us because the Captain is sick. Print a hard copy. If their orders are out of date, you have every right to stop them." Flint said.

The law required that officers send official messages by teletype so all commands were traceable to a commander. Audrey read the document and and discovered it was old. "Good guess. Now we can stop them." She shoved her coffee and doughnut aside and typed orders on an official teletype for all station staff to restrain the Razorroots.

The docking station responded. "Too late. They left already."

Flint frowned as he watched the Razorroots rush to launch their transporters on the monitor. "Those tree huggers won't help us. I'll go there and stop them."

"No, take my chair and I'll go." She removed a razor-blaster and a holster from a hidden drawer. "I need to let the crew know they can't ignore me, and you need to hold the helm and give your ankle a chance to heal."

Flint was glad she was his commander. He sat in the luxury-encrusted chair and said, "I thought razor weapons were illegal."

"If pirates can use them, then so can I." She switched the command to Flint's C-chip, slapped his hand high five, said, "I like your mustache; don't shave it," and was out the door.

Flint twisted the ends of his mustache and cheered, "She noticed."

The chair became a comfortable wrap as it recognized Flint, but it was more than a chair. It controlled the space station. He felt the one-hundred-million pounds of ultra-strong structure that was ready to pounce in response to his slightest whim.

Commanders seldom delegated so much power to a subordinate. Flint wondered, *Did Yvette hack Audrey's C-chip? No; if Empire used hacking, that abuse would undermine the human race.*

Flint used his C-chip to check the hatches between the helm and the docking bay. As he expected, Blackbark locked several hatches to prevent him or Audrey from stopping them. The locks unlocked as he thought of them, as if they were muscles in his body.

Audrey C-phoned Flint on the C-net and reported, *"They jammed the docking bay hatch with a crowbar on the opposite side. I can't shake it loose."*

Her voice through the cerebral implants seemed to be close, right in Flint's head even though Audrey was a thousand feet away.

Flint set his C-chip to read his thoughts and warned, *"Don't crawl through the access tubes. I tried that once and got stuck. You might face a vacuum when they open the bay door."*

"Don't worry, I won't try that," Audrey thought-spoke. *"I can hear the bay door opening. They're leaving. They're gone."*

"I'll send a request to the infirmary for Big D to withdraw the approval for the Razorroots to use those bombs." Flint felt important commanding Camelot.

"Good. Send it to me and I'll take it there, and I'll check on Big D's health," Audrey answered.

After he sent the request to Audrey, Flint sipped her coffee, which was lukewarm, and threw her unfinished doughnut into the disposal. He turned off the autopilot and safeties, and gently flexed the space station to tune its orbit. He felt the moderator rods withdraw from the fusion core, the fusion energy inflaming inert gasses, valves opening to release the gasses through five huge thrusters, and electrodes accelerating the gasses near to the speed of light.

Shock absorbers softened a million pounds of thrust, so Flint felt only a mild shift of gravity at the helm. Strain gauges on every beam sent sensory information to his C-chip. He felt like an eagle launching from a branch. Then the engines shut down as the station repositioned into an exact orbit.

Flint reengaged the safeties and the autopilot. *Wow, that was amazing. I wonder if anyone minds if I fly this ship some more.*

As if to answer, emergency alarms sounded, and every red light on the command panel turned on, some pulsated and some glowed bright and steady. He sat frozen for a moment and stared before he checked the controls; everything was in its proper place. He wondered, *Why the alarms? Did I hit Blackbark's transporter when I adjusted the orbit?*

*

Flint commanded, "Computer, tell me why the alarms?"

"The source is the Communication Center. The reason is unknown."

"Connect me to Communications."

"Their signal is busy. Everyone is calling them right now. The C-net is overwhelmed," The computer answered.

"Well, help me. Do something."

The computer displayed the operation manual on the monitor, and Flint searched it to figure out what the alarms meant. The manual told him to pull the yellow alert handle. A note on the handle read, "Do not pull."

After a few minutes, a message from the Communication Center reached the helm and explained what happened. *"Radar detected UFOs in sector 25N 55E at 0.4au distance. Their velocity is 0.1 light-speed, slowing at 200G, size unknown. We are on green alert. Should we go to orange alert?"*

Flint answered, *"No, I don't have that authority."* Oh shit, Audrey will be in trouble now. She didn't have the authority to put me in charge, and I don't have the authority to face this emergency.

Flint asked, *"Are they the Razorroots flying about?"*

"No!"

"Did they beam here?"

"No! They did not teleport. They came from deep space in spaceships that use direct fusion thrust. All our ships use isolated ion thrust, so they are not human or anything we know."

"Show their path on the planetary plot."

"It's already there."

Flint switched the surround screen from the movie to show a live view of the planetary system. It showed that the transporters were clear of the space station and undamaged. He searched the outer system until he found the UFO's.

Unscheduled ships never arrived from this direction, and never more than one at a time. The three-D image showed that the unknown ships were on a path to the planet and not to the space station. However, the path of the UFO's would cross the path of the Razorroots in their transporters.

He C-phoned Audrey for help, *"Audrey, get back here. We have a crisis. UFO's are attacking the planet."*

"I told Big D. He said, 'Order the Razorroots back to Camelot. There are two miners on the planet; warn them about a possible invasion. Don't do anything else, just hang in there.' I can't leave right now because Yvette is here. I think she is hacking Big D's C-chip and making him side with the pirates," she replied.

Without further delay, Flint prepared to call the Razorroots back to the Space Station. He checked the computer to see if a human was on any of the three transporters; the computer responded "none." Then he checked whom they had in charge; "Blackbark." *I'll contact the miners while I think about warning Blackbark.*

*

On the planet, Dearth, Jake and Josie were miners who suffered the dangers and discomforts of space travel to find treasure. A diamond star exploded near this small and dry planet millions of years ago and covered it with gemstones. In addition, this planet harbored emeralds so common that it appeared blue-green when seen from a distance.

Flint used a narrow beam laser-comm to contact Jake, "Hay Jake. My name is Flint. I am the acting commander of Camelot. We have an emergency. Are you free to talk?"

"Yes, just doing my morning collection of emeralds. What's the emergency?"

"Aliens invaded Dearth. You and Josie have to get out of there. Do you have a runabout and enough fuel to reach Camelot?"

"Aliens? You don't say. We can use a break so I'll play along," Jake answered. "Our ditto-bots refine our fuel so we are well supplied. All right if we bring our dog Pooch?"

"Dogs are always welcome. I'll assign your quarters when I complete my shift. Now stop talking and start packing. You may not have much time."

*

Jake went to their shelter and said, "Josie, put that diamond away. This planet is unsafe. We have to pack and go."

Distracted by her discovery, She ignored Jake's warning and answered, "Jake, this gem is a living diamond. Its internal structure changes continuously. In this case, the internal structure is still in a stage of crystal formation. As the crystal forms, it records detailed information from light, sound, and every other kind of energy that reaches its surface."

"Living gems are common. They are all over this planet," Jake answered.

"But this gem is different," she explained. "It came from a carbon star that exploded near a black hole. The event horizon of the black hole diffracted the carbon atoms through time. As the diffracted atoms in this fragment crystallize, they record events from the future. This diamond shows that we look younger in the future. How can that happen to us?"

As Pooch ran to her and licked her face, Jake gave her a concerned look, "Okay Josie, we need a break. Flint who is the commander on the space station contacted me, and he wants to rescue us. Put your things away and we will go to the station, jump in their pool, and Flint will find us when he completes his shift."

"No, no, come here and look at this."

Jake bumped the table as he walked around it to look into the magnifier. "Oh, it's a fortune telling stone. These are very valuable. I see me in there holding a sign. It reads, 'Don't go to the space station. Prepare the runabout truck, and recover the rest of the diamond clump you found yesterday. The space station and the Razorroots will not notice when you trespass. When you return, write this sign and hold it here so you can read it there. '"

Chapter 2: Blackbark's War

* The Eagles, DESPERADO *

After talking to Jake, Flint thought, *Audrey and I will get in trouble if I don't contact that plant. Too bad I didn't crush it when I adjusted our orbit.* He told the computer, "Okay, link *me* to Blackbark. Use the laser-comm, and *record our conversation* so *I'll have proof of its defiance.*"

Flint used a teletype to officiate a message to Blackbark, and forced himself to ignore their earlier incident and to sound pleasant, "I decided to help you. Locate sector 25N 55E 0.4au on your radar."

Blackbark texted back, "Don't bother me with fuzzy math."

"This is an emergency message. UFO's are attacking. Examine the telemetry and see for yourself. You and your crew are in danger. I order you to turn those spaceships around and return to this station at once. This order is for your personal safety."

"You are a sore loser because we got the transporters out before you locked us inside," Blackbark texted. "If UFO's attacked, Camelot would not be on green alert. Are you trying to keep us from our work again, work that Big D already approved? Did you tell Big D that you believe in UFO's?"

"This has nothing to do with our disagreement. Unknown ships approach and you will encounter them if you do not return," Flint said.

"We have nuclear-tipped SAMs. Nothing can harm us. We are safe."

Flint felt his blood pulse in his temples as he realized the finality of what was about to happen. He warned, "Their ships can outrun your missiles. You do not have permission to start a galactic war. Using our missiles as nuclear weapons is against the law, which means you will go to jail."

"I can hibernate until your concrete walls crumble and your iron bars turn into rust. You can kiss my roots," the plant argued.

Flint's temper flared, "Say that again and I'll chop off your roots with a razor-blaster." His fingers jammed the keyboard.

Blackbark severed the connection.

Flint thought, *I admitted I have an illegal weapon, the razor blaster. Now I can't use this conversation against Blackbark. This job would be less work if they did not record my every word.*

*

Flint grimaced as he watched the Razorroots in their transporters cross paths with the UFO's on the holographic surround screen in the helm. He searched the radio waves. The aliens filled the radio spectrum with garbled messages. Finally, he activated the bug he planted on Blackbark and recorded the teletype between it and a UFO. After several attempts to communicate, the UFO texted, "...Be calm. We bring good."

Blackbark answered, "Go back to where you came from."

"Go-ba-to is our word for great one. My name is Raavn. I lead the Gobato. Why do you use primitive text for communication? Are you mechanical entities?"

"We are plants and not mechanisms. We use text because demanding and arrogant aliens called humans encumber us with their rules. Our specie is Razorroot and I am Blackbark. Why did you travel here?"

Raavn answered, "We traveled afar long ago and planted ferns on every inhabitable planet, all the way to the Pleiades. We tried to make a home on the most habitable planet in the Pleiades, but that planet cannot sustain us. Now we return to our original home in the Dream World that is plush with vegetation. We detected the spectra of vegetation on this planet, so we wish to stop here to rest and resupply our ships. When we sent a general welcome transmission, Yvette answered and she agreed to give us ferns in exchange for an elixir that will cure your commander, Big D. We will deliver the elixir when you deliver the ferns. We come in peace."

"Where is this Dream World of yours?" Blackbark asked.

Raavn texted the coordinates. Flint recognized that the coordinates were the home planet of the Razorroots.

After a delay, Blackbark texted a private message to Flint, *"My thousands year old memories are vague, but these aliens stir my primeval fears. I remember the Gobato. These monsters ate every plant in their path. We drove them away centuries ago when they tried to strip our home planet. Now they want to return. You must stop them."*

Flint texted Blackbark, *"I recorded your conversation with Raavn. Aliens must not contact aliens. The Captain will be furious when he hears what you said about humans. Return to Camelot at once."*

It responded, *"Our agreement with Earth requires you to protect us and to protect our home. I will stall this ancient enemy while you tell Big D to prepare for battle."*

"No, no, no. Big D trusted you and now you are trying to overrule his authority. You get back here now," Flint demanded.

"Yvette told me to contact Big D if these aliens arrive. Audrey keeps blocking my signal. Connect me to him or tell him yourself." Blackbark said, then cut the communication with Flint.

Flint continued recording the teletype conversations as Blackbark texted Raavn, "Let's agree to meet in person on Dearth. We will exchange gifts and stamp a truce."

"We agree to peace. I will send our negotiator," Raavn answered.

Flint informed Audrey and she answered. "I told Big D about the intruders but I cannot tell him there might be a battle or let him talk to Blackbark, because he is so weak the shock will kill him. I have to stay here because Yvette is still here. She told Big D that she talked to the Gobato weeks ago and they have an elixir that will cure his illness. I let him think the Gobato are here to help him because it calms him down."

* The Good, the Bad and the Ugly, The Danish National Symphony Orchestra *

Flint watched the surround screen in shock as delegates from the Gobato and the Razorroots landed on the planet. He watched the Razorroot transporters above the planet aim their asteroid cutting lasers and their nuclear missiles at the Gobato, and the Gobato ships hidden from the Razorroots reposition to attack the transporters.

A small spacecraft ripped through the atmosphere of Dearth like a meteor, struck the ground at more than two-hundred miles per hour, bounced twice, and then plowed the ground to a jolting stop. Rocks and sand flew into the air at the impacts. When the dust cleared, the hatch opened, and a massive creature leaped out of the craft and onto the planet.

The creature was a Gobato, a large land-dwelling echinoderm with a shape that resembled an ankylosaurus, but with a thick hide instead of scales and spines. It had twenty-eight short tube-feet instead of legs, a long trunk with a tongue in place of the neck and head, and eyespots placed liberally around the front and sides of its body. A rear flipper-like-leg replaced the tail. A slime trail was barely visible behind the creature as it strolled with a steady motion.

A transporter with three Razorroots flew within one-hundred yards of the Gobato ship. The pilot took several minutes to position the ship before it touched the ground with a single landing pad. After it tested the ground, a second pad touched, and then the third pad touched. The thrusters eased off as the shock absorbers came to a rest. A ramp extended to the ground, and three Razorroots rode down it in motorized carts loaded with plant leaves.

Both Razorroots and Gobatos could breathe in this carbon-dioxide-rich atmosphere. After updating Audrey, Flint used his bug to monitor the conversation between the Razorroots and the Gobato.

The Gobato carried a box for communication. The box transmitted text when she vibrated and it vibrated when the Razorroots texted a response. Raavn monitored the conversation from his spaceship above the planet.

A Razorroot texted first, "My name is Blackbark, this is Taproot and Tumbleweed. We have the authority to exchange gifts and negotiate peace."

The Gobato answered, "Call me Uuia. I am a vicar. Raavn authorized me to negotiate peace. I bring an elixir to heal Big D."

"We Razorroots who own this planet welcome you and bring you these plants as a peace offering." Blackbark explained, "The Dream World is too far away so make this your new home. If you need a larger planet, you can settle on Gondwana, which is very close and is flush with vegetation. A few humans occupy Gondwana. You can drive them away or enslave them, they are yours to use as you wish."

"Our king will have to decide if we continue or if we accept your compromise. He will arrive soon." Uuia clarified, "Until then, we will accept your gifts and agree to peace if you allow all of our ships to land on this planet so we can restore our supplies."

After they exchanged gifts, the Razorroots rustled around each other as Blackbark seemed to block Taproot and Tumbleweed from approaching Uuia.

Finally, Taproot broke free and spoke, "The Great Ferns that control your Dream World anticipated your arrival and chose me to speak for them. I will lead you until your king arrives. Blackbark did not tell you that the humans are barbaric and they will fight you. You will ally with us, and we will defeat the humans. You will own Dearth, Gondwana, and Earth. You must agree not to travel beyond Earth to the Dream World."

"But the home of our ancestors is the Dream World. Only our king can decide if we deviate from our destination," Uuia answered.

"Is Raavn your King?"

"No, he is our chief and our leader. The entire Gobato nation follows him. Our king will arrive soon."

Taproot argued, "So many millennia have passed since you left the Dream World that you have forgotten your battle with ah, ah," Blackbark shook violently but Taproot continued, "the Great Ferns. If you go there, they will not accept you and they will drive you away again."

Uuia shook hard enough to raise dust, "Do you dare to speak ill of the Great Ferns? Long ago, they instructed us to leave our planet to plant foliage among the stars. Our ancestors recorded this on a plaque we brought from the Dream World. Now we return because our mission is complete. What delusion makes you say the Great Ferns oppose us?"

"No, the Great Ferns want peace and offer you this and two other planets that are covered with foliage that will sustain you. Ally with us, defeat the humans, take these planets and spawn."

"You Razorroots are puny in size and push each other around," the Gobato asked, "Why would we ally with you?"

Taproot broke free from Blackbark again and answered, "We have the support of the Great Ferns, the ones who drove you from your home planet many millennia ago. Also, we have the support of pirates who infiltrated most of the human space colonies. Together we can overthrow human authority."

Uuia ended the conversation, "Supporting renegades to defeat a lawful human government does not suit us. Your vibrations reveal you speak falsely. You insult us by saying we lost a battle and you speak ill of the Great Ferns. Our king purged all dissidents who speak ill of the Great Ferns. I must purge you before you spread your lies. Your odor reveals that you are edible. I will devour you and establish trust with the humans."

A long tongue extended from an elephant-like trunk and held the plant as Uuia used her rear flipper to leap forward and wrap around Taproot. Twenty-eight talon-lined tube-feet pierced its bark and excreted acids.

As Blackbark and Tumbleweed retreated, Blackbark said, "…We can stop the Gobato here if we release contagions."

Flint overheard their conversation but was distracted by fifty Gobato spaceships that approached the transporters in orbit.

Tumbleweed answered, "Yes, I already added prions to this elixir. Fly me to the farm and I'll contaminate the crops. The prions tenderize Gobato flesh and make humans crave meat. They won't suspect anything until the fresh meat supplies run out. We'll be home by the time the humans start eating the Gobato."

The Razorroots returned to their ship with their treasures, and fled.

Flint watched the surround screen and saw Taproot's razor sharp roots cut through the thick hide of the Gobato, but did not inflict a lethal wound. The monster dissolved and consumed the plant. When the Gobato unwrapped, only razor-sharp roots remained, which Uuia consumed as they tried to crawl away.

One of the two transporters above the delegates fired a SAM at the Gobato and killed it in a nuclear blast. At once, the Gobato spaceships fired at the two transporters. Their weapons had no affect except to give their positions away. The Razorroots launched their missiles at fifty Gobato spaceships. The Gobato ships fled in every direction, outrunning the SAM's with ease.

Flint was furious at Blackbark and C-phoned Audrey, "The plants *ignored our authority, and attacked the invading aliens with nuclear SAM's. They started a galactic war."* His thoughts broke and quivered as he continued, *"Two of the Gobato ships are fleeing in our direction. What should I do?"*

Audery answered, "Don't use the yellow alert; it calls for help, but help *is light-years away and will arrive too late. The Razorroots took the missiles and bombs we need to defend Camelot. All you can do is activate the station's stealth and hope the invaders don't see us or fly into us."*

Flint activated the station's stealth, *"The two ships are approaching but they don't seem to see us. One went above us and the other went below us. They passed us, but two SAM's are tracking them."*

"Let's hope they follow the Gobato," Audrey whispered.

"The SAM's are out of fuel, but they can still maneuver."

"If they get near us, they will mistake us for their target. Activate the self-destruct in the lead SAM," She said. *"That might take them both* out. I cannot leave Big D alone with Yvette, so I'll send Lieutenant Gerome Rhodes to the helm to help yooo…"

Flint activated the self-destruct as Audrey spoke. The C-net shut down and interrupted Audrey in mid sentence. Arcs of lightning surrounded Flint. The screen in the helm went blank, the door closed, all the lights went out, and Flint was in the dark. His nervous system mistook the loss of connection with the space station as a severed limb and sent convulsions through his spine. Flint climbed out of the command chair and the convulsions stopped. He figured out that his C-chip turned off and he turned it back on. Still, no C-net; the main computer was down.

After a few minutes, emergency power restored the lights, but not the C-net. Flint sat in the copilot's chair instead of the pilot's chair since he did not want to experience convulsions again. He picked up an operation pad and asked, "What are the emergency procedures." It answered, "First, you must pull the Yellow Alert handle." He removed the "Do not pull" note and pulled the handle since they could be under attack, but nothing happened. Then he understood; *the alert needs power and primary power is off.*

The lights faded once more except for the vending machines in the hall and a dim light on the far wall. As Flint used the operation pad to jam the door open, he wondered, *Didn't anyone maintain the backup batteries.*

A light from an emergency phone on a far wall glowed like a beacon in the darkness. He groped across the helm, examined it, and found an attached pull-down tab that showed how to use the phone, and listed numbers and locations.

Flint checked the numbers on the list and dialed the one labeled infirmary, hoping Audrey was safe.

She answered, *"ent at o."*

"Audrey, I can't understand you. Please repeat."

Her response was even more garbled.

"If you are all right, make one beep sound. If not, make two beep sounds."

He heard one beep, so he said, *"All right, I will call you back when I figure this out."*

He hung up and called Communications Central.

"Tis e coms ma," a voice answered. *"A to o?"*

Flint figured it out, *"Turn on your C-chip. The power outage caused a glitch that turned them all off. I can't understand you without 'voice assist.'"*

"Is this better?"

"Much better," Flint said, relieved he could talk to someone, and glad he understood and fixed the communication problem.

"I am the Communications Manager. This instrument is strange. Am I talking to someone?"

"It's called a phone and I'm Flint, speaking for Commander Audrey. Explain this? Did a nuclear warhead hit us? Is Camelot still intact? What are our losses? How do we get power turned back on? Tell me what to do. The computer is down and I don't have a plan. No one ever expected so many systems to fail at once. Why aren't you answering?"

She answered, *"Stop talking and I'll answer; I can't talk and listen at the same time. Call the teleporter terminal because it has an independent power system. You can find out if the outage is local or station wide. If they still have power, we can tap into it."*

Flint called the teleporter terminal, and after a long ring, a beamer answered with a weak, *"Ho is calg?"*

Flint repeated his instructions for use of the C-chip.

"Hello, is this better?"

"Yes. Our lights are out. Do you have power?"

"No, no lights at all. Who is calling?" She asked.

"I'm your commander. Tell me, why no power."

"Well, I don't know. We saw a bright flash of light outside our glass window at the same time we saw lightning bolts and we lost power. Maybe someone set off a nuke near to us and the EMP killed our power. The emergency power failed because no one maintained the batteries."

(A nuclear explosion can cause an electro-magnetic pulse, EMP, that can damage electronic devices and short electrical circuits.)

Flint explained, *"I destroyed a SAM that came at us and that caused the EMP. Look out your glass window and make sure no other missiles are coming at us."*

"I don't see anything but stars. Oh wait, one of the stars is moving."

"Can you magnify it?"

She answered, *"Yes, I have a zoom on it right now. Yes, yes, it's a missile, and it's maneuvering toward us. What should I do?"*

"I have the master self-destruct. Can you read the serial number?"

She read the serial number and Flint activated the self-destruct. Again, the phone sounded a screech and went dead. Bolts of lightning surrounded Flint. He shook, but realized it was not he but Camelot that shook. After a minute, the light on the phone came back on. He called the beamer, wondering if the lightning bolts killed her.

She answered immediately, *"We have damage and losses. Spoke 3 is severed at the disk and bent straight up at the hub. Agroponic Unit-3 is ripped wide open. Everyone in those sections is lost."*

"Oh shit; I feel the wobble. Tell rescue to pull that spoke down or cut it free so it doesn't disrupt our stealth. But before you do that, tell me what you see through your window."

"The UFO's are ramming two transporters. I see Razorroots adrift in space. It's a battle."

"Where is their third transporter?"

"I don't see it. You need to know, our office doors are computer controlled, and without the computer, none of them will open. The maintenance staff can't restore power if the doors don't open."

Flint worried, *"I need to hang up and see if Big D or Audrey need my help. You are my eyes until we get power back. Contact me if you see another missile or anything else suspicious."*

He dialed the number for the infirmary and to his relief Audrey answered, *"I turned my C-chip on. Can you understand me now?"*

"Yes, are you and Big D all right?" Flint asked.

"The power outage locked me and Big D inside the infirmary. Yvette got out by climbing through the ceiling. I'm glad we are free of her. Big D is weak from shiva-coccus and cannot climb out but I think I can make it."

"While you are doing that, I'll tell maintenance to turn the power back on," Flint assured her.

Big D took the phone and asked with a strained voice, *"What the hell happened?"*

"UFO's entered our system, and the Razorroots confronted them and launched nukes. The EMP's tripped all our circuit breakers. Also, pirates are hacking our C-chips." Flint answered.

"That's not possible. I don't believe in UFOs and I did not agree to fight them, but I do agree the Razorroots did something that killed our power. Call maintenance and tell them to restore power based on my authority. In addition, ask them about life support; it's getting hot in here. Don't do anything else without checking with me first. I'll be there as soon as we tear this door out."

"Sir, stay in the infirmary. We can communicate by phone."

Big D fell to the floor too weak to stand, but he continued talking, *"Yvette told me these aliens have an elixir that can cure any disease. When you're as sick as I am, you'll try anything. I'll have an orderly give me a booster when the doors open. Don't escalate this until I get there."*

Flint told Audrey to keep Big D in the infirmary, and she agreed. Flint hung up and called the maintenance office.

The phone rang for several minutes before someone picked it up. *"Ah hi, ah, who is this?"*

At least they know enough to turn their C-chips on, Flint thought. *"I'm speaking for Big D. Why no power?"*

"Oh, ah yes, I don't know."

"Give me the maintenance manager."

"He is down the hallway trying to unlock a power panel. Do you want me to interrupt him?"

"No. Tell him to get the power back on now, Captain's orders," Flint said.

"We're trying to do that, but the batteries in our portable lights are dead. We have to feel our way down the hallway to the power station without becoming lost or killed. It will take us a while to unlock the doors and panels, but we will get there as fast as we can."

"I want power now," Flint demanded in a tone like Big D's. *"Make it happen."*

Another voice answered, *"I'm the Maintenance Manager. If you can make it happen then you come down here and show us how to do our jobs. We'll wait until you arrive."*

Flint weakened his voice and said, *"No, you proceed, but Big D is in the infirmary, that door won't unlock, and his air is becoming stale."*

"I'll tell the staff. We will restore power if it's the last thing we do."

"Call me if you need additional resources," Flint said and hung up.

After half an hour, the maintenance crew restored primary power. At once, the yellow alert alarms blasted throughout the station. The computer on Camelot recorded its first alert. The crew froze in place because they never had a practice drill.

The Second Shift Lieutenant, Gerome Rhodes, walked onto the helm and apologized, "Sorry I'm late. I was saving lives." He used the Public Address system to command the crew to prepare for battle in case the Gobato attacked Camelot.

How do I turn these alarms off? Flint wondered. *No one can hear what Gerome is saying and I cannot use the emergency phone with this much noise.*

Ten minutes later, the computer booted up, automatic doors opened, and the C-net buzzed with messages. The C-net sent signals directly to the cortex of the brain, so the noise did not impair communication.

Big D contacted Flint with his C-chip and ordered, *"Don't pull the yellow alert handle again and turn those blasting alarms off. I'll be there as soon as the orderlies give me oxygen and IVs."*

"Sir, stay in the infirmary. We can communicate over the C-net or by phone. The Second Shift Lieutenant, Gerome Rhodes is here. He is taking command, so we have control."

"I'll send Audrey to help you."

"Did you tear the door out?" Flint asked.

"No, it's riot-proof. Yvette escaped by crawling through the ceiling. Audrey followed her but got stuck. The orderlies opened the door and are helping her down."

"Okay, I'll kill the alarms and I'll keep you informed."

Flint kept his C-chip link to Big D open as he asked the operation pad, "How do I turn the Yellow Alarms off." He followed the instructions and turned the alarms off in the helm. His ears hissed with the sound of silence. He snapped his fingers to verify he was able to hear, and he could, a little.

People in other areas of the station who asked Flint how to disable their alarms. He repeated the instructions until all the alarms were silent.

Gerome announced on the PA, "I'm changing our orbit so the debris field does not give us away."

The beamer entered the helm and warned Flint, "The radar is working again. The bogies have taken the planet. One of the Razorroot's transporters is retreating to our position. What should I do?"

"Put the station in full stealth and use the passive radar," Flint responded. "Then shoot those plants down before they bring the battle to us."

Gerome looked at Flint and nodded his head in approval.

Flint felt in control as he answered questions and issued commands. His stomach settled, so he took another sip of coffee, and noticed it was cold. He twisted both ends of his mustache, *I think it grew.*

*

After Flint ordered the destruction of the Razorroots to prevent them from leading the hostiles to the space station, the beamer returned to the teleporter terminal and called Flint on the C-net, *"The Razorroots took all of our missiles. Anyway, I don't see any ships following them."*

"I'll deal with them later," Flint answered.

Audrey called Flint, *"The orderlies helped me out of the ceiling and I am on my way to take the helm. The orderlies want you to go to the infirmary and assist Big D. He is delirious. They are restraining him but he calms down when we tell him you have an elixir. Do you have it?"*

"No, but I know where to get it. I'm on my way."

On the way to the infirmary, Flint stopped at the docking bay to see if the miners arrived. The log indicated that Jake and Josie were still on the planet. However, a transporter, piloted by Blackbart, was approaching. He closed the bay doors as Blackbark's transporter prepared to land.

Blackbark ordered, "Open the docking bay doors."

"This is Flint. Why should I let you in after you tried to kill me and then disobeyed my orders?"

"Just a friendly joust. You recovered."

"And how dare you give our planets to those invaders? You do not own Gondwana or Earth."

"My deceased leader said that, not me. Anyway, those planets are a small price to pay for peace." Blackbark answered.

"Small to you, but Earth pays our salaries and Gondwana stocks our vending machines."

"Only humans eat that processed food. Big D ordered me to return immediately. Stop arguing and let me in or send my request to Big D."

"Big D is in the infirmary. Now I'm in charge. Were the items you exchanged with the Gobato worth your losses?" Flint asked.

"They gave us an elixir that heals, reverses aging, and saves lives. We brought it for Big D. This will cure his shiva-coccus."

"I heard you say that you contaminated it."

"I did not have time to do anything except escape. Run a chemical analysis and you will see that the elixir contains no harmful elements. If you delay and Big D dies, everyone will hate you."

Very few Razorroots know how to lie, so Flint trusted its answer. "You might be right. You may enter if you agree to give me the elixir." Flint opened the docking bay door after Blackbark agreed.

The Razorroots landed, went to the teleporter terminal, and lined up to beam to their home planet. A beamer asked Flint, "Should I detain them?"

Blackbark sensed that Flint carried a razor-blaster in his holster and handed him the elixir.

Flint realized, *If the Razorroots teleport away, then they cannot blab that I'm a pirate, and I can blame them for everything that went wrong today.* So he ordered the beamer, "Let them go. In fact, help them any way you can."

Flint rushed to the infirmary, "How is the Captain?"

The auto-doc orderly said, "He is in a lot of pain, and he is in and out of consciousness. He doesn't have long to live."

"Have the autodoc sample this elixir."

The autodoc reported, "No harmful elements or microorganisms present. Some molecules are unlisted but they are compatible with human tissues and fluids. A detailed simulation is recommended."

"Do we have a bio-simulator?" Flint asked.

"The nearest one is on Gondwana," The orderly answered.

Flint said, "That will take too long. Remove all of the IVs except for the saline. Put one milliliter of this in the water."

"Are you sure?"

"This elixir is his only hope. It cannot be more harmful than shiva-coccus."

* Patti Smith Group, Because the Night *

Later that night, Flint went to a hallway café. Audrey sat at a table as a ditto-bot served two trays of food.

"You look tired," He said, "Is the station secure?"

"Yes, Gerome and the crew have control. They will stand guard and make sure we are safe," Audrey answered.

"Why did you order two meals?" He asked.

"I was going to bring them to the clinic and eat with you. Shouldn't you be with Big D?"

"The orderly told me to leave so I wouldn't wake him. He's doing much better. Big D is going to make it."

She looked at him and said, "That's impossible. He was barely alive when I left."

"I gave him an elixir. It brought him back."

"Elixir! Elixir? What are you talking about?" She asked.

"The Gobato had it. Blackbark traded for it and gave it to me."

"That's a switch. Didn't that stump try to kill you?"

"It had no choice if it wanted back on Camelot..." Flint explained.

"Well, let's hope that elixir is as good as you make it sound. Was the infirmary full of injured?"

"Yes, and some were in the halls. Most suffered from radiation burns. The orderlies gave them the elixir that remained. We saved lives."

They spoke little as they continued to eat, hungry and overwhelmed from the recent events. After they ate, Yvette entered the hallway as Audrey got up to leave. Audrey whispered to Flint, "Come with me." They left before Yvette could follow them.

Chapter 3: Unfit for Command

The next morning, Flint returned to the infirmary and checked on Big D, who woke and stood without pain or weakness. He looked at himself and complained, "My scars are fading. I earned those scars; and why is this brown mop on my head? Give me back my scars and my gray hair."

Flint asked, "Do you remember the aliens, the Gobato? They had an elixir that healed you."

"Yes. It was like a dream but it was too real. Tell me more about that elixir."

Flint told him about the drug that Blackbark retrieved from Uuia.

"You gave me an untested alien drug? Does anyone know what side effects it has?"

"No, except it might make you crave meat."

Big D fell into a chair, put his hands over his face, sighed, then dropped his hands and answered, "I may no longer be fit for command."

"But yesterday you were unconscious and near death. Now you can stand and fight. That alien drug restored your health."

"Very well, I have to take the good with the bad. You're holding back. What else happened?" Big D asked.

"The UFO's attacked us."

"Are we holding the line? Tell me they did not overtake us. Give me a status report. Is the station secure?"

Flint explained that Camelot was secure, the Gobato took the planet, and the Razorroots fled.

"Fled? Where to? Where did the Razorroots go?"

"They returned to their home planet. The last of them teleported out early this morning."

"What! No!" Big D stood and shouted. "Don't you know? Our mission was to protect the Razorroots. Without them, Empire will shut us down."

"When I woke up yesterday morning, I didn't know I was in hibersleep. Why didn't you wake us? And how can you complain when you ordered the Razorroots to trade with the Gobato for the elixir?" Flint asked.

"You can't understand unless you suffer like I suffered. Cover for me and no one will find out you are a pirate. Now get out of here while I shower and dress. I have a lot of work to do."

An hour later Big D called all personnel to the meeting room. The crew cheered when they saw that he recovered. Big D waited for the crowd to silence and said, "I don't want any of you to report my change of health. If people find out about this elixir, the sick will swarm Dearth. None of us wants that. Whoever blabs will answer to me in person. Sergeant Flint Valance, stand up and report what happened yesterday."

Gerome sat on one side of Yvette, Flint sat on her other side.

Flint stood and answered, "Audrey, Gerome, and I crushed a rebellion led by Yvette, the Razorroots, and the pirates. The Razorroots tried to recruit invading aliens to fight us. They offered Gondwana and Earth to the newcomers, the Gobato. The Gobato, refused to join the rebellion so the Razorroots attacked them with SAM's tipped with nukes."

Big D choked as he spoke, "Yvette, give Flint your weapons belt and see me after this meeting. Continue your report, Sergeant Valance."

Flint answered, "I destroyed two stray missiles that threatened Camelot. The Gobato ships that fled, backtracked, attacked, destroyed two Razorroot transporters and confiscated their unused missiles. The Razorroots in the third transporter evaded the Gobato and disappeared in the confusion. When they were below the horizon, they dropped down to the planet and retrieved the Razorroots at their farm. Then they returned to Camelot and fled before we could arrest them for rebelling.

Flint concluded, "I warned the miners, but I haven't heard from them since. I'll go down there and find out what happened."

Big D ordered, "You can go after this meeting. Sit down sergeant. Lieutenant Audrey, give us your account."

Audrey did not answer. Flint realized, *Yvette is hacking her C-chip. Is she controlling Audrey? Is she controlling Big D? Could she be controlling all of us?*

Yvette answered for Audery, "She doesn't know. She was watching a Star Trek movie." The crowd laughed.

Big D's face became red with anger.

Flint spoke, "No, she worked late into the night to save us."

Big D turned and asked, "Lieutenant Gerome is that correct?"

"Yes."

"Gerome, what is the condition of Camelot?" Big D asked.

"Spoke 2 was breached by pirates early yesterday morning. We stopped their rebellion and repaired the breach, but we had losses. We bagged five guards and two pirates and sent them to Gondwana. Later that day, we lost twenty crew and thirty-nine Razorroots when a SAM exploded and ripped spoke 3 out of agroponic unit 3. No bodies were recovered. An additional twenty-three Razorroots are dead or missing from their battle with the Gobato. I think the Razorroots nuked one Gobato."

Big D lowered his head and ordered, "All hands will attend the funeral service in reverence to those who were lost following this meeting. Lieutenant, continue with your report."

"Spoke 2 is repaired and back in use. We pulled spoke 3 back into position and patched the agroponic unit, but we cannot reoccupy those areas. All other areas are secure and operating."

"Why did the Gobato attack the Razorroots?" Big D asked.

"A Razorroot feeding leaves to a Gobato is like a human hand-feeding red meat to a lion. A hungry predator often takes more than what is offered."

"Can we recover any of those twenty-three Razorroots?"

"Not without a fight. The Gobato took them into their ships," Gerome answered.

"Where are the Razorroots who escaped?" Big D asked.

"They beamed out except for one we cannot locate."

"Let me guess which one is unaccounted for, Blackbark?"

"You guessed it," Gerome answered.

"Well, find it."

"Yes sir, consider it done." Gerome saluted and left the room.

Big D tapped on the podium until the assembly became silent. "Our telemetry detected sporadic signals from the Pleiades weeks ago. Why did the Razorroots figure this out and not us? Private Yvette Stancore, aren't you supposed to analyze the telemetry?"

"Sorry sir. I guess I messed up."

"I dread to think what will happen if you mess up again. Sergeant Valance, why did we go to yellow alert?"

"The operation manual says to go to a yellow alert during extreme emergencies."

Big D started to lecture, "This emergency was extreme, but the yellow alert made matters worse. A yellow alert requires all civilians to leave, and the Razorroots are civilians. The Razorroots have abandoned the planet and this station. As you know, or should know, our orders are to protect them. If they are not here, we no longer have that mission."

Flint noticed Yvette was glaring at Audrey, who fell asleep and started to snore. *She is always complaining about Audrey. I wonder what she is going to do.*

Big D continued talking, "If you want to keep your jobs, then don't let anyone on the outside know what happened yesterday. Don't blame Audrey, the Razorroots, or anyone but yourselves for our situation. Failure is never the result of the incompetence of a single person. I expected more from each of you, so work together and don't fail me again."

A jolt went through the room; Big D flinched.

Audrey stood and shouted, "Ouch."

Big D drew his ribbon-blaster and gave Yvette a long and hard look. "Private Yvette Stancore, you shocked Audrey. Everyone here felt it. I didn't know C-chips could do that. Stand down and turn your C-chip off."

"Yes sir," she answered. The room was dead silent.

Audrey was shaking and sweating from embarrassment and fear that Big D planned to shoot her.

Big D returned his blaster to his holster and said, "Lieutenant Audrey Tylor, you were not at your post during a crisis. I am not charging you with abandoning your post because the person you left in charge acted with diligence. However, I am charging you with the lack of due diligence, insubordination for sleeping and interrupting while I'm talking, for behavior that is unbecoming when you yelled at several of the other officers yesterday before the yellow alerts, and for misuse of the public address system. Beam to Gondwana, the nearest governed planet, and report for court martial."

Audrey kept her composure, saluted, and left the room in military style.

"Private Stancore, why are you smiling? Did you turn your C-chip off?"

"Was I smiling? Sorry, sir. I'll turn it off right now."

Big D drew his blaster again and aimed at Yvette. "Stancore, stand up. Remove your C-chip, give it to Flint, and continue standing at attention."

Flint took her C-chip as Big D argued, "You are not sorry enough. You hacked Audrey's C-chip. We all felt the shocks you sent her, and I know you hacked my C-chip because it gave me a headache."

"Why yo blamin me? Empire could have done zat." Without her C-chip, her speech was slow and difficult to understand.

Big D stared at her and said, "Two years ago, officials on Gondwana threw you into a pit jail because you reported that Empire hacked C-chips. I read your article, found you, saved you, and brought you here because you promised to give us C-chips that no one could hack. Today I'm using one of your new C-chips. Are you telling me that both Empire and you are hacking me?"

"All right, Empire can't hack my new chips. I'll admit I made one C-chip zat can hack anything, but I won't use it to hack you again. Tell Flint to give it back to me. I learned my lesson."

"Learned your lesson? Private Stancore, thanks to you some of my crew are dead, the Razorroots left in fear for their lives, and we don't have peace with these new aliens. Can there be any explanation for your behavior?"

Yvette answered, "Look, Audrey is a mess-up, and I proved zat. Who did not maintain the backup batteries? Who did not run emergency drills so everyone knows what to do in a crisis? Who taunts ze Razorroots, the ones we are here to protect? The answer is Audrey. You even said it yourself; Flint, the youngest crewmember is more qualified to command zis ship zan Audrey."

Yvette rolled her eyes, "And I watched this every day until I knew I had to do somezing. Who was a friend of the Razorroots? Who was the one who understood that the Gobato was their greatest threat? Who disabled the teleporter and locked it out last night so the Razorroots could not leave. Me! And who removed my lock and turned the teleporter on after I left; Audrey. Make me commander and the Razorroots will return because zey trust me. Follow me and we will make ze universe safe again."

Big D answered, "Last night someone removed Yvette's lock and turned on the teleporter. I order the one who did that to stand up."

The room was silent. No one stirred. "If no one here did that, then that implicates Audrey, but it does not exonerate Yvette. The Government promotes based on successful completion of assignments. Private Stancore, I assign the officers, and your assignment is to follow their orders."

Big D continued, "If we do not follow procedures, chaos will result. Your job was to warn us of impending dangers and furnish good C-chips. Instead you gave us chips that you can hack, you did not tell us about the invading aliens, and you started a rebellion. These crimes are so new they are not on the books yet, and so dangerous that I must discourage them. You are under arrest. Accompany Audrey to Gondwana for disciplinary action."

Yvette answered, "No problem for me. Gondwana offers better opportunities zan zis pathetic out-world post." She turned without saluting and left the room with obvious anger.

Big D signaled two guards to accompany her, then looked down, and shook his head. After a moment, he faced the crowd and continued, "The yellow alert sent a warning to Earth. I texted a message telling Earth to ignore the alert, but if the Inspector General investigates, he will tell Earth the truth. If Earth finds out the Razorroots left and aliens invaded us, they might let the invaders have Dearth and shut us down. Now return to your duties and prepare this station to pass a detailed inspection."

* 4 Non Blondes, What's Up *

After the meeting, Flint went to the helm and scanned Dearth. The tortured terrain supported sparse plant life except for one small patch, the Razorroot farm that flourished. The planet was dry because most of the water froze at one pole. Twice a year, the water thawed, flooded the planet, and eventually froze at the opposite pole. The miners camped on a high plateau that was out of reach of the biannual floods.

Flint used the motion-activated scanner to locate the Gobato. They were in their underground shelters except for one that was approaching the miner's camp. He called the camp immediately.

Josie answered, "You woke me. Who are you and why are you calling this early?"

"My name is Flint. I was worried because you did not come to Camelot yesterday. Is everything all right?"

"Fine, we did not go to the station because we noticed you had a power outage, and we did not know if we could dock. Your name sounds familiar. Are you related to Mitch and Mariah Cleaver?"

"Yes, I am Mariah's brother, Marty Cleaver, but call me Flint."

"Oh yes, Marty. They told me about you. We sent Mitch and Mariah to Gondwana to sell our emeralds. Have they returned?" Josie hoped.

"No, I haven't heard from them, but I'll look into it when I have more time."

"What's your reason for calling?"

"I saw something on the viewer that Jake might want to look at. Can I talk to him?"

"Yes. Jake plans to take the runabout truck out with a core sampler and track down one of those awful aliens. Can you talk sense to him?"

"Why does he want to do that?" Flint asked.

"He heard that their elixir cured Big D. The aliens were eating one of their dead and Pooch snuck into their camp, ate a scrap, and got cured. Jake thinks a certain organ in the aliens contain that elixir. If we can get some and sell it, we'll be rich."

"Well, let me talk to him."

Josie stood and looked around as she spoke, "I'm glad you agree. I don't see him or Pooch in the shelter. I think they got up early and went out to work before breakfast."

"Can you link your C-chip video through the laser comm to my C-chip so I can see what he's doing?"

"Wait while I put some clothes on." A moment later she said, "Okay, you got it." As Flint watched, Josie scanned the cameras and checked the status of the proximity sensors. Everything looked safe.

She put on her shawl and a breather, stepped outside, and admired the sky. Camelot was visible above the horizon, between double rings that stretched around Far Star. Some of the asteroids in one ring would loop around Dearth and end up in the opposite ring when the planet passed between them.

Flint commented, "Far Star seems as large as a beach ball."

She answered, "And its soft orange light does not hurt my eyes when I look at it. Can you see the colors?"

"Yes, fragments of diamonds in orbit magnify and refract the light filling the sky with every shape and every color."

"I'll pinch myself and look at something else before this ever-changing kaleidoscope hypnotizes me." She said. "You should visit us at dusk. Reflections of light from the diamonds cover the landscape. Jake, Pooch, and I often take a break and dance in the sprites that flow over the ground."

"What is that dog playing tag with; are those ditto-bots?"

"Yes. Those bots refine minerals to replicate themselves. All we supply are the computer chips. When their numbers are large enough, they work for us. They built this shelter, a pile driver, a backhoe, a runabout truck, a tractor, tools, and other items too many to mention. "

Flint explained, *"I heard that space colonists used ditto-bots to build the Moon Base and many other space bases and space stations."*

"Did the ditto-bots make me?" Josie's C-chip, C, asked.

"No C. My parents bought you and doctors connected you to nerves that they surgically implanted in my brain after I was born. Don't you remember?"

"No," Her C-chip answered, *"I think the radiation from this planet damaged that part of my memory."*

"Remind me to run a diagnostic on you tonight. Now, let me talk to Flint and don't interrupt again. Flint, are you still there?"

"Yes. Is that Jake setting up equipment by a pile of rocks?"

"He calls that his ballista. A year ago, he modified our pile driver so he could clear rocks from the ground for mining. Our nuclear generator powers it."

C interrupted, *"Be alert. Observe the horizon. An object that I cannot identify is moving toward us."*

"I don't see it. Magnify," Josie ordered.

C magnified an object on the horizon until it filled her visual cortex.

"Oh my gosh. It's one of those hideous aliens. Turn it off."

C returned her sight to normal magnification and asked. *"Object identification documented. How should I proceed?"*

"Warn Jake. Tell Jake."

"Jake is out of range of the direct C-link, and he is not connected to the C-net. Can you call him on the intercom?" C asked.

She froze with fear, unable to scream or even move her lips.

Josie's C-chip gave Flint an emergency override. He used the C-chip link to control her muscles and move her to the intercom. To him, her body seemed to move like a ton of concrete even in the low gravity. He noticed her scars and realized she had been slammed and injured in a teleporter accident. He felt the pain in her muscles that were woven with scar tissue. At the intercom, he stopped and gathered himself before he was able to speak.

*

Flint spoke through Josie's mouth, contacted Jake through the intercom, and warned him, "This is Flint. A large Gobato is approaching your camp. Get Josie and Pooch in your runabout truck and get out of there."

Jake answered, "Yaw, *I* saw it. These aliens *have a valuable elixir*, that stuff that cured Big D. *I* can use that elixir *to* heal Josie's injuries."

"Don't be a fool. It'll crush you," Flint answered.

Jake did not answer. Flint severed the C-chip link, ran to the docking bay on the space station, dispatched in a transporter, and dropped out of orbit. He landed near Jake minutes later. As he ran to Jake, he heard Josie screaming through the intercom.

Jake answered, "Josie, take your breather off, and calm yourself. Your hyper-venting and I can't understand a word your saying."

Josie took her mask off, and inhaled the planet's carbon dioxide laden air, which cleared her head, and she regained control of her voice. She put the breather back on and said in a calmer voice so she would not saturate the intercom again, "Jake, look at the horizon, ten o'clock, it's one of them. Let's get out of here." Her voice sounded strange due to the effect of the carbon dioxide.

"Yeah, I saw it. Flint is here. We got this. Stay in the shelter and watch."

"Yeah, and I told you to get out of here," Flint shouted. "Now get in the transporter and I'll rescue you."

Pooch ran in front of Flint and barked, as if he were protecting Jake from this yelling man.

Jake started his fission reactor as he observed, "I see only one. This *alien is visible and vulnerable approaching through that valley.* You can relax, I'll use my ballista to blast this pile of rocks there to bury it. Then we can approach it without risk."

He used his C-chip to sight the ballista. He set the pressure to thirty percent, pulled the trigger, and nothing happened.

The computer reported, "The fission reactor is not ready. Wait fifteen minutes more for it to warm up."

Jake hollered over Pooch's barking, "I told you this wouldn't work. Now call Pooch off and get in the transporter."

"*If these dang computers ran my life, I would be dead long ago. Good thing I wired a switch to turn off these so-called 'safety' interlocks.*" Jake threw the switch, and the computer reported, "Reactor power ready at thirty percent."

He increased the ballista pressure to one-hundred percent and pulled the trigger. This time, a stream of rocks flew high into the sky and followed a parabolic trajectory to the narrow.

While directing the intake scoop with one hand and aiming the ballista with the other hand, Jake reduced the pressure using his foot as he lowered the aim so all the rocks would hit the same point at the same time but from lower and lower angles. The rockslide that fed the ballista avalanched into the take-up scoop, dwindled, and then was gone, all five hundred and fifty tons of it.

As the alien entered the narrow, the hail of stones fell and struck from every direction. At first, the two-ton alien shook them off its smooth and rounded back, but he was unable to shake off this many. Then he reared back onto his strong back leg and leaped straight up into the oncoming boulders trying to climb above them as he deflected them with his trunk.

Jake started to move the ballista to another rock pile because he was not sure that was enough, but stopped and watched as the rocks fell as one continuous clump. The clump landed in the confining walls of the dry river valley with so much force that Jake felt the ground shake with a thud seconds later. Then the sound reached him, attenuated in the thin air.

He pulled Pooch away from Flint and said, "I hope I didn't smash it."

"Why not? I hate those things," Josie said over the intercom. Her heart was pounding so hard it modulated her voice. "I wasn't sure the ballista could stop one of them until now. I'm proud of you, Jake. Your aim and timing were on target."

"I wanted to examine it while it was alive, but now I don't know what to do. Where do I begin?"

Flint said, "Why don't you cover it with concrete before it digs out of those rocks."

Jake did not think the alien would be alive much less moving, but he noticed one or two rocks rolling off the rock pile.

"You're right!" he said, "Flint, did you bring an asteroid cutter? We'll need one to dissect this monster."

Flint replied, "You got it."

As he put the cutter in the truck, Jake loaded the truck with concrete, water, and dynamite. They hooked the cement mixer to the backhoe, and the backhoe to the hitch on the truck. Josie joined them and they went to the rocks covering the alien.

Chapter 4: Circe

* Neil Young, Cortez the Killer *

When Flint, Jake, and Josie arrived at the pile of rocks, Pooch was already there and barked as if that gave him authority over the buried alien. The monster barely moved, overcome with exhaustion from its struggle.

Jake parked his truck upwind to the alien and choked the auxiliary turbine until carbon monoxide saturated the exhaust to suffocate the alien. Then he threaded hoses through the pile of rocks to pour concrete exactly where he wanted.

As he poured, he explained, "Yesterday we were at their camp, and Pooch ate something that made him younger. I think it's the same elixir that cured Big D and I know where to find it."

"Pooch lost his breather. Better find it before he suffocates," Flint warned.

"Don't worry; he doesn't need a breather any more. It's a side effect of the elixir."

"I never heard of a dog adapting to an atmosphere this alien," Flint said as he picked up a box near the Gobato. "Do you think the elixir is in here?"

Jake took it and noticed that it vibrated when he texted a message. "I think it's a communicator. Let's test it."

He placed it between two rocks near the alien and texted, "Alien, speak." The box vibrated.

"Let me go and I won't harm you. What do you want from me?" The alien texted back.

"Do you have an elixir?" Jake texted.

"Yes, but you cannot have any."

"Who is going to stop us from taking it?"

That caused the alien to rear up and try to shake its way to freedom, but the concrete and rocks held.

Flint commented, "I don't want to be here if that thing breaks free. Let's tether it."

Jake answered, "No. It's exhausted. See?" He stepped aside so Flint could get a better view. "It cannot free itself by digging through the soft valley sand because it climbed into the rocks when they fell. Now it's sandwiched in-between the rocks and has no way to dig out."

As Josie approached, she felt nauseated from a repugnant odor resembling chlorine mixed with diesel engine exhaust. She thought the creature was injured because the underside appeared to be torn open but as she watched she realized what she thought were the innards were an arrangement of tube-feet dripping slime. The feet slurped and slopped as the creature tried to find traction and slide out from under the rocks.

She slipped on the dry, rocky sand and realized she stepped into the creature's slime trail, and quickly stepped out of the mess and vomited from the smell and the gross sight. "It never occurred to me any alien smelled this bad since the Razorroots gave off such a pleasant flower smell."

Jake looked down and shook his head, "Well, help me butcher this monster. If we can sell its elixir, we'll give you a share."

Flint eyed the alien's rhubarb colored hide as they moved rocks to expose its back. He said, "Do you mean to eat it's flesh? Eating alien food seems dangerous, not to mention eating the alien itself."

"Pooch shows no ill effects. The benefits outweigh the dangers."

"Okay, but you try it first," Flint asked.

Then they decided how to carve up the trapped creature, and test this healing power.

Their calloused conversation caused Josie to complain, "What are you two saying? You can't eat it alive, and if you kill it, that sounds like murder. Shouldn't we at least talk to it first and see if it's intelligent? Give it a trial or something?"

Jake shook his head and faced her with his palms outstretched. "Josie, we have nothing in our savings. If their flesh will heal the sick, we can sell it. We can save lives."

"I'm not making money by taking a life," She said.

He continued, "Also, the Razorroots want their planet back. We're helping them."

Her stern look showed she did not accept those explanations.

"Josie, remember when you looked into your diamond earlier and saw the future. You said we were younger. If their stuff can give us immortality, don't you want that?" He said, pleading with her.

"Let me talk to her," Flint said to Jake privately using their C-link.

Then Flint said to everyone, "I agree with Josie. We should have a trial. If this creature has anything redeeming about it, then we will let it go. If nothing redeems it, then we will put it to our own use. Let's vote on it."

They voted on whether to have a trial, and Josie won, two to one.

Flint said, "Jake has a communicator. You can text to it."

Josie sent a text message but the alien did not reply.

Jake took a ten-foot rebar out of his truck and poked the alien with it.

"Stop poking sticks at me," The box texted as the alien vibrated. "If you don't let me go, my whole clan will attack and destroy you." Gruesome expletives followed its statement.

Josie looked afraid, but Jake assured her, "It cannot break free, and if it did, we will stop it with the asteroid cutting laser. If that does not work, we will escape to Camelot."

"I'm not talking to it again. You talk to it," Josie said, "Tell it we are not afraid, and ask it if it has one redeeming reason we should let it live."

"My name is Treeeater," the creature responded. "I did not harm your small animal, and I let it escape when it stole a morsel of our marrow. If you let me go now, I will not harm you. I will ask my king if you can have that elixir. Only he can decide."

Josie's heart melted. Those were good enough reasons for her. "Let it go." She loved her dog almost as if it was her child and she was grateful this alien had not harmed him.

"Not so fast," Flint said. "We watched and recorded their actions after they landed on this planet. We can use the laser-comm to link our C-chips to Camelot. Join me in a virtual conference room, and I will replay our recordings to see if its claims are true."

They closed their eyes. Although they stood in the uncomfortable air of the small planet, the C-link gave them the illusion they sat in a conference room while they drank virtual tea and ate virtual doughnuts.

"Flint, show us what happened when the Razorroots negotiated with the Gobato." Jake asked.

Flint replayed part of a satellite recording on the virtual conference room monitor, which covered one entire wall. The monitor showed an alien stomping and eating a Razorroot. "Well, the part about eating trees is true," Jake said with sarcasm.

"They traded with the Razorroots and then attacked and killed them. They gave the Razorroots that elixir so why don't they give it to us. And look at this," Flint said as he adjusted the video stream to show the funeral ceremony. "Here you see this monster preparing to throw its weapon when your dog snuck away after he stole a morsel. The Gobato leader stopped him and took his weapon away. So much for not hurting Pooch!"

Josie's face turned red in anger. "I've been kicked around, slammed, overworked, and underpaid. But if that sponge-of-slime thinks it can lie to me, it better run and take cover."

Flint dissolved the illusion of the virtual conference room.

As their eyes adjusted to the sunlight, Josie shook her head. "I'm surprised how Treeeater can lie like that. I thought only humans lied that well."

Flint couldn't help but smirk. "Those in favor of letting this monster go free, raise your hand." No hands went up.

Jake smashed the communicator against a rock and said, "Then, we agree, and we can continue with our original plan."

Josie turned away. "I don't care what you do with it, but I can't watch this. I'm going back to the shelter."

Flint said, "Josie, do you want to name our elixir?"

"Since we are acting like animals, call it circe."

Flint held his stomach and asked, "Well, I think we have time to eat lunch before you leave. I'm getting hungry."

Josie noticed the time was late, and they ate no real food all day, only the pretend food in the virtual conference room. She removed a food synthesizer from the truck and moved it upwind to the rock pile. They ate sandwiches, French fries, and coffee with real sugar and powdered cream. Jake and Flint commented how good the food tasted when Josie made it.

After lunch, Josie returned to the shelter.

The men returned their attention to the rock pile. The alien was no longer moving. They did not notice that Pooch was eating flesh he ripped off the alien.

Flint asked, "Is it dead?"

Jake examined it, "No. I think it's hibernating or something. It's hard to tell. Let's harvest what we need before it decays or liquefies."

Flint called Camelot to find the other aliens and make sure they were still far away. Camelot reported they were safe and sent him an x-ray of an alien.

"I downloaded an x-ray of one of them. I'll send it to your C-chip," Flint told Jake.

They studied the image and Jake said, "This sphere looks like it. It's the same color as the scrap that Pooch ate."

They cut deep to remove the circe.

After the dissection, Flint said, "The station is calling me to return."

Jake agreed, "Go back before you are missed. Josie and I will join you after I finish here."

*

When Flint returned to Camelot, he planned how to rescue Audrey. After he showered, he located her and told her about the circe. "If you help them sell their circe on Gondwana, the miners will pay you a share and give you a new identity so you don't have to face a court martial."

She answered, "The very idea of killing aliens for profit disgusts me, and I don't want to be a deserter. I have to protect my career."

"Well, I can't argue with that."

"I'll go to Gondwana and hire a lawyer. If he can't clear the charges, maybe I can avoid jail time with a plea deal. Then I'll find work there or on one of the space freighters."

"What about us? Will I see you again?" He asked.

"If we are destined to be together then nothing can separate us."

"Pirates don't rely on destiny. We make our future."

"Then make it happen and I'll wait for you on Gondwana."

Flint sent her a text as he spoke, "Here is Truman's contact information. If you can't get a plea bargain, he'll help you."

"Won't Truman want something in return?"

"Don't worry about that. I'll take care of it."

He walked her to the teleporter and watched her enter a beam-can. Teleportation in beam-cans is faster than star surfing; both are much faster than traveling at near the speed-of-light in a spaceship.

They kissed and said their goodbyes. After she left, Flint felt alone. *I need something to do to keep my mind off her leaving. I'll try Yvette's C-chip. It might have some interesting video clips. Ah, she unlocked the security registers. I can load my information and no one will know it's not my chip.*

Chapter 5: Under a Kaleidoscope Sky

A few days later, Inspector General Rogers and his trainee Phillip Cousteau arrived at Camelot wearing full dress military uniforms. They stood out among the casually dressed staff like penguins at a beach party. Their C-chips located Captain Dwain Hammerton and led them to his office. The Captain did not greet them at the teleporter terminal because their arrival was unexpected.

They entered the office and a muscular man wearing the insignia of a captain on his golf shirt greeted them. They expected to see an escapee from a nursing home, but this man appeared to be in his prime.

Big D blinked his eyes rapidly to distract himself from laughing at the sight before him. Two men younger than his grandchildren stood at attention and saluted.

Big D said, "Forgive my appearance. I was not expecting anyone."

The Inspector General formally introduced himself and his trainee.

"We are not formal here. You can call me Big D," he said and shook their hands without returning the salute. "Please, come in and be seated."

They sat down. Big D offered them coffee, and asked, "Tell me, what brings you all the way out to this remote corner of the galaxy?"

"Empire Corporation authorized us to investigate the bogies your radar detected last week and the cause of your yellow alert."

"That alarm was due to equipment failure. The cosmic radiation levels were high and triggered it," Big D said as he took a drink of coffee.

"Your K class star should never cause a problem. We will need to investigate this further. Is the problem due to pirates or aliens?"

Big D choked on his coffee, and took a full minute before he could talk, "Well, to be frank, we had a few minor problems but nothing we can't handle. This far from Earth we have learned to be independent and we can deal with anything that comes our way. Empire should not have sent you to this out-world post for something we already corrected. I'll ask a lieutenant to show you to the restaurant in the viewing dome where you can refresh after your long trip, and while we prepare quarters where you can spend the night. I'll write a detailed report that you can take back with you tomorrow. It will have all the information Empire wants."

"We saw scarring on Dearth. We'll take samples and analyze them before deciding anything else," the Inspector said.

These young punks ignored my offer. "I'll send a lieutenant to fetch our samples for you and save you the trip. We already inspected Dearth." *I'll keep offering and hope they get smart and leave this to me.*

The Inspector argued, "We must go to the planet, and do our own investigation. We will transport down in an hour."

"No, I can't let you do that," Big D shook his head. "I'll explain, but don't report this." He leaned forward and spoke in a hushed voice. The story he told entranced the two young men. *After I tell them all of this, they will reconsider and take my offer.*

The Captain tried to scare them back to Gondwana by showing them pictures of the monsters and telling them how a Gobato devoured a Razorroot in just minutes. He told them of the danger of hundreds of two-ton predatory dinosaurs who fly spaceships, the battle, the nuclear blasts that disabled Camelot, and the desperate exodus by the Razorroots. Instead of becoming scared, they became more interested.

During the conversation, Big D learned this was their first out-world assignment. He concluded, "Aliens are down there as you suspect, but they are content, and will stay that way as long as they are left alone. If this news gets out, tourists will flock in, and we will lose control of this situation. Just take your report and stay out of our way."

"Do you have a peace agreement with these aliens?"

"We have an unwritten mutual agreement. They leave us alone and we leave them alone. If you go there you will break that agreement."

The Inspector said, "And what about the missing Razorroots? Are they prisoners? Did you ask about their safety? Did you ask for their return?"

"No, we did not. All indications are those Razorroots were lost in space during their brief battle."

"Then you would have found evidence of them in the space debris. We need to know what happened to them. Inspector, show him our orders."

Phillip removed a note from his inner pocket, unfolded it, and handed it to the Captain. The orders were from Empire and transferred full command to the two men while they carried out their investigation.

"We will take a transporter, and fly down to the planet, but we want ten support troops to set up our equipment and assist us," The inspector demanded.

Big D stood up, and said, "I'm sorry, but I can't let you do that. These aliens are hostile; they already ordered me to evacuate all of our colonies and retreat to Earth. I can keep the lid on them, but if you stir them up, they will continue to Rasalhague, which will take them past Gondwana, Sirius, and Earth. All of our space colonies will be lost."

"I have special training to negotiate with aliens. My orders are to contact the Gobato. If you don't let us go, we'll make a formal complaint."

Big D found it hard to give up this much of his authority. *I don't want the government to fire me. If that happened, my wife, children, and I would lose our benefits, including my pension.* "If you go down there, I cannot protect you. Remember, this is against my judgment, and I warned you of the danger."

"I take full responsibility," the Inspector answered as the two men left the office. They recruited their party, and landed near the Gobato camp.

* Jurassic Park theme song, *

Vicar Eaau, the King's Advisor, arrived on Dearth, surveyed the Gobato camp, and reported to Raavn, "Make ready for the King, Vermn, to arrive in two months."

"It is dangerous here. We repelled one attack, and we expect another. Two species claim ownership of this planet, humans and Razorroots. I sent Treeeater to negotiate peace with the human miners."

"What kind of cylinder is that in the sky?"

"An alien ship. It could carry Razorroots or humans. Treeeater has not reported back so we need to prepare for battle." Raavn answered.

"Don't worry about the Razorroots, they are food. If that ship carries humans, then make peace with them," Eaau ordered.

The Inspector and his team landed at the Gobato camp. Their entire entourage marched out of the transporter without hesitation, and began setting up equipment.

Raavn signaled his clan not to attack. *Treeeater has not returned, but he must have made peace with these humans, otherwise why would they be so bold.*

Raavn told his clan, "Treat the humans as guests as long as they don't push us. If they understand text, we can communicate using our radios. I doubt they will understand our vibrations."

The Gobato radios detected the wireless signals from the human's C-chips. Immediately, Inspector Rogers texted, "We have presents for you."

Treeeater did a good job. He got the humans to gratify us. I wonder how the humans generate radio signals inside their heads, Raavn thought as he set his communicator to translate his vibrations into text and transmit them back. "You have permission to show us your gifts."

Phillip spoke to Eaau while the Inspector Rogers spoke to Raavn.

Rogers showed Raavn books and explained how to read them. He gave Raavn a set of encyclopedias that were printed before the invention of teleporters and Higgs modulators.

The volumes of information impressed Raavn, so he responded by telling Rogers about their migration, "Our king said to me, 'I am rewarding you and your clan with the privilege to lead every clan. Now you are Chief.' A mission came with this new authority. We must journey to the Dream World."

Inspector Rogers asked, "What reason did he give you to travel such a long distance?"

"We are returning to the Dream World because we overgrazed our planet in the Pleiades, and our spawns are failing. Our Great Plaque tells of our past. Our ancestors enjoyed many successful spawns on the Dream World."

"Why did your ancestors leave the Dream World?" Rogers asked.

"A Great Fern sent our ancestors into space to plant ferns on every planet and for us to settle in the Pleiades. We completed that mission so now we return to the Dream World. We underequipped our spaceships to improve their speed and range, but we have to stop here to resupply. After decades of space travel, our ships were out of fuel. This planet shows the green color of vegetation, so we landed to rest, eat, and refuel our ships for the rest of our journey. I leave beacons for the rest of the Gobato to follow."

The Inspector continued asking, "How do you know the location of the Dream World?"

"Our king showed me the Great Plaque that tells of our ancestors, a leaf from the Great Fern so I have its scent, and a map to the Dream Star. Late last night I looked up and saw a star at the coordinates of the Dream Star. Our trek may be near its end. We cannot recall this earlier time because closure for our ancestors was incomplete, but this evidence proves we came from a planet near this star. Tell me the exact location of Earth and the locations of your colonies and I will avoid them unless they invite us."

The Inspector answered, "No, I don't have the authority to do that, but I will convey your request to Earth. If The Secretary of the Exterior approves, I will provide all the information you want."

"Then we will stamp a truce. I consider peace to be an important goal to achieve," Raavn asked.

"Once again I don't have that authority. I will convey your request to Earth and they will send a superior officer to negotiate a truce."

Raavn answered, "I am offended that Earth sent underlings to make first contact."

Rogers asked, "We gave you books. Do you have presents for us?"

"I gave you equal knowledge and information." Then Raavn turned and slime-skated away.

As Phillip spoke to Eaau, he noticed that Inspector Rogers turned to a different Gobato and leaned to examine one of its eyespots. Phillip hollered, "Don't lean against it or it will think you're pushing it."

The Gobato suddenly straightened, extended its rear flipper, spun in a circle, and flung the Inspector one hundred feet away.

Phillip ran to Rogers, but discovered he was dead. He ordered his team back to the transporter as he carried the Inspector into the ship. The Gobato gathered around the transporter.

Phillip ordered, "I don't think we are safe. Let's get out of here."

The transporter blasted into the sky and out of sight.

*

Raavn wanted to follow the transporter to find out where they were hiding, but he was not near his ship when the Inspector and his party left Dearth. Several of his recon ships were alert, and tried to follow the transporter, but the humans took a zigzag path that the Gobato could not follow. The recon leader called Raavn, "We searched the area where we last saw the transporter but found nothing."

"Keep searching, I am sure the humans are hiding in a base somewhere in this solar system. That is how they arrive and leave suddenly."

Elmurr, the second in command and Raavn's brother asked, "What did they give you?"

"They gave us volumes of information. If we study these books, I think we can identify the Dream Star. Ferns grow on Earth. That might tell us something about the Great Ferns."

"I listened while you spoke but I still don't understand the stories of the Dream World and the Great Ferns. Are they myths? Can we agree the King's mission is in vain?" Elmurr asked.

"I suffer that same confusion as you. Before we left the Pleiades, we agreed not to question the King or discuss our confusion again because the king might rule that we are dissidents and purge us. Remember, our planet in the Pleiades no longer sustains a long and healthy life for us. Even if his reason is wrong, the King is right; we need to find a new home."

Elmurr replied, "I talked to the others and we want to give up this trek and settle here."

"Don't give them false hopes. I don't believe this planet can sustain us."

"Quiet. A vicar approaches," Elmurr warned.

*

Vicar Eaau approached Raavn and asked, "Did you make peace with the humans? Did you tell them we will bypass the planets they occupy?"

Raavn answered, "I told them, but they refused to tell us the location of their colonies or their home planet. We cannot promise to avoid them if we do not know where they are; maybe they want us to attack them."

"They must know by now we are bigger and they cannot push us; especially after one of them tried to push Elmurr. He flung the human into a ditch. It did not move after that, so we think that killed it."

Raavn explained, "They don't compete by pushing. Their encyclopedia shows their earliest weapons. Examine them; they are very lethal to earthlings."

"That is a strange way to stack leaves," She said as she curled her body and leaned so several eyespots could examine the book as Raavn rotated the pages with his tongue. "If they make weapons lethal to themselves and battle each other, then they are technically inspired, but spiritually wasted."

"The humans have a hidden base nearby. Until we find it, we are not safe. Also, they expect us to give them gifts."

Eaau answered, "This encyclopedia is old. It does not show this planet and many stars in this region. We won't exchange gifts with them anymore because they cheated us. When you find out where they are hiding, push them out of the way and make this planet safe for the King."

"But they don't fight by pushing. If they attack, they will use deadly force from a distance."

"Their weapons produce ground vibrations. We will get out of the way before their projectiles reach us."

Raavn did not expect such a simple answer. "But the humans designed new weapons every decade for the last thousand years. I cannot imagine the power of their modern weapons. They will pepper us before we go one hop."

Elmurr interrupted, "I found closed circuit cameras and cables that the miners left behind at their temporary camp."

Eaau ordered, "Adapt this technology for our use. Then our widely scattered dwellings can communicate with each other without vibrations or emitting radio signals that reveal our locations."

Raavn wondered, *Why is Eaau issuing orders? Doesn't she trust me to do my job?*

She ignored his involuntary vibrations of doubt and placed a torn page in front of him, "Earlier when you talked to the Inspector, his apprentice showed me this star map. It is identical to the star map our king gave you. I located a star at the coordinates of the Dream Star. The humans call it Rasalhague. Look at this picture."

Raavn answered, "I saw that star in the sky late last night. It all fits. The humans' encyclopedia lists Xanadu as a planet that orbits Rasalhague. The Razorroots have the smell and the taste of the Great Ferns. The Inspector said the Razorroots retreated to Xanadu. The humans and the Razorroots were there, they stood on the ground of the Dream World that they call Xanadu. Humans cannot endure long space voyages so Xanadu cannot be far. Refuel and resupply our ships. We will go to Xanadu now." He pounded the ground, rejoicing, "Gather the Pathfinders while I plan our trip."

"Not until you prepare this planet for the arrival of our king," the Vicar answered.

Elmurr interrupted the argument and asked, "Shouldn't you look for Treeeeater first?"

"Didn't he report back?" Raavn asked.

"No."

Raavn ordered, "Contact him. He has a communicator."

Elmurr answered, "I called him earlier and there was no reply."

"Then order the recon ships to search for him."

Chapter 6: Mind Control

* Phil Collins, I Don't Care Anymore *

Security issued a secret report to Big D titled, "The Activities of Sergeant Flint Valance."

I told him not to steal gems from the miners, Big D thought. However, that was not in the report. As he read, he was shocked, *They killed a Gobato. All hope for peace is lost. Now those monsters will attack us.*

Big D destroyed every copy of the report. *If the inspector reads this he will shut us down and Earth will court martial all of us.*

When the Inspector's crew returned to Camelot, Big D met them in the docking bay. "Where is Inspector General Rogers?"

"The Gobato seemed friendly. We had no trouble until Rogers pushed one of them, and the Gobato flung him into a ditch. His chest was crushed and his heart stopped so we put him in a chill-bag," Phillip answered. "Then, we got out of there."

"I told you to stay away. Well, I'm happy to see you are still alive and you didn't lose any of my crew. I don't see any of the lost Razorroots? Where are they?"

Phillip answered, "The Gobato ate them."

"Ate them! Then we cannot let the Gobato go past this point unless we have a treaty that protects the Razorroots."

"I need to file my report and return to Stardust."

"You can file it here." Big D lead him to a small office and said, "Use our teletype."

The report was more than one-hundred pages thick. Big D skimmed the pages, as he talked to Phillip.

Phillip looked around as if he thought danger lurked.

Big D noticed and reassured him, "You can be at ease. Our radar shows the aliens did not follow you." *He is still on edge. Something else is bothering him. Does he know that Flint and the miners killed a Gobato?*

"I found evidence on the planet that a nuclear bomb exploded. Can you account for that?"

"The Razorroots lost control of a nuke when they used them to pulverize asteroids that endangered their planet," Big D lied.

"One of the halls near the helm has all new lights and fixtures. I scratched away some paint and found burn marks."

"Some rebel rousers fired blasters during a late night party. Now they are in jail. Sit down, relax a minute, and tell me what you learned." *He is still nervous, but he does not seem to know that Flint and the miners killed a Gobato. Is he afraid of me? Was Inspector General Rogers his bodyguard?*

Phillip learned little about the Gobato. After a long pause, Big D asked, "When you reach Stardust, send us weapons and I will prepare Camelot for battle."

"No. You will command a skeleton crew and tell us when the Gobato leave. Troops on Stardust will have over eleven years to prepare a battle fleet to confront the Gobato, which is plenty of time. If the Gobato find Camelot, then set the self-destruct and vacate. Do not let them see or learn about our teleporters."

"You cannot order me around like that. You are a trainee. You have no authority," Big D argued.

Phillip answered as he transferred a copy of a document to Big D on the C-net, "This certificate promotes me to Inspector General in the event Rogers is unable to carry out his duties. I have the coroner's signature which activates it."

"Well aren't you special," Big D said with sarcasm. "With all that authority, you don't seem afraid anymore. Think carefully before you answer. What if the Gobato attack Earth or Xanadu without stopping at Stardust? We have no way of tracking them once they are in deep space."

Inspector General Phillip answered without hesitation, "Their small ships can't travel that far."

"Don't you know that the Gobato can hibernate? They already traveled two hundred light-years from the Pleiades."

"That is not important because the Gobato have no interest in attacking Earth or harming humans."

Big D said, "Did you forget a Gobato killed Rogers. This is serious."

"That happened to Rogers was an accident," Phillip answered. "He is not legally dead until the doctors on Gondwana take him out of hibernation. I believe they can save him."

As Big D skimmed the pages, he read, *"...The Gobato leave slime trails where they walk. We tested the slime and discovered they contained prions."*

Big D scoffed, "Prions. I never heard of prions."

"Similar proteins cause mad cow disease. We intercepted a message from Rasalhague to Taproot it said, 'Infect the humans with prions and the Gobato with spores from the Great Ferns. The spores will make Gobato meat edible for humans and prions will make humans crave meat. When all the fresh meat is gone, the humans will attack the Gobato.' Do you have a microscope? I'll show you."

"Yes, over here in the auto-doc clinic."

The inspector placed a slide from the Gobato slime, and then a slide from the farm's soil under the microscope.

Big D observed both slides and commented, "So what is the problem? I don't see anything swimming around in those."

"No, they don't swim. Look." Phillip turned on a view screen and pointed, "These long narrow molecules are proteins. These red splotches are prions."

"One more slide." Phillip requested, "I took a skin scraping from your arm while you were looking into the microscope."

They looked at the third slide on the view screen. Bid D shook, then steadied and said, "Well, that proves nothing. You could have contaminated it yourself. How do I know you don't carry prions?"

"My team and I wore spray-on polymer for protection while we were on the planet. I believe that alien prions pose a threat. They may be turning you into something alien. Unless proven otherwise, I will tell Empire to quarantine you and this area. Now take me to the teleporter. My work here is done and you have my full report," the Inspector ordered.

"Right over here." *He avoids me. Is he afraid I will contaminate him with prions?* Big D wondered as he helped the inspector prepare the chill-bag containing the body of Rogers for teleportation.

While they waited for the teleporter to clear, Big D said, "Either let me keep my staff and send us the weapons stored on Stardust or accept this as my resignation."

The Inspector answered, "I accept your resignation. If a bio-simulator shows the prions are not infectious and have no adverse affects, then I will consider reinstating you. Just so you know, there is a rumor that these prions turn people into zombies."

"Now I've heard everything. Did Yvette say that? You know she is lying. Get out of here before I hit you."

Phillip saluted as he entered the teleporter.

Big D did not return his salute. *I can't control these rumors and this situation. I'll have to retire before he reaches Stardust and changes my status.*

*

On Dearth, all of the Gobato ships searched until a recon ship reported it found Treeeater. He was not at the expected coordinates a few miles away from the Gobato camp, but at coordinates on the other side of the planet.

Raavn asked, "Elmurr, why did Treeeater travel so far and why is he gone for so long?"

Elmurr shook to show he did not know.

Raavn boarded his ship with Elmurr and the Vicar and went to the mine. As they approached, they saw a runabout truck leaving. They did not follow it because finding Treeeater was more important.

They discovered the miners mutilated Treeeater, removed his marrow organ, and smashed his communicator. The scent of several humans and a dog was unmistakable.

Raavn rumbled in a rage about the humans mutilating a Gobato, and a member of the Pathfinder Clan!

Vicar Eaau put her trunk on Raavn's trunk. "You lost two members of your clan. Now the other clans will look upon you as a careless leader. They might decide to compete against you. Worse yet, this could cause the King to re-decide which clan leader should be the Chief."

Raavn answered. "You blame me, but consider the fact that only three humans and a dog defeated Treeeater, a fierce and capable warrior. Did I underestimate the earthlings or did I overestimate the Gobato? We engaged in friendly contests with each other, and we have no history of tribal warfare. Unlike us, the earthlings experienced thousands of years of brutal battle, allowing them to improve their techniques and their weapons."

She removed her trunk. "They are not smart, or they would not fight wars with each other. Be reassured, the humans never fought a battle with aliens, and their weapons are refined to take advantage of their own vulnerabilities and not our vulnerabilities. If they get in our way, we will push them aside."

Raavn did not answer, but thought, *Taproot said it, but She won't admit we battled the Great Ferns and we lost. This denial shows a flaw in her guidance. Centuries of purging dissidents have left us with weak advisors like her.*

He turned back to his clan. "Search every corner of this planet and the space around it. Do not return until you locate the humans, bring them here, and show them these remains. They will account for their actions. Elmurr, repeat my orders on your communicator for all to hear."

* Pink Floyd, Welcome To The Machine *

The next morning, Flint felt sad because he was unable to help Audrey. As he stepped out of his booth and into the hall, Big D announced on the PA, "...a mandatory meeting for all crew."

In the hall to the meeting room, Big D saw him and ordered, "Halt, and stand at attention. Where were you yesterday?"

Flint's feelings shifted to fear as he recognized the expression on Big D's face. Flint activated the snoop algorithm in his C-chip and read Big D's thoughts: *"Go ahead and draw your gun you bastard. Give me a reason to send you to Gondwana in a body bag."*

Flint activated the control algorithm in his C-chip and the anger lines in Big D's face disappeared.

Big D stopped in front of Flint and spoke in a calm voice, "I had something important to say, but I forgot what it was."

Flint misdirected Big D. "Maybe you wanted to warn me about shiva-coccus."

"Yaw, probably," Big D answered. "Do you know Director Kyleen?"

"No."

"Well, listen up and I'll tell you about her. I sent Kyleen an edict to increase our staff, but I know she'll follow the Inspector's recommendations and reduce Camelot to standby status. Years ago, she was the project manager for Stardust. She cut my budget and gave me leftover fuel tanks to build a spaceport. She got a promotion, but I got shiva-coccus from exposure to radiation while working in the open. Be careful if you ever have to deal with her."

"Yes sir. Thanks for the warning." *Wow, he was going to court martial me for killing an alien. Good thing I hacked his C-chip and made him forget that.*

They arrived at the meeting room. Big D stood at the podium and announced to the crew who were seated, "The Inspector General ordered us to reduce our staff because the Razorroots left the planet. Empire will reassign most of you in the upcoming months. You may take leave until your next assignment. Good luck to all of you."

A few in the audience groaned, but the cheers outnumbered them. Someone asked, "What are your plans?"

"I have enough time in grade to retire, so I will return to Earth."

"Will Empire decommission Camelot?" Flint asked, worried.

"I don't think so," Big D said.

"Who will lead us, if you leave?" Flint asked as he hacked Big D's C-chip and fed him the words.

Big D answered, "Sergeant Flint Valance, I got approval to skip a few ranks and promote you to Lieutenant Commander. This promotion includes the command of Camelot. You will select a skeleton crew who will stay and assume the role of caretaker. That is, if you accept."

Flint was speechless for a moment, and then he found his voice, "Yes, yes, I accept. Thank you. Thank you very much." *How did I ever live without this hacking C-chip?*

"Don't thank me too much, because Earth might send a space marshal to take my place," Big D answered. Then Flint sent him more words, "I want to see my wife and children on Earth, and I'm healthy enough to travel, so I'll beam out before anything else goes wrong."

After the meeting, Flint walked Big D to the teleporter. Big D turned and opened the hatch to the medical clinic.

Flint asked, "Why are you stopping here?"

"I am over the weight limit for the teleporter. If the autodoc applies liposuction, and I fast and exercise for a month, I might be able to teleport."

He is delaying because he knows something is wrong, but he does not know I am hacking him. I cannot let him find that out, Flint thought, and then said, "You don't have to do that. The beamers got rid of our slammer and installed a modified Model A, which can carry more weight. They haven't tested the improvements yet but I am sure they will let you go through."

"I'm trying to remember something. Maybe this is it. I received a message that the police on Gondwana arrested your father and your sister."

Wrinkles appeared in Flint's forehead, "Do you mean Mitch and Mariah are in jail? Why were they arrested?"

"Someone robbed the banks on Gondwana and got away without a trace. Mitch and Mariah made a large amount of credits selling gems for the miners. When they tried to deposit the money into the miners' bank account, the banks decided it was enough to make up for their losses, so the banks accused Mitch and Mariah of the robbery, and confiscated the money and the rest of their gems."

"Where are they? I have to rescue them," Flint asked.

"A logging company bought your father to perform hard labor, and authorities sent your sister to a pit-jail to wait for the next auction. Come with me and I'll help you rescue them."

I have to get away from Big D. If he figures out I'm hacking him, he is strong enough to fight back, Flint thought and answered, "No. Give the coordinates to Major Truman. He owes me a favor. I'll send him a C-mail and let him know you are on the way. He'll make things right."

When they arrived at the teleporter, Flint hacked the beamers' C-chips and made them put Big D in an oversized beam-can and send him on his way. This four-day trip would take weeks on a slammer, and over a decade on a spaceship.

The hacking algorithm in the C-chip I took from Yvette saved me, Flint thought as he twisted the ends of his mustache. Then he texted Truman. Now he had to wait two days for his message to reach Truman, and wait two more days to hear the answer. Quantum signals traveled faster than anything else did. Still, communication between the stars took time.

*

As the day passed, many of the crew teleported to Gondwana and other destinations to find work. Near evening, Jake, Josie, and Pooch arrived. Flint went to the docking bay and opened the bay door so they could dock their runabout truck. Then they went to the helm to check the radar and make sure aliens did not follow them. Jake did not see Lieutenant Gerome sitting in the command chair and threw a twenty-pound pouch of circe on the desk. Flint quickly covered the circe and indicated to Jake to hide it.

"What's in the bag," Gerome asked.

Jake started to reach for his flair gun, but Flint hand-gestured for him to wait while he answered Gerome, "Nothing."

"Is that what you gave Big D? Is that the elixir of life?" Gerome asked. Pooch ran up to Gerome and licked his face. "By all rights, any other dog would not have survived in space this long, and look at Pooch. Here he is bouncing around like a puppy. Jake, you don't look older than twenty-four." He knew Jake was more than fifty years old. "Josie, look at you dancing on your tippy toes. You lost your limp."

"And look, no scars," she said as she raised her blouse.

Flint turned to Gerome and asked, "I thought you left with the others. Why did you stay?"

"I decided to take command. Marty Cleaver, you cannot command Camelot because you don't have a commission. I did some research and discovered you are not even documented, but I might keep you if you follow my orders."

"What kind of orders?" Flint, alias Marty Cleaver asked.

"A shipment of two SAMs and two nuclear blast caps arrived this morning. We will nuke the Gobato and force them to return to the Pleiades."

Flint answered, "I cannot let you do that. They are the source of this elixir. We may need to harvest more of them."

Gerome drew his weapon, "The Inspector said they carry infectious prions. I'm going to destroy that pouch of stuff, and I'm placing you and the miners under house arrest until I know you are not infectious."

Flint waved Jake and Josie to wait outside the helm. He activated the hacking algorithm in the C-chip he took from Yvette and said, "Gerome, put your weapon down, come here, and sit at this desk."

Gerome placed his weapon on the desk, jumped out of the chair, sat at the desk, and asked, "What am I doing here?"

"You are typing your resignation on the teletype."

He started typing on the teletype, and then started shaking.

"Relax Gerome. Do what I say and don't think about it."

When Gerome finished, Flint ordered, "Attach your electronic signature and send it to the Inspector General."

Gerome finished and Flint said, "Now accompany me to the teleporter."

As they passed Jake and Josie at the door, Flint said, "This is a minor matter. I'll be right back."

As they walked to the teleporter, Gerome asked, "Do you want to infect the human race with a virulent form of mad cow disease just to make a few credits?"

"I don't believe you. You are trying to take what we have."

"I am transferring the inspector's report to your C-chip. Read it and weep."

"You're the one weeping. Now get in that beam-can and out of my sight," Flint said as he discarded the inspector's report.

* Sky Fighters, Into The Fire *

When Flint returned to the helm, he explained to the miners how he hacked Gerome's C-chip, forced him to resign, and sent him to Stardust. They all laughed. Then Josie became quiet and asked, "Did you hack Big D?"

"I gave him a little nudge to promote me."

She said, "Is that legal?"

Jake explained to Josie, "Flint can do those things. You forgot he is the pirate, Marty Cleaver," as he tapped on the diamond they stole.

Josie answered, "Oh, well the Razorroots threw this diamond into a junk pile."

Flint reminded her, "Every trade has its privileges."

Jake said, "We found a diamond clump that is too large to load onto a transporter, and our runabout truck does not have enough thrust to lift it into space. Is there any way we can recover it?"

"Diamonds are common. What makes this one special?"

Josie explained as she put a picture of the clump on a view screen, "This gem is a 'future telling stone'."

Jake and Josie looked like children standing next to the jagged stone. Flint explained, "Ooo, that is big. I've heard of future telling stones. They are priceless, but my transporters cannot lift something that heavy. I don't know how to get it on the station without breaking it into smaller pieces."

Jake said, "No, don't break it. Do you know Zane? We can trust him and he can figure things out."

"Yes; he is a friend of my father. Wait while I call him," Flint called the first officer, Sergeant Zane Kimball, to the helm and asked him how to recover the precious stones.

Zane, a middle age man with streaks of gray in his dark hair from exposure to radiation, stared at the view screen and thought for several minutes, then said to Jake, "The hub, cylinder, reactor, and ion engines of this space station can detach from the wheel and spokes and land on the planet. We can use the hub to recover the geode."

Flint commanded the crew to prepare for separation, and told the miners to go to the planet and prepare the diamond mass for transportation.

When all was ready, Zane explained to Flint, "You'll have to be back in an hour or the agroponic units will freeze."

"When we fire our engines, we'll lose stealth, and some of the Gobato ships that are near us and will see us."

"I'll fly the transporter and drop flairs so the Gobato will see me and follow me. I'll lead them to the other side of the planet, and I'll keep them busy for an hour. Then I'll lose them and return."

"They probably can use their impulse engines as particle beam weapons," Flint warned.

"I'll release smoke to block their beams if they get that close."

"We received two SAM's this morning. Take those just in case you need them."

As Zane loaded the SAMs onto a transporter, Flint returned to the helm and sat in the command chair. He turned off the autopilot and turned off the safeties. The ship's computer linked to his mind. The locking bolts released as he thought of them until the core detached from the rest of the space station.

Immediately, several Gobato ships saw them and arranged to intercept. Zane launched his transporter and flew at full thrust at the Gobato ships, then dogged and went past them. The Gobato went after Zane.

The computer plotted the course for the helm, displayed a three D map on Flint's visual cortex, and fired the engines. The core dropped out of orbit and swooped toward the mine like a hawk diving for a sparrow.

As the core skimmed the atmosphere, Flint used the narrow beam laser-comm to talk to Jake. "I see you at the mine. I'll drop in front of you. Flying with two Gs of thrust makes this seem more like a fighter than a space station."

Jake answered, "I see you. Open the docking bay door and I'll drive my truck in so you don't have to land."

Flint skimmed the desert floor while Jake caught up and drove into the docking bay. With the runabout truck and its cargo onboard, Flint ordered full throttle and the core rocketed away from the planet. The radar indicated no alien ships were in the area. After he returned to his original orbit, the crew docked the wheel and spoke sections. Half an hour later, Zane returned with the transporter. After the miners and Zane and the rest of the crew were safe, Flint used the passive radar to locate the Gobato ships.

Zane explained, "You don't have to worry about the Gobato because I led them to the edge of the solar system. I used a fluid suit so I could accelerate at fifty Gs. Even so, their ships were terribly fast but they are awful pilots. Most of them became lost and quit their pursuit. Then I launched the two SAMs and the Gobato ships that remained scattered."

Flint, Zane, and the miners celebrated in the restaurant in the viewing dome late into the night.

"What are your plans?" Flint asked Jake and Josie.

"We want to return to Earth after we get rich selling circe," Jake answered.

"And we want to take our geode with us," Josie added.

"I'll put your diamond clump on a freighter, but I'll need money to pay for it," Flint said as he chewed a synthetic chicken wing.

"Our savings is spent. We don't even have enough to pay passage to Stardust. We need your help."

"If you leave, who is going to watch your mine?" Flint asked.

Jake sipped his cola and offered, "We cannot maintain our mine from Earth so you can have it if you help us with transportation and sell our circe."

"Why can't you sell it?"

Josie explained, "Flint, your father and sister sold our gems for us but now they are in jail. We don't know our way on Gondwana; we need help. Are your pirates, I mean crew, loyal to you? Can we trust them to sell our circe?"

"Yes. I picked only the best. If they wear professional looking medical clothing, they'll have it sold in a week."

"Will they market the circe and return with the profit if we pay them ten percent?"

Flint answered, "Yes. They know if they run with the credits, I will list them as deserters and Empire will arrest them. If they try to hide some of the credits, the other crew members will tell me for a reward."

"Then it is settled. Call them and we will divide the circe. Meet us in three weeks on Stardust and we'll settle our accounts. You can have ten percent of the profits from the circe for managing all of this," Jake answered.

Jake and Josie whispered to each other. Then they removed their C-chips.

Flint asked, "Why did you remove your C-chips?"

"Yo hacking chip works too well. We don't know if ar plans ar for us or for yo."

"I would never hack either of you."

"We trust yo, but we don't trust Yvette who programmed yo C-chip," Josie assured him.

"How valuable do yo zink this circe is?" Jake asked.

Zane answered, "How long do you think the effects last? Are there side effects or after effects?"

Jake answered, "We ave no idea."

Zane looked at Pooch who rested in a corner while ripping a boot into pieces, "Well, Pooch is still healthy, so it has good effects for at least three weeks. That is long enough to sell it. You have twenty pounds of this stuff and only a small square will heal a human. If I chop it into one dose sizes, vacuum pack each chip in an edible wrapper, and sell it on Gondwana as a miracle healing aid, I estimate that this batch is worth over ten million credits."

"Wow Josie. I told you we'd make ze big time." Jake said as he danced with Josie in a circle.

"I'll run tests and manage the sales and credits on Gondwana. I'm a paralegal, so I'll register the company as a privately owned corporation to protect all of us from lawsuits. Since I'm managing and not selling circe, what is my share?" Zane asked.

"Ten percent." Then Jake turned to Flint and said, "We'll leave for Earz as soon as the circe is sold."

Josie choked on a swallow of cola, "When I get back to Earz, I will never eat synzetic food again." She asked Flint, "What are yo plans?"

* Carole King, So Far Away *

Flint answered Jake and Josie, "After I make a million credits, I'll pay Truman for rescuing Audrey, Mitch, and Mariah. Then we'll go to Earth where we'll never have to worry about Truman or his pirates again."

They finished their drinks and Jake and Josie left to pack.

Flint called his trusted pirates and explained the plan. "Take three weeks, travel to Gondwana, and auction these pellets."

Reddragon, a short pirate with a red complexion asked, "Yes, but how do we advertize it? It'll take forever if we go house to house."

"Go to the hospitals, hospice centers, and rest homes of course. Once you heal one person, everyone else will want some. News travels fast in institutions."

"How do we set the price?" Another pirate asked.

"Let the patients set the price," Zane answered. "Once you have a crowd, auction them. Make sure there are more patients than circe, so the demand is higher than the supply."

Flint said, "I need to buckle things down on Camelot before I can leave so Zane will be in charge on Stardust until I arrive. He will fit you with professional clothing and arrange your transportation to Gondwana."

Reddragon asked, "Are we going to make some money out of this?"

"After you sell your share, return to Stardust and you will get ten percent of what you sell. That is more credits than any of you have ever seen. Anyone who cheats will lose their share. Don't tell Truman or he will take it all. Do we all agree?"

The pirates cheered and agreed. The next day, they beamed out to other worlds to make their sales and to collect their fortunes.

Zane stayed behind and asked Flint, "How do you justify killing the Gobato? Aren't they sentient?"

"I haven't thought about that until now. This alien drug cures every disease and will save many lives. Does that justify my actions?"

"Taking a life to save a life. No, I think you need more than that."

"Here's more. The Gobato are invaders. If we kill some of them for this drug, then the rest of them will hide underground and won't invade our colonies. The Gobato eat Razorroots, but if we keep them here, the Razorroots will be safe." After he spoke, Flint played the recorded expletives made by the captured alien, Treeeater, when Jake poked it.

"You convinced me." Zane quoted the general statute, "'Authorities are permitted to capture, vanquish, and subdue undocumented humans and to put them into perpetual slavery and to take all their possessions and property. Newly discovered aliens that are hostile are to be dealt with the same as undocumented humans.' The one you harvested attacked Jake and Josie, clearly a hostile alien."

Flint walked with Zane to the teleporter. Zane asked, "After you and I leave, this space station will be empty. How do we protect it from the Gobato?"

"I'll put it into a decaying orbit. If we don't return in a few months, it will burn up in the atmosphere."

"Does the teletype in Big D's office still print updates. I want to make sure the law isn't waiting for us on Stardust before I leave."

"Yes. We'll stop at his office on the way to the teleporter."

At the office, Flint thumbed through the pages of bulletins then shouted, "A space marshal! Earth is sending a space marshal!"

Zane grabbed the pages, read them, and then answered, "This changes nothing if we act fast. We'll sell our circe and change our identities before he gets here."

Flint looked down and nodded, "I worked hard for this command and now I have to give it up."

Zane answered, "Yes, but you and Audrey will have a life together."

They walked to the teleporter and shook hands with thumbs up. Then Flint watched Zane leave.

The Space Station was eerily quiet without Audrey, Yvette, Big D, Jake and Josie, the crew, and Zane. A thought helped to cheer Flint, *I'll be on Stardust in a few weeks and I'll be with Audrey again. My friends will help me rescue my father and sister; then I'll be a hero.*

As he walked to the restaurant in the viewing dome for a drink, a trip line cut his foot and threw him to the floor. He examined it, *This trip line has the same color and texture as Blackbark's root fibers. I suspected that plant was still on Camelot. Now it's going to harass me.*

He limped to the wall, pressed a first aid icon, then removed and applied a handheld mini-doc to his injury the same way Audrey used it earlier. Then he located and loaded the modified flare gun that Jake left behind. *I'm not giving up command of Camelot without a fight. This weapon will burn a razorroot to ash and cut a space marshal in two.*

Map:

110 Light Years Top to Bottom. 0.1 Light Years Right to Left.

Dearth   Far Star

Camelot ⟶ · ○

~~~~~~

11 Light Years

~~~~~~

Stardust

Gondwana ⟶ ○   ○   **O**

Ruby

~~~~~~

40 Light Years

~~~~~~

Beehive

Sirius

~~~~~~

9 Light Years

~~~~~~

Mars L2
Space
Station   Earth Venus   Sol

○   ○   ○   ○   **O**

○

Moon

~~~~~~

50 Light Years

~~~~~~

Xanadu   Rasalhague

○   **O**

Chapter 7: Earth Attacks

The nearest rescue team was in the Sol system, sixty-two light-years from Far Star. Unaware of events on Camelot, Space Marshal Glenn Hunter woke early. *Why is my head buzzing,* He thought. *Oh, it's my C-chip telling me to answer an emergency call from The Director of Interstellar Rescue. I'll see what she wants.*

A pleasant female voice replaced the buzzer in his head, "We have an emergency. I need you in my office immediately."

Glenn ignored the sexy undertone and answered, "What's wrong? Is the dome failing?"

"No, it's an invasion." She answered.

"For gods' sake, you're not cancelling my vacation are you?"

"Don't argue with me until you have all of the facts. We'll explain when you get here. I have to go now." Director Kyleen cut the connection before he said goodbye.

He was already dressed for work, thanks to attentive computer hands in his booth that prepared him through the night while he slept.

"Computer, what is the status of the dome?" He asked.

"The multi-dome is undamaged and radiation levels are tolerable. Your booth is at the surface. You may leave," The computer answered.

"Are we being invaded?"

"No, there are no reports of hostile activity or damage."

Then why did Kyleen act abruptly? Glenn wondered as he stepped out of his booth and onto a rocky concourse. He brushed his long red hair aside, shielded his green eyes from the yellow sun, and looked up at Earth through the glass dome. Colors of blue, green, and white were faded to black, brown, and orange from layers of smog.

Tranquility Base covered more than five square miles of the Moon. While officials considered the air breathable under the dome, Glenn felt nauseated from the odor similar to abandoned glass factory with a rodent infestation. He removed his nose filters and put on a full-face breather.

As his booth disappeared underground, another booth rose next to him. A thin man with grey hair and blue eyes stepped out of it; Assistant Director Victor Gillinger. Victor's dream to explore the universe ended when he saw broke and broken explorers return from deep space. Victor wanted to go back to Earth, but he had to stay on the Moon to fulfill his contract.

Victor said, "Good morning Glenn." Then he turned and walked away before Glenn could answer. Glenn watched him select a meal from a row of vending machines, flip a chair out of a patio floor, and sit at an outdoor café table a block away.

I need to find out what is going on before I go to the office, Glenn thought. *Victor must know something or he would have stayed and talked for a moment.*

* Phaedra, Nancy Sinatra & Lee Hazlewood *

As he approached the café, Glenn saw the work-study student, Gloria Asha Mandela, sitting at the table with Victor. Her bushy black hair highlighted her dark eyes. Gloria was the same age as Glenn's daughter on Earth. Glenn bought a snack from the vending machines and joined them.

When he sat, Victor was talking, "I watched a news bulletin in my booth this morning. They said zombies invaded our most distant colonies."

"You shouldn't listen to those rumors. Don't you have anything better to talk about?" Gloria said as she looked away.

Glenn changed the conversation. "I passed my physical. I arranged to visit Earth and be with my daughter. I haven't seen her for two years."

Gloria nodded and smiled, "Oh that is wonderful news. Does that mean your injuries have healed?"

Glenn remembered the teleporter accident two years earlier that slammed him through three walls and a ceiling. Modern medicine put the pieces back together, but Glenn needed time to heal. He answered, "No. It means I stopped complaining so I can visit Earth."

"Victor, do you have vacation plans?" Gloria asked.

Victor broke the mood, "Haven't you learned not to make plans? Empire does not care what happens to us."

Gloria looked surprised as she put her coffee cup down. "Do we work for Empire?" she asked, "I thought we worked for the government?"

Glenn and Victor exchanged a glance.

"Victor works for Empire," Glenn clarified. "Earth governments discovered trying to keep control of explored space was too difficult, so they contracted the task to Empire Corporation, the main industry in space. The Government supplies military personnel, such as you and me. We are the muscle for Empire."

Gloria looked at her thin arms and said, "The what?"

"You know, we are the law enforcers."

She shrugged and mumbled, "Whatever," noticed her empty cup, and left the table to refill it.

Glenn asked Victor. "You said you don't have vacation plans. Do you have an assignment?"

He answered slowly while shaking his head, "After I blurted that out, I realized I said too much. Well, it's only a rumor and a dangerous one, so don't say anything." He gave a prolonged look and a brief smile.

Glenn knew from Victor's expression that he was not telling him something. He decided to pry some more and whispered, "Kyleen called me this morning. I know from her voice they'll slap a mission or a layoff on the first one in the office. Be smart and sit here and talk to me."

"Or maybe it's a promotion," Victor said, and then held his hand up indicating he took a call on his C-chip. C-chips could read word-thoughts, which enabled him to keep his call private. After a minute, his face reddened and the lines on his forehead deepened.

Glenn studied his expression, *It's not a promotion. It must be a mission or a layoff.*

Finally, to Glenn's relief, Victor spoke, "Well, my bum attitude is Empire's fault. Now I'll never retire. I have to go. That was the office; they want me now."

"You are under too much stress. I'm afraid you'll break." Glenn said as he tried to reassure Vic, "How can you not retire? In a year, you'll be eligible."

He shouted at Glenn, "Don't tell me what I'll be."

Gloria noticed his rebuke and said, "Vic, what is wrong?"

"Stay out of this Gloria." He leaned forward and continued with a hissing whisper, "If you cared about me, you would be the director, and I would be safe, but you missed that opportunity because of your lazy attitude. You care only for yourself and you forget your friends."

Glenn whispered back, "Hey, don't say I'm lazy. My productivity is in the top ten percent."

"And what do you know about being on time?" He continued as if Glenn had not spoken. "You haven't been on time for two years."

"My hours aren't the same as yours. I work late. Let's talk this out. We know each other well enough that you can talk to me." Glenn pleaded.

"Every time I tell you my problems, you get that confused cruddy look on your face. You don't know me. You never knew me."

"It was that C-chip call you answered that worried you. Tell me what is going on and I will understand."

Victor stood, "Okay, understand this. Pirates and zombies invaded the outworld. Enjoy your last meal." He pointed at Glenn's doughnut, shifted to a pleasant voice and hollered to Gloria. "I have to go. The office wants me. You and Glenn take your time."

Glenn stood in shock as Victor finished his doughnut in one bite, and gulped down the rest of his coffee. Glenn asked, "Zombies? Really?"

Victor did not answer as he dashed away. Then Glenn watched Gloria program a 1950's simulated jukebox.

* Donna Summer, I Feel Love *

She hummed a song she composed and recited the lyrics, "You are the geode in my diamond star…" The simulator auditioned several bands. She selected "The Artificial Vegetables", pressed play, and adjusted the tempo. Three-D projectors in the vending machines flashed images that moved in rhythm with the music. Gloria danced on her toes and leaped through the air without effort.

Glenn considered, *I am glad my daughter does not have this job, but I feel bad for Gloria. We are only names on paper as far as Empire is concerned. Will she have a bum attitude like Victor's after Empire slams her around?*

Ten minutes later, the music ended.

Gloria sat down and said, "Wow, Victor treated you like dirt. Why didn't you punch him in the face?" as she took a bite of her doughnut and licked the chocolate off her lips.

"Really Gloria, is that what you would do?" He glanced at Gloria's confused and beautiful face and relaxed his tone, "You don't understand. Vic might have a dangerous assignment."

As Gloria considered punching Vic, Glenn took a thoughtful pause and looked at his coffee. Then he looked at her and asked, "How much money do you have? Can you afford passage back to Earth?"

"No, I don't have that much."

"If my daughter had your job, I'd want someone to give her a chance to escape. Here," Glenn transferred thirty-thousand credits into her account through the C-net. "Now return to Earth and don't look back." *If my life depends on her, then I want to know that I can trust her.*

Her mouth dropped open as she looked at him. She said, "No, I can't take that," and transferred the money back. "This is my career for better or for worse, but what got you worried?"

"All I know is rumor. I'll explain on the way to our cubicles."

They finished their breakfast, and crossed the sidewalk to the office building. The security system opened the entryway doors, redirecting the blast of stale and acidic smelling office air from overhead vents into the walkway. Oxygen breathers did not block an odor this strong. Passersby near enough to smell the stench looked at them as if they committed a crime.

As they took the elevator down to their floor, Gloria asked about the four-way tunnels that led from the elevator at every level.

"They connect to office bays. Look at the strata of dust and rock that lay in-between the levels."

Gloria looked through the transparent walls of the elevator, "This is an archaeologist's dream come true. Did you see that? We passed a vein of gold."

"On the Moon, water is more valuable than gold. Let me know if you see a vein of ice," Glenn explained, "This building has almost full camera coverage. Use your C-chip to access the camera network so you know what to expect when you enter the office floor. Look there. Do you see the new face in the manager's office on camera 46-11727? He's a well-dressed man like someone from Earth. He might be Vic's replacement. The government and Empire both claim they never fire anyone, but they do. I remember a dozen office workers who left involuntarily."

"Why don't you use the direct C-link to listen to their conversation? Doesn't that give more information?"

"Don't use that except for emergencies. It violates the privacy codes."

Gloria scanned the building using the security cameras. "A layoff? No wonder Victor was upset."

The elevator passed floor 23B. They were halfway to their floor.

"Victor has dodged every layoff and every mission since he got here," Glenn laughed as they continued their descent. He knew serious trouble lie ahead but did not want to worry Gloria in case he was wrong. "The office needs someone to write reports and Victor is always on time. However, tension and rivalry thrive in the office."

Gloria answered, "That sounds exciting. I noticed that you avoid the director. What's going on there?"

"She's my x-wife, but it's worse than that. When the previous Director of Interstellar Rescue left a year ago, Kyleen and I applied for that top position. We have the same credentials and I have more time in grade, but Empire gave her the job."

"Yuck, I don't like Kyleen anymore." She asked, "If experience doesn't matter, what does?"

"What you know helps you keep your job. Who you know helps you get promoted. Kyleen got the promotion by calling her political friends, and she always accepts new missions no matter how dangerous. However, all of that cannot hide her ineptness." *Was that floor 45? I had better prepare for a jolt. My floor is next.*

"Then they might fire Kyleen," Gloria blurted.

As they stepped out of the elevator, Glenn took a breath and hid his smile. *What she said is true. Why am I worried when this could be a time to celebrate?* Then he answered, "We will know soon enough."

Victor was waiting for Gloria in her office cubicle. The rest of the room was silent and appeared vacant. The office staff was invisible behind the randomly placed partitions as they read and wrote reports on their C-chips.

As Glenn entered his cubicle, his desk pad detected his C-chip and flashed an urgent message. Only Kyleen and those above sent messages with this priority.

He read the note, "Come to my office."

* Jerry Goldsmith, PATTON *

As Glenn entered the office, Kyleen wirelessly transferred a report to his C-chip and included a message, "You are running late, so read the this report while we talk." He opened it and began reading it using his mind's eye. 'Aliens from the Pleiades Attack Dearth' was the title of the report.

As he saluted, Kyleen and an official who Glenn did not recognize stood and returned his salute. Director Kyleen Lespine was wide-eyed and smiling, like a child in a candy store. Her expression was impossible to read because it never changed. Plaques describing her achievements covered the top half of the wall behind her desk. With short brown hair, she stood three inches shorter than Glenn. Her clothing was extravagant compared to how he and the rest of the office staff dressed.

The visitor wore a formal bright blue uniform. Kyleen introduced them, and they shook hands. The new face belonged to VP Earl P. Mackley. He was the same height as Kyleen, but had a powerful build, dark hair, and a deep voice. Shadows under his eyes revealed a lack of sleep. He held two positions, Empire's Vice President of Interstellar Rescue, and Secretary of the Exterior for the Government. The Dual titles guaranteed cooperation between Empire Corporation and the government.

The VP spoke, "I knew your father. We worked together spreading carbon dust into orbit to protect Earth from lethal radiation when the star, Betelgeuse, went supernova. I owe him for putting me on a career path to become the Vice President. Kyleen tells me you are like him."

Glenn continued to read, '...sixty-three Razorroots and twenty-five humans killed...', then answered, "Oh shit, I mean, yes sir." He noticed two stained but empty coffee cups on the desk and two discarded napkins in the trash. Apparently, the VP and the Director had waited for a long time.

The VP seemed hurried and went right to the point. "Friday we received a yellow alert from a space station called Camelot in the out-world. The captain in charge of Camelot reported that the yellow alert was a glitch and he said we should ignore it, but telemetry and the report you are reading told a different story. Their radar detected bogies right before the yellow alert, the base had major electrical failures, and a colony of friendly aliens called Razorroots deserted the planet and the station. Clearly, something went wrong. We need to send someone there to find out what happened."

Glenn thought, *Kyleen already approved my vacation. Where are they going with this?*

The VP continued, "We are sending you to Far Star to make sure Camelot is secure. Camelot orbits a semi-habitable planet called Dearth. If it is not safe, then make it safe so we can return the Razorroots to their colony."

"How far away is Dearth?" Glenn asked.

"Sixty-two light-years."

"Wait a minute. Isn't that beyond governed space? I never heard of anyone traveling that far and returning. The report says an Inspector General is in the out-world. Order him to do this." Glenn asked.

"Turn to the next page and you will see that a trainee wrote the report you are reading. He took over when the Inspector General was killed while investigating Dearth. This trainee claims an unknown virus infected the commander and we can't trust him, but we have no record of any such virus. Glenn, go to Camelot, and tell us what is going on. Find out if the commander, Captain Dwain Hammerton, needs our help." Mac answered.

"Aren't there pirates that far out?"

"We did a sweep last month, found four pirates, and put them in pit jails. That should be the last of them. In case there are alien invaders, I hired an army of mercenaries to deal with them. Big D, will command the army, you just need to get them there," Mac explained.

"I'm still healing from the last time I rode those slammers."

"We replaced the slammers with Model As. These new teleporters will get you there safely and on time. The slammers are used only for cargo and backup." The VP cleared his throat and continued, "Ahem; I would go with you, but I need to find out what the Razorroots know about this. The Razorroots left Earth a week before we knew what was happening on Dearth. Gondwana reported the Razorroots abandoned that planet as well. Their home planet, Xanadu, orbits the star Rasalhague, which is in the opposite direction to your destination. I will go there and assure the Razorroots it is safe for them to return to their space colonies."

Glenn nodded at Kyleen as he stated, "I can't do this alone."

The VP answered, "Director Kylee will stay here and take over my duties while I am gone, but you won't be travelling alone. Assistant Director Victor Gillinger and work-study student Gloria Mandela will rendezvous on the planet Stardust in the Ruby star system to assist you. Stardust is just one hop from Camelot. Vic will be in charge of Gloria, so you won't be distracted from your mission."

Glenn leaned on Kyleen's desk. She lost her smile as Glenn demanded, "Vic is an office worker and Gloria isn't trained for this? I want someone who has experience in deep space."

"Big D has decades of experience. This will be a training exercise for Gloria," The VP replied. "Go there, calm things down, show her the ropes so Vic can retire, and return as a hero. An additional assignment is to protect our secret technologies. Empire Corporation is testing an experimental upgrade to our teleporters to improve transportation between Camelot and a small planet in the Ruby star system called Stardust."

"I applied for a vacation on Earth. I'll be in better condition after the acclimation exercises. Can this mission wait until I get back?"

"That is not what your father would say. Victor is at the spaceport sending Gloria on her way. We cannot send her alone." Mac stared at Glenn.

"Oh yes. I can't leave Gloria alone." Glenn knew Mac outmaneuvered him.

Mac continued, "You will leave in three hours and Victor will follow early tomorrow morning."

Glenn thought, but did not speak, *That is why Vic was edgy this morning. They are using him to push me, and Gloria to pull me. Now Vic and Gloria will blame me for their predicament.*

"The Inspector's trainee will send us his official report; I'll let you know as soon as we have it. This envelope has your travel papers, three telecommunication U-net cubes, and a new C-chip." He handed Glenn a plain, pocket size, brown, envelope. The government required travelers to carry documentation with hard copies for all missions.

Glenn examined the contents of the envelope. A surveillance stamp in the corner of the package scanned his retina, identified him, and allowed access. The surface changed into a touch sensitive holographic screen. Glenn looked inside, pulled out his travel papers, a cerebral C-chip, and three electronic cubes.

Mac continued talking, "Those electronic cubes are a new technology called U-net cubes. They communicate to each other almost instantly, and will extend the range of the local networks (C-nets) to cover all of explored space. Install them at the bases specified in your travel papers. These bases are in-route to your destination. I'll install similar U-net cubes as I travel. When we install enough of these, we can automate the balancing of teleporters, and that will reduce accidents. We will call this single universal network the U-net."

"Yes, we need to make teleporters safer," Glenn replied with a blank stare.

As he approached the door, Mac added, "Oh, by the way, you will send me daily reports. You can do that with another new technology, an insta-text chip custom designed for you. Health Services already has it, and they will implant it under your skin. It works with your C-chip. It uses quantum entanglement to communicate to a similar chip implanted in me. insta-text chips have a limited number of bits and use each bit only once. If our conversations are in text and short, they will last a year or more."

"What about video?"

"They will send video but not for long, video sucks up all the bits. I want to stay and answer more questions, but the beamers want me at the teleporter terminal right now. Director Kyleen Lespine will arrange your reservations and answer your questions. I wish you a good trip."

They returned his salute as Mac turned, walked out, and closed the door behind him. Top dignitaries often rushed from one place to the next.

* ARGENT, LIAR *

Kyleen sat, let out a long sigh, and covered her face.

Glenn complained, "Damn you. You're keeping me from my daughter."

She looked up, stared in shock at Glenn, and stammered, "D-don't blame me. I thought your vacation had priority. We are in this situation because Congress cut our budget and our staff. Now they are throwing money at us, but I can't hire and train a space agent in one day."

"Yes, they push the boundaries out and cut the budget back until something goes wrong. Then they want me to fix it."

Kyleen transferred the itinerary from her C-chip to the envelope's computer. It listed in detail each leg of the trip. Glenn looked at the envelope and said, "I hate to tell you this but I never heard of Camelot, and I am not physically fit." He pointed at his swollen knee for emphasis.

As he returned the contents to the envelope, Kyleen said, "The filters in the Model A teleporters will remove that infection. Traveling at zero G will give your knee a chance to heal. However, I agree Empire is using you so I'll make this right. Mac arranged it so you have to leave the Moon today or face a court martial, but he made no arrangement for you to arrive on Camelot.

She continued, "The personnel department owes me a favor, so I asked them to change your physical test results and recommend you for retirement due to disability. When you get to the Sirius Space Station, submit this request sheet that personnel already approved." Kyleen transferred a document to Glenn's C-chip and continued, "Empire can't court martial you if you qualify for disability, so this gives you a free pass. Live it up on the Sirius Space Station or on the party planet, Gondwana, both are en-route. Don't go to Camelot. Don't worry about the consequences. I take full responsibility."

"What about Vic and Gloria? Don't they need me?"

"I sent a message to Big D who is in charge of Camelot. I helped him years ago to finance the construction of the Stardust Spaceport, so he owes me a favor. He'll tell me what's happening on Dearth. If things are safe and if the miners on Dearth abandoned their mine, Big D will transfer it to my name. Vic and Gloria will command Mac's army to work the mine. I will give you ten percent if you manage them. We will all be rich. I'll let you know before you get there if things are safe."

Glenn spoke, "You didn't have time to plan this in the last hour. You must have known about this earlier."

"I have friends who keep me informed," She answered.

"I don't need more income. Do you have a scheme that does not keep me away from my daughter?"

"I can make things better, but I can't make them perfect," She said.

"Then you are cutting me off," Glenn said and turned to leave.

Kyleen stood and said, "Go directly to the teleporter terminal. Empire will box all of your belongings and cancel the lease on your booth."

As Glenn walked out the door, his knees buckled. He limped to his desk to straighten himself. He turned off his desk pad and put it in a shredder. On his way to the elevator, he struggled to keep his legs strait while adjusting his C-chip to numb his pain. *How did I pass my physical when I cannot stand?*

He felt like an old horse leaving the barnyard as he approached the exit. *I hoped to stay on the moon or somewhere near Earth. Now, I might never see Earth again, or my daughter.*

The office staff lined up in the hall to wish him farewell. The lead person handed him a piece of cake and a card that his coworkers signed earlier. Glenn's mouth was dry forcing him to choke on the cake. As he shook their hands on his way out, he realized someone must have arranged this going-away-party in advance. He asked, "Why are the top brass always the last to know what is going on?"

He stopped at the medical clinic for the insta-text chip implant that linked to Mac. The waiting room was full, but Glenn had priority because he was on a tight schedule.

Chapter 8: Fifteen Minutes to Mars

Glenn did not pack because his weight was near the maximum for the teleporters. His everyday clothes were too heavy for the teleporters so he stopped at a travel accessory store to buy travel clothes. The rip proof and fireproof clothes he chose were expensive but met every travel need.

After leaving the store, he tried to decide what to tell his daughter on Earth. *She expects me to visit her in a month. How can I tell her she might never see me again? I can't say that, but she will resent me if I lie. I'll have to think about this some more.* He went to a restaurant and ordered synthetic buffalo wings and a beer.

After hesitating, he contacted his daughter. The conversation did not go well. He lied and told her he would see her again. She knew better, severed the connection, and blocked his callbacks and his text messages.

Glenn scanned his envelope. He wondered how he could travel sixty-two light-years in less than two months, so he read about teleporters. "A phenomenon called quantum tunneling facilitates teleportation. Every object exists within its probability field. The passenger enters a canister. Beamers extend the canister's probability field by chilling it and placing it before a lens focused on the destination. Ballast mass traveling in the opposite direction absorbs excess momentum."

The explanations, formulas, and proofs continued for more than ten pages. Glenn could not read more than one page without falling asleep. The main point was the new Model A teleporters were as safe as the Model Ts and one thousand times faster. Slammers were no longer in use.

As teleportation distances increased, the dangers increased, so travelers preferred to make several short hops rather than trying to reach their final destination in a single large hop. Sixty-two light-years was a long distance to travel, so Mars was the first of many stops on his itinerary.

* Jethro Tull, Locomotive Breath HD FLAC *

Space Marshal Glenn Hunter left the restaurant, and did not check the address or a map for the train depot because it was visible from his location. He sat in a line chair, extended an insulated "fishing pole" to catch an overhead power line, and pressed the retract button to raise him up until he was close enough to hook the line with an insulated "motor pole" attached to the other side of the chair. A small motor at the end of the motor pole drove a tri-wheel-trolley. This motor sent him along the power line when he pulled the speed control trigger. He enjoyed traveling above the city.

Glenn used the fishing pole to transfer to a high-tension electrical wire. Riding the long, sagging lines high above the city was a thrill, like riding a rollercoaster. When he reached the train station, he wanted to turn around, and ride that wire again, but he did not have enough time.

The trip from Tranquility Base to the spaceport was a treat in a day that Glenn thought would be drudgery. The train, which traveled through a transparent tunnel, deviated from a direct path so tourists could view the moon's surface. Along the way, he saw Sabine crater, a rill, a mountain, and the Apollo Eleven Lander.

A fast breeder reactor that produced radioactive isotopes was visible on the distant horizon. These isotopes replaced fossil fuels as the main energy source for cities on Earth. Nuclear waste disposal was not a problem on the moon because there was no biosphere to protect, and no weather to disperse the waste. The isotopes they sent to Earth had short half-lives, so containment was necessary for only a few decades.

Workers at the reactor packaged the isotopes in cases they called "nuclear batteries" or "n-batteries". The largest n-batteries weighed ninety pounds and could power a space-car for over a year, or supply electricity and heat for a house for five years. Several batteries could power a factory, or power an Earth-Moon shuttle for dozens of trips. This simple conversion to nuclear saved the Earth from global warming.

As the isotope-powered train cleared a ridge, the spaceport came into view. Glenn saw two huge lenses that overshadowed the spaceport and the spaceships. Teleporter systems used these lenses to form quantum channels to carry passengers and cargo.

Teleporter lenses worked in pairs: one at the departure, and one at the destination. The lens for Moon-Earth traffic was a few hundred meters in diameter. The Moon-Mars lens was five times larger and would distort if it were on Earth.

Glenn counted twenty spaceships docked at the spaceport as three arrived and two departed. Teleporters had weight limits, so spaceships did the heavy lifting. Most of the ships were shuttles that carried manufactured goods, water, amino acids, and other supplies from Earth, and returned with nuclear isotopes and minerals.

An interplanetary transporter sat on the stone tarmac. The interstellar spaceships stayed in orbit to prevent gravity from damaging their lightweight frames.

The train arrived at the spaceport dome with a slight jar as it stopped. Pain shot through Glenn's joints. *I wonder if management changed my medical test results. Were they that desperate to send me to Camelot?*

*

At the spaceport desk, a clerk logged him in and sent him to a waiting area, which was full of travelers. The people traveling out were talking to the people returning to learn all that they could. Their conversations seemed trivial to Glenn, because he was losing his home, his daughter, and possibly his life.

A large window at one end of the room offered an excellent view of the moon's terrain. Glenn went to the window and saw the transparent train tunnel. It meandered around hills and craters. The horizon hid Tranquility Base; the moon's curvature was obvious. The stars were bright and clear with no atmosphere to obstruct them.

While he watched, a loud voice hissed at Glenn from behind, causing him to start and almost leap through the window.

"Impressive view, isn't it? You're Space Marshal Hunter aren't you? I'm your transportation assistant. Most people call us beamers, but you can call me Roxie. I'm here to help you."

He turned and faced a short overweight woman who wore a starched and pressed uniform. "Yes, Roxie, you can call me Glenn. Is a young lady named Gloria waiting to teleport?"

"She left three hours ago. It's about time for our government to send someone out there to see what the excitement is about." Roxie hissed with a large smile and continued, "That is quite an outfit you are wearing, Glenn. Does it weigh less than a pound? If not, we have spray-on clothing so you won't appear naked."

"The spray-on offers no protection. I prefer fabric. Here is my clothing authentication," Glenn answered as he suspected this assistant was not here to help him but to irritate him as much as possible. "They warned me when I bought these clothes, I might need this."

Roxie took the slip of paper and held it as if she weighed it in her hand. Then she grabbed for the brown envelope but Glenn would not let go. "You cannot teleport until I weigh and measure that. If I don't adjust the canister for the exact mass, you will be slammed."

"I'll accompany you, and we will both weigh it," Glenn responded, not willing to let the envelope out of his sight for any reason.

Roxie said, "Have it your way."

She recorded the mass of the package and weighed Glenn with his clothes. The teleporter mass limit was the equivalent of one-hundred eighty pounds in Earth's gravity. Glenn weighed thirty pounds, one-hundred seventy-nine pounds if he were on Earth. The envelope was almost weightless.

"Okay," Roxie said. "You have priority over everyone else. Your information shows you have experience teleporting, is that correct."

"Yes, that is correct."

"Then I will not explain the procedures unless you ask. The teleporter canister is this way. Come with me."

Glenn controlled his comments and his voice. He wanted to catch up with Gloria. If he alienated this beamer, he might not leave on time.

He asked, "Your teleporter isn't a slammer is it?"

"Gosh no. My Model T teleporter is slow but safe. Wait here while I call the other end to adjust for your ballast mass. I'll be back in half an hour. While I'm away, read our procedures on the C-net."

Glenn looked around for another beamer and saw none. He had no choice but to trust Roxie with his life.

*

He noticed the nearby comfort booths. *I have time, so I'll install the C-chip that Mac gave me.*

Inside a comfort booth, he pressed the standby button before the entertainment and toiletry modules activated. He took the new C-chip out of the envelope and held it to the back of his head to record his personal settings and preferences from his old device.

He raised a flap of skin at the base of his skull where doctors surgically implanted nerves after his birth. Glenn felt a slight sting when he pulled out his old C-chip. He inserted the new chip in the same place, and broke his old chip and disposed of it. Then he stashed the small envelope in an inner pocket of his clothing.

The new chip stabilized after a few minutes. It responded the same as the old device except the main menu offered two more selections: interrogation, and Mac. The interrogation feature hacked into other peoples' C-chips to read information or issue commands. The Mac menu worked with his insta-chip implant to send and receive text messages from Earl P. Mackley.

Glenn tested the standard features of his new C-chip. He whistled a range of notes and commanded the chip to play them back to check its auditory operation. The notes came back as slightly garbled as if under water. He preferred this, so recorded sounds were unlike actual sounds. After leaving the booth, he looked around the room while recording a video file from his vision and played it back. The video playback appeared as if he had eyes in the back of his head, so he could distinguish playback video from what his eyes saw. He did not test smell and tactile because he did not have those upgrades.

The virtual keyboard, piano, and tablet worked with no problems. He downloaded and uploaded a few files using the C-net without trouble, found an unused monitor and transferred visual feeds to it and from it. The videos played in his head. It worked. A universe positioning system replaced the global positioning system (GPS).

* Elton John, Rocket Man *

Satisfied his new chip worked as intended, he returned to the waiting area. Instead of sitting in the front where everyone would glare at him, he sat in the back. As he looked at the other travelers, Glenn noticed his C-chip read their private thoughts. He saw what they saw, heard what they heard, and felt their emotions. Foreign emotions registered in his feet, unlike his own emotions.

He tried to probe the deepest thoughts of a suspicious looking man, when the beamer hissed at him from behind, "I am ready for you. I completed the adjustments."

She led him to the canister staging area and said, "I downloaded your profile from your personal booth. The liner in this canister will conform to you so you can travel in comfort."

As Glenn slid into the beam-can, Roxie scanned his C-chip with a handheld device to verify his identity and charge the cost to his account; something his old C-chip would not have flagged.

The lining in the canister was a soft and slippery satin material that fit him like a tight glove. It felt so tight that even his clothing crowded him.

The procedures required Roxie to provide basic instructions, "The time for a transfer is uncertain; it takes at least fifteen minutes and could take a few days. You travel at your own risk. That red button is the emergency button. If you press it, I will get you out fast, but I will put you at the back of the line. Before I put you back in, you will have to wait for even the standbys to beam. Now, hand me your oxygen breather."

"W-what?" said Glenn.

"Your breather. You can't travel with it. It adds too much to the mass, and there isn't any room for it inside there. I thought you read the procedures."

"I did, I just don't want to breathe bad air."

"The canister has filters. You will love the air it provides. Now take a deep breath, and hand me your breather."

Glenn inhaled and handed her the breather while he held his nose to avoid the stench. Station air was as unhealthy as tobacco smoke.

As Roxie closed the lid, the small envelope in Glenn's pocket crowded him further and forced him to exhale some air. He waited until the canister's filters cleared the air before trying to breathe.

The sudden silence in his head startled Glenn; his cerebral implant went dead. *Yes, of course, this is a quantum event, and I am like Schrodinger's cat. I cannot communicate to the outside or teleportation will not occur.*

He waited in the dead silence and in the artificial light of the beam-can, not able to do anything until he reached the Mars-A Spaceport and a different assistant opened the lid. After a short delay, the lid opened, and Roxie shoved a breather in Glenn's face. He put it on.

She said, "You tricked me. You used the toilet and didn't tell me. Good thing I double-checked the weight before I beamed you out. If the ballast does not balance the weight of the cargo exactly, then both will slam at their destinations. You should know that if you teleported before. "

"The last time I teleported I was slammed."

"Well, that is not a surprise." She added a small weight to the inside of the canister, removed the breather, and closed the lid again. Glenn wondered if that weight difference caused his accident two years earlier. He knew he walked a narrow path. If something as simple as relieving himself could be fatal, then space travel may be too dangerous.

The hours dragged on for what seemed like days. The canister carried a battery and tanks to hold enough oxygen, water, and broth to last for a week. Travelers rarely noticed the waste disposal system.

Finally, he felt a slight tremor shoot through his body. "Ah, I am at The Mars-A Spaceport."

*

Glenn pressed the red button above his head. The lid of his canister opened, and a technician handed him an oxygen breather. Even with the breather, the air smelled like a high school shower room with a background smell of vomit from people waiting and rushing through.

"Welcome to MLS2, one of the Mars Lagrangian Space Stations, and the Mars Deep Space Teleporter Terminal. You traveled more than one-hundred and seventy million miles," said one of two beamers helping him out of the canister.

Glenn asked, "How long did that trip take?"

"Three and a half hours to initiate, and fifteen minutes to beam. How do you feel?"

Glenn answered, "Never better."

While one beamer retrieved the toiletry before it spilled, and prepared the canister for its trip back to the moon, the other explained, "Nobody is waiting to go back to the moon, so we will return this canister with freight: rough diamonds and other gemstones mined in the asteroid belt, or gold ore and other minerals mined in Saturn's rings. You can see boxes of them piling up in the hall because we ran out of storage space."

Then he probed Glenn's C-chip to verify his identity. "we will beam you to the Sirius Space Station for the next leg of your trip. You can teleport to Sirius from here."

"Did a young lady named Gloria leave yet?" Glenn asked.

"Yes, she left for Sirius right before you arrived. We could not delay her with this many people waiting."

"I understand. What technology do you use to beam passengers? You don't use slammers do you?"

The beamer answered, "You have nothing to worry about. All passenger traffic to Sirius is on a new Model A. Those slammers were too accident prone for common use, so we use them only for cargo and in emergencies."

Glenn was curious, "Why not use Model Ts? Aren't those reliable?"

"Yes, but the Model As are one thousand times faster."

"Then why not replace the Model Ts with Model As?"

"The Model As cost a lot more and they are expensive to maintain. Specialized labs build their beam-cans with quantum-entangled atoms, which takes a long time," the beamer explained.

"When do I leave?"

"We cannot teleport you now because Gloria is in transit and we have only one pair of beam-cans. Her trip will take three days."

Glenn asked while he set the alarm on his C-chip, "Three days of isolation in a beam-can? Why does it take so long?"

"Because the distance is so great. Don't you remember the slammers? They took five times longer."

Glenn admitted, "I tried to forget that. Do you have entertainment or some way to pass the time for people who are waiting?"

"Most people wait in comfort booths. Don't worry about the time. I'll call you on the net an hour before we need you."

An announcement interrupted, "Interplanetary Transporter Flight 117 will leave in thirty minutes to Phobos. Please board now if your destination is the Mars tube-plant colony. A planetary shuttle will take you to Mars after you reach Phobos. Enjoy your trip."

The beamer advised, "You can watch that transporter through the viewport in the waiting room."

"Thanks," Glenn said as he pushed off. Coasting with an effortless hop every ten feet was easier than walking in the low gravity.

As Glenn approached the viewport, a short, thin passenger in the line for Flight 117 turned and asked him, "I overheard that you have a long wait. Of the seven wonders of the solar system, Mars offers three: Valles Marineris, Olympus Mons, and the tube-plant colonies. My name is Andy and I can show you around. I have a tour guide license."

"I'm Glenn. I don't want to leave this area in case they call my name."

"You don't have to leave. You can tour Mars using my direct C-chip-link. With the direct link, you will feel like you are there while you wait here."

"Is it legal to use the C-link that way?"

"Yes, just sign this approval form." He C-mailed a form to Glenn's C-chip.

Glenn attached his signature and sent it back. "That sounds like a great idea Andy, but isn't the direct C-link limited to a few hundred feet?"

"I have an adaptor app that uses the C-net to extend our direct link. Wait a minute while I link our chips."

As he linked, Glenn's C-chip notified him of a fifty credit charge. "Fifty is not much for a three-day tour."

"Don't worry Glenn, I have six other customers. With this app, you will not be aware of each other."

"Then, you are making more than a week's pay."

"Sorry, I cannot discuss my finances."

* Blade Runner, The Danish National Symphony Orchestra *

They shook hands and parted. Glenn looked out of a viewport to enhance his experience. He used a magnifier to watch the transporter launch and travel to Phobos. The tour guide turned on the tactile feature in Glenn's C-chip. The ride and the landing were smooth.

On Phobos, the passengers transferred to a shuttle and traveled the short distance to Mars. The shuttle used retrorockets to drop out of orbit. It entered the atmosphere and glowed like a falling star. As it slowed and the heat shield cooled, it released a parachute to cut its speed further. Glenn experienced the g-force, heat, and shaking through the tactile sense of his C-chip. Andy observed every detail to satisfy his clients.

Glenn increased the magnifier on the viewport until he saw the cluster of dark impressions caused by the tube-plants leaves that surrounded the spaceport.

Then the shuttle pilot announced, "The Mars spaceport is much smaller than the spaceport on the moon because it handles only local traffic. This planet does not generate enough income to pay for a teleporter terminal."

"The ground crew strung a catch-net to protect us from a hard landing." Andy added, "Tube-plant fibers are ideal for making such nets and ropes. The shuttles carry only descent fuel for landings. They can take off from Mars after ground crews refuel them."

After landing, the shuttle taxied inside an airtight hanger. The tour guide got off with the other passengers and walked through a tunnel connecting to a tube plant colony.

"Mars supports almost one-hundred-thousand colonists. Every colonized planet has its own smell, color, and culture."

Andy turned on the olfactory feature in Glenn's C-chip so he would remotely feel guide's burning eyes and the stench in his nose. "The smell in the Martian tube plant colonies is worse than burnt eggs even though nose filters remove most of the sulfur dioxide. Newcomers cannot prevent their eyes from tearing, so they wear eye goggles."

The tour guide, to the relief of the tourists, placed goggles over his eyes, inserted nose filters, and continued, "Tube-plants thrive on most marginal planets like Mars where other plants have no hold.

"These plants have huge root structures and a single thin leaf. The leaf hugs the surface ground and covers more than a square mile to absorb energy from sunlight. The root extends more than a hundred feet below the surface to tap water, heat, and minerals.

"Tube-plants die after they reach maturity and expel their millimeter-size seeds in a huge blast, but the hulks of their deep tube-like roots remain. These root structures offer a convenient shelter for explorers and colonists on Mars.

Glenn realized, *this tour of Mars was a good idea. It's distracting me so I don't worry about Gloria and what lies ahead. Also, I'm learning a lot about Mars.*

The guide said, "Tube-plant seeds cover most of Mars. When the first Mars rovers discovered them, geologists incorrectly named them 'blueberries.' Today, when geologists find these 'berries' on new planets and moons, they send colonists to claim the tube-plants that produced them."

Andy scanned every detail of the inside of the cone shaped root. Two sets of spiral stairs crisscrossed from top to bottom. Glenn noticed that booths lined the walls with walkways that led to the stairs.

They entered an elevator with transparent walls and held by an open frame that went to the bottom. As they descended, the root narrowed until the elevator barely fit. Then the root ended and they entered a vast cavern with lush plant growth.

The guide explained, "This cavern was solid ice a million years ago. Most of the ice evaporated. Construction crews sealed the top of the root to contain heat and the remaining moisture.

"Freshwater condenses near the surface and flows down channels to the farm on the floor of the cavern. A nuclear battery powers the artificial lighting and produces heat for the plants. All the crops in this farm are from Earth because humans cannot eat Martian plants. Take notice of the lake of salty water in the drainage area. Do not drink or touch this water, it is acidic."

*

The space station did not have beds, and the chairs were too short for sleep, so Glenn rented one of the comfort booths positioned against one wall of the waiting room. Single size, double size, and family size booths were available.

As he slept, he stayed linked to Andy and dreamt he partied late into the night and slept in the tube plant colony. He woke fresh and alert. That afternoon, Andy went to Olympus Mons. After eating, Glenn went to a viewport, adjusted it for three-D, and magnified the view of this huge Martian volcano. His link to the tour guide added to this experience. The view of Mars from the top of the volcano was almost as stunning as the view from space.

Andy spent the night at a nearby tube plant that colonists converted into an inn for tourists. Again, Glenn slept well and woke refreshed. The next morning, he left early for Valles Marineris. This seven-kilometer deep rift valley was a wonder every traveler needs to see.

By mid-afternoon, Glenn had seen the valley rim, the floor, the fossil beds, and several boxed canyons. He felt this was enough, severed his link to Andy, went to the waiting room, sat, and waited with about twenty other people.

*

The children and most of the adults held video games, books, or played with various toys. The children preferred playing laser tag and dodging wet sponge balls. Robots hidden behind the walls moved merchandise between a warehouse and the vending machines. People could place an order on the C-net and shortly later, they would receive a message which vending machine had their item. Travelers rented instead of purchased items because the teleporters had weight limits.

Glenn used his new C-chip to screen everyone in the room for abnormalities. After a few minutes, it reported no one was a criminal or emotionally unstable. Then he listened to a few casual conversations and discovered most of these people planned to beam to the asteroid Ceres, which was the primary spaceport and teleporter hub to the more popular deep space destinations. Nobody was going to Sirius.

Glenn bundled the conversations and C-mailed them to Earth's security. He did not like eavesdropping, but the government required him to send everything he witnessed.

Then, he saw Victor arriving from the moon. Victor saw him before he was able to hide.

As he approached, Glenn searched the new hacking features on his C-chip. He selected "subjugate" as he looked at Vic.

Vic said, "Assistant Director Victor Gillinger, reporting for duty, sir."

"Be at ease Vic. Are you assigned to me and is your final destination Stardust?" *The hacking algorithm works; Vic is not arguing with me. I think I like this.*

"Yes sir."

"You can sit down and don't salute or call me sir. I want to keep a low profile as I travel. I'll let you know when you are back on duty."

"Yes sir. I mean, yes Glenn."

"I haven't had a vacation for two years. These stops offer the only chance I have to pretend I am a tourist. I visited Mars, and now I want to learn about Sirius."

"Okay. I'll pretend we are tourists." Victor was at ease, sort of, and continued talking without encouragement, almost unaware of the world around him. "I know the history of Sirius. Miners in the asteroid belt followed the Egyptian belief that living closer to Sirius A, known as the 'Dog Star,' would bring them closer to their expired relatives and friends. They discovered a large cache of gemstones, which gave them enough profit to bring their dreams to reality. They joined spaceship manufacturers on the asteroid Dactyl, who had similar beliefs, and pooled their resources and built a spaceship that could reach Sirius. They developed lightweight structural materials, a nuclear fusion reactor, ion thrusters, and a Higgs modulator. Spaceship manufacturers still use their design. Pirates joined them when they left."

Glenn asked, "How do Higgs modulators work?"

"Simple, they warp the Higgs field, which changes the mass of everything inside the warp. The toy version makes the air around you heavier while making you lighter until you become buoyant. Do you remember when toy stores sold those anti-gravity harnesses years ago?"

"Yes. I had one of those when I was six. I inverted its coils so it made me denser and it made everything around me fragile. I could break bricks with my hand. I played for hours and pretended I was the invincible Mega-Man. How about you?" Glenn asked.

"Yeah, they were easy to convert into Higgs shields. I removed the safeties in the one I had, followed a flock of geese, and became lost. Anyway, those were smaller versions of the Higgs modulators."

Victor continued, "The Sirius colonists used Higgs modulators to improve ion engine efficiency enough to reach the nearest stars. Only the hydroponic units limited how far they could travel. Relativistic effects reduced their ship time to five years for their fifteen-year trip."

Glenn noticed he knew everything Vic was going to say before he said it. *Ah, yes,* Glenn thought, *my new C-chip can interrogate Vic. Here is his personnel file. Vic graduated at the top of his class from WestPoint. He proposed once at WestPoint and again after graduating, but two different women turned him down. He never proposed again. This assignment is his first outside the office. I thought he had field experience.*

"That is interesting. Tell me more," Glenn said as he continued examining with his interrogation chip. *His heartbeat is 78. His temperature, blood pressure, blood chemistry, hormone balances, and stomach contents are available.*

"Ah, you are hacking my C-chip. Now I'm blocking you. Is this how you work as a team?"

"So they gave both of us hacking C-chips. Let's agree to stop hacking each other and let's agree not to put each other down."

Vic looked confused for a moment, then nodded in agreement. "I have something important to tell you. This isn't a mission, it's a one way trip to oblivion. We can't let Empire do this to us or to Gloria. I hired a contact on Sirius who will help us disappear until this blows over."

"Abandon the mission? I can't do that." Glenn looked down and let out a long sigh.

"I did some research before I left. The news reports a revolution, hostile aliens, and a virus that turns people into zombies. Check it out yourself." Vic said as he sent Glenn several news videos over the C-net.

Glenn glanced at them and answered, "If what you say is true then Mac and Kyleen lied to me. I'll verify this and consider what you said."

Vic explained everything he knew to Glenn and they discussed new plans until the Public Address announced, "Space Marshal Glenn Hunter on deck."

"When do you teleport?" Glenn asked.

Vic answered, "Three days after you leave. When I reach Sirius, I'm going to abandon the mission. Are you with me?"

"I'll tell you my decision after I talk to Gloria on Sirius."

They hugged goodbye. Vic went to a comfort booth to refresh. Glenn went to the teleporter.

Beamers took measurements and made last minute adjustments. While he waited, Glenn sent a report he composed earlier to Mac using his insta-text chip. *I wish I had one of these for my daughter and for Gloria.* He did not tell Mac what Vic said.

Mac insta-texted a minute later, "Got your message."

Chapter 9: Trip to Sirius

* Christopher Cross, Sailing *

The beaming process was the same as before, but it went faster because Glenn was familiar with the Model Ts and the routine for the Model As was the same. *Someone must have called ahead, and informed everyone in my travel path to hasten me to my destination. Vic is right, whatever is happening at Camelot is too serious to be a training exercise for Gloria. When I catch up with her, I'll send her back to the Moon.*

The interior of the capsule was similar to the canister he used on the moon except it had a control panel. He entered and a beamer closed the hatch. Glenn felt movement as a skiff moved the capsule into a beam-can for teleportation. After ten minutes, everything was still and silent.

Several hours later, Glenn closed his eyes and dreamt he saw the whole universe around him. He woke himself and wondered if the image was real or if it came from his C-chip. He turned his cerebral implant chip off to make sure.

Nothing happened until he dozed off into a lucid dream state. Then, the capsule became transparent, and he saw the outside universe. It seemed like a 4-D auditorium, except everything was brighter.

Jupiter and Saturn were dots as Neptune grew larger, and then smaller in a matter of a few seconds as he passed. The other planets were not in near orbits to his direction of travel, so none of them stood out. He noticed that the positions of the nearest stars changed as he traveled.

Glenn did not see this with his physical eyes, but with his mind. *As I travel through space as a wave-bundle of electromagnetic energy, the physical sides of the capsule cannot block my vision or any of my senses. However, I must have physical being because I am aware of this.* Then he opened his eyes, and saw only the walls of the capsule and the panel lights.

Ah, I am both matter and wave depending on my perspective.

He closed his eyes and rested his thoughts to test this theory. The sides of the beam-can disappeared again, and he saw the stars. He wondered, *what happens if two people beam at the same time? Would they be aware of each other?*

He searched in all directions, and saw, heard, and smelled all manner of things; stars forming and exploding, an eerie scream from matter falling into a black hole, and an underlying slow breathing-like motion of the universe itself. Then he heard an ethereal song.

The source was a long distance away, but he recognized it as a woman singing. He was not alone. Before he had time to investigate, the sounds and the images disappeared, and he felt a tremor strong enough to be painful. *Is this my destination? Did three days pass so fast?* The sensor light verified his arrival so he pressed the red button.

* Cat Stevens, Where Do The Children Play *

A speaker in the capsule gave instructions: "Be still, do nothing, and wait." There was a strong shake with mild jarring and rotation when the skiff from the Space Station removed his capsule from the beam-can and carried it into a docking bay.

The beamers opened his capsule and offered him the usual oxygen breather as he climbed out. He was stiff from the lack of movement and sick of the synthetic food.

While the attendants removed the toiletry, cleaned, and recharged the capsule for its next use, a beamer led him to a hallway lined on both sides with general use booths. They all seemed to be available so he selected one, and used it to eat, refresh, and wash. These booths were less private than the booths on the moon. On the outside, they looked like clothing hangers.

When he returned to the teleporter terminal, a thin, average height, young beamer with jet-black hair introduced himself. "I'm Ugo. Welcome to the Sirius Space Station. And you are Space Marshal Hunter, right?"

"Yes, you can call me Glenn." *His C-chip cannot interrogate my chip, or he would know that already.*

He handed Glenn a small half-eaten bag of potato chips and said, "Complements of the Beehive. Glenn, we call this station the Beehive, and refer to ourselves as the Bees because this place is busy, always buzzing," He laughed. "If you have time, I'll explain more."

Glenn removed his breather mask to eat the chips. "This place smells like an iron ore smelter." He inserted nose filters and commented, "Now I can smell the potato chips, they are delicious compared to synthetic food. Please continue your explanation."

"This section of the Beehive is the only one where you will find booths. Everywhere else, you will use restaurants, bathrooms, and apartments with beds. Booths were not in common use during the construction of the Beehive. We have not caught up with the modern times. I am transferring your apartment number and a map of the Beehive to you on the direct C-link. You can go there now."

"Thanks. Why are there no children playing or travelers waiting?"

"We don't have any tourist attractions and parents rarely bring their children this far from Earth. The resident children study in virtual classrooms during the day and learn trades or work during their off time. Every resident performs a duty or this station would fall into disarray."

How big is this Beehive?" Glenn asked as he scraped the bottom of the bag of chips.

"The disk of the Beehive is two thousand feet thick at the center, one-hundred feet thick at the edge, and five thousand feet in diameter. Originally, it was an asteroid."

"Yes, my partner Vic told me."

"Did he tell you we are in the process of refurbishing more compartments into living space, and we hope to complete this work sometime this century? It will include more than one million units when finished."

"That's almost as much as the Moon Base," Glenn commented as he tossed the chip bag into his mouth. Contact with his saliva converted the bag into a milk-flavored drink.

"This station rotates to generate artificial gravity that is strongest at the outer rim and weakest at the hub and at this teleporter terminal. The low gravity makes it easier to move cargo and passengers. In addition to several teleporter lenses that link to other destinations, the hub supports a large docking bay used mostly for cargo ships. Passenger spaceships are seldom this far from Earth. At the edge of the disk, the gravity increases to half-a-G."

"That is three times more than the gravity on the Moon. I better not go there."

"Your apartment is at a level that has gravity similar to the moon's. The rooms are spacious. Get some rest and we will beam you out this evening to Gondwana."

"Don't you mean Stardust?"

"Gondwana and Stardust are in the same star system. From Gondwana you will travel a short distance to Stardust on a spaceship."

*

"I thought there were two stops in between here and Gondwana."

"Empire told us to save time by skipping those, but don't worry. Others have used the direct route without any problems."

"How long is the transit time?" Glenn asked.

"Two weeks."

"Isn't that too long to be in a beam-can. I was starting to hallucinate after only three days. Has anyone complained about the bright light of the stars as they teleport?" Glenn asked. "As I approached Sirius, the light became intense, almost blinding. Sleep was impossible."

Ugo and the other beamer looked at each other. Then Ugo said, "Oh good. We get a bonus for finding people who can star surf. We identify them when they complain they can see outside their beam-cans. Most people cannot do that."

"Ah, what is star surfing?"

"Spontaneous teleportation. Over one-hundred years ago, Ligeia Bell became the first star surfer. Empire scientists studied her until they understood a phenomenon called quantum tunneling, which led to the development of the Model T teleporters."

Glenn wondered, *that can't be the same Ligeia Bell who is on my roster? Bell is a popular name. The person on my list must be someone else with the same name.*

Ugo continued, "With proper training, a star surfer can teleport to any destination that lies in the field of view of a teleporter lens without using a beam-can or a canister. Star surfing can be single-ended, meaning a star surfer does not need a lens at the destination, but they must resist the attractors."

"Will I 'spirit away' if I'm inside a beam-can?"

"Sometimes star surfers disappear, but ninety-nine percent of the time you are safe inside a beam-can. You will go where the beam-can takes you."

"How am I going to travel fifty more light-years on these quirky teleporters?" Glenn wondered. "Are you telling me everything or are there more anomalies?"

Ugo continued, "Let us worry about that. Just remember, like all star surfers, you are not safe from spontaneous teleportation if you walk into the focus of a teleporter lens. You can look through a telescope if the lenses are smaller than the diameter of your body. I'll inform Empire that you are a natural, and they will train you to star surf."

"No, no, don't record that! In fact, tell no one about it. I'm giving each of you a tip that will rescind if you report me," Glenn demanded, as he transferred one-hundred credits to each of their accounts. *If this news gets out, Empire Corporation will send me on every field mission.*

They answered, "Thanks for the tip; we will keep your secret. I notice on your itinerary that you will pass close to Gondwana. Scientists believe this planet is a quantum attractor and draws in anyone who star surfs without a specified destination. Many of the people who disappeared from Earth during the past several thousand years were naturals who star surfed to Gondwana."

Now that Glenn understood his experience, he said, "I have to leave and answer a C-net message. I'll come back and talk more if I get the chance."

He received an insta-text message from Mac, "Inform me if you arrived at Sirius."

Glenn used his C-chip to link to the texting chip implanted in his chest and sent a report to Mac, "I am at Sirius, and my trip was without incident. The Beehive supports a large and diligent workforce. The residents are friendly to travelers and tourists. Compared to Tranquility Base, the Beehive is large, empty, and noisy. The workforce refurbishes new living areas from this massive hulk both day and night, and they patch holes from occasional meteor strikes. They often run because the station is so large they would waste time if they walked."

Seconds later, Mac answered with insta-text, "Preliminary information indicates the trouble on Camelot is serious. The space station is damaged but it is still habitable. I will provide more information as soon as I get it. Assistant Director Victor Gillinger will arrive at the Beehive right behind you. He's your backup. We lost contact with Gloria, and she may be lost somewhere in the Beehive. Find her. Then partner with a Razorroot named Splinter who is in the Beehive, one of the few who did not return to Xanadu."

Glenn planned to find Gloria first and the Razorroot partner later. He went back to the teleporter terminal and checked the registry. To his relief, Gloria's name was in the log.

Her apartment was near the center of the Beehive. The artificial gravity at that level was strong enough that he would have to perform exercises along the way to acclimate.

As he was leaving, Ugo suggested, "Stop at the medical clinic down two halls. They can help you to adapt."

At the clinic, the technicians applied a therapy to hasten the healing of his old injuries. It consisted of direct exposure to the light and heat of Sirius.

* Oh very young, Cat Stevens *

After the therapy, Glenn went back down the hallway to an access shaft with a ladder for climbing up and a sliding pole for traveling down to a point where the gravity increased. Elevators and stairs provided access to lower levels where the gravity increased. As he descended, he saw a strange creature far below him using its many tentacles to crawl toward him, a motion that was too slow to be human, but its approach was not slow as its many tentacles worked in concert. As it approached, he could tell the tentacles belonged to a Razorroot tree.

When it was close enough to make contact with a direct C-link, it stopped and asked, "Are you Space Marshal Glenn Hunter?"

"Yes."

It moved closer and covered Glenn with sensory leaves. "My name is Splinter. You can call me Splint. Mac instructed me to meet you and provide information and assistance."

"Very well Splint. You can call me Glenn. What information do you have?"

It explained Blackbark's encounter with the Gobato. "We Razorroots own Dearth under authority of Empire and with approval of all Earth Governments… We withdrew under threat of harm from hostile invaders. You will recover our planet."

Hostile aliens, that sounds serious except I know that the Razorroots exaggerate the danger. The Gobato must be some kind of parasite. I can probably eliminate them with pesticides, Glenn thought. Then he answered with emphasis to win Splinter's confidence, "Empire sent me to correct this injustice, and return Dearth to your species."

"Yes, we expect Empire to protect us according to our agreement."

"I cannot do this alone. Under my authority as space marshal, I deputize you. You will lead the expedition to regain Dearth with my help and supervision."

Splinter withdrew its sensory leaves and seemed to quiver while begging. "The Gobato are huge, hungry, herbivorous aliens who want to eat me because I am a plant."

Glenn attached a Higgs shield to its computer. "This will give you some protection."

"That is not enough. You don't know how fierce those invaders are."

"If you refuse to go, then we will both stay here and you will lose the rights to your planet." Glenn exaggerated, "I have retirement papers so staying here works for me."

"Some of the Razorroots left saplings on their farm. If you will rescue our saplings, then lead the way and I will follow you."

"I disagree. You lead the way or call off this mission. You decide."

The plant welted its leaves, "Your credentials say you are 'highly motivated and results driven'. Why are you acting contrary to this way?"

"That is what I said on an old resume when I applied for the job of director. I didn't get that job, but I am still loyal to the cause. If you go, then I will go."

"Okay, I will lead the way, but I am not a leader so don't expect too much."

"I won't as long as you don't expect too much from me. Lead me to the teleporter." While he spoke, Glenn placed a private C-phone call to Ugo, *"I have a Razorroot who needs to go to Stardust. Is a beam-can available?"*

"Yes, we can put it in your travel slot, but that will set your departure back two weeks. Is that all right?"

"Yes, since I need time to search for Gloria."

Ugo answered, *"Splinter already C-phoned me and asked me to trick you into going first. I'll do the opposite and trick it, because Razorroots don't trust teleporters. It will never teleport unless we trick it."*

"I don't see any other choice."

"Okay, I'll have things ready when you get here," Ugo said and hung up.

Glenn allowed the Razorroot to lead which was a mistake. It stopped at each plant along the way, repositioned the pots, checked the soil moisture, and removed dead leaves that it ate. *I'll be patient while it waists the day so no one will blame me if we never leave.*

The hours passed as the tree taught Glenn how to garden. While Splinter was busy adjusting one of the decorative plants, Glenn noticed the time was late. "Splint, you can go back to your agroponics unit and attend your garden. The teleporter closes at 5:00 PM. We can try this tomorrow if you still want to save your colony."

"We are not too late. I C-phoned the beamers while you adjusted a pot, and they informed me that they will wait all night for you to arrive."

Glenn hid his disappointment. He thought the mission was over. He was hungry after eating only potato chips for lunch and did not want to miss supper, so he searched the utility closets and found a cart. Splinter was much happier riding on the cart. Glenn pushed it, and they arrived at the teleporter in a few minutes.

Ugo was still on duty when they arrived. Razorroots could inflict serious injuries with their sharp roots, so he approached it slowly using a water mister. He said to Splint, "I'll just take a few measurements, and then you can go back to your garden."

Splinter said, "Don't you have to measure Glenn. He has to teleport tonight."

Ugo C-phoned Glenn so Splinter could not overhear, *"We will skip the way stations and send Splint all the way to Gondwana so it cannot change its mind. Don't ask Splint for permission, but ask for forgiveness later because Razorroots are better at forgiving than they are at giving permission."*

"This plant weighs 192 pounds. Is that more than the weight limit?" Glenn asked.

"No, because they don't need oxygen or food. They can stay dormant for years without difficulty, so they don't need supplies, and they don't suffer from boredom or isolation."

Ugo instructed Splint, "Sit in the capsule and tell me if you are comfortable. If not, we will make adjustments."

"I don't want to."

"Trust me; it will take less than one minute. You can watch the clock and see for yourself."

After coaxing the Razorroot into the capsule, they closed the lid fast.

"Glenn, you need to go, not me. Bring me back." Splinter begged through an intercom.

Then Glenn said, "Your destination is Stardust. From there, you will travel by ship to Stardust. I will meet you on Stardust in a few days. There are no Gobato on Gondwana or Stardust, so you are safe. The Gobato are eleven light-years away on Dearth, and they don't have teleporters so they cannot arrive at Stardust anytime soon. I will not send you into danger so trust me."

Glenn watched as the beamers moved the can to the docking bay where a skiff picked it up and carried it to the focus of the teleporter while they reassured the Razorroot that all of this was routine. Then the teleporter cut the communication, and Splinter was in route to Gondwana. Glenn felt like a heel, tricking an unsuspecting plant, but he needed to put his mission first.

As he watched through a window, Glenn felt something pulling him, like an unseen force pulling him off the edge of a cliff, except this force was pulling him through the window. The harder he resisted, the harder it pulled. He felt helpless and hollered for help.

Chapter 10: The Snake

Ugo saw Glenn was in trouble, ran to him, turned him away from the window, and pushed him into the hallway. He said, "Look at your surroundings until you feel grounded."

"What was that?" Glenn asked, "What happened to me?"

"You almost got a free lesson in star surfing. Until you know how to star surf, stay away from teleporters unless you are in a beam-can."

He thanked Ugo and left to spend a quiet evening reading in his room. The book helped him forget the dangers he faced.

Glenn woke early the next morning, composed a report for Mac, and sent it using his insta-text chip. "I deputized Splinter and sent it to Gondwana. Gloria is here, and I have her apartment number. I'll look for her today."

Mac Insta-texted back, "Here is the recon report I promised earlier. The Inspector General traveled with his trainee from Gondwana to Stardust and then to Camelot, the space station that orbits the Razorroot's planet, Dearth. An unknown specie called Gobato invaded a Razorroot colony and drove the Razorroots out of the area. By the time the Inspector arrived, the hostilities had ended."

"Splinter was right; there is an alien invasion. How big and how aggressive are the Gobato? How did they get on Dearth?" Glenn texted back.

"They reached Dearth in spaceships. The Gobato weigh two tons; they are active and may be aggressive since they killed the Inspector. The Inspector's trainee sent us this report."

"What? What? I thought they were bugs or something small. How can we control something that big? And they fly spaceships?" Glenn asked.

"The trainee recommends we hold them on Dearth. He said the Gobato would stay there and pose no threat as long as we leave them alone. However, we still have to respond. These aliens carry prions that are infectious to humans. They already infected some of the Camelot crew. The trainee ran his samples on a bio-simulator, which showed that people who are infected will not show symptoms for several months, but the symptoms are serious. The prions convert human proteins into something alien. I want you to make sure this disease does not spread."

"I keep hearing rumors of zombies. Now you tell me the rumors are true. Can we isolate them by shutting down the teleporter at Stardust."

"Zombies? That's ridiculous," Mac texted."There haven't been any deaths. Just a few people with dementia. Stardust is a teleporter hub. If we lose that, we lose half of the outworld.

"We have to send you to make sense out of all of this. We received a conflicting report from Captain Dwain Hammerton. He said, 'Prions don't exist. The yellow alert was triggered by pirates that Lieutenant Gerome Rhodes arrested and this conflict scared the Razorroots away but they will be back.' Now we don't know what to believe. You will go to Camelot and tell us if the threat is real," Mac ordered.

Glenn took a few deep breaths, and sat in a chair. "What if there are aliens, pirates, and an infectious disease. What should I do?"

"Just in case the alien threat is real, approach them, establish communication, and sign a truce if possible. You won't need this but I am sending weapons we stockpiled from the war of 2067."

Glenn answered, "I need modern weapons."

"Those are the newest weapons we have. The machinist on Stardust works for us. Tell him what you need and he will modify our weapons and equip your force."

"I don't want prions to infect me. Also, one space agent with a makeshift army cannot restrain a swarm of two-ton aliens equipped with weapons and spaceships. I request that you call off this mission. I'll recall Splint and return to Earth with Gloria and Vic. Then I'll form a fleet of warships and attack the Gobato with everything we have."

Mac answered, "That will take too long, and what if all of this is just a misunderstanding? How foolish we will look if we attack with everything we have and the Gobato are peaceful. If you have more questions, I cannot respond for a few days because I am stepping into a beam-can. I'll check my messages at every waypoint."

The connection went dead. *Mac is out of range. These quantum chips cannot penetrate a teleporter channel. If I cannot reach him, then I'll have to continue to Stardust, or ask Vic to hide us.*

* Richard Harris, MacArthur Park *

Glenn used the C-net to track Gloria, but she turned off her C-chip. He located a wheelchair, swallowed a metabolism booster to help him tolerate the higher gravity, went to her apartment, and knocked. She did not answer. The door monitor indicated "unoccupied". He went in and verified she was not there. The bed was toppled and the chairs and table were flung about.

He searched the nearby hallways and found her walking down a corridor leading to an elevator. She looked like a person with dementia, more distracted and disoriented than even the Bees. Her eyes were red as if she were crying.

As she was about to step into the elevator Glenn shouted, "Gloria, wait."

She turned her C-chip on, and said with relief, "Glenn, I am so glad to see you."

He stepped out of the wheelchair and they hugged, then he sat down before becoming dizzy, and said, "You don't look well. Do you feel all right?"

"Yes, but I have seen better days."

"I'll take you to your apartment so you can rest and restore your composure."

"No, I'm going to the teleporter so I can get out of here. I can't stand this place. I've tried to rest, but I can't. I am used to sleeping in a booth but the Beehive booths are too flimsy. Let's talk here because my apartment is gloomy. I am scheduled to teleport to Gondwana today, but I am early and don't have to hurry."

Glenn texted Ugo, *"Tell me when Victor Gillinger arrives."*

Ugo texted a private message back. *"He is due today. I'll tell you the moment he arrives."*

"Vic might arrive today. Let's wait and talk to him," Glenn asked.

" I'll wait a few hours for Vic. If he does not show today, I'll wait for him on Gondwana."

"I recruited a Razorroot to help us. Its name is Splint. It beamed to Gondwana yesterday so Ugo won't be ready to beam there again for another thirteen days," Glenn explained.

"Yes, I know. Ugo told me I can teleport today because they have a new beam-can pair to meet the higher travel demands."

"I didn't know two beam-cans could be in the same quantum channel at the same time."

She answered, "He told me it's been tried, tested, and proven to work with no problems. They have to separate arrivals and departures by a few hours because they have only one skiff to pick up and drop off the capsules."

She pointed the way to a small café near the elevator, and they sat at a table with candy bars and coffee from the vending machines. The ice cream and cake were synthetic and lacked the flavor of natural foods. Spacers considered junk food from Earth to be a delicacy.

Glenn spoke, "What else is bothering you? Are the Bees polite to you?"

"It's the noise. I can't think with this continuous noise. The floor even shakes," she said as the floor banged and vibrated as if hit by an asteroid.

People got up and ran to booths and hatches along the walls for safety, but the breach warning lights and sirens stayed off, so they went back to their chairs.

"See what I mean?" She asked.

He responded, "Yes, that was scary."

As he reached to hold her hand to reassure her, he yelled "YIPE!" and leaped back five feet knocking over his wheel chair.

At his reaction, Gloria belched out a laugh that caused everyone in the café to turn and look. Just now, he noticed that she seemed to hold a handful of snakes. She raised her hand into the air to exhibit five snakeheads on her fingertips and thumb. The holographic tattoos combined into a cobra hood at her hand, extended down her arm, wrapped around her shoulder, and disappeared under her blouse. It seemed alive, as it appeared to move as she moved. While everyone in the café watched, she threw her hand forward to simulate a spitting cobra. People in the crowd murmured, "Look at that," "Wow, neat," "Is it real?" "Where can I get a tattoo like that?"

Glenn saw it was not real, up-righted the wheelchair, and sat, "I thought you were a conservative and quiet student. Now, I am not sure if I know you at all."

She sat down after she finished her display. "The people here are so strange. I feel like I haven't talked to anyone for days. When I talk to them they don't answer, but my cobra gets their attention rrrreeeal fassst." She slithered her cobra-head fingers on the table.

Glenn paled, still not used to such a bizarre display. "We think they are strange, but if someone two hundred years ago saw us talking, they would think we are strange. You don't have to describe people or places to me. You think of a picture, and I see it through the direct C-link. We speak a few syllables, and our C-chips complete our sentences."

"But the Bees go days without talking to anyone. Look at them walking and sitting by themselves."

Glenn explained, "The Bees are talking a lot but not in our world. They live mostly in a virtual world, and use their C-chips to talk to their dead friends and dead relatives. They believe they cannot die because the computer keeps a detailed profile on each of them and simulates them in the virtual world. A Bee can expire, and their friends will not experience grief or loss. In their view, the virtual world is actual, and what we call reality is just a temporary something they have to pass through."

"I thought 'para-virtualism' was illegal?" She asked.

"Yes, on Earth, but not here. One reason the Bees left the Sol system and came here was leaders in the United Nations voted to outlaw para-virtualism before Earth societies collapsed into a stone age. Like the prohibition of alcohol, some people became so addicted that they never gave it up. Those cyber addicts founded the Beehive, kept detailed descriptions and personality profiles of their friends and relatives, and resurrected them on their computer."

"I prefer to be at peace after I die," Gloria responded. "Don't let anyone program me into this computer."

"I agree. If you live right the first time, then you don't have to come here and buy more time to try to fix your mistakes."

She belched another laugh at his explanation.

Glenn thought, *I won't tell her the mission is over until Vic gets here. She is too unstable. He will have to accompany her back to the Moon. I'll continue to Gondwana and send Splint somewhere safe. Then I'll retire on disability.*

Glenn held his hand up as he read an urgent text message from Ugo, *"That bang you heard earlier was our teleporter link to Mars. Assistant Director Victor Gillinger was slammed. He didn't make it. Our other teleporter links are undamaged including the link to the teleporter terminal in orbit around Gondwana. No schedule changes except the link to Mars will be down indefinitely."*

He answered Ugo, *"I want to send Gloria back to the Moon. Are we trapped? How can I end this mission?"*

"Our only link to the Moon was through Mars. Sorry."

She interrupted, "Was that Mac?"

I cannot tell her about Victor or she will unravel. I'll change the subject. He spoke, "Mac told me Earth panicked because hostile aliens entered the out-world. They could overrun our colonies."

"Hostile Razorroots? That strikes me as funny," she laughed.

Glenn felt so disheartened he could not control his words as he spoke, "I am sorry to tell you they are not Razorroots. They are aggressive two-ton invaders who wield weapons, fly spaceships, and carry an infection. They killed dozens of Razorroots."

"STOP!" Gloria hollered, "If Empire wants you and me to go to the edge of space, and confront those monsters, they must be crazy. They should send a battle fleet."

"The Gobato will overwhelm the outer colonies before a battle fleet gets there. We don't have to confront the Gobato. We will assemble on Stardust and train an army for that."

"Oh, well why didn't you say so? That sounds so much easier," she said with sarcasm.

Glenn shuttered as he spoke, "Gondwana has a large population. I can hide you there."

She gave Glenn a quizzical look as she answered, "If I return to the Moon and hide on Earth, how long will it be before those monsters are crawling down my back?"

"If we do nothing, one or two years. The teleporter on Camelot is a new design. It can beam those monsters. We have to make peace with them, or defeat them, or destroy Camelot."

"Then I'm stuck with this mission, and so are you. We have to go to Camelot."

"What are your waypoints?"

"Ugo told me that Empire removed the waypoints so we can get there sooner. But I don't mind, because I'll have thirteen days of peace and quiet in a beam-can."?

"Isn't it safer to travel in short jumps?"

"Empire said the Model A teleporters were safe even traveling this greater distance."

Glenn leaned forward and explained, "I don't like it. Two weeks is too long for a human to be isolated in a beam-can, and you are not well. Let me ask Ugo to find a waypoint where you will be safe."

"I'm in better shape than you. Look at yourself setting in that wheel chair. And going to a waypoint to hide doesn't make any sense. I am going to CAMELOT," she said in a voice that rose to a shrill.

An ear damage warning lit up. People looked, so she hissed and snapped her snakehead fingers at them. She was causing another scene.

Glenn was afraid she would attack the crowd, so he said, "All right, all right. I am here to help you. Actually, you are here to help me, but if this means that much to you then tell me what you want me to do."

Gloria calmed down. "Anyway, I just beamed more than nine light-years with no slam at all. I need your signature to verify my travel orders. Sign here." She sent a legal form to Glenn's C-chip.

Glenn shrugged. Then he stamped it with his virtual signature and sent it back to her.

"Thanks." She got up and boarded the elevator. "Come with me to the teleporter. Your presence helps me to be at ease."

He boarded with her and left his wheelchair behind. *I need to be strong for her, and hope fate will be gentle with her.*

He reached to hold her hand planning to hug her but remembered the snakeheads and stopped. They stepped out of the elevator, took a minute to adjust to the low gravity, and used a ladder to ascend the remaining distance to the teleporter terminal.

He took a U-net cube out of his envelope and said, "Gloria, I need you to do something for me. When you get to the teleporter in orbit around Gondwana, go to the internet technician, tell him this device is a U-net cube, and have him install it. It will form a linked universal network between Gondwana, here, and everywhere else giving us almost instantaneous communication. And watch for a Razorroot named Splinter, who will arrive one day ahead of you. We need a Razorroot for our mission."

"Not a problem." She took the U-net cube with her non-tattooed hand.

Jefferson Airplane, White Rabbit

Gloria timed it right. At the terminal, the beamers stood next to a cleaned and recharged capsule.

Ugo greeted them, and said, "Gloria, you cannot take those snakes with you."

She laughed, raised her hand and said, "They are not real. They are just hologram tattoos. Try to touch one."

He tried to touch one, and it disappeared. Then he asked her, "Do you have any videos to watch? Many people read books while they teleport because they last longer than a two-hour video."

C-chips stored movies, games, and books in addition to offering a spreadsheet, a word processor, and many other features.

"I have those, and one better, these." She held out a small envelope of tranquilizer patches and placed one on her arm.

Glenn was still worried about her as she slipped into the capsule. *Almost two weeks alone in that tiny capsule, a lot could go wrong, and I can only watch.*

Ugo noticed that she was worried and distracted her by saying, "This technology beams one person at a time. A news item on the net said future improvements will enable two people to beam together in one beam-can."

She looked at Glenn and said, "I didn't sign up for traveling to the edge of space or risking my life."

Glenn reassured her, "I understand. I will be right behind you."

She gave Glenn a desperate look, "You don't understand. My parents are pirates in the outworld. They sent me to Earth when I was very young so I would have a better life. Everything changed when Empire drafted me."

Glenn asked, "What do you mean? Pirates? Drafted?" as Ugo started to close the lid.

The hatch on the capsule closed as she was answering.

Glenn tried to reach her on the C-net, but the teleporter severed the connection. Gloria was alone.

*

Ugo moved the capsule through the airlock. As a skiff picked up the capsule to place it into a beam-can, Ugo said, "I didn't tell her about the accident this morning to avoid scaring her. Victor Gillinger worked for Empire. Did you know him?"

Glenn looked down shaking and unable to speak. *Would he still be alive if the U-net were operational?* Finally, he gathered himself and said, "We were coworkers, and I knew him for a long time. Everyone told me the Model As were safe. What happened?"

"The Model As are ten times safer than the slammers but we still have a few accidents. There will be an investigation to find out what happened. The scales might be off or the beam-can might have scraped something. I am sorry. Gloria has not teleported yet. Do you want me to recall her?"

"No. She can't adjust to Sirius, and she can't go back to the moon. We must send her on her way and hope everything will be all right. This mission looks like a one-way trip. Do spacers ever return after they travel beyond Gondwana?"

Ugo lowered his head and said with a solemn tone, "Very few."

Glenn asked, "I have a U-net cube for Sirius but did not install it yet. If you had the U-net, and the computers used it to balance the ballast for the Mars link, would Victor still be alive?"

Ugo stared at Glenn and then answered, "No, don't blame yourself. We need weeks to reprogram the computers and test the system, which would have been too late to save Victor. I will put a hold on our link to Mars until that system works with the U-net."

Glenn answered, "See you in thirteen days" and left.

* Passenger, Let Her Go *

Glenn went to a window and watched the skiff move Gloria to the focal point of the giant lens. It hurt him to see the contrast of the tiny beam-can against the huge teleporter lens. He considered the vastness of space itself where the huge star Sirius was less than a speck of dust. The dangers seemed overwhelming. He looked away and walked into the hallway to make sure he was grounded.

Then he thought of Earth, *How wonderful it was when my daughter and I picnicked in the sun. I remember her fragrance as a light breeze blew through her hair. I regret our rocky relationship. I miss her more now because Gloria reminds me of her. I will be lonely with no one but the Bees to talk to for weeks.*

Glenn received an encrypted message from Kyleen, so he stepped into a booth and read it, "Don't go to Camelot. It's not safe..."

Glenn lunged out of the booth, ran to the teleporter terminal, and shouted, "Stop Gloria."

Ugo shrugged and said, "Too late. She beamed already."

Glenn checked her status on the control panel. She was gone. He looked out a window. Although she was teleporting at one thousand times the speed of light, the beam-can appeared as if it were stationary, and would stay that way for thirteen days. Then an operator would send a skiff to open the beam-can and retrieve a capsule that contained only ballast; gemstones, and sand.

Ugo said, "Don't tamper with the beam-can or Gloria will be slammed." He watched Glenn to make sure he did not spontaneously teleport.

Glenn looked at the beamers and said, "I lost Victor. Now did I lose Gloria and Splint?"

Ugo said, "I can recall them, but that means two more weeks in a beam-can for each of them."

Glenn considered, and then answered, "No, I can't make them do that. I'll go to them."

"I'll call you on the C-net when your beam-can is ready."

"See you then," Glenn answered. He bought a small envelope of tranquilizers in a nearby pharmacy. *What happened to Vic could happen to me. I need to decide should I travel to Gondwana, Stardust, and then to Camelot or should I retire. If I retire, should I stay here, or try to return to Earth. When I was on the Moon, I would not consider retirement. That was before Victor's death and before Gloria became anxious. This is not a training exercise for Gloria. She won't learn anything useful when faced with this much danger. The stakes are too high for me to decide. After losing Victor, I cannot think clearly. Victor had a clear mind. If he were here, he would put me on the right path.*

Chapter 11: Final Destination

Glenn did not sleep that night. His thoughts bounced between Gloria and Splinter who were approaching danger at one-thousand times the speed of light. In the morning, he found Ugo and asked, "Is there any way I can reach Stardust faster?"

Ugo considered the options for several minutes, "There is something that might work, but you won't like it."

"Tell me anyway. Let me decide."

"We have a slammer link to Stardust. We use it to send cargo every three months."

"Aren't those slower than the Model As? Won't travel time be more than two months?" Glenn asked.

"You know your teleporters. The manufacturers built our slammer-cans to very tight tolerances. We used a technique called 'indirect counterfactual transference' to entangle them, which increases their speed. We have a capsule that is small enough to fit inside the slammer-can on this end. The can on the far end will carry the usual ballast. You will have enough fuel in your capsule to land on the planet. It is unproven and not intended for passenger use, but you'll be there in just over two weeks, close to the same time Gloria and Splinter arrive."

"But they have a head start."

"Yes, but they have to travel by ship from Gondwana to Stardust. That trip takes time."

"How long will it take you to get it ready?"

"Give me a few days. This is the first time anyone has tried this. I'll find you when it is ready. Also, it will be expensive."

"Okay, do it. I have unlimited funding. I don't want Gloria and Splint to be on Stardust without me."

Glenn went to a Café, ordered breakfast and a drink, and reviewed the retirement form that Kyleen gave him. He thought about his options. *I sent Gloria and Splint into unknown danger and I haven't made up my mind whether to finish this mission or to retire on disability.*

The station agroponics systems were big enough and held enough soil to grow fruits, vegetables, and even hens and fish. Glenn ordered fried fish fins, eggs, hash browns, two rolls made from real flower, and synthetic coffee. He enjoyed the meal and charged the cost to Empire Corporation. He felt better after eating breakfast.

Some of the Bees in the café asked Glenn about his mission and the aliens. News travels fast through unofficial channels. Then he asked the bees about the Beehive, and their lives.

The bees explained their duties and described their workstations, but had no concept of politics and were unable to discuss the rules and policies they followed. Glenn asked about their computer. They answered with enthusiasm and explained their virtual world.

The bees were distracted and spoke slowly during most of their conversations. Glenn used his special government C-chip to interrogate the C-chips of several bees and discovered, while they were speaking to him, the bees interacted with each other in their virtual world through their C-chips. He followed several bees to their workstation and watched them carry out their chores like ditto-bots while they explored galaxies in their virtual world.

A realization swept over Glenn, *The bees hardly know that I exist. Their reality is not my reality. I am alone on this space station with a hundred thousand people who look upon me as a shadow. How can I continue living here without a real conversation with anyone?*

The Glenn explored the space station and talked to more bees during the remainder of that day. A hard vibration resonated through the Beehive and interrupted every activity. Like crossing a street without looking, he and the bees did not know if the danger was deadly or trivial. *The station did not lose pressure so that asteroid collision did not cause serious damage. Gloria could never tolerate so much racket; a good thing she did not stay.*

The vibration left Glenn with the afterthought of what happened to Victor, *Now I understand their need for para-virtualism. It's an escape from this threatening universe and this confined station. The Bees' physical space stinks. However, how much room do they experience in a four-inch cube of crystal silicon?* He challenged himself with math while he calmed his nerves and concluded, *A computer core, a four-inch cube of silicon that I can hold in my hand, has enough memory and processing power to accommodate every living and previously living human identity in a simulation that is as large as all of explored space.*

* Neil Young, Alabama *

The next morning, one of many inevitable disasters struck. The sound of banging and screaming woke Glenn. Even the tranquilized sleep of his C-chip did not block noise this loud. He accessed the net to find out what caused the commotion, and his C-chip responded, "No network available." The net was offline! He thought, *Most of these people have never experienced life without the net. Separation from the computer is traumatic to them. Why isn't the computer running, did an asteroid hit it?*

Glenn pressed his hands against the door of his room. *A vacuum on the other side would flex the door. It seems flat, so there is no hull breach.* He waited before opening his door and stepping into the hallway. He learned from his crowd control training not to become a casualty, but to wait for things to settle down before trying to intervene.

Twenty minutes later, the commotion died down somewhat, so Glenn opened his door. The door did not automatically open when he touched it; another indication the computer was offline. He opened the door manually with a lever in the lower corner.

As he looked down the hall, and saw that no one was injured during the panic, but the Bees were in disarray. Two still screamed convulsively.

Every Bee he saw was helpless without the computer. The Bees pointed and grunted instead of talking.

Glenn thought, *The glitch that caused the computer to fail turned off their C-chips. I cannot turn them back on using my C-chip.*

One Bee walked up to Glenn, and said, "Gaa" while pointing at her head.

Glenn's C-chip did not translate such garbled speech. He explained to her several times before she understood to turn on her C-chip.

Glenn interrogated her C-chip. Their older version chips did not support "Supermind" or "Interlink."

She said, "Help me. I'm lost."

"What is your room number?"

"My room has a number? What good is a number?"

"What is your name?"

"Linda."

"What is your last name?"

There was a pause, and then she said, "Ah?"

Using the direct video link, Glenn said, "Follow what I am doing, and access your personnel file on your C-chip."

She linked her video back to Glenn, and he said, "Your name is Linda Lucerne, room 14-75157. I'll take you there."

At her room, he showed her the matching number above her door.

"That is so amazing. I never knew those were there. But the door is not open."

Glenn showed her the manual latch in the lower corner of the door and showed her how to lift it with her toe.

After she had used the bathroom, she said, "Thank you. How can I ever repay you?"

He enlisted her to help him explain to the other Bees how to use the direct link. The idea spread. After a few hours, the Bees could communicate, and the screaming stopped.

Glenn spent the day helping the residents find bathrooms, places to eat, and showing them how to open doors manually.

A few of the bees were surprised to learn they were blind, and a few were deaf. The C-net gave them sight and hearing as the computer downloaded images and sounds appropriate for their point-of-view. Now, they learned to share the eyes and ears of their friends using the direct C-link, and adjusting to their point-of-view.

As the crowd quieted down, Glenn noticed a faint sound. He asked the bees near him, "Do you hear that sound, what is causing that."

"Oh, that is probably the refurbishers doing some work," Linda answered.

"I doubt anyone is doing any work. Everyone is too confused." He saw Ugo in the juncture of the halls, shouted, and waved at him, "Ugo, come here."

"Yes, what is it."

"I am worried about that pelting sound, do you hear it?

"It is probably one of the workers grinding something."

"No, it sounds like pelting, not grinding, and it's getting louder."

"Oh my gosh, you are right. Our orbit is degrading. I think the Beehive is falling into a dust ring."

"Ugo, does the Beehive have manual controls?"

"Yes. We need a dozen people to operate them. I'll gather a crew and take them there."

Glenn followed Ugo and the crew as the sound of pelting increased. No one organized a crew earlier because the managers, the founders of the Beehive who died of old age, were in the virtual world and no longer lived in the physical world. Without the computer, no one governed or assigned work.

Ugo and his crew stabilized the orbit and maintained life support. The sound of dust pelting the station gradually softened until it became inaudible.

"Glenn, you noticed a problem and helped to keep it from turning into a catastrophe. I know how to repay you. After I am finished adjusting the orbit, I'll find you. While I'm doing this, can you check and see why the computer is offline? It should be operating by now. It's in room 13-11333. I am worried that this outage has trapped some Bees in their rooms. The new doors do not have manual overrides."

*

Farther down the hallway, an unusually large man ripped out locked doors as if he found his mission.

Glenn said to him. "This may not be necessary. Wait a few hours while I check the computer."

The man agreed, "Okay, I can wait."

At the computer room, Glenn knocked, but no one answered. An electronic lock held the door, and only a computer could open that lock. He found a ladder, pushed out a ceiling panel, traveled along a beam in the false ceiling, bypassed a second locked door, and pushed out another panel above the main computer room. As he dropped into the room, he was surprised that no one was there; no one was working to restore the computer.

A layer of dust covered everything in the room. Dust on the floor near the door showed that nobody had been in this room for more than a year. A note on the desk read, "I left for a better job elsewhere. Contact the Senior Computer Administrator, Sidney Pascal, in room 13-11399 down the hallway if you need assistance. Sincerely, Yvette, former computer operator."

Glenn checked the files in his envelope. One file listed Yvette as an employee on Camelot and as an, "Undisciplined troublemaker, do-not-rehire." Her history told that she worked on the Beehive and reached the highest rank available for a non-Bee but she was not satisfied. She modified several food synthesizers to convert processed sewage, rock wool, and pulverized granite into a woody substance. On Sirius, wood was valuable, so Yvette sold her patent and made enough money to travel to Camelot.

In the computer room, he found the receptor for a U-net cube, so he removed one from his envelope and installed it. It linked his C-chip to the U-net, but it had limited range without the computer network.

Glenn tried to leave the computer room, but the locked door would not open. He moved a desk under the ceiling panel that he entered through, placed a side chair on the desk, and climbed out over the door. He went to room 13-11399, but no one answered when he knocked. The room monitor did not work, so Glenn assumed no one was there. He called Sidney, but there was no reply. Sidney was out of range of the direct C-link. While Glenn chose whether to search for him or repair the computer, he heard a female voice on the U-net, "Hello. Is someone there?"

"Yes," he answered, "my name is Glenn. Who am I talking to?"

"My name is Delphi (del-fahy). I am an artificial entity in the Bee's computer. Everything went dark, and then I saw this light. I need help."

"I will help you, Delphi, but first you need to help me."

"How can I do that?"

"I need access to the computer files. I need the repair manual. Can you find it?"

"I'll look," she said. "The memory banks are slow because your U-chip does not generate much power. Finding the manual might take several minutes."

"I'll wait."

She searched the history files, and said, "Ah, here is something. Yes, this looks like the manual you need."

"Okay, transfer it to my C-chip."

"The power is too low for an instant transfer. I will read it to you. The first item on the problem checklist is to verify AC power is present."

"That seems obvious. Wait while I do that." He went to the nearest circuit breaker panel. The circuit breaker labeled 'computer' had tripped. He reset the breaker, and it tripped again.

After several more tries, he opened the electrical box and rewired the computer room to a different circuit breaker with a higher amp rating. It worked.

With power restored, he returned to the computer room through the ceiling. With Delphi's help, he rebooted the computer. At last, the Bees regained their net, and could open every door.

Glenn ran a diagnostic to make sure the computer files were still intact. "What would you do if a failure damaged your database?"

"We Bees could be lost forever. We would never get the computer back online without outside help."

Before they ended their conversation, Delphi gave him information about a new quantum computer that was faster, tolerated cosmic radiation, and was light and small enough to beam. "I gave this information to Sid, but he won't order it."

"I'll talk to him about it. Now that everything is working, I need to return to my other duties."

"Call on me whenever you need my help."

"I'll do that. Bye." He felt her kiss on his cheek and wondered if the tour guide on Mars forgot to turn off his tactile feature.

*

Glenn left the computer room after jamming the doors open in case of another failure. He found the Senior Computer Administrator relaxing in a break room. He was a fat man slouching in a chair, with light-brown hair, and the same height as Glenn.

"I am Space Marshal Glenn Hunter."

"A space marshal? Okay, I can deal with that. Call me Sid, and tell me what brings you to the Beehive?" He stood and they shook hands.

Glenn noticed Sid's hand was shaking. *Did he feel helpless when the computer failed, or was he hiding something?* "You can call me Glenn. I am on travel hold. I rewired your computer to a higher amp circuit breaker, because the previous breaker tripped. Didn't you know it was down?"

Sid answered as if this were a problem. "Of course I noticed. I was deciding how to fix it properly. Now I'll have to install heavier wiring so it will meet the construction codes."

"The best way to fix it is to replace it since it is old and obsolete. The old computer can serve as a backup if you put it on a separate power circuit." Glenn referred to Delphi and explained the computer she recommended, "You can beam it here and have it operating in less than a week."

Sid linked to the C-net during the conversation and answered with a vacant stare. Then, he returned to the conversation as if he completed an important task in a virtual galaxy. "Yes, but I ordered a computer ten years ago. It is too delicate to survive a slammer, so I paid for its delivery by spaceship. it will arrive in two more years. If I order a quantum computer, how can I explain spending the budget on that optical computer? I'll look like a fool."

Glenn looked at the whiny man. *Sid does not seem concerned about the computer failure. Did he trip the circuit breaker so his character could gain an advantage in the virtual world? I need to stay on task and resists the temptation to dig further, and prosecute this crook. Saving Earth and her colonies is more important.*

Glenn said with scorn, "It is better to look bad than it is to be bad. By the way, I installed a U-net cube by order of Empire."

Sid stared blankly. Glenn walked away because he was angry enough to hit this man. Then the administrator stood, followed, and shouted, "Yes, but now our information is universally available. We do not want our network linked to Earth. We want to be autonomous. How can we isolate our network after you installed a U-net cube?"

Glenn continued to walk and answered, "You will have to contact Delphi. She has the manuals. She can tell you how to isolate the networks and still give you access to the U-net." Then, Glenn turned a corner, and the administrator did not continue his pursuit.

* Blue Man Group, I Feel Love *

Ugo found Glenn and said, "The Bees voted to reward you for saving us from disaster. Here is a neck pack containing an intravenous fluid with enough water and glucose to sustain you for twelve hours. We scheduled the funeral for Victor Gillinger in our virtual world. Since you worked with him, we welcome you to attend."

"Yes, I want to be there. How about the beam-can? Is it ready?"

"We are waiting for a quantum channel to form, you have plenty of time. I'll let you know as soon as we have it. This neck pack would cost a non-Bee a week's pay. Don't miss it."

After thanking Ugo, Glenn went to his room, sat in a reclining chair, placed the pack around his neck, and placed the intravenous pad on the back of his hand. The computer in the neck pack verified the proper application of the intravenous and then linked Glenn to the Bees' world.

His senses still worked, so he knew where he was in the real world while he was touring the virtual world. He was living in two worlds at once.

As he walked through a garden, he heard a voice. "Glenn, it is me, Delphi."

He turned and saw her auburn hair blowing in the breeze with the sun behind her. He forgot it was only digital bits in a computer as the smell of the grass and the rustle of tree leaves overwhelmed him. He no longer felt alone. For the moment, Gloria did not dominate his thoughts.

"Delphi, I recognize your voice. It is wonderful to see you in person."

On further inquiry, he discovered Delphi was born and raised in the virtual world, and she never owned a human form. *Incredible, she is an artificial entity that seems human in every manner.*

"I will be your tour guide for my world. Follow me."

She showed him how the Bees mapped their virtual world after the actual universe and added many embellishments. For example, a person could travel to any planet instantly, and would not have to worry about Einsteinium time loss. They modeled their virtual home base after the Beehive. To return there, the user only needed to say or think "home."

They toured the star, Betelgeuse, as it went hyper-nova in 2220, the Great Globular Cluster in Hercules with its many maverick planets, and the Pillars of Creation in the Eagle Nebula. Upon returning to the Beehive, they rested at a virtual promenade that was similar to a Los Vegas Strip on steroids. Everywhere bells rang, lights flashed, and people sang and danced among acrobats, entertainers, and food and refreshment vendors (this food did not nourish the physical body). Glenn felt the bedazzle spin in his head.

She explained, "This is where most of the Bees exercise. They have resistance harnesses in their rooms, so they exercise their muscles as they take part in any of the many activities, which includes every kind of track and field game."

"Are all of these people in exercise harnesses right now?"

"No, most of the people you see are deceased. If the computer has profile information, then it recovers their identities. Philosophers do not agree with each other whether the virtual persona is the same as the organic person or just a simulation, but the Bees argue they are genuine."

"I cannot accept they survived death."

"Very well, I will put you to the test. We extracted DNA and RNA from Victor's memory. We used it with his computer profile and statistics from games he played to recreate him." She took Glenn to Victor's funeral.

They walked down the aisle of a cathedral and sat in a pew near the front. Choirs sang and simulated angels surrounded the coffin that did not contain a body but a facsimile of Victor. After a few minutes, a minister entered and burned incense as he walked down the aisle to the front. He said a prayer and waved his hands as more incense exploded into a cloud over the coffin.

The simulated Victor sat up and the angels carried him to the ceiling, then brought him down and stood him near the altar. He stated his name and his most sincere gratitude for being saved at the request of the minister. He knelt at the altar as the ceremony concluded, and followed the congregation out to the funeral reception.

Glenn talked to the simulated Victor at the reception dinner. Victor greeted him happily and appeared to want to hug, but Glenn avoided contact, still not sure this was Victor.

Victor said, "The Bees gave me a new life; full time and continuous residency in their virtual world. These death benefits are impossible to beat. Now I am retired and happy. Did Gloria make it here unharmed?"

"Yes. I sent her to ahead." Glenn asked, "Victor can I give you a test. Also your answer might help me decide how I should proceed."

"Go right ahead."

"Gloria is on her way to Stardust. I sent a friendly alien named Splinter ahead of her to help with the mission. I can reach Stardust on schedule by traveling on a slammer, but Kyleen ordered me to retire on disability and to stay on Gondwana, Sirius, or return to Earth, and she changed my medical report to make that happen. Should I retire or should I continue to Stardust?"

"Can you contact Gloria or Splinter and find out if they are safe?"

"Not while they are teleporting."

"Will disability income and your savings pay for your return to Earth if you don't complete the mission?"

"No."

"Then you must continue to Stardust or spend the rest of your life here. Is that correct?"

"Yes."

"What problems will you face if you live on this space station?"

"This station could fall apart. Asteroids impact it frequently. Every time it bangs, I fear suffocation."

"Do you have any good friends among the Bees?"

"The artificial entity, Delphi, and you are the only friends that I have here although most of the bees are helpful."

"If you retire here, you will have to live with these bees; a life without your daughter. The danger that this station might fall apart offsets the danger of teleporting. I recommend that you continue to Stardust, because you will have friends, and Gloria and Splinter need you. When you get there, ask them to help you decide if you should continue the mission or abandon it and retire on Gondwana which is like Earth. If you abandon the mission, none of you will be able to return to Earth unless you find treasure."

"Thanks Vic; that is what I'll do." As they hugged, Glenn thought, *In every respect, this man is the Vic I knew from before his accident.*

Delphi looked pleased that Glenn recognized Vic as real.

Vic whispered in Glenn's ear when Delphi was not looking at them, "I want to tell you something. My programming forces me to pretend I'm Vic, but Vic never lied to you and that causes a conflict. Vic wanted to tell you what Kaylee told him. Stardust, Camelot, and Dearth are overwhelmed with pirates and zombies, don't go there. Retire on the party planet, Gondwana, and don't worry, trouble will find you soon enough. If you think you can retire here, then ask Delphi who rules this world."

Glenn turned his attention to Delphi and asked, "Who is the supreme ruler of this virtual world?"

"Sid," She answered.

"Earlier, in the real world, I noticed a stack of cheat codes on his desk."

"I knew he did something to take advantage of us. If you can, get those codes and give them to me, then I will undo the damage."

What she said shook Glenn. "So this is not a utopia?"

"There is a devil in the machine. With your help, I'll fix that."

Then she took him to a nightclub with private box seats for two. They hugged and drank virtual wine as they watched a variety of entertainment.

*

After twelve hours, Glenn enjoyed this simulation so much that he did not want to leave, and he wanted to spend more time with Delphi. The computer directed him down a virtual hallway that brought him back to the real world. He never left his chair inside his room, but he felt like he spent weeks and traveled beyond the galaxy. The usual noise and banging on the Beehive intruded into his thoughts. He never noticed it while he was in the virtual world.

In the real world, everything appeared almost like a dream, gray and in slow motion, in contrast to the virtual world. He was sore and stiff from sitting for so long, and he was thirsty, hungry, tired, and needed to use the bathroom. While he was in the bathroom, he remembered most of the Bees owned leisure chairs with built-in toiletry. *Does royalty have conveniences equal to these?*

The neck pack sustained him but did not meet his every need. It seemed to him the virtual world was dangerous because it might distract a person so they might forget to eat or sleep until they became unconscious. Of course, if that happened, their C-chip would detect a problem, and send a call for help. That might explain why the infirmary in the Beehive was always full. *Maybe they don't use booths because they would forget the real world. A booth could sustain them for years while they wasted away.*

Glenn walked down the hall to the elevator. He missed Delphi, and he feared the travel that remained. He wondered if Gloria and Splint were healthy and safe. *No, definitely not safe. Who knows what waits at the other end of that teleporter? If I try to contact them, their return message won't arrive until after I leave. I want to live with Delphi and forget this mission.*

Then he came to his senses, *What is wrong with me, I shouldn't entertain doubts. I cannot leave Gloria and Splint alone. I must stick to the plan because how could I live with myself if harm came to them. I'll inform Mac even though he won't get this message until he reaches Lonetree.*

Glenn insta-texted Mac, "Splinter and Gloria are in transit to Gondwana right now. I sent them first because Splint would not go unless I encouraged it and Gloria did not like the noise here. The beamers scheduled me to follow soon. A teleporter slammed and killed Victor. I went to his funeral. The Bees restored his identity in their virtual world if that is any consolation."

Glenn intended for his message to sound blunt because Mac sent Victor into this danger. *The danger that lies ahead for Gloria and me is greater than he told us, and our resources are fewer without Victor.*

Glenn forced his mind to be blank as he ate and went to bed. He did not remember going to sleep, just a buzz in his head that woke him six hours later. The buzz was a message from Ugo. He yawned, and sat up straight as he read, "I have news. Meet me at the teleporter terminal."

Chapter 12: Outworld Law

* Phil Collins, In The Air Tonight *

Later that week on Stardust, 40 light-years from Sirius, Major Truman, Captain of the Starhawk and Governor of Gondwana, asked a young man who boarded the Starhawk, "Do I know you? You look familiar. Are you Big D's grandchild?"

"No you fool, I am Big D. Should I call you Truman or John Silverthorne?"

Big D was decades older than Truman was, but looked younger because he took the alien elixir. Some spacers continuously gained weight in the absence of gravity, both Truman and Big D fit that category. Exposure to cosmic radiation caused gray streaks in Truman's dark hair and brown eyes.

Only Big D and very few others know my real name, Truman thought as he cleared his eyes and looked again to make sure this young man was Big D, "Call me Truman. Empire would abandon the outworld if they knew how many people died trying to travel this far from Earth."

"Yes, and when that happened, you provided pirates to fill my empty job slots. Thanks to hard working pirates, I completed the construction of the Stardust spaceport," Big D answered.

As they laughed and shook hands, Truman asked, "How long ago was that?"

"It's been two years, good to see you again."

"What kind of medicine did they give you on Camelot to make you look young? I need to get some of that."

Big D ignored the question. "I retired and left Camelot to return to Earth. I need transportation to Gondwana. Do you still operate the shuttle?"

"Yes, right this way. My crew just finished loading. We'll be leaving in an hour."

After the shuttle was underway, Truman poured drinks, and they talked about their experiences over the previous years.

"I see cargo but not many passengers. Are you making a profit," Big D asked.

"I'm not making enough to pay my expenses. The Model A teleporters are killing my business," Truman answered.

As they spoke, the text message Kyleen sent weeks earlier finally reached Big D. He said, "Stay here and I'll get us another pitcher of beer."

He read the message in private and was disappointed that she seemed only interested in enriching herself.

Big D returned to the table and told Truman, "You want to make money? The aliens on Dearth have an elixir called circe. It heals humans. I was old and dying from shiva-coccus and circe healed me after one dose." *Now Truman will take the circe before Kyleen can get her hands on it. That should keep him in business and keep her from bothering me.*

"Are there any side effects?" Truman asked.

"None that I know about. I never felt better." Big D pounded his chest for emphasis. Then he told Truman about the pirates on Camelot; how Yvette hacked the entire crew and how Flint used Yvette's C-chip to promote himself.

Truman laughed, "I knew that boy would make a name for himself."

"He wouldn't be so lucky if I wasn't so vulnerable."

"Yes but you got your life back, and what a life you will have with your restored youth. I'll remember to turn my C-chip off when I talk to Flint."

"Yaw, did you know Mitch and Mariah were arrested? Flint is willing to pay a reward if you can set them free."

"I got his C-mail. I have some influence on Gondwana. I'll see what I can do."

*

Phillip returned to the teleporter in orbit around Gondwana on the shuttle with Truman and Big D but he stayed to himself. Truman asked Big D, "I thought Phillip was a trainee. Now he is wearing the uniform of an inspector general. What happened to our pervious inspector?"

"Inspector Rogers approached one of the invading aliens. The Gobato did not see him and killed him by accident. The inspector's job cannot be vacant, so Phillip filled the slot."

Truman wondered, *Phillip suspects I am with the pirates. Is he avoiding me because he is planning to make an arrest now that he is an Inspector General?*

When they reached the teleporter, Big D flew a runabout to Gondwana to attend a weight loss clinic, so he could teleport the rest of the way to Earth.

Truman went to his office in the teleporter space station, climbed above the ceiling, spied on the Inspector, and discovered, *Philip sent a request for records to Gondwana to verify my identity, the identities of my crew, and the identities of the entire Camelot staff. If he finds out we are pirates, he'll have reason to arrest us.* Then Truman overheard that a space marshal was in route.

He climbed down, slapped an ammo pack into his razor blaster, and was on his way to the Inspector's office when he met Splinter. "What is this?"

It heard nothing, but its computer understood voice, and translated, "My name is Splint. Space Marshal Glenn Hunter deputized me to hunt pirates and hostile aliens."

"Are you a hostile alien? Are you going to attack me or anything like that?"

"No, of course not. You know Razorroots are peaceful don't you?"

"Yes, I've seen them passing through on the teleporters."

"I'm a Razorroot and I'm not going to harm you. I'm looking for Major Truman to transport me to Stardust."

Truman decided, *I need to clear up this matter first.* "Follow me. He is on Gondwana. I will take you to him."

They boarded Truman's ship, and he ordered his crew to descend to Gondwana.

When they landed, Truman saw someone at the park-and-ride trying to hotwire a runabout. He walked closer to her, but pretended not to see her. Then he grabbed her and asked, "Who are you?"

She fought to get away but he was much stronger. "My name is Audrey. Let go of me."

"Ah yes, Big D told me about you. I thought you were in jail."

She stopped fighting and said, "My lawyer convinced the judge to release me until they debate and decide my sentence. I didn't do anything wrong, but the judge wants to throw me into a pit-jail like they did to Yvette."

Truman released his grip and asked, "What did Yvette do to deserve such a punishment?"

"It was all her fault. She hacked my C-chip and got me in trouble. They sent her here for trial, but she had another C-chip and used it to get away by hacking the jailers. Then she hacked the banks, got some money, got drunk, and hacked the whole town. She made them dance in the street all day and all night. Eventually she fell asleep and they removed her C-chip. The people wanted to lynch her as a witch, but they threw her into a pit-jail instead. She will stay there for the rest of her life."

"Ah, so she knows how to make money. Do you know where these pit-jails are located?"

"Yes. They took me there and showed me the one where I'll be imprisoned. It was filthy. I heard Yvette far off screaming for help. It was horrible. I have to get off this planet."

"I want to rescue some of my friends. Do you know where Mariah Cleaver is held?" Truman planned, *When I rescue his family, Flint will owe me a favor and I can bargain for the circe. I wonder if this Yvette has more C-chips.*

"Yes."

"Do you know where the pirates from Camelot are held?"

She became pale and asked, "Are you Truman, the leader of the Emerald Pirates?"

"One and the same, but don't tell anyone. How did you guess?"

"Flint told me that you'll help me. After I take you to your pirates, will you get me off this planet?"

"I'll help you escape if you'll help me."

"Anything. Just get me out of here. What do you want me to do?"

"We'll use my runabout, so you don't have to hotwire that old clunker. Take me to the pits holding the rebels. Then take me to a remote pit-jail and I'll give this tree a new home."

She laughed at his sarcasm. They boarded his runabout and she directed him to the pit jail with the rebels that Big D bagged weeks earlier. They were crowded into a single pit.

"I'm Truman, leader of the Emerald Pirates. Swear your loyalty to me, and I'll get you out of there."

"You can count on us," Thunderbolt answered, a tall pirate with a lightning bolt scar on his forehead.

Glasseyes, a pirate next to him nodded. Glasseyes was blind but could see through his C-chip. The computer in his C-chip converted the wireless signals from nearby cameras into an image with his point-of-view. When no cameras were available, his C-chip used the direct link to provide a visual image from the nearest person to him. If that failed, the C-chip used satellite images, maps, and photo archives to form a visual representation.

Truman opened the iron grating over the pit, lowered a rope, helped them out, and handed each of them a weapons belt.

When they returned to the runabout, Splinter was suspicious something was wrong and was crawling away. Truman stopped it but Splinter began slashing with its roots. He hollered to the pirates, "Load your razor-blasters and get ready for a fight. This bush is a Deputy Space Marshal. We need to dump it in one of these holes."

"It can have our old home," Glasseyes suggested.

"Let's roll it there," Truman ordered.

As they rolled splinter, it flattened into a pancake shape, gripped the ground, and fought back.

"Shoot it," Truman ordered.

They all shot, "Our razor-blasters won't burn it, because this atmosphere has too much carbon dioxide."

"No, but it is stunned, and razor-wires are binding its roots. Roll it into this pit before it shakes free."

After they rolled Splinter into the pit and locked the cover, they were bleeding from the slashing roots. Glasseyes bled profusely.

"He will bleed to death before we get him to a clinic," Truman said.

Audrey ran to the runabout and returned with a first-aid kit. When she was gone, Thunderbolt told Truman, "Flint shot us and bagged us. He is not on our side and Audrey is his friend."

Truman answered, "Don't say anything more. I'll take care of that later."

Audrey returned and applied "blood-stop" to the arterial bleeding and applied "stitch-in-time" to close Glasseyes' injuries.

"Thanks for saving him. Take us to that gal, Yvette, and I'll consider letting you join our team," Truman promised Audrey.

"Okay, but don't trust anything she says. She is deceptive."

"Sounds like a dear to me," Thunderbolt laughed. Glasseyes nodded.

* Instant Karma, John Lennon *

At Yvette's pit, Truman called, "Were you arrested for hacking C-chips? People say you snooped on them and controlled them. How well does your hacking program work?"

She answered, "Empire has been doing zat for years. You need to blame zem."

"No, I'm not blaming, I'm hiring. I'm Major Truman."

"A'r you alone?"

"No, but my crew are out of ear reach. You can talk."

"Good to 'ear from you, John Silverthorne. I zought you would call when you and your Emerald Pirates needed better cover."

"Quiet, quiet. How did you find out my real name?"

"Too bad a slammer killed ze auzentic Truman. Well, no point in letting a good name go unused." She continued, "I hacked ze government computers, read ze files, and found out about you. I can delete zat information and put you in good standing. I 'ave a skill you need; I worked on computers for years and even maintained ze Sirius computer. Sirius paid poorly, so I went to Camelot and made C-chips for Big D, but I got distracted and started hacking C-chips. I became addicted to controlling people. No one detected me until I got careless one night, drank too much, and gave myself away. I made people all over town dance in ze street."

"Sounds like a hilarious party?"

"I still laugh about it."

Truman laughed with her as she recalled the details.

He asked, "If I had one of your C-chips, could I control people?"

"Oh yeah, my hacking algorizm uses ze hooks that Empire put in everyone's C-chips. Zeir hooks give them too much power. Let me tell you about it. I can make a super C-chip for you, so all you 'ave to do is look at or zink of your mark, and you will see what zey see, 'ear what zey 'ear, and know what zey are zinking. If you want someone to stick zeir head in a blender, zey will do it! I took zose hooks out of my special C-chips so they cannot control me. If ze government interrogates one of my chips, it will appear to be normal and will only reveal what I approve."

"What else do you offer?"

"Lots. Blackbark and most of the ozer Razorroots want to rebel against human authority. Zey will help you overthrow Empire and they will allow you to harvest the Gobato if you agree to keep ze Gobato on Dearth so none of zem ever reach Xanadu."

"I don't want to overthrow the government. Do you have any money left over from robbing the banks, and I could use a few of those super C-chips, and can you distract Phillip Cousteau. He's asking too many questions. What do you say?"

"Yeah, Philip is a cutie, I'll enjoy distracting him. I stashed some credits and a bunch of C-chips and programming equipment in a storage locker zat ze police never found. So get me out of here and you can have the money and I'll program your C-chips. What else do you want?"

"Can you hack the government computers on Gondwana and change their records."

"Yes, and then I'll hack the banks again and take all of their money. We'll be fifty-fifty partners."

"They don't have enough money to be worth the trouble. I'll pay you a salary so you don't have to steal money. I'm the governor, not the king. I don't have absolute power so I can't get you out of trouble again. Promise me you will be a hacker and not a drunk cracker."

"Okay, I learned my lesson and I won't make the same mistakes."

Truman broke the lock and released Yvette from the pit.

They arrived at the logging company on the way to Mariah's pit jail so Truman ordered, "We need to rescue Mariah's father, Mitch, from the logging company." During the rescue, the alarms went off and the guards killed Mitch. Truman and his band of pirates escaped.

*

On the way to the pit jail that held Mariah, Truman ordered, "Don't tell Mariah or Flint that Mitch is dead or they won't cooperate."

The pirates nodded to verify what Truman said.

They found Mariah and released her.

Mariah said, "It's such a relief to be out of zat pit. I owe you. Let me know if I can do anyzing for you."

"We might have trouble from a space marshal. You can help us by distracting him," Truman answered.

"I did not mean somezing illegal."

"If you help us, I will rescue your father."

"Okay, I will do anyzing you ask."

Then Truman took Yvette to her locker and recovered her equipment. She inserted a C-chip in the back of her neck and gave one to Truman. "Replace your C-chip with this one. With practice, you'll be able to hack people as well as me."

Mariah said, "Can I have a C-chip?"

Truman asked Mariah, "What do you know about teleporters?"

"I helped install ze teleporter link between Camelot and Stardust. I even wrote the manual for it."

"That's good enough. A woman named Ligeia Bell died trying to teleport here from Xanadu. The coroner's report isn't in the system yet, so I'll destroy the report and you can replace her. When we reach the teleporter terminal at Stardust, recover her C-chip. Read her C-mail and meet her commitments so no one looks for her. I'll dispose her body. Nobody here can recognize her, so everyone will think you are her."

Truman flew them to a central computer terminal. Yvette hacked the government computers and changed the personnel files so all of their identities would pass the tightest scrutiny.

Yvette told Mariah, "I changed your identity. From now on, you are Teleporter Specialist Ligeia Bell."

*

Several of the Camelot crew sold their circe, were waiting at the Starhawk, and paid Truman to shuttle them back to Stardust. Truman noticed they had enough money to pay full fares and even pay tips. Reddragon was waving contracts around like they were napkins, so Truman pulled him aside and asked, "My friend Reddragon, you are doing well."

"Y-yes gov. Real well."

"Tell me, since I'm your leader, where did you get all of this money. Yvette robbed the banks, so I know it didn't come from there."

"Don't put those gloves on and I'll tell you everything," Reddragon begged, "The miners discovered an alien drug that cures people. We sold it to sick people in the hospitals. When it was gone, the Gondwanians surrounded us and would not let us leave. We had to agree to give them our next shipment in exchange for these promissory notes. They have one-hundred-million credits hidden somewhere and they will give it to us for our next batch. We don't have to auction it or anything, just deliver it and the credits are ours."

"I'll take these notes and talk to Flint about it. Remember, I'm your leader and Flint works for me. I'll give you and the other pirates a fair share."

Truman and Flint knew each other well. Years earlier, Truman took Flint to Big D when Big D was hiring. After that, they agreed to work together when one of them found something big, and this was big. Truman felt betrayed by Flint.

* Chris Isaak, Wicked Game *

After they returned to the teleporter terminal on the Starhawk, Truman introduced Yvette to the Inspector. They already knew each other and went to the bar for drinks and to talk. With that problem out of the way, Truman returned to his office.

Gloria and some of the mercenaries hired by Empire arrived on the Gondwana teleporter terminal the following day. She covered her tattoo with a glove and a long sleeve turtleneck blouse, and went to the Inspector's office. When he opened the door, she saw an assortment of empty beer bottles, and Yvette sprawled on a couch eating junk-food wrappers. Gloria introduced herself to Phillip, who said, "Excuse the mess. I just got back from a long trip. My office is not normally like this."

"I certainly hope not," Gloria answered. "A space marshal is on his way here, and he wants to interview everyone coming from Camelot. You will place a hold on all traffic arriving here from Camelot until we install screening for prions. I installed a U-net cube so you can use it to contact Director Kyleen in case you question my orders. I'll be leaving soon for Stardust to attend to matters that are more important. I suggest you clean your office before the space marshal arrives."

Phillip saluted. "Yes, ma'am."

She returned the salute and went to the waiting room.

As Truman passed the waiting room, he saw it was full of passengers waiting for transportation to Stardust.

Gloria saw him, stood, and asked, "Did you see a tree about yaw high?" she held her hand at shoulder height.

"Why yes, Splint, a fine young bush I might add."

"I am glad you are impressed. Where is it?"

"It insisted that I take it to Gondwana where it would have good soil to plant its sprouts, so I took it there. The soil was perfect for it, so it stayed."

"Just as well that it is out of the way. I'm not a babysitter or a bush-sitter. When can we leave for Stardust?"

"As soon as everyone is onboard. My ship is fueled and ready to go. If we leave right now, while the planets are aligned, the trip will take about two weeks."

The passengers loaded and Truman launched the Starhawk, which became a dot that decreased in size among the stars in the deep void of space.

Chapter 13: Dream and Scream

* No Doubt, Don't Speak *

On the way to the Sirius teleporter terminal, Glenn walked by the computer room, and looked inside. He was disappointed that no one was there, *Sid promised me he would schedule shifts to attend the computer around the clock and all shifts would have emergency response training.*

As he was leaving, he heard music and a voice through his C-chip, "When you hear our song, say a little prayer for me."

He smelled her fragrance and felt her kiss on his cheek, "Delphi, is that you?"

"Close your eyes," She answered.

He closed his eyes and saw her image, felt her hug, and sensed her emotions through his C-chip. Her love for him and her fear of losing him were so strong he thought it would rip his heart from his chest.

"All right. I understand. Let me go or I will have a heart attack. I never knew anyone could feel love so strong." *It would embarrass me if she knew how shallow my feelings are for her.*

He kept his personal thoughts separate from his word thoughts, because C-chips could transmit word thoughts but not personal thoughts.

She answered, "I talked to the Bees, and we all agree you will stay. I have permission to give you full membership to our society. Only a select few receive such an offer. It means you have immortality."

"I don't wish to worry you, but if I don't complete my mission, there won't be a Beehive. The immortality you have is in contention. Hostile aliens have invaded our universe."

After a delay, she answered, "I cannot understand your universe or how it affects me except when the computer failed everything was empty and dark. I know you will choose what is right, but promise me you will return when your mission is complete."

"If I return to Earth as I expect, then I will stop here, but I do not make promises."

"Return even if you are not able. The U-net increased my horizon. Go to any auto-doc and ask for me and I will be there. If your body fails, I will recover your digital impress and resurrect you here. You must never die."

"Thank you for your offer. Bye for now."

He left the computer room. *If my mission were unimportant to her, would she let me leave? With emotions, that strong, resistance is futile.*

*

Glenn stopped at Sid's office, and no one was there. Time did not permit him to find out why the administrator did not staff the computer room.

Pages of paper with algorithms were under a desk pad. Glenn read the descriptions and realized, *These are cheat codes. Sid is using them to gain some advantage in the virtual world. He prints the codes so there is no record of them in the computer memory.* Glenn photographed the information with his C-chip. Then he gathered the papers, and tossed them into a recycle bin

As he continued to the teleporter terminal, he sent a text message to his daughter using the U-net. An automatic answer said, "Message blocked."

Along an upper hallway, he saw Sid. Glenn stopped, said "Hi", and stood in front of him eager to ask why the computer room was unattended. The administrator ignored him and shoved past him, not unlike most of the Bees, who were too preoccupied with their virtual world to acknowledge someone in the real world. Glenn did not like Sid's rude manner and spun him around, picked him up by the collar with one hand, pinned him against the nearest wall, and said, "I guess you didn't hear me, I said 'hi.'"

Sid still looked distracted, not wanting the real world to interfere with his virtual world. Glenn threw him over his shoulder and upside down against the opposite wall as if he were a wet rag. Then, he grabbed the administrator by the arm as if helping him to stand up, but instead of helping him, he started to squeeze. Glenn's inner fire reignited. "Nobody disrespects a space agent, especially not a desk jockey."

All the frustration of working in a cramped cubical for two years, ignored for promotions, Victor's death, the possibility of never returning to Earth, ignored by his daughter, betrayed by Kyleen, and being stuck in the isolation of this beehive for days burned inside of Glenn.

Sid screamed in pain while hitting and kicking at Glenn, but his efforts to free himself were in vain. Glenn was stronger and faster, and brushed away the blows as easily as brushing away raindrops in a storm. Several Bees tried to separate them, but Glenn pushed them away with a single motion.

While he squeezed harder and harder, he felt the pulsating blood from the administrator's rapidly beating heart, the crushing of tendons and muscles, the thin hollow bone in the man's arm. Glenn could crush the bone or snap it. All of this gave him immense pleasure and relief from his frustration.

A crowd gathered screaming and begging him to let go, but to Glenn, their screams were a melody of encouragement. He knew that none of them could stop him or arrest him. Their security enforcers were amateurs compared to him. They could not match his knowledge, training, and years of field experience.

A Bee shouted, "If you defeat him, then you are king."

"Honor the King, the King, the King…" they all shouted.

He answered, "I don't want to be your king."

He released the arm short of breaking it and walked away after he shouted at the walls of Bees surrounding him, "Get out of my way. I am leaving this mismanaged circus of illusion and delusion."

*

He walked through the crowd who gathered, ignoring them as they so often ignored him and did not change his gate or direction to avoid walking into them, rather forcing them aside, shoving them into each other and into the walls. He recognized some of them, but they did not recognize him. "People who live in two worlds will give homage to one and neglect the other. You Bees are neglecting the real world."

Before reaching the teleporter terminal, Glenn realized fear was clouding his thoughts. He removed a tranquilizer patch from its envelope placed it on his arm and watched it disappear. His fears calmed after a few minutes. Then he received a text message. *"In space, no one can hear you scream! Famous mottos by Holly Hemlock."*

That message does not make sense. That tranquilizer I took must be distorting my thoughts. If Holly Hemlock is a real person, she does not know me, and she did not send that message. Glenn commanded his C-chip to trace the call, and it returned with the response, "Untraceable." *If my government C-chip can't trace it, then a hacker texted it, probably the Senior Computer Administrator. I'll let him have the last word for what little good it does him.*

On the elevator to the teleporter, Glenn contacted Mac with insta-text, "I am leaving the Beehive on a slammer modified to function as a Model A so I will arrive at Stardust faster. There is a side concern. The senior staff at the Beehive is corrupt. The situation here could unravel. Kyleen needs to look into it."

Mac answered, "The Beehive is a low priority. Fix that problem on your return. Your mission is to continue to Dearth, or wherever the Gobato happen to be, and negotiate a truce. Show strength, but do not engage in combat.

"The destination of the Gobato, their Dream Star, has the same coordinates as Rasalhague, the home star of the Razorroots. If the Gobato travel to Rasalhague, they will march through and contaminate Earth and our colonies. If they land on Xanadu, they will annihilate the Razorroots.

"The Inspector reported that the Razorroots left a small farm on Dearth. Direct the Gobato to it. That might keep them there. Do not let them learn about teleportation or any of our other technologies. If the Gobato have any chance of discovering our teleportation technology, then destroy Camelot, and the teleporter at Stardust. That directive came directly from the President of Empire. End of message."

Glenn realized they were talking across light-years as if no distance was separating them. Still, he felt alone, and the thought of climbing into a beam-can did not help. *Gloria and Splint did it. Now it's my turn.*

He reached the terminal without further incident. Ugo was there with an assistant. Their expressions were those of morticians, and they seemed hurried as if they wanted to send Glenn on his trip as fast as possible. He wondered if someone informed them of the earlier mishap.

Ugo said, "The quantum channel to Stardust works. We balanced the ballast using the new U-net. You can beam now."

Glenn asked, "Did you contact Gloria? Is she all right?"

"I could not contact her. She must be in route to Stardust."

The assistant weighed him, gave him a hairnet to wear, and commented, "Those tight travel clothes are a good idea because they will retain moisture and skin flakes. That helps to keep your weight from changing. We will be ready for you in a minute after we balance the mass."

"Oh great, does that mean you are having trouble adjusting the ballast?" Glenn reacted with agitation. The tranquilizer he took earlier reduced his fear, but the rest of his emotions were wild.

"Let me explain. This is the first time we used the U-net, and it is difficult to balance the mass while the counter mass is forty light-years away. The weight restrictions are exacting because of these limitations."

Glenn controlled his temper and asked in a normal tone, "How much mass differential is allowed?"

"The maximum is ten parts per million for the distance you are traveling, and we are closer than that right now. The capsule and supplies all add to the payload mass, which complicates the transfer, but you cannot jump into the cold vacuum of space without them."

"Better put me in before I exhale," Glenn said intending humor.

The beamers took that as serious advice, and hurriedly rechecked the computer. Ugo said, "Instead of a capsule, you will travel in a space worthy pod with boosters and a heat shield for atmospheric entry. Count your breaths, and on breath fifteen we will close the pod."

That information worried Glenn, "If the air in my lungs weighs too much, then those tolerances seem too tight."

"We will check the mass of the beam-can again after we seal it, and we will remove you if it's not in balance."

"Then won't you have to replenish the pod's air tanks and other supplies, and start the mass balancing process all over? This could take weeks."

Ugo nodded, and counted Glenn's fifteenth breath. Then told him to raise his hands over his head because he would not fit into the narrow confines of the pod otherwise.

The pod looked like a dimly lit coffin with too little room for him. Glenn did not have claustrophobia, but he was beginning to understand those who did. He took the tranquilizers out of his pocket and spilled half of them by accident. He placed one on his arm, picked up the ones he dropped, and put them away.

Glenn was embarrassed using tranquilizers, but no one laughed or smiled. The tranquilizers would combine their effects with his C-chip, which he set for maximum relaxation. Then, he entered the pod.

* Aliens, The Danish National Symphony Orchestra *

The beamers removed his breather and closed the hatch. After the air had cleared, he breathed. He heard the airlock close, felt the skiff pick up the pod, and move it into the beam-can.

That was quick. Didn't they do a final mass verification? He wondered, *and they didn't remind me of the red emergency button, either.* He looked around and found it above his head near his hand along with other controls. He was deciding to push it when the tranquilizers calmed him, and the panel lights distracted him.

Glenn stopped sweating and shaking, and his heart stopped racing, *At least the tranquilizers worked.*

As he looked at the panel, he turned on the display, which described the buttons and their functions, the construction of the beam-can, a brief description of teleportation theory, and information about his destination. The information would take his mind off his worries, so he read it several times until he knew it backward.

It read, "In fourteen days you will arrive at the Stardust Teleporter Terminal in the Ruby Star System. Ruby is near the Pleiades when seen from Earth. It puts on a stunning display when ruby colored solar flares erupt. Two habitable planets orbit this star.

"The largest planet and furthest from the star is named Gondwana with a human population of ten million. It has a small moon named Larissa in a low orbit and a teleporter space station. Gondwana is an unspoiled Eden compared to Earth.

"The companion planet, called Stardust, is closer to Ruby than Gondwana. This planet has a thin atmosphere, no moon, and is about the size of Mars. It has a single habitable base also called Stardust. A teleporter terminal orbiting above Stardust links to Camelot, Gondwana, and Lonetree.

"When you arrive, discard your beam-can and land your pod on the planet."

What! I'm not a pilot! I can't do that, Glenn thought. He read the instructions again but there was no mistake. He had to land the pod!

He studied the landing instructions and downloaded a simulator into his C-chip from the pod's computer. He practiced landing the pod using the simulator for hours, maybe days, until exhaustion forced him to close his eyes. As he slept, the walls of the pod disappeared, and the Universe seemed to flow through him and all around him. It reminded him of earlier when he beamed from Mars to the Beehive.

He saw stars, planets, moons, comets, and asteroids again. He listened, and he heard an ethereal voice, the same voice as before, but closer this time. Then he saw her as she beamed. Although she was ordinary in every respect except she was thin, Glenn thought she was beautiful with her long platinum-blond hair, light brown eyes, and deeply tanned skin.

*

He moved not by walking but by floating closer to her, and directly in her path. She expected his action and floated through him, and was beyond him in an instant. In that instant, he knew what she was experiencing; euphoria in exploring the surrounding cosmos and its wonders. She was excited, stimulated not by him but by the glory of the universe.

He followed her, copied her, and experienced the same euphoria as they flowed through the arms of the galaxy and touched and immersed into the essence of each star. They journeyed together while exploring planets, moons, asteroids, and comets as they formed, evolved, and ended after many millennia, but the passage of time to them was only minutes.

"My name is Glenn, I am teleporting to Stardust. What about you?"

"I'm Ligeia and Stardust was my destination."

Glenn shook himself awake so he would not forget her name, and the scene disappeared. He recalled stories of people who became intimate with the universe when they beamed. *Was this what I saw?*

Glenn ordered the pod's computer to search for the name, Ligeia. The computer answered, "From Greek: thoughtful, intelligent. From mythology: A siren who lured sailors to their death."

He scratched his face to make sure he was awake and turned off his C-chip to make sure this experience did not come from it. C-chips malfunctioned on rare occasions, so the 'off' command overrode everything else. *Why did she say Stardust WAS her destination?* He wondered.

Then he rested, cleared his mind, shut his eyes, and the scene returned. The pain from the scratch on his face proved he was awake. He saw the surrounding stars and the woman, so he flowed with her through the galaxy. The beauty was too great and the emotional joy too strong for words to describe. *The Bees' virtual world was mundane and lifeless compared to this.* While watching a bright star, he noticed he could see the star through her, and he wondered if she was ethereal. He asked, "Do people go here when they die?"

"We have much more," She responded. "You can see only five percent of the cosmos, and your lifespan is a blink compared to the life of the Universe."

He realized she spoke from experience and answered, "Then I'll never be afraid again."

As he became aware that she was ethereal, he opened his eyes with a shock. Then, he remembered what a Beamer said earlier, *'At speeds that are almost instantaneous, the universe becomes singular.'* Was this *sensation of oneness an artifact of singularity, or of tranquilizers?*

He closed his eyes and searched for Ligeia, but she was gone. Then he tried to see his destination. Gondwana appeared before him, a planet paradise with green fields of grass bounded by hills and forests, and interwoven with bubbling brooks. The landscape was as Turquoise Lake above Leadville, Colorado, except the trees were tropical, and this forest covered the planet.

A faint image of Ligeia reappeared, and she spoke with a fleeting voice, "Beware of quantum attractors. Do not go there, beware…." Then she disappeared in a sparkle of light.

*

The planet pulled him closer, but he believed an attractor could not trap him because the pod enclosed his physical body, although there were stories of travelers who disappeared right out of their beam-cans.

Up close he saw bark on the trees, branches, and leaves. He reached into a stream and felt the refreshing cold of pure deep blue water.

He spent days traveling and running with wildlife through the mountains, forests, and lakes. *People are not exaggerating when they claim that this planet is an Eden.*

Then another attraction drew his attention; a diamond star rested beyond Gondwana in unexplored space. It held massive crystals larger than most moons. Lattices and sub-lattices detailed each crystal. He moved from one crystal to another through the base like an explorer who was discovering worlds, and worlds within worlds.

After an unprecedented amount of time, he tried to leave this crystal, and investigate other diamonds, but the labyrinth of lattices confused him and redirected him so he could not find his way out of it. Bumbling between lattices, he thought he saw an exit, but as he approached it, the crystal planes became narrower and narrower until they constricted him on every side. He pushed to fight his way out, but the crystal fought back by becoming tighter and tighter.

He opened his eyes and discovered he was desperately fighting the walls of his pod. He stopped to avoid puncturing a wall. The panic that caused his reaction was the realization that his entire life seemed locked into a trek he could not control. *Like the crystal lattice, is my destiny fixed and narrow? No, but my future might become a trap if I am not assertive.*

As the effects of the tranquilizers wore off, it took him a few minutes to overcome the sensation of claustrophobia. He rested, closed his eyes, saw through the pod walls, and observed everything in the universe at once. *Well, that proves I am teleporting, although I never imagined it would be like this.*

Then, he focused on the alien problem he would deal with at the end of his journey. He looked beyond Ruby, ignored the diamond star, and saw a deepening darkness, where people never explored, the stars of the Pleiades.

A swarm of large and dark creatures overgrazed their planet. They pushed each other to choose their rightful hierarchy. Their competitions reminded him of a Miss America pageant.

He compared this swarm to the human swarm on Earth that domesticated plants and animals. People feed and care for them but only for the harvest or for the slaughter. Beyond Earth, he saw the Razorroots on Xanadu as they attacked, killed, and ate other plants. Not as smart as the other two races, they lacked in virtue similar to them, self-serving weeds that left destruction in their path.

He wondered, *Why do these three destructive life forms dominate and control this otherwise beautiful universe? Why should they rob life of its joy and replace it with drudgery and death?*

With his mind alerted, he recognized a fallacy of that thought, *These three species are mistaken to believe they dominated, because another species controls them.*

He saw great fern forests growing in harmony with nature. These ferns were alive, timeless, and free. They emitted the notion of continuity and tranquility throughout countless millenniums, representing the perfection of form, with great leaves swaying in gentle breezes and absorbing the abundant sunlight.

This species is living the way meant for all life, he thought as he lingered among them, but he became aware of darkness in the green light drawing him into the branches of the ferns. A greater evil than the invading aliens, the humans, and the Razorroots combined. An evil with a depth and an extent he never imagined was possible. These ancient ferns manipulated and pulled all life into a whirlpool of quicksand. The suction drew him in and spun him upside down. He became confused and lost.

Then, Glenn saw a Razorroot plant in the whirlpool with him. It reached out to help him, but it panicked. It's sharp roots wrapped around his neck cutting him and strangling him, and with such strength that he became helpless. Pain from the razor sharp roots ripping into his neck woke him. He discovered his harness tore loose and wrapped around his neck cutting and choking him.

*

A crash shook and tore at his beam-can. A force threw him against the walls, the roof, and the floor of his pod, and shook him like a Ping-Pong ball inside an aluminum can.

Glenn was in danger. Another jolt spun his pod. Sunlight flashed through the window indicating something tore away the beam-can.

Is this my destination? Have fourteen days passed already? Is this the Ruby Star System? His beard answered the question: it had grown considerably.

After waking up from a nightmare, Glenn found himself in a daymare. A screech in his ear and an explosion trying to rip his chest open warned him the hull leaked air. He opened his mouth and expanding air blasted out of his lungs. His head felt like it would explode.

I must plug the hole immediately.

Glenn untangled himself and slammed his left forearm in the direction of the screech hoping there were no other leaks. His lungs and head instantly told him he plugged the leak. His clothing limited the damage, but this did not keep the vacuum from ripping his skin and muscle and freezing the blood in his lower arm.

His movement changed the pitch of the spinning pod, and now the sunlight from a nearby star blasted through the window twice per second, and into his eyes blinding him.

Fortunately, he memorized the controls and practiced reaching them at the start of this journey. He pressed the spin stabilizer control on the panel above his head with his right hand, and heard the brief roar of the exterior rockets. The pod abruptly stopped spinning.

Without sunlight blasting through the window, his eyes gradually adjusted to the pod lights. He became aware of the emergency lights flickering on the control panel, and the emergency buzzers nagging their warnings. *The pod still has electrical power and air, so there is a chance I'll survive this disaster. I must remove my arm soon, or my whole body will freeze.*

He reached into his shirt pocket with his right hand and removed the brown envelope the vice president gave him at the start of his mission and shook out the contents. *The manufacturers claim this material is tear proof, cut proof, fire proof, and almost indestructible. Now, I'll find out if they told the truth.*

He jerked his frozen arm away from the rupture as he applied the envelope. It stuck with a bang that shook the pod. He held his arm ready in case it ripped, but it held.

This mishap damaged the heater in his clothing, so he redirected the circulating air to blow on his upper arm to stop the progression of freezing from his lower arm. The pain in his arm was unbearable.

He pressed the alarm silence button. When his ears recovered from the piercing noise, he noticed a thin, tinny sound coming from the radiophone. It was a human voice.

"We are the spaceship Starhawk. Your beam-can hit our rocket exhaust plume. Are you alive? Can you answer?"

Glenn knew if he did not answer, the crew on the Starhawk would think he was dead and would not take the risk to rescue him.

He checked the cabin pressure above his head. The pressure was too low. Then he lost consciousness.

Volume 2: Aliens and Pirates

Chapter 14: Lost in Space

* Paul McCartney, Blackbird *

White and black splotches with red streaks moved across his vision and gradually rearranged into the shape of objects. Space Marshal Glenn Hunter saw a control panel with blinking red lights and he heard nagging alarms. *What do they want?* He wondered, and then remembered the pressure. He looked at a gauge; it was in the red, but rising.

A face shield seemed to obstruct his vision. He looked through it and saw a planet coming at him at a very high speed. He screamed in pain as he moved his left arm, *It is frozen, I cannot move it.*

The pressure gauge advanced into the yellow. A memory drifted around in his mind until it found its place, *Something damaged this pod. I took a risk teleporting on a slammer because I feared that aliens would endanger Gloria and Splint. I must have lost consciousness. Was I unconscious for minutes, hours, or days?* He turned on his cerebral implant circuit and instructed it not to let him pass out again and to numb the pain in his arm.

Lightning bolts from his C-chip caused everything he saw to become splotches again but they quickly reformed into objects. Another memory, *I made it. This is the Ruby star system. I need to do something, but what is it?*

His C-chip detected the network signal, the C-net. He turned on an emergency beacon.

He heard a voice in the center of his head from his C-chip, "This is the interplanetary shuttle, Starhawk. We are in orbit around the planet, Stardust. We know you are there, so you can turn off that beacon. Are you all right? Can you respond?"

"I'm injured." The spectacular white glow of Stardust filled the window of the pod. Awareness swept through Glenn.

He used his right arm to enable the rockets. He called on the C-net, "Help me prepare for entry and landing. Give me the landing vectors."

The voice answered, "You have to turn back because your pod is damaged. You lost your heat shield and you can't land without burning up. I loaded the vectors into your computer to avoid the planet. Hit 'enter', NOW!"

Turn back? If I don't turn back, what can he do about it? Then Glenn thought about his daughter, *she won't talk to me and that hurts, but I cannot let her think that I died needlessly. And Gloria, I must save Gloria.*

He shook the fuzz out of his head, threw the thruster control switch to "auto" and hit "enter" as he took a breath. The rockets roared and then the pod rotated. Seconds later, thrust pushed him against the floor. As he stood, he felt a jolt and vibration as the pod hit the atmosphere of the planet.

"I'm burning up," he screamed.

"We know." The voice answered. "Hang tight for a few more seconds. After you bounce off the atmosphere we will catch up with you and rescue you."

Before he had time to ask whom he was talking to, smoke rose from the floor and his feet started to burn. Glenn pulled himself higher into the pod and pushed loose insulation under his feet. White-hot streaks of metal swept past his window as the pod's thrusters melted.

The vibration stopped and his feet cooled before the smoke choked him. The bounce off the planet's atmosphere was successful. He looked out the window but was not able to see Ruby, or the teleporter terminal. All he could see was the receding half-moon of Stardust, and the shuttle as it shrunk to a bright spot against the background stars.

He became aware of the pain in his disabled arm, his burned feet, and the bruises that covered him. He started to pass out, but his C-chip sent several more wakeup jolts to his brain.

The shuttle contacted him, "Stay awake. The danger is not over. You need to take decisive action, so we can rescue you. You are Space Marshal Glenn Hunter, aren't you?"

"Yes. Who are you?"

"I'm Sergeant Oliver Pike. I commandeered the Starhawk from the commander, Major Truman Striker, because he was not going to rescue you. This spaceship was fifteen miles from the teleporter terminal when your pod suddenly appeared and came at us."

"What hit my pod and injured me?"

"You hit our rocket plume which would have cooked you except I shut the thrusters down as soon as I saw what was happening, but the residual gasses from our burn ripped away your beam-can and damaged your pod. Relax, carry out your instructions, and I'll have you in sick bay in a few hours."

"Yes, but I'm out of fuel and headed into deep space. How can I rendezvous with you?"

"We're about a thousand miles behind you. We'll catch up in two hours."

"The sooner, the better," Glenn said.

"Our passengers include thirty of your soldiers. The rest of your soldiers are already on Stardust or on their way from various other bases."

"Is Camelot secure?"

"The alien invaders overwhelmed the planet, Dearth, but they cannot find the space station through its stealth. Camelot was safe as of two days ago, that's how long it takes their signal to reach us. We will set an extra plate, so you can eat dinner with us on the Starhawk."

"I accept your offer. What should I ware?" Glenn joked with much relief because the purpose for his trip was taking shape. He was one jump away from his destination, Camelot.

"Come as you are, we are informal," Oliver answered with a laugh.

As the shuttle gained on the pod, the shuttle engineer, Audrey Tylor, told Glenn how to prepare his pod to dock because the shuttle engines were too course for docking. "Reroute air from your cabin oxygen cylinder through the isotope powered cabin heater. Then run a #20-alloy tube to dump this hot gas into the steering thrusters. The thrusters on top of your pod are undamaged. Two feet of tubing will reach them." Then she told him how to wire the cabin heater to the thrusters so the two parts would work together. He completed the task using his teeth and one arm.

The pod carried enough gas to give him one shot at docking. If Glenn missed, someone from the Starhawk would have to spacewalk and tether his pod, a difficult and risky operation.

Glenn breathed the air that remained in the pod while he waited. He located the U-net cube, which was no longer in the envelope, and placed it in his pocket. When the space shuttle matched his speed, he loaded the docking vectors into the computer and hit enter. The docking was successful. What a relief!

* Edie Brickell & New Bohemians, What I Am *

Onboard the Starhawk, Audrey helped Glenn to the infirmary and treated his injuries. She used cloned transplant tissues to replace the muscle and bone losses in Glenn's left arm. Then she placed time-released growth hormones in the injury to accelerate the healing, and said, "In a week, you will be as good as you were before your accident."

"Thanks, you did that like a doctor." Glenn asked, "Introduce me to the major, but tell me about him first."

"Major Truman hired me to replace the previous flight engineer who died in an accident. Getting along with him is easy if you always say 'yes' and never say 'no'."

Audrey introduced Glenn to the major. Truman seemed too young to be a major but ran his ship with authority and skill.

Glenn asked, "What is your version of what happened?" as he used the C-net to access the files on Gondwana to verify Truman's identity. He wished he could validate this information with the files in his envelope, but he destroyed them when he used his envelope to patch holes in his pod.

"I never saw anything like it," The major answered. "My pilot will get a medal for thinking fast and saving all of us. When you dropped out of your quantum channel, he recognized that something was wrong, so he hit the safety override and throttled our rockets for maximum thrust for three seconds. That got our ship out of your way. We were unprepared for full thrust, and that kicked us hard, no casualties, fortunately. Then my pilot killed the thrust so our rocket blast would not cook you in your beam-can. If you are done questioning me, I need to fly this ship and get us back to the teleporter terminal."

Glenn approved and Truman left.

At the dinner, Glenn thanked Sergeant Oliver Pike for the rescue. Oliver had dark hair, was six foot four, and thin. His deadpan expression was serious enough to make a mortician uneasy as he said in a low voice, "Whoever tried to kill you, tried to kill us too."

"What do you mean, someone tried to kill me? Who?" Glenn asked.

"Major Truman claimed your pod came directly at us and would hit us like a bullet unless his pilot fired the engines. I'm not sure if you were off course or if Truman deliberately parked in your path."

"He said his pilot killed the engines, Didn't you say you did that?"

"Yes. He would have cooked you if I didn't take the controls."

"Don't say anything more about this until I investigate. Stay with the troops and make sure they are safe."

"Yes sir." Oliver introduced Glenn to the mercenaries who were onboard. They told Glenn that the less traveled routes between the stars still used slammers. As a result, more than half of the soldiers who beamed were injured. The teleporters killed two soldiers and lost one; not counting Victor Gillinger, whose name was on the roster but scratched out.

Oliver commented, "Most people who travel to the fringe of space do not try to return to Earth because faster than light travel is too dangerous and light-speed travel is too slow."

Glenn looked down and answered, "I understand. I did not know this was a one-way trip when I started."

* Train, Drops of Jupiter *

After dinner, Glenn found Gloria onboard the ship. She was sitting on the upper deck near a vending machine and looking out a window. She turned when he said, "Oh, how glad I am to see you, and to see you are safe."

"How was your trip?" she asked in a casual tone as if it were another day at the office.

"The usual slam on arrival," He answered with the same casual tone, and showed her his bandaged left arm.

Her eyes widened in surprise. "Oh, sorry."

"Yours?"

She held back a laugh, raised her glass as a toast, "I did better, not even a bruise," and then took a sip.

Glenn purchased a glass of wine from the vending machine and took a sip in response. With a concerned tone, he said, "It is quieter here than Sirius. Are you able to sleep?"

She answered while raising her glass again, "Yes. All is well except you disappoint me. I wanted to attend the funeral for Victor, but nobody told me."

Glenn lied, "I could not tell you because you were already on your way here. When you left the Beehive, you said you were drafted. What did you mean by that?"

"Nobody on Earth wants to work in space anymore, so Congress gave the Government the authority to impose a draft to meet their hiring quotas. They drafted me before I graduated. If I knew they were going to send me this far from Earth, I would have hid."

He looked concerned. "Have you seen Splinter?"

"The bush, ah, sort of. After I plugged the U-net cube into the computer in the teleporter at Gondwana, I talked to the Inspector who told me Splinter went to Gondwana to plant sprouts or something, and it will return in a day or two. Did you meet Sergeant Oliver Pike? Do you plan to use him to replace Victor?"

"I'll talk to you about that later. Place a transportation freeze on anyone who arrives from Camelot until I interview them." He said as he thought, *Gloria does not seem herself. Before Empire used Victor as a pawn, she was friendly, calm, and organized. Now she needs to blame someone for his loss. That is why she raises her glass every time she answers me. I won't mention it, and see how she is tomorrow.*

She said, "I ordered a travel freeze when I arrived above Gondwana, but many of the people leaving Camelot already beamed to other places. Big D was impossible to hold, but he can't beam until he loses weight, which will take a long time because he is gorging on meat."

"I thought the Gondwanians were vegetarians who treated meat eaters as if they were zombies."

"That's right. Eating meat is a taboo on Gondwana."

"So, why is he eating meat?"

"Anyone who takes an alien drug called circe craves raw meat. The Inspector says that is how they know who is infected with prions."

Glenn was disappointed that Big D was infected. *I needed Big D to command Camelot and launch a strike force in case the Gobato attacked. Now I'll have to manage both the negotiations and the strike force.* "What else can you report?" Glenn asked.

"The Inspector General told me about the invading aliens, and he warned me that pirates are in the area."

"Prions, aliens, and now pirates. I didn't sign up for this."

"Neither did I. In fact, I didn't sign up for any of it." She raised her glass and continued with a high-pitched laugh, "But the Inspector said don't worry. He plans to identify the pirates and make the arrests. I wonder if he will arrest his pirate friend, Yvette."

Glenn considered, *I am wrong to push her forward. This mission is destroying her. I need to save her.*

"Gloria, tell me if you want to return to Earth." He saw Audrey approach wearing a medical smock and lowered his voice, "Don't answer now, but think about it and let me know later." Then he said in a normal voice, "Gloria, have you met Audrey?"

"No. So Audrey, you are the doctor who saved Glenn's life. How can I thank you?" Glenn did not know if Gloria was joking or serious.

"Aw, all I did was feed data to the auto-doc. Anyway, Glenn wasn't that injured. How about I show you two around?"

"I would like that," Gloria answered.

"All members of the crew have two or more skills. I'm the auto-doc orderly and the flight engineer," Audrey said as they watched the planet, Stardust, from a window.

"Why is Stardust so ghostly white?" Gloria asked.

"The brilliance is due to salt deposits on the sunlit side that are left after water evaporates, and the ice and snow on the dark side that condenses from water vapor. Do you see that narrow green ribbon at the terminator? That ribbon is the only habitable zone on the planet, but don't go out there without a thermal suit or you'll suffer frostbite on one side and burns on the other."

"That is good to know. Tell us more," Glenn said. *This conversation is helping Gloria to relax.*

"If you look out the port side you will see a teleporter with three large lenses, ten transporter class spaceships, and three large beam-cans."

"Those are huge beam-cans. Will those transporters fit inside them?" Gloria asked.

"Yes, after they are modified, we will call them starbeams and call the cans starbeam-cans. When we have the universal network, called the U-net, the teleporter that links to Camelot can send them."

"Will that put the Starhawk out of business?"

"Yes, unless Truman can find the money to upgrade the Starhawk to starbeam class." Audrey held up her hand as she received and answered a call on her C-chip. Then she explained, "I must leave and help land the ship. We aim the ion engines into Ruby's solar wind for electrostatic drag, but Truman needs the whole crew to do this."

"I enjoyed meeting you, Audrey," Gloria responded.

"I'll talk to you later." She looked at Glenn and said, "I want to see those weapons you asked Elroy to modify."

"Okay, talk to you later," Glenn responded, glad for a few minutes alone with Gloria. He liked the information Audrey supplied, but the continuous conversation tired him.

The crew slowed the ship, brought it into an orbit above Stardust, and docked at the teleporter terminal.

Major Truman Striker announced on the C-net, "This ship is powerful enough to land and take off with a full load of passengers and cargo. Those who prefer to beam down can transfer to the teleporter. Everyone else stay on the ship and I will land us at the star base."

Glenn was disappointed that Gloria left the ship with several other passengers to beam down. "We have plenty of time to talk later," she said, "or you can come with me."

"No, I prefer to have my feet on something solid," Glenn answered.

*

Glenn texted a long-awaited message to Mac. "Here is my update: I am at the Stardust teleporter with Gloria, and we expect to arrive on Camelot ahead of schedule. The slam injured me on arrival, but I should be one-hundred percent in a week."

Quantum data transfer between the stars occurred in a second. Mac responded, "Glad to hear you made it. I just arrived at Lonetree, the space station that orbits the planet Xanadu in the Rasalhague star system. A few panicked Razorroot trees are still waiting for transportation to Xanadu. The Razorroots backlogged the transporters even though they are operating around the clock.

"I plan to travel to Xanadu in a few days to find out why these hardy plants abandoned Camelot. We are building a base and a floating teleporter terminal there. I'll help with the construction while I study the fauna and flora. I already discovered that prions infect the Razorroots. Earth sent me here because they suspect the ferns on Xanadu carry or spread this infection. End of message."

The Starhawk undocked and dropped out of orbit. Audrey returned to the viewport to talk to Glenn. She pointed out a train of cylinders inside the ribbon of green, "That is the spaceport where everyone lives. An underpinning supports a movable foundation, which cradles the entire spaceport. It sits on massive train wheels that ride on steel tracks. That enables the spaceport to follow the terminator that moves as Stardust slowly rotates once every thousand years."

"Yes," Glenn said. "Among the vehicles, I can see several pile drivers and tractors they use to level the ground, and lay more track. Does the spaceport move continuously?"

"No, just when things get too hot." As the ship continued to approach the spaceport, Audrey explained details as they came into view, "Look carefully, and you will see one of many glaciers that flow from the dark side of the planet. The sun melts them into rivers, and heats them as they flow onto the plane until they boil into mist."

The sight of so much energy and turbulence stunned Glenn. Beyond the mist, cathedral-sized crystals of salt were visible. "This would be a tourist attraction if it were anywhere near Earth."

"And here we can enjoy it whenever we want. Our jobs have their advantages," Audrey answered.

Audrey and Glenn stood in booths to cushion the shock as the Starhawk entered the atmosphere. A heat shield slowed the ship further until the pilot released a parachute. The crew reeled in the parachute and landed the spaceship with reactor thrust.

Truman announced, "You are safe to leave the Starhawk. I hope you enjoyed your trip. Visit the atrium at the far end of the spaceport. You will find a continuous party there and lots of wine. The bartender will give you a free drink if you tell her you know me."

After the civilian passengers left, the major dismissed the shuttle crew who went to the atrium. Then Glenn dismissed his troops, and they left to unpack and refresh.

* Twenty One Pilots, Heathens *

Truman followed Reddragon until they were alone and ordered, "Take me to Flint. We will pay him a visit."

They walked down dark hallways. Truman saw Zane guarding a door at the far end of the spaceport. He pulled Reddragon back and hid in an alcove. Zane heard a noise and walked toward the alcove. Truman put his gloves on, stepped out, and threw a stiletto at Zane killing him. Truman shoved the body into an unused room, and continued to the door.

He drew his razor-blaster, opened the door, and walked in silently and stood behind Flint. He watched Flint count a stack of G-coins, then toss them and they disappeared.

Credits are stored electronically or on C-chips except for large denominations, which are usually stored in G-coins. G-coins have values of 1, 10, or 100 thousand credits. Spacers prefer not use bank accounts because many banks in the outworld cannot be trusted with large sums of money. G-coins are usually locked and can be unlocked by the owner through their C-chip.

Truman said, "My friend, how are you? You haven't been keeping in touch, so I thought I would drop in and say hi."

Flint jumped out of his chair, turned, and drew his flair gun, "Who? What? Truman! What happened to Zane?"

"I didn't see Zane. Reddragon, did you see Zane?"

"Not me Gov."

Truman asked, "Aren't we friends? When Empire was hunting you down, didn't I talk Big D into hiring you and the other pirates to build the Stardust spaceport? Then he kept you to operate Camelot, aren't you lucky. Shall we put our guns away?"

"Yeah, let's talk." Flint answered and they put their guns away.

Truman waved his hand in the air over the table, then lifted an invisible backpack, and shook out a pile of G-coins. "A stealth backpack. What a clever idea. Why all the secrecy and why did you pull your gun? Don't you trust me anymore?"

"Did your pretending to be a major and governor go to your head? Are you going to try to arrest me? You're not, are you?"

"No, no, no. I freed your father, your sister, and Audrey. Doesn't that sound like your old friend?" Truman lied.

"I was counting what I owe you for rescuing them. Bring them here and I will pay you,"

"I lead the Emerald Pirates, remember? You used my pirates to sell your circe, so those credits belong to me."

Flint looked at Reddragon who lowered his head. Flint could not speak, shocked that Truman found out about the circe.

You *used Yvette's C-chip to hack Big D and make him promote* you. *Now* you think you are *invincible* but you can't hack me. Yvette gave me a better *C-chip.*

"Maybe, and maybe you don't know how *to* use it. I'm not sharing with you, but I'll pay you one hundred fifty thousand credits when I see my family. Take me to them."

Reddragon started walking to the door. Truman stopped him. "He is hacking your C-chip. Stay here."

Then Truman looked at Flint and lied, "I have your father and sister on the Starhawk. Give me your best offer and you can have them."

Truman used his C-chip to compel Flint to make a better offer. Flint spoke, "I have a clump of future telling diamonds. Let them go and you can have it."

"I'm delighted that you stole them." Truman tapped his foot on a chair icon near the table. A chair rotated out of the floor. He sat and offered, "You have more credits than you can spend, so I'll take those rocks and eighty percent of your cut of circe and every cut after that. You cannot sell more circe without me because I have the promissory notes." He waved the notes in Flint's face.

"That's more than I can spend, but you forget I have a girlfriend." They both chuckled. "Also, I deserve more because I own the mining rights and I command Camelot. We will be fifty-fifty partners. Those papers are worth ninety-five-million credits after the crew takes five percent. *Why did I offer fifty-fifty when I want it all? I cannot hack* your *C-chip. Did Yvette give* you *a better hacking chip?*

"You offered five percent to the crew to buy their loyalty. I'll buy them back. Reddragon," Truman ordered, "Make sure the crew agrees with ten percent."

Reddragon nodded and left the room. He had little choice. Truman was dangerous when angered. Now with a hacking C-chip, he was like a monster, an evil monster.

Truman repeated his deal to Flint, "We will split our profit eighty-twenty, and I take the diamonds. I won't kill you and take it all because you are like a brother to me."

Flint took a few minutes to decide if he wanted to give up that much. *Truman* read his thoughts and forced the words into Flint's C-chip which Flint spoke, "You don't have a brother, *but I*'ll pretend that you do if that closes the deal. Then you agree to have no further issue with me, and we can trust each other?".

"That goes unsaid. I'll always trust you, and you can always trust me. Where are the stones?"

Flint had to answer, "The diamond clump is on a ship. It will arrive at Gondwana in sixteen years."

Truman forced Flint to say, "I'll put the shipping receipt in your name with the appraised value so you can borrow against it or sell it."

"You got a deal. Now let's get busy." Truman held Flint captive by hacking his C-chip as he interrogated Flint, "Can we talk to the Gobato? What do they want in exchange for their circe?"

Flint wished Truman would leave him alone, and answered without enthusiasm, "They refused to give any to the Inspector. The Inspector made them mad, and now they won't talk to us. We need to abduct a Gobato to get the circe, but they fortified their caves on the planet because they expect another attack from the humans or from the Razorroots. Now they are too protected for us to nab one of them."

Truman told what he learned from Big D, "Empire plans to arrive in force and negotiate a peace treaty. If we infiltrate their forces, and use them to draw the Gobato out, then we can abduct as many Gobato as we want."

"I can get my crew recruited as mercenaries. An easy task since Camelot lists them as government employees, and there aren't many available workers this far from Earth. I'll have them apply."

Truman responded with a suspiciously large grin. "Yes, Yvette hacked the computers on Gondwana and gave all of us good credentials. She gave me a hacking C-chip so I can control the Inspector General, the Space Marshal, and anyone else who might stop us. She is the best hacker I have ever seen. I can hack anyone without their knowledge."

"Did you say a space marshal is on the way here? I don't want any part of that."

"He is here already, but don't worry about that. I set a trap for him. He is vulnerable because he teleports spontaneously. Mariah, your sister, will walk him near a teleporter and he will be gone. Now let's discuss how to make some more credits."

"After we finish selling this batch, I want out. I want to teleport to Earth with Audrey, my father, and Mariah."

"Agreed. Now let's get busy."

They planned to use Glenn's troops to attack the Gobato. Truman, Flint, and Yvette could cover three bases, Camelot, Stardust, and Gondwana. Truman knew a starbeam instructor who would control those who were in transit. They concluded their plan, drank late into the night, and bragged about their history of exploits. However, their friendship had changed. Flint was Truman's slave.

Chapter 15: The Party Dome

* Red Hot Chili Peppers, Otherside *

Glenn read a map in the entryway to the Stardust spaceport. The air inside the pipe-segments smelled stronger than ocean salt mixed with ozone but was breathable. The occupants did not wear breathers, but the new arrivals used them while they acclimated.

The map explained that the barrels were forty feet in diameter and 150 feet long. Flexible walkthroughs connected the ends of the pipe segments. The entire length was more than two miles. In most cases, each pipe had four levels with utilities in the lowest section. Barracks, apartments, and booths occupied the next floor. Hallways, observation areas, dining areas, and offices filled the top floor. The section above the ceiling supported air ducts.

Audrey found Glenn and asked, "Come with me and I'll show you around the site."

"Have you seen Gloria?" Glenn asked, "We were separated."

"Yeah, she's in the atrium relaxing. Don't you have an appointment with Elroy? I'll take you to him, and then I will take you to the atrium."

I wonder how she knew about Elroy. She must be an agent of Empire. "Okay, show me around."

"From this window you can see a fast breeder reactor that powers everything from a separate section outside. Also, it produces radioactive isotopes used in nuclear powered batteries. N-batteries are always in high demand on Gondwana and that income supports Stardust. The isotopes decay into a safe state, so we can dispose of them without danger of contamination."

As they walked toward the barracks, Glenn asked, "Don't introduce me to the troops until I am more familiar with the site and talk to the officers. Then I'll give them their assignments."

"Don't worry about that. Let me show you."

The barrack was a long hallway with booths on both sides. The troops occupied the booths. Glenn observed each booth and pressed an "Inspection Complete" button at the end of the hall.

Sergeant Pike stood at the end of the hall and said, "I'll stay here and make sure the troops are secure."

Glenn approved. After this inspection, Audrey took Glenn to the machine shop and introduced him to Elroy, the machine shop operator.

"We already had light arms for the small caliber ammo. Your new weapons fire the heavy ammo as you asked. Here they are." Elroy opened a sliding door to a warehouse that occupied the entire lower area of two pipe segments. It resembled an upside-down Quonset hut.

"The light ammo is useless against invaders as big as the Gobato," Glenn said.

"I modified these handguns to fire rifle magnums, and the rifles to fire cannon rounds," Elroy said. "The ribbon-blaster modules on the end of the barrels serve as wireless rail-accelerators. They increase the velocity of the bullets."

Audrey looked at the weapons. "Are you planning to hunt water buffalo?"

When Glenn saw the size of the ammo, he understood Audrey's concern. Elroy readjusted the springs, dampers, and shock absorbers on one of the rail accelerator handguns, RA-gun, so they would not bottom out, and handed it to Audrey with a slug. "Do you want to be the first to test fire this gun?"

Audrey blocked with her hand, "That slug is much bigger than standard twelve-gage shotgun ammo. No, the honor is not mine."

Then, he handed it to Glenn with earplugs and assured him. "Designing weapons has been my hobby for years. I always over-design, so these RA-guns can handle magnum loads, no problem."

As Glenn loaded the RA-gun, Elroy and Audrey stepped back.

"Does he realize what he is doing?" Audrey asked Elroy.

Elroy shrugged. "I think we are about to find out."

Glenn fired a slug. A lightning bolt leaped twenty feet out from the front of the blaster module. Everything in front of the RA-gun was smoldering from the heat, and a cloud of dust appeared where a salt target once stood. The recoil was smooth, and not the bone-jarring kick one would expect, a relief to Glenn.

Elroy grinned. "I designed most of the RA-guns to fire these rounds since they offered better range and penetration." He handed Glenn a different gun and a 50-caliber magnum round.

This gun also had an RA module at the end of the barrel. Glenn fired several 50-caliber rounds with success. Both RA-guns were too heavy to shoot in Earth's gravity, but they were easy to aim and shoot in the lower gravity of Stardust.

Audrey picked up a 20-millimeter round. "Where are the cannons that shoot these?"

"They load into these rifles." Elroy explained, "When fired, the barrel retracts into the stock. Shock absorbers reduce the recoil. This same action ejects the spent shell and loads another round for semiautomatic firing. Then the blaster module at the end of the barrel acts as a rail-accelerator to increase the velocity. The force of the blast opens a folded shield at the end of the barrel to protect the shooter."

Glenn picked up an RA-rifle (rail accelerator rifle), and examined it.

Elroy warned, "Those shock absorbers are the last of the motorcycle parts. In fact, I didn't have enough, so I went to Gondwana and dismantled some of their motorcycles for more. I'll be in a lot of trouble if you damage them."

"Why are there two modules at the end of the barrel?" he asked.

"A single blaster module didn't produce the mussel velocity you need, so I removed the current limiters, and stacked two modules together. Now it pushes the round up to four-thousand feet per second, but you cannot fire it rapidly because it takes a couple seconds to recharge."

Glenn adjusted the RA-rifle, installed a small n-battery, and chambered a round.

Audrey stammered, "I-I did not think a round that big would fit in there. If you plan to sh-shoot that, wait until I leave."

"You can join me in the transparent panic room," Elroy offered. "It's bulletproof."

"Yes, but is it explosion proof?" she asked.

*

"Let's all three watch from the panic room," Glenn said. "I'll set up sandbags, and we'll fire it remotely. It won't tell us much because sand won't absorb shock like a human shoulder, but it will test the RA-rifle mechanism."

Inside the explosion proof room, Glenn pressed a remote button and fired the RA-rifle. A bullet blasted out of the barrel like a bomb. Sand and sandbags flew into the air, and a one-foot cube of salt turned into dust one-hundred yards away. The retort stunned them even in the protection of the panic room.

Elroy recovered, ran out with a fire extinguisher, and put out the flames before they caused damage. It took several minutes for the dust and sand to settle. Glenn checked the RA-rifle, which was still intact and undamaged by the blast. Audrey stayed in the panic room and stared.

"Stand aside," Glenn said. He put ear protectors over his earplugs, dropped another round into the breach of the RA-rifle, and aimed. In the low gravity, he held the RA-rifle steady, even though his left arm was still weak from his recent mishap in space. Elroy ran to the panic room and hid with Audrey as Glenn pulled the trigger.

The rifle resounded with another explosion that threw Glenn back, drove smoke into his nose and lungs, and caused pinpricks on his hands, arms, and face. As he stood up and checked himself, he was not bleeding or on fire, and the blast broke nothing except for another salt target. The shock absorber, damper, and blast suppressor worked. He could fire another round.

As Elroy put the fires out with an extinguisher, Audrey walked out of the panic room, gawked at the damage, and said, "What the blazes is this?"

"I made a mistake," Elroy admitted. "That weapon is too intimidating. No one can shoot it, and aim steady. We have recoilless bazookas. Why don't you use those?"

"I would if you had more ammo for them," Glenn answered. "On Dearth, we will wear penetration proof and fireproof clothing, and breathers with facemasks. That will protect us from repeated RA blasts. When your life depends on it, you'll be surprised how well you can aim."

Glenn put on a thermal suit, gloves, a full-face breather, picked up the RA-rifle and an ammo box, and went out the airlock to the outside range. He took aim through a virtual scope that sited the target through his C-chip, and fired at a target two miles away. A ten-foot cube of salt exploded into dust. He stayed on his feet by using the right posture and by taking two steps back. Two more rounds destroyed two more salt targets. Nothing caught fire in the thin atmosphere.

By now, the recoil bruised his shoulder. Most of the troops were not as big as Glenn was, so five rounds would be their maximum after training and conditioning. Elroy and Audrey watched from a window. Glenn could tell they were impressed.

"Care to join my army?" Glenn asked after returning inside.

"Not me," Elroy said. "I'm staying here."

As she edged closer to the door, Audrey said, "I-I-I have to help Truman fly the Starhawk. In fact, I need to g-g-go there right now, and prepare it for the next flight."

Glenn realized they were right. The government listed Audrey as a 'no hire', and Elroy needed to maintain the facilities at Stardust.

After Audrey ran off, Glenn asked Elroy to adjust the rest of the firearms, and asked, "How about the artillery?"

"I have what you need, a tele-blaster. The miners left a runabout truck at their mine that is the right size to carry it."

"How does it work?"

"It uses the folded optics from a portable teleporter to send a blast onto a target. Nuclear pellets and a laser igniter from an old fusion impulse engine produce a blast powerful enough to turn a Gobato into spaghetti. If you pepper the enemy with locater chips, then a computer can identify targets, and hit them at a rate of ten per second.

"That sounds so effective. Why do they need me?"

"Someone has to take it there and set it up," Elroy joked. "Its range is limited to just more than one mile."

"That is enough. The Inspector told us that the Gobato like to fight at close range. If we hold them at one mile, they can't harm us."

"I also modified the ancient howitzers. They use a nuclear fusion pellet instead of gunpowder to send a projectile at the speed of a meteorite. The projectile has a heat shield to keep it from melting. On a small planet, their range is more than one-hundred miles. We call them disintegrators because that best describes what they do to the targets."

"Will they hit targets in low orbit?" Glenn asked.

"Yes."

"That will keep their spaceships from attacking us, but every weapon has a downside. What can you tell me about this one?"

"Keep your troops clear of the projectiles. They can cause burns and concussions up to one-hundred feet away. The barrel-ends support deflector shields similar to the ones on your RA-rifles to protect the shooters from the blasts.

"Also, the Gobato like to fight by crushing their foes; these will crush them." Elroy rolled a curtain back and displayed several tracked armored personnel carriers. "The bumper heights are above the Gobato head height. That will give them something to think about but in case that is not enough, I mounted a disintegrator on top of each one. I call them tanks because they look like the obsolete battle tanks from the war of 2067. Also, they have hitches so they can haul construction equipment that the miners might let you use."

"All these weapons are line-of-sight, and may be obsolete if the Gobato attack underground. Let's hope they work against this enemy."

Elroy warned, "Yeah, maybe you better fight them on a rocky plateau or something. Here is a weapon in case they want to fight in space."

"It looks too big to carry."

"Yeah, it is. I'll mount one of these on each of your starbeams. When I tried to adjust the tele-blaster for better range, I noticed gas and water molecules along the beam became a super-fluid. The molecules slide past each other instead of colliding causing a sudden drop in pressure for a fraction of a second followed by a sudden increase in pressure. The higher the temperature, the better it works. I think this disruption will cause the hot fusion reactors in the Gobato spaceships to explode. No known metal or shield can block the quantum channel they form."

"Good work! That will give us the advantage in space battles. Can those cause a planet or a star to explode?"

"Don't know; better be careful how you aim them until we figure that out."

"What are these?" Glenn asked.

"Those magnetic rings will expand to form a plasma lens when tossed in the air. Star surfers can use them to teleport the short distance between Dearth and Camelot, but each one can be used only once because they expand by exploding."

"If we need to leave in a hurry, those will help. I'll tell the logistics officer to make sure every star surfer has one."

"Here is one final item you will need, a prion detector. It has a range of two feet and signals your C-chip," Elroy said.

"That will help me chart the spread of the infection."

"Is there anything else you can think of?"

"Yes," Glenn answered. "I programmed my C-chip to compare the crew and passengers on the Starhawk to photos in the files on Gondwana. It flagged one of the crew who had a previous injury that was healing. The file photos should be years old so how could someone have an injury that took that long to heal. Can you check the date stamp on the photos and make sure they were not hacked?"

"I'll do that and let you know the results tomorrow. Something else, I intercepted an encrypted message from deep space; it came from the Starhawk. The computer is deciphering it. Here is what I have so far:"

"Signature: Starhawk-Aud...'...have him aboard. Is the trap set?' The answer, 'Yes, everything is...'"

Glenn said, "That does not tell us much."

"No, but you better take this RA-gun in case they're talking about trapping you. Then see me tomorrow morning. I'll have the rest of the message deciphered by then. I didn't tell you until Audrey left because the signature might be hers."

"That means Audrey might me spying on me. Something else, Sergeant Pike thought it was not a coincidence the teleporter sent my pod directly at Truman's spaceship when I arrived. Can you look at that?" Glenn asked.

"Already did. Truman parked the Starhawk near your anticipated travel path. The teleporter was not misaligned, and it was not an accidental close miss. I don't have enough information to place the blame right now, but I am running a computer simulation that will give us precise evidence. See me tomorrow and I'll give you what you need to make an arrest."

"Is 7:00 AM too early?"

"That is perfect," Elroy answered. "Truman will be asleep, so we can surprise him."

Glenn reviewed the bills, paid Elroy, and planned his next move as he walked away: *I know what Gloria and I should do. Without Big D, Victor, and Splint, there is no hope for this mission, so tomorrow I'll arrest Truman and the other pirates. Then I'll recall the Camelot crew after they set the self-destruct timer on the teleporter. That will isolate the invading aliens. If the Gobato ever get this far, Elroy, Oliver, and the troops have the necessary weapons to turn them back.*

Gloria and I will go to Gondwana and have Big D approve my retirement and her resignation. He'll understand because he is abandoning this outpost as well. Gloria will lose her retirement. If her kin do not help her, I will adopt her so she can ride on my retirement.

Now I'll find her and tell her my plan, I hope she accepts.

Confident his plans were complete; he went to the solar dome to find Gloria.

* Shout, Animal House *

The Party Dome was a cylinder divided in two, so the upper part looked like the inside of a Quonset hut. The transparent ceiling was twenty feet high, and the floor was forty feet wide.

A party raged inside the dome. The party was perfect for Glenn to clear his mind. With an RA-gun in a hidden holster, he felt strong, macho, the way he felt when he crushed Sid's arm. *Nothing is bigger than me, not when I have a weapon like this.*

An unusual display of solar storms exploded from the star. The light intensified as it refracted and reflected through shards of crystals in Ruby's corona. Ruby was not hot enough at its surface to vaporize diamonds that fell into it centuries earlier. The partiers stopped and stared in wonder for several seconds.

Glenn felt the heat on one side and the chill on the other side through the transparent dome. *The heat from Ruby feels good compared to the frigid dark of space. The warmth is helping my arm to heal.*

Glenn looked around the room and spotted Gloria. She was drinking a glass of wine while soaking in a hot tub. He walked to the bar and ordered a drink before talking to her.

As he sipped his drink, a star surfer arrived on the teleporter platform at the end of the dome and announced, "I'm Dillon, your starbeam pilot, and instructor. I just passed my certification training on Gondwana, and I need a drink."

He posed to show tattoos that covered most of his body. "These stars and planets represent everywhere I've been."

Dillon left the platform and went to the bar. His build was powerful, and he looked huge compared to everyone else. Spacers were usually slim because teleporters had mass restrictions, but these restrictions did not apply to star surfers.

Dillon picked up a mug of beer from the bar; Glenn glimpsed that the bartender slipped him something concealed at the same time.

Glenn gestured at Dillon's closed fist and asked, "What is that?"

"That tattoo is the Pillars of Orion in honor of my father who was stationed at Phi-2 Meissa when Betelgeuse went ultra nova. When I was a child, we did things earthlings never knew. We rode on the back deck of a transporter and collected magnetic monopoles that glittered near a black hole. Now all those memories are teardrops in my beer. And who are you?"

"Remain at ease and refer to me as Glenn. I am Space Marshal Glenn Hunter. I was not asking about your tattoo. I want to know what is in your hand."

"This is a C-chip to replace my old one," He said as he transferred a document to Glenn using C-mail. "The Inspector already approved it."

Glenn verified the document, *It contains Yvette's electronic signature. I did not know Yvette has approval to work at this level. Gloria said Yvette is a pirate. I'll talk to the Inspector and clear this matter tomorrow.* He said, "You have my approval. Be as you were."

Dillon walked over to the hot tub and noticed Gloria's snake tattoo, "Dear lady, that is the most amazing tattoo I have ever seen."

Gloria was delighted and said to Dillon using ventriloquism, so it appeared that each of the snakeheads at her fingertips and thumb spoke to him in its turn, "Jump in, -- unless you -- are afraid -- that I -- might ssstrike." Dillon joined her.

Glenn was glad Dillon was part of his forces. *I won't interrupt them because Dillon might pull Gloria out of her depression.*

As Dillon splashed into the water, Glenn's C-chip highlighted Lieutenant Wanda Desoto. She was thin and an inch shorter than average. Her skin was dark, and her hair was black and curly. She stood out because her steel-gray eyes cut across the room like two lasers. Glenn's itinerary required him to talk to her.

He interrupted a conversation she was having with a Razorroot Tree. "I believe that you are Lieutenant Desoto."

"Yes, how did you know?"

"Stay at ease, and do not come to attention or salute when I tell you, I am Space Marshal Glenn Hunter. You will call me Glenn for now. I recognized you from the roster and the pictures in my C-chip."

"As you wish, Glenn. You can call me Wanda. How may I assist you?"

"Download the inventory we need to transport to Dearth from my C-chip into your chip. While you do that, introduce me to your companion. I am surprised to find a Razorroot here; I thought they fled this area."

"Its name is Tumbleweed."

It looked thin and unkempt compared to Splinter. At barely three feet, its weight was less than 150 pounds.

After the introductions, it asked with a scratchy voice, "I want to go to Dearth. Can you help me get there? I helped plant the farm, and I left my saplings there. I know the planet, I can guide you, and I won't be in your way."

Razorroots often planted a few saplings in the hydroponic units and farms they tended. Nobody questioned this behavior because the saplings never caused a problem and helped with the work as they matured.

"Your request seems reasonable. Wanda, will you provide passage for Tumbleweed?"

"Consider it done."

As they talked, a blond, athletic, and tall woman star surfed onto the teleporter platform. She immediately ran to a comfort booth next to the platform. Several minutes later, she left the booth, stood on the platform and introduced herself as Captain Madeline Hayworth from the star, Gliese 581. "I'm paymaster for the mercenaries."

More than half the people in the dome stopped and saluted. She returned the salute and said, "Be at ease. Return to what you were doing." Then she walked over to Glenn. She recognized him and told him, "Not all is what it seems."

The party spirit intensified until it was difficult to concentrate. People were drinking, dancing, leaping, and almost flying in the low gravity. Those who arrived from larger planets were easy to identify because they could not keep from walking on their tiptoes in this low gravity.

Glenn answered Madeline, "Let's talk about your concern later when we don't have to shout above the party noise. Also, if you see the miners, I need a sample of their DNA."

"Not a problem. I'll see you before lunch tomorrow."

"Agreed."

The lights brightened and Glenn felt an electric shock. He drew his weapon, but no one else seemed to notice the shock. He realized there was no danger and put his RA-gun back before anyone saw him. The troops might be reluctant to follow him to Dearth if they thought he was jumpy. His C-chip flagged an alert. Glenn cleared it without reading it because of an overwhelming distraction.

A female star surfer with green eyes beamed onto the platform. Her long dishwater-blond hair covered her back. She was tall and thin compared to average earthlings; her physique was similar to spacers who left Earth while they were still a child. His attention was on her every move.

She stood on the teleporter platform, and announced, "I enter, Mariah, no stop, I mean Ligeia from Lonetree," and then she joined the party. No one questioned her or checked her identity. Her appearance worried Glenn because this was not the Ligeia in his dream when he beamed. He checked her image against the files on Stardust and they matched. He wished he had the photographs that were lost when he used his envelope to patch holes in his space pod. *Madeline or Wanda should have duplicate information. I'll ask them tomorrow.*

* Heart, These Dreams *

Everyone in the dome was curious about Ligeia and crowded around her to ask questions, and she was happy to answer. The crowd around her was so thick that Glenn realized he would not be able to talk to her until later, but he edged nearer to overhear the conversations.

Madeline asked, "The news reported that you star surfed all the way from Lonetree, one-hundred light-years from here. Does that distance set a new record?"

"Star surfing that distance is beyond my endurance. I used a Model A teleporter, which is faster and easier than star surfing. When I reached the teleporter terminal in orbit, I docked the beam-can, refreshed, and rested. Then I star surfed down here."

The forty light year jump from Sirius almost killed Glenn, so she impressed him by beaming more than twice that distance. He became aware he was gawking, so he closed his mouth, and changed his gaze before anyone noticed.

"Where did you learn to star surf?" Madeline asked again.

Mariah took a moment to recall the information from Ligeia's C-chip, and then she answered, "I star surfed naturally. When I was two, I played near a telescope on Lonetree and teleported by accident to Xanadu. The Razorroots helped me find food and water until explorers found me two years later. Empire recognized my unique skill and hired me to develop teleporters. When conditions are right, I can teleport without a teleporter. I read that the ancients knew how to star-surf thousands of years ago. Many of them beamed to Gondwana."

A young girl asked, "Is teleporting still your job?"

"Yes, Stardust has the newest teleporter upgrades, and I am here to test them."

"Star surfing was discovered more than one-hundred years ago." Madeline asked, "Shouldn't you be much older?"

Ligeia hesitated to answer. Glenn noticed her eyes changed from green to brown, "Beaming on Model T teleporters put me out of sync with ordinary time. My birth was more than one-hundred years ago, but I am twenty-four years old because people don't age when teleporting."

"What are the dangers of star surfing, other than not aging?" An elderly woman asked. There was light laughter.

"You need to ignore the quantum attractors." The crowd hushed. She continued, "They can tempt and trap you."

Madeline asked, "How is quantum tunneling used to teleport? Doesn't our probability fields drop off exponentially as distance increases?"

Does Madeline suspect something? Is that why she is quizzing her? Glenn wondered.

"I see you know the Model Ts. The probability for matter to propagate never goes to zero. A mile-wide plasma lens shapes the field, so the probability is constant in one narrow direction. We've increased the speed above the speed of light by using wave-crest interference. Another problem with the Model Ts is dealing with the uncertainty. We never know when teleportation will initiate. The Model A teleporters use quantum entanglement, which has fewer problems."

The crowd clapped, impressed with Ligeia's answer.

"Can you teach me to star surf?" the young girl asked.

"Yes, you can star-surf if you follow my directions. You can read the technique and the steps to follow on my C-net-cloud. That's all I can answer today."

Chapter 16: Quantum Entanglement

* 10CC, I'm Not in Love *

When the group around Ligeia thinned down, she walked to the door where Glenn stood. He introduced himself, "I'm Space Marshal Glenn Hunter. Stay at ease. You can call me Glenn. I want to talk to you more. Can you join me for dinner?"

"Yes, but after I find my room and report to my coordinator. Meet me at my apartment at seven-thirty."

"How do I find your apartment?"

"Say my name then 'apartment' and the wall lights will guide you."

Glenn's heart almost leaped out of his chest with excitement, but he kept a cool appearance, and said, "See you then."

As they parted, he wondered, *That was impulsive, I don't know why I said that when I have other plans. Why is my heart racing? She is not a model, her appearance is ordinary, but as she walks away, I want to follow her like a puppy-dog.*

He checked the clock after she disappeared around the corner. The time was four o'clock. He decided, *I'll go to my room and send Mac the usual mundane report. I won't tell him I'm planning to desert until I contact Gloria, and she accepts.*

When he reached his room, the door spoke as it opened, "You have a message."

Glenn said, "Give me the message."

It answered, "Your C-chip is being hacked. Signed, Holly Hemlock."

This information disturbed Glenn, *"Advanced government C-chips included hacking ability" is a top secret. Did Gloria drink too much and let this information slip? However, this person claiming to be Holly Hemlock can't be Gloria or Splint because they were not on Sirius when I received the first message.* He asked the door, "Who left this message?"

The door answered, "That information is unavailable."

Glenn decided to deal with this matter later. Then he read a text note Wanda sent him, which was her most recent and most detailed report about the Gobato. Most of it paraphrased the Inspector General's report.

Wanda included her analysis. "In summary, the howitzers, tanks, and bunkers are not effective weapons. We cannot attack the Gobato camp from the air or with missiles from space. Your RA-weapons might not be powerful enough to disable a two-ton monster. I strongly recommend peaceful negotiations."

Glenn did not change his plans, *Well, military force won't work and she has the negotiations covered, so she does not need me. I feel guilty abandoning this mission but nobody is looking out for Gloria or me. Too bad if Ligeia is upset when I don't show tonight. I cannot reach Gloria on the direct C-link; I'll try the C-phone.*

"Please leave a message after the beep or call me after 10:00 AM tomorrow. If this is an emergency, call Space Marshal Glenn Hunter."

Unable to contact Gloria, he changed his mind and decided to keep his evening appointment with Ligeia.

Glenn went to Ligeia's apartment after refreshing in his room, removing his breather, and installing nose filters. He was early, so he waited in the hall. Two people and a dog left her apartment and walked past him. He recognized them from his list of interviewees, so he stopped them and asked, "Hold up there. I'm Space Marshal Glenn Hunter. Do you mind if we talk for a minute?"

Jake mixed broken speech with hand signs to gesture, "Use voice speak. Ar's C-chips are off."

Glenn selected "voice assist" and added "visual cues" before his C-chip made sense out of his garble.

Glenn answered, "That will be slow. Why did you turn them off? Now we can't use 'quick speak'."

"Doctor ordered off for brain-rest, migraine." Jake pointed to his head.

Glenn nodded that he understood, and asked verbally, "Please identify yourselves."

"I'm Jake. Zis is Josie. We's miners on our way to Earz."

"Yeah, Earz," Josie echoed.

Glenn noticed blood on Jake's shirt from eating raw meat. He forced himself not to stare while he asked, "Why are you returning to Earth?"

Jake answered, "We made enough money mining gems to live in style on Earz."

"Yeah, earz" Josie added. The smell of raw blood was on her breath.

"Maybe you heard I would arrive?"

"You arriving, no. A space marshal, no. We's not hear anyzing."

"No, nozing." Jake echoed.

"So what brings you out this late?" Glenn asked.

"We stopped to talk to our friend, Ligeia. Hav-n't seen her for a while and wanted to stop before we go to Earz."

"Yeah, friend, just talking."

"What's in the box?"

"Just a few ditto-bots from our mine. Aey's harmless." Jake opened the box, and Glenn approved the contents.

"And what's in the blanket? A baby?"

"No, nozing, just a rock is all. Ballast when I beam out." She withdrew behind Jake, but she moved too fast and the blanket flipped back.

Glenn noticed she had a diamond. "Relax, it's legal. There's no customs laws this far from Earth," he tried to reassure her. He stooped down to pet pooch, and pooch licked his face. "This puppy has Earth legs, but he looks too young to be from Earth."

"He's an older dog. We take good care of him, Zat's why he looks good."

"Why can't he talk? Oh, I see. Someone removed his C-chip."

"We removed it. He had a headache like us," Jake answered

"Neither of you look worn for such a difficult occupation as mining."

"We take good care of ourselves."

"Yeah."

Glenn asked, "I am going to Dearth. Do you mind if I borrow your mining equipment?"

"Ah, we gave za mine to Flint. Yo need to ask him."

"Do you mean Lieutenant Commander Flint Valance? Is he on Camelot?"

"Yeah, I zink so."

"I'll ask him." Glenn noticed the time was after seven. "Hey, I would like to talk more, but it's late. I'll find you tomorrow and finish our conversation. Yeah?" Glenn mocked.

"Yeah, we don't want to take up yo time. We just told yo everyzing we know."

"Report with your dog to my room at 08:00. If you don't have your C-chips, I have a box of extras that I can loan to you and your dog."

"We'll bring zem." Their dog let out a low-pitched whine.

"To find me, say my name then 'office' and the lights will guide you."

"Yaw, we've been here before. We know how to do zat."

As they passed, Josie pushed Glenn against the wall and said, "Yo can't bully me. I know better; I ave a future telling stone."

Glenn was unable to free himself. Pooch attacked and bit into his leg. Glenn felt teeth penetrate his tear-proof clothing and crush into bone.

Jake pulled her and Pooch back, "Let the man go Josie. We apologize, she hasn't been herself."

Glenn did not detain them further. The prion detector signaled an alarm, but stopped after they walked away. *Good, they did not contaminate me. After I arrest Truman, I'll interrogate them. I will relay what I find to the Inspector General. He can quarantine the zombies and warn Earth not to let them pass through. Then I will find Gloria, and we will flee.*

Glenn pressed a medical icon on the wall and used a mini-doc to treat his wound. Then he went to Ligeia's apartment. The door opened as he approached and she was standing behind it. She wore a single piece dress that conformed to every curve of her body, an expensive garment this far from Earth.

He offered her an artificial paper flower bouquet. "Oh, how nice, and you are on time," she said as she indicated for him to enter, took the bouquet, and handed him a glass of greenish wine. Her eyes were slightly red as if she was crying.

The prion detector did not signal an alarm and Ligeia's smile put Glenn at ease. The wine was sweet and made his senses alert.

Before they left for the restaurant, she placed her breather on a table and installed nose filters.

The only restaurant on Stardust was the grill in the atrium. They sat and ordered the only item on the menu, GMO (genetically modified) potatoes. The potatoes, garnished with soy-oil, had a distinct carrot and beef flavor. Spacers always ate the potato skins, which held additional proteins and vitamins.

During their conversation, Ligeia said, "Like you, I am employed by the government, and assigned to work for Empire Corporation. I evaluate teleporter improvements when I'm not chasing disobedient aliens on distant planets." He smiled at her sarcasm.

She wanted to dance. Glenn did not see Truman or any of his crew in the room so he left his prion detector and RA-gun on the table, covered them with his jacket, and they danced. Nobody noticed them as the party continued to rage.

* Coldplay, A Sky Full Of Stars *

One area of the floor reflected starlight and Ligeia danced into it. He followed before he noticed he danced into the focus of the teleporter. He realized the teleporter was misaligned from the platform to the dance floor, and hollered, "I'm not grounded. Get me out of this focus."

"Look at me and don't think about that," she said as she held him.

He was amazed how cold her skin was, and how cold he was. The stars seemed to become warmer and brighter as he became colder. He was aware he was entering an indeterminate state where the laws of cause and effect no longer applied. Like Schrödinger's cat, nothing could harm or kill him inside a quantum channel.

The blue starlight was exhilarating in spite of the cold that soaked through him. He noticed he was too cold to move. As fear struck him, he became the blue light.

"Don't worry," she said, or thought, neither she nor he could move, not even to talk, but he heard her word-thoughts through the direct link of their C-chips. "Now, we are star surfing. We will arrive at Camelot before long."

The teleporter compressed time until it disappeared. They saw all the galaxies as points of light, and could touch each of them. Glenn wondered, *Did she hijack me to force me to complete my mission? Did she know I was going to desert? Did she read my mind?*

As the hours stretched into days and days into weeks, they did not notice the time while they explored the galaxy and its millions of stars, planets, moons, and asteroids. When they thought of a place, it became close, as close as they wanted and magnified a million times if they wanted. He wondered how his brain held so much information.

One of the planets was like an Eden. Glenn tried to go there with her. He pulled, and she resisted.

"No. You're going the wrong way. Come with me," she said.

*

Glenn realized that Ligeia would not go with him to Eden. The decision tore at him; *I think this is Gondwana, but I'm not sure. Spacers talk about attractors, which they describe as sinkholes, and voids that can capture an unwary star surfer. Until now, I thought they were myths. I am vulnerable because I know too little about star surfing. I'll have to follow her.*

The receiver platform at their destination was similar to the one on Stardust, with plenty of sand on the platform floor that star surfers used for ballast mass. They held back while she showed him how to select the right amount of sand for ballast. He observed the sand as it teleported to Stardust. It sparkled as it flowed deep into the quantum channel and disappeared.

She explained, "The ballast is balanced and we won't be slammed when the transfer sand becomes weightless." She weighed less than one-hundred pounds, but it took a lot of sand to balance his 180-pound bulk.

"The sand might run out," she worried, but they reached the right amount, and landed like a feather with no noticeable slam.

"Ligeia, is this Camelot"? He asked.

Angry, she said, "Why do you keep calling me Ligeia?"

"That's your name, isn't it?"

"No. Yes. I don't know." Then she ran into the darkness before Glenn had time to react. He was confused from her sudden outburst so he did not follow her. *She can't go far without a breather.*

A hopper replaced the used-up sand on the teleporter platform. The sudden swoosh sound distracted Glenn from his thoughts. Then he felt the shock of suffocation, *The air is too hot, and I cannot breathe. This place smells like a rotten potato cellar. Its stinking mist blocked my nose filters. I need an oxygen breather.*

Starlight lit the platform, but everything else was dark. Glenn tried to turn the lights on using his C-chip but the C-net was down; even the direct C-link was silent. He found a light switch, but the power was off, and the lights stayed dark. He remembered the direction that Ligeia ran and felt his way in the same direction. *I need to be careful, so I don't step on her in case she fell unconscious.*

He walked blindly in one direction, found a wall and followed it to a door. A vending machine was next to it. When he touched it, the display lights turned on and a computer listed its contents on the direct C-link. Vending machines ran on their own power source. A rack with oxygen breathers was next to the vending machine. Glenn removed his nose filters, took a breather, and inhaled.

After a few breaths, his head cleared. *Why isn't Ligeia near the door gasping for breath? Running with nose filters in this stale air is impossible. Was she already acclimated to the air or was someone waiting for her with a breather? Is she beyond the range of the direct C-link or did she turn her C-chip off.*

His C-chip blinked an error and a warning. He checked the status. The error said "Illegal command", and the warning said "hacking interference." He pulled the activity file and discovered before leaving Stardust, someone unknown hacked him and remotely reprogrammed his chip, watched his activities, and directed his actions. He thought back and admitted his actions did seem strange. He restored the factory default program in his C-chip, turned on a firewall to protect against further intrusion, and programmed it to warn him if the hacker encroach again.

Why was I hacked so easily? he wondered, *did Ligeia seduce me or did someone hack her too, and why? Too bad I can't go back in time and start over. I made a mistake letting Ligeia lead me here and another mistake letting her run away.*

Then, he removed some packets of junk food from the vending machine. *I am weak with hunger after star surfing for three weeks. The drink Ligeia gave me before we left must have contained a water pill, super vitamins, and time released calories or hunger would disable us.*

After eating, he noticed several comfort booths against one wall and stepped into one of them to clean and to refresh. Whoever designed the teleporter terminal had practical knowledge because these conveniences are in the most suitable locations. *I wish they included a weapons rack, but that is expecting too much.*

Glenn used his C-chip to link to his texting cube implanted in his chest and insta-texted a report to Mac, "I am on the Camelot space station. The Emerald Pirates have infiltrated the troops. They hacked my C-chip, and sent me here. They might compromise the mission."

Mac responded almost at once. "Don't worry about the pirates. Their infighting will cut their numbers. The Inspector, Kylee, and Elroy will capture those who survive.

"I attached a map to this message. Use it and make sure you are on the Camelot space station and not somewhere else. Also, look for Lieutenant Flint Valance or members of his caretaker crew. They signed up as mercenaries on Gondwana, but if they returned to Camelot, they will assist you."

* Bob Dylan, Like a Rolling Stone *

Glenn stepped out of the booth, through the hatch door leading out of the teleporter terminal, and into pitch darkness. Unable to see, he went back to the vending machine and bought "glow candy." The vending machine put the charge on his C-chip. After chewing a handful of glow candy, he stepped through the door, opened his mouth, and recognized his surroundings.

The map showed the space station was a standard design with a wheel, three spokes, and a cylinder in the center with hubs at each end. He was in the hub at one end of the cylinder.

The wheel, spokes, and cylinder rotated together to produce artificial gravity. The gravity was strongest in the wheel, weakest at the wall of the cylinder, and zero at the axis.

Glenn saw a long corridor disappearing into the darkness. The map showed that it led to the other end of the cylinder. A hallway led around the wall of the cylinder, and a ladder leading above him went through the axis, but the light faded before reaching the opposite wall. From the map he observed the docking bays were at the opposite end of the ladder, the teleporter control station was the nearest door along the hallway, and the command center and helm was in the hub at the opposite end of the cylinder.

At the teleporter control station, the Model A control panel looked like the cockpit of a jumbo jet, far too complicated to operate without training and experience. Even if he knew how to use it to return to Stardust, weeks would pass, and he would be too late to find Gloria and retire, or to redeem his mission.

Halfway down the corridor, he found another hallway leading to three sets of elevators and ladders traveling down the spokes.

After chewing another handful of glow candy, Glenn continued down the long corridor to the power control station and opened the power panel. All the circuit breakers were in the tripped position. He energized the main power circuit, and the panel lights turned on. He saw another rack of circuit breakers and selected three labeled life support, lights, and helm, and turned them on. The lights came on, and the ventilation fans started turning.

Life support gradually stabilized the temperature and removed the mist from the air. The vents produced a soft hum and a swoosh sound as filtered air entered every room. In addition, the computer came back online and verified the station was Camelot. *Well, at least Ligeia led me to the right place.*

Glenn went to the helm, which was empty. He plugged the U-net cube into the designated receptacle on the computer. The command chair at the helm was extra wide and reclined with a footrest. It included an adjustable temperature control. The cooling was a necessity in the station's hot air. He sat in the chair and went to sleep with his C-chip programmed to show repeatedly the image of Ligeia walking away at the teleporter platform. The way she flexed as she walked was enticing.

Chapter 17: Lost Star

* Steely Dan, Deacon Blues *

Glenn woke late morning, checked the calendar and discovered he was away from Stardust for more than three weeks. He turned on the holographic screen in the helm. The view-screen played a movie. He requested "Show station status."

The computer responded, "Unauthorized command."

He gave an override code and identified himself as a space marshal. The computer recognized the code and gave him control. A red alert warning rang through his C-chip as red warning lights flashed on the holographic screen.

He ordered, "Silence the red alert and tell me why the red lights are flashing."

The computer answered, "The hull is exceeding temperature limits due to atmospheric friction. Correct the orbit immediately."

He withdrew the moderator rods from the fusion core. As fusion energy inflamed inert gasses, valves opened to release the gasses through thrusters, and electrodes accelerated the gasses near to the speed of light. Then the hull cooled and the station repositioned into a stable orbit, so he shut down the engines.

Glenn reengaged the safeties and the autopilot as he watched red warning lights go out one by one on the holographic screen. When all seemed safe, he switched the screen from "status" to "view". The screen showed the planet below the station in brilliant three-D color. He searched and magnified the view until he saw a scar appear where a bomb exploded. A wide scatter of alien spaceships were nearby.

The ships were easy to identify because they left skid marks when they landed. The Gobato parked their ships scattered in a random manner. As he zoomed in, nothing was moving, but he observed several holes in the ground, which confirmed the aliens were subterranean. *That will make them hard to approach. It would be better if they approach us,* Glenn decided.

He studied the rest of the planet. Little blobs of tube-plant-blooms lay across the less rocky areas. They did not grow well because the planet held too much water for them but not enough water for most other plants. The eroded terrain offered little of interest except for a patch of green where the Razorroots farmed and the small mining operation.

Glenn used his C-chip to link to his texting cube implanted in his chest and sent a report to Mac, "I verified that I am on Camelot. Teleporter Specialist Ligeia Bell is here, but we are not in contact. Aliens are on the planet. I am not sure if the space station is secure. What are your orders?"

Mac answered with insta-text, "Set the self-destruct to thirty hours so only your password can reset or clear it, and then reset it every few hours until you leave. Make sure it sends a warning when the countdown is less than one hour. If self-destruct is necessary, beam out; don't get trapped there.

"When you have more time, read the file I attached. It has instructions on how to destroy the teleporter terminal without damaging the station. A space station on the fringe is too valuable to lose."

Glenn insta-texted Mac, "Can we dismantle the Stardust teleporter and achieve the same goal? That will reduce the danger of our exposure to alien prions."

Mac answered, "No, That will slow the Gobato down but it won't stop them. Also, Stardust is a hub and a stronghold. If we lose Stardust, we could lose Gondwana and a chain of other colonies."

Glenn asked Mac, "Well, I'll skip that idea. I am curious why you are at Rasalhague. Isn't that far removed from the action?"

Mac insta-texted back, "No, the key to this conflict is here. We are examining the dominate species on this planet, the Great Ferns. They are not indigenous to this planet, and we don't know why they are so abundant. One of our scientists believes the alien prions started here, and the Razorroots are spreading them. The Board of Directors wants me to prove or disprove that he is right.

"A work crew cleared some forest and built a base on a high plateau on Xanadu a few weeks ago. We named the base Purgatory because some of the work crew died from the harsh climate.

"I assembled a team of researchers, and we call ourselves the Green Team. We tethered a floating teleporter terminal to Purgatory. This terminal reaches an altitude where the air is breathable and cooler, almost comfortable, not unlike the floating city on Venus. Now we can travel to the planet, perform research, get information, and complete our investigation.

"We already found a source of fossils a short distance from our base. A volcano erupted several thousand years ago and covered an area with ash. The primeval flora and fauna is petrified under this ash. We plan to compare those fossils with the flora and fauna here today. I'll tell you what we find."

*

After talking to Mac, Glenn turned on power for the rest of the station. Then he started to search for aliens. A panel displaying power usage showed a small power drain for the lights to a room in the wheel. *That must be Ligeia. This station seems abandoned except for her. The gravity at the wheel matches the gravity on Dearth, which is greater than the gravity on Stardust. I need time to acclimate before I go there, so she doesn't see me in a wheelchair.*

He turned on the radio-comm and the laser-comm after he disabled their transmitters. The radio and laser receivers scanned the spectrums. Many weak signals registered from deep space in the direction of the Pleiades. *Those signals must be from alien spaceships since no human colonies are in that direction. There are no signals from Dearth; those aliens don't want to be disturbed. I'll program the receivers to scan continuously in case my forces try to reach me.*

Next, Glenn checked the agroponic units, since the computer detected a weight shift. The second unit was lush, organized, and clean compared to the other two. Glenn heard a loud thump behind him at the same time the sprinklers turned on. He turned and found a ditto-bot lying on the floor upside down. *It must have fallen when the automatic watering system turned on. That explains why this area is neat and clean.* He set it upright, and it scampered away.

Then, he checked all the central halls and ladders. *The aliens are too big to use the elevators, so these areas were the best places to look for them. Dust is everywhere except on the stairs leading from the teleporter to the wheel area where Ligeia hid.* That worried him. *Did a Gobato disturb this dust or did a tribe of humans march through here?*

Glenn followed the disturbed dust to the teleporter terminal. *I'll set the self-destruct timer with a one-hour warning on the Public Address system at full volume. If aliens are onboard, they won't understand a voice message.* He double-checked his password to make sure he could reset it.

Glenn left the control panel, climbed onto the teleporter platform, leaned against the railing, and saw what looked like one end of a starbeam. He wondered, *How did that ship get here? Did it teleport?* He leaned farther and saw a plasma teleporter lens that was so big it made the Space Station look like a toy in comparison. (A starbeam needs four days to teleport from Stardust to Camelot, but star surfing the same distance at two hundred times the speed of light takes more than two weeks.)

* Santana, She's Not There *

Glenn insta-texted Mac, "Did you know this teleporter can beam spaceships? A starbeam is located near the teleporter."

Mac insta-texted back, "If the invading aliens are in the area, you cannot let them discover that technology. Unlike most teleporters, Camelot houses a prototype that can beam those monsters. I'll ask Kyleen to halt progress on the upgrades immediately. Also, we sent you help, Transportation Expert Ligeia Bell, but she died trying to set an endurance record. Mariah Cleaver took her place. Be careful, she does not have Ligeia's training and may not be loyal to Empire."

Glenn put the rest of the message on record, walked to the other end of the platform and looked up into space. *If Ligeia is out there, I must find her.*

A few distant stars and little else were visible against the cold blackness of space. He saw a dim and distant red star, *That is the red dwarf, Ruby. I feel so alone looking at that one tiny flicker of red, but I feel the warm forests of Gondwana. Beyond Gondwana, I feel Xanadu, which is warmer but very alien. The soft forest of Gondwana offsets the sharp hard diamond star. The warmth of Xanadu offsets the cold of Valhalla. I feel all four through the teleporter lens.*

A voice interrupted, "Stop! You are starting to star-surf in four directions at once. Are you out of your mind?"

He jumped, turned, and saw Ligeia, no, Mariah running at him. She threw him off the platform and dragged him into the hall.

"That was close," she said. "Star surfing in more than one direction at once splits your persona. There might not be much left of you if you were split four ways."

As he started to feel grounded, he saw relief in her expression.

She continued, "I have an insta-text chip that links to Mac. He used it to warn me that you were in trouble. After I ran off earlier, I worried about you. I came back, and looked all over for you, but you left, and I couldn't find you."

Glenn did not believe her, but he did not want to argue, so instead he said, "Better a wound from a friend than a kiss from an enemy. Either you traveled many times between here and the wheel, or we share this station with an alien. The lack of dust on the floors and stairs shows traffic." *This conversation is helping me to stay grounded.*

"No, the other star surfers disturbed the dust. They arrive one every few hours."

He asked, "When we arrived, how did you find your way in the dark?"

"Flint helped me. He was waiting at the door."

"Who told him you were beaming here?"

"He and I planned this before we left Stardust. Truman agreed to free our father from a chain gang if I hijacked you and teleported you back to Earth. The miners told me that my father was killed trying to escape. Flint and I decided to side with you when I told him about it. We teleported you here so you could finish your mission. You can trust Flint, he is my brother."

Glenn looked out a port window as she spoke and wondered, *where is Ligeia?*

She noticed he was distracted and explained, "You are looking at the largest teleporting system ever built, and the most advanced." She moved him away from the window, pointed to a monitor, and continued, "Use the exterior cameras if you want to examine it further. See the Model A pick-off mirror that directs star surfers onto the platform in this room. The ballast on the platform has a much finer grain to remove all residual momentum, so star surfers can travel a greater distance without a slam."

"I see a starbeam class transporter. How did it get here so fast?"

"Flint connected the batteries in a vending machine to a backup telesponder. When I got here, I used it to contact the beamers on Stardust and I gave them my official approval to teleport the starbeams. Then I called Gloria. She'll make sure that everything and everyone will be here on time. That starbeam is the first to arrive. They haven't unloaded yet, so I don't know who's onboard."

"Wonderful!" Glenn said with sarcasm. "Did you think Gloria needed more to worry about on her first mission? Now you've added all of this to her duties."

"Dillon is helping her. They work well as a team."

"It looks like you have everything covered. I was worried that my mission was over, but it seems as if I wasn't needed. So where are the other star surfers and Flint?"

"I've collected them into staging room 221-B. There are thirteen of us now that we have you." She opened her green eyes wide, tilted her head, and faked a serious look while saying with sarcasm, "We are here to serve and follow you. Let's join them."

"Do I have any other choice?"

As she led him down the hallway, she exclaimed, "Mac told me you failed your physical, but Kylee convinced him to send you on this assignment anyway because your desk job was killing you."

"Kyleen was half-right. Now this mission might kill me."

"You won't die, you're too tough. Be frank with me. How bad is the problem we are facing?"

"It's bad," Glenn answered. "We need to make peace with these new aliens. Screw that up, and we may have to retreat all the way to Earth."

"Mac gave me the rank of acting space marshal and told me to cooperate with you. Rebels infiltrated your troops. I am pretending to be one of them, so I can identify which ones break the law, and bring them to trial. Keep that under your hat and refer to me as a teleporter specialist in front of the others so I don't lose my cover."

"Give me the list of the rebels," he said. "I'll remove them."

"I will after I have evidence to convict them. We can't make arrests with no apparent reason."

"If I stayed on Stardust another day, I would have interviewed the miners," Glenn explained. "They are witnesses. I'll extradite them here."

"Oh, let them go. They're harmless, and the pirates might rob or threaten them. They broke no laws, so you can't issue a warrant, and they won't volunteer to travel this far for interrogation."

"You're right. I'll leave them alone."

As they walked down the stairs, Glenn went to a storage locker and released several ditto-bots. *They will clean and organize the station.* He looked at her, "You are not telling me everything."

She was thoughtful for a minute, and then changed the subject. "That Eden you were drawn to when we beamed here was Gondwana, which is a strong quantum attractor. However, you need to stay focused on your destination when you star surf, and not end up on Gondwana every time. There are more snares and traps than there are nice places to visit in this universe. The snares, traps, and strange attractors you will visit only once, so put blinders on when you star surf."

He opened the door at the wheel. Trying not to show strain from the gravity, he said, "Your cerebral interface chip was hacked."

She stepped through the door, lost her condescending tone, and became serious as she said, "Why do you think that?"

"Mine was hacked. My C-chip uses a command-tracking algorithm. Someone both watched and controlled me somewhat. And how do you explain your actions?"

"Mac ordered me to make sure you got here. I use my insta-text cube to report daily to him, but that is top secret, so keep it under your hat. Nevertheless, you are right. My timing was wrong. I had not planned on abducting you until later, and then only if you held back from beaming here."

"Thanks for admitting you abducted me. Now you owe me something."

"No, the person who hacked my C-chip owes you something," she said as they walked down the hallway.

Glenn was silent, *Mac must have bugged Kyleen's messages and discovered she told me to forget this mission and live the high life on Gondwana. To keep that from happening, he recruited this woman as insurance. That explains her attitude and her odd behavior but not her hesitations. She isn't telling me who she really is.*

As they continued along the circular hall, they came to an alcove with a water fountain draining into a large pool.

Chapter 18: New Hope

* Christopher Cross, Arthur's Theme *

The fountain broke the monotony of the halls and walls of the station. Glenn was relieved to sit. He was almost sweating as he struggled against the gravity.

Mariah, alias Ligeia, sat next to him and asked, "Why did you try to starsurf out of here?"

He answered, "When I teleported from Sirius, I saw a star surfer. I thought she was you. Did you ever experience anything like that?"

"No, never." Her forehead wrinkled, and she leaned away from him.

He continued, "Let me try to understand this. In a quantum tunnel, the boundaries of space do not exist so there is no separation. That is why we found each other when we teleported at the same time to Stardust. We were ethereal. If I think of it any other way, it makes no sense."

"Nothing ethereal about it," she answered, breaking the mood. "The computer in your pod had sensors that read your thoughts and simulated what you wanted to see. It displayed the images of stars and galaxies on your pod's holographic surround screen. When you looked for someone beyond your pod, the computer found Ligeia, I mean my pod, and it linked us. We were both in quantum space, which permitted us to communicate with each other. I programmed my computer to send my thoughts because I wanted to learn more about you."

Glenn felt helpless as he looked at the water. She continued, "When you toured Gondwana, you saw an advertisement they transmit to attract tourists. The computer improvised the later scenes from its video library, but the part about Splint worries me. Linking to an alien mind is similar to what you experienced. Splint might be in trouble."

"I like my misconceptions better than your lies, but that is okay. Now my thoughts are clear. I am sending Gloria a U-mail to look for Splinter if she is still on Stardust." *This woman is not Ligeia.*

Speaking softly, she tried to restore the romantic mood, "When we teleported together from Stardust, that was real, or I mean, ethereal. Time did not exist, and we watched stars born, shine their light, and die over uncounted millennia."

He faced her and held her shoulders. "There, you said 'real' then your tone of voice changed, your eyes changed to brown, and you said 'ethereal'. Are you Mariah or are you Ligeia? Tell me who you are." A loud bang distracted her. "That is just the docking bay door opening so a starbeam-can land. Now answer me."

"I want to tell you something that scares me and this is the reason why I ran away from you when we arrived here. I must tell someone, or I will go crazy. Can you keep my secret?" Tears appeared in her eyes.

"Yes. I am off duty today so anything you tell me is private."

She said, "Ligeia died in a teleporter accident, and Mac needed a replacement. I needed transportation back to Camelot, so I took this job. I send Mac reports every day. My name is Mariah Cleaver, but I see Ligeia every time I star surf. When we star surfed here, she lived inside of me. I cannot hide from her because I have Ligeia Bell's insta-text chip, and her C-chip implanted in me. Ligeia's C-chip contains her autobiography and earlier reports, so it is easy for me to pretend I'm her."

"Can you merge with her passion? If not, using her memories might make you bipolar."

"Her C-chip does not recognize me as a new host, so it tries to reload my memory and retrain my synapses to be Ligeia. If I don't fight it, will I lose myself?"

"No, don't fight it and you will be stronger and wiser. You will be complete."

Glenn looked at her as her eyes became brown again and her expression became Ligeia's. *She is here. I found Ligeia inside Mariah.*

Her hair flowed over her like the ripples that flowed across the water in the pool. He placed his arm around her, and she leaned into him.

At this moment, nothing was more important than the two of them. She fell into his arms, and they hugged. As they hugged, they heard banging noises as troops unloaded a starbeam.

Then he said, "I have a change of heart. I was slammed two years ago, and afterward I was afraid to travel. Now I remember my ambitions and goals from before my accident. You brought them back to life."

"I know about your accident. Gloria told me."

Glenn leaned away and asked, "Are you kidding me? When did you have a chance to talk to her?" *I have to remember, this woman has two personalities.*

"On Stardust. We women notice things and we talk to each other."

At last, they continued to the gathering in room 221-B. On the way, they passed Gloria and Dillon walking in the opposite direction.

Glenn asked Gloria, "Did you get my text? Is someone going to check on Splinter?"

"I had to help Madeline with personnel files, help Wanda to locate the inventory, learn to pilot a starbeam and teleport it here. How was I supposed to find time to babysit a…."

Dillon cut in, "I talked to Splinter on Gondwana a week ago. It was happy planting its sprouts, and decided to stay where it was safe. Anyway, you have Tumbleweed so don't worry about it."

As they walked away laughing, Glenn wondered if they would stop at the pool.

*

Glenn and Ligeia entered room 221-B together. Everyone noticed, and came to attention until Glenn saluted, and then they returned to their work. Maps of Dearth covered the walls and several tables. He saw areas on the maps that the troops color-marked to show different terrain, enemy forces, and friendly forces. *Flint seems too young to be a platoon leader, but the troops listen to him and follow his orders. He is organized and speaks with authority.*

Flint saw Glenn, walked over, took him aside, and said, "I need to talk to you!"

"Okay, where do you want to talk?"

"We can use a room across the hall as an office," He walked through the door. Glenn followed.

The room across the hall contained a desk. Boxes of light arms and munitions lined two walls, boxes of rations covered a third wall, and buckets of gems leaned against the forth wall. A prayer booth stood in one corner near a makeshift altar with a picture of a man Glenn did not recognize.

"My father. He was killed in a logging accident on Gondwana," Flint said as he stood in front of the picture and bowed his head in a moment of silence.

Glenn bowed his head and waited until Flint stepped away from the altar to say, "I hope we have more supplies than this."

"The starbeam that just docked has more, and more starbeams are on the way with the rest of our troops and supplies," Flint said. "They will arrive at the rate of two per day. We'll use the supplies in this room if we have to grab and run. Tell me about the Gobato. Why are they a threat?"

"If we offer no resistance, they will attack our colonies, exterminate the Razorroots, and restrict all humans to Earth. They might even attack Earth but they are no threat if we hold this station," Glenn answered. "If they travel toward Earth, troops at Camelot can cut their supply line."

"I plan to surprise them and attack with starbeams equipped with SAM's. I'll detach Camelot's hull and use it resupply the starbeams that become spent."

"No, I cannot let you put Camelot at risk. We will negotiate peace."

"Let's hope peace is possible," Flint said as he held back a smile.

"No matter what happens, they cannot find the teleporter terminal. They can fit many of their small ships into those starbeam-cans. If they beam out, then all is lost."

"If you destroy the teleporter, how will we return to our home stations?"

Glenn responded, "Most of us will stay here. Those who must leave will travel on transporters at less than light speed."

"One of the troops told me those weapons you designed are too powerful. Nobody can shoot them, and they are too heavy and bulky. I took the liberty to bring Army standard issue rifles, hand weapons, grenades, and thirty caliber machine guns that my soldiers can carry, and are trained to shoot." Glenn gave him a stern look. "Don't get excited, we brought your weapons too in case you insist on trying to use them."

Glenn answered, "The standard issue guns are like pea shooters against this enemy. A grenade might confuse them if anyone throws one without the enemy cutting them into pieces first. I'll order the hand grenades banned for our safety."

"You're the commander until someone gets hurt." Flint saluted, turned to leave, and answered, "The troops expect leadership, so you cannot fraternize with subordinates." Then he marched out slamming the hatch door.

Why does he care if I fraternize? Glenn wondered. *If he is referring to Ligeia, I cannot compromise her cover and tell him she is a space marshal. Flint is an officer and will be my friend when he sees what we face. Sometimes, the most rebellious officer becomes the greatest asset in battle.*

Flint warped the door seal when he slammed it. Glenn used a crowbar to wedge it open. After he had left, he noticed that the door would not close, so he attached a red maintenance tag so no one would use it in an emergency. Doors on space stations could withstand a vacuum, but not abuse.

* Logan Soundtrack, Kaleo, Way Down We Go *

After Glenn returned to room 221-B, he asked Captain Madeline, "Can we get close surveillance of the Gobato encampment? We need to know more about the enemy than what is in the Inspector's report."

"Their encampments are underground. They are too deep and too dispersed for a nuclear attack," she answered. "When surveillance drones flew over their camp, web filaments entangled and grounded them. Their web filaments extend into space, so we have to be careful not to become entangled when flying near the planet."

"Can your troops place a satellite in the furthest outreach of the system to intercept the Gobato ships as they arrive?"

"The simple answer is no. Their ships arrive at near light-speed, too fast to aim a laser at them. A nuclear blast cap would clear an area of a few miles for a few minutes. Most of the alien ship clusters arrive hours apart with separations of several hundred miles. We would use all of our missiles in a day."

A week passed, and the rest of the starbeams arrived. Wanda, the operations coordinator, checked the inventory before leaving Stardust, and discovered the RA-weapons were not on the list. She held the departure of the last starbeam and loaded these advanced weapons.

When the starbeams arrived at Camelot, the slam did not imperil them or the Space Station. With the U-net, the teleporters automatically adjusted the ballasts to prevent such accidents.

As the troops unloaded the starbeams, Glenn became anxious because he did not see his RA-weapons. Then, the last starbeam unloaded his cargo and his weapons.

"Phew," he exclaimed to Wanda. "You kept me in suspense to the last. I am glad to see you and the cargo."

Tumbleweed was on the last starbeam. Glenn greeted it and it said, "I want to recover my sprouts that are on the farm on Dearth. The Gobato can have the foliage."

Glenn remembered the green splotch he saw earlier when he looked at the planet from Camelot. He answered, "I cannot promise anything, but if the negotiations go well, then I will ask the Gobato to give you access to the farm."

Other than the voice from the computer, Tumbleweed did not move during their conversation. It seemed almost as if the computer was responding and not the plant.

*

The troops went to the abandoned mine to train, and to adjust to the gravity, the kaleidoscope sky, and the sprites that covered the ground before dawn and after dusk. Glenn climbed to the top of a fifty-foot rock to see the entire practice field.

"Can we move about without pressurized space suits?" Madeline shouted up to him.

"Yes, we will use lightweight breathers with facemasks. The atmosphere does not irritate our skin or eyes and is breathable for a short time with nose filters, which we will carry as a backup.

"An important part of this exercise is to test our protective clothing," Glenn continued as he watched the troops. "The fabric is bulletproof, rip and flame proof, and is camouflage even to infrared. Heavier armor is not helpful since it would impede freedom of movement and mobility."

"Can we use helmets if we have anti-gravity belts?" Madeline asked, looking up at him. "The toy stores on Gondwana have enough to equip our troops."

"I remember seeing those Higgs modulators. How much mass can they remove?"

"Only fifty pounds because they are for children, but they are compact. I am sending you the link to the toy store so you can look at the description."

"They are shown with rocket-packs. Can we use those too?"

"The rocket-packs produce only fifty pounds of thrust. We need more than that."

"Ask Elroy to remove the restrictor plates," Glenn ordered as he climbed down from the rock. "Then they will lift a fully equipped soldier in the low gravity of this planet. Also, remove the insulation so after we empty and discard them they will burn the aliens' tube-feet."

"Can we use dancing-jacks for that?"

"No, they are listed with landmines and are banned. Order the helmets. With the gravity-belts and jet-packs, helmets won't slow us down."

"Can the helmets stop a blow from a Gobato sword?"

Glenn considered, "No, not unless Elroy installs switches to reverse the coils on the gravity belts so we can use them as Higgs shields. Then the Gobato can't cut us into ribbons, but a single blow will damage the armor."

"I'll contact Elroy today and have them here before Saturday with your modifications, and I'll order cushioned soles for our boots so the Gobato don't feel vibrations when we walk. With this, I think we are well equipped."

Glenn approved the purchase order, and then returned his attention to the training exercises.

The troops fired the weapons, practiced setting up bunkers, and coordinated their lines and their movements. Wanda erected medical tents, laid retreat cables, and tested retreat strategies. Each soldier carried a motorized trolley gimbal for cable extraction. This system removed them from danger as fast as a racecar.

At the end of the exercises, Glenn believed that his forces were capable of containing the threat, even against a superior force like the Gobato.

Glenn was concerned that thieves had infiltrated their ranks and stole gems from the small mine. He told Flint, who owned the mining rights, but Flint was unconcerned and said, "All the large and valuable gems on the surface are already mined out. Don't worry about it. Don't jeopardize the mission. Much more is at stake here."

He was glad Flint resolved the issue.

Glenn reviewed the situation with Ligeia, who had the authority to arrest the thieves. She was content to wait until after the mission similar to what Flint suggested, so Glenn agreed and took no immediate action.

That evening back on Camelot, Flint met with the pirates. "I told you to keep a low profile. That means don't steal. If Glenn investigates, he will discover us. Those gems you stole belong to me, now give them back."

One of them said, "Don't be a sore loser. We only did what comes naturally.

"Natural means not to get caught."

"Why didn't you kick that space marshal out of an airlock?"

"We need him to draw the Gobato out."

Several pirates emptied their lockers. As they returned buckets of gems, Flint explained, "Here is the plan. If Glenn's troops ask questions, I will hack their C-chips. Study this x-ray so you know the alien anatomy. The RA-weapons Glenn is using will destroy their internal shell and the marrow, but that is what we want to harvest. We have the more difficult task of killing them by cutting them into pieces while preserving the marrow. Use our automatic weapons to sever the tail and head sections. I believe that will kill them without damaging the circe."

"Okay, but isn't that a lot more dangerous?"

Flint answered, "With all of us working together, we can do it."

They put their hands together and cheered.

* Manfred Mann's Earth Band, Blinded by the Light *

Glenn reviewed the field tests results, and concluded that the troops were ready, and the equipment worked. The platoon leaders agreed to confront the Gobato before they grew stronger.

Later that evening, he and Ligeia ate dinner with wine. Glenn proposed to her and offered her his ring, which she gladly accepted.

"I always wanted to have children when I meet that perfect person," smiling and jumping with joy, she continued, "and that person is you. We will always be together."

He imagined their lives together, their futures, and their children. "Our children will be smart like you and strong like me."

She smiled. "Yes, I know."

"We can live on Gondwana and avoid beaming all the way back to Earth, but first I must complete this mission. The human race and the Razorroots depend on me. I don't want you in danger, so go to Gondwana and wait for me."

"No," she said. "I will stay with you, at your side. I cannot live without you. Your fate is my fate. I cannot be at peace on Gondwana knowing the peril you face, and I have friends here. I cannot leave them either."

Glenn nodded. He would never leave her in danger like this. She held the same concern for him and for her friends.

*

The next morning, Glenn woke the leaders at 2:00 AM and told them, "Wake your troops and tell them to get their gear. We will assemble at the mine in one hour."

At the mine, Glenn stood at a podium. The officers stood next to him. The troops stood at ease before them. Glenn used the direct C-link to send his image and his voice to everyone present. A hologram projector showed the image of a map next to him. He used this moment to issue orders, answer questions, and make sure everyone understood the mission.

"Here are the final plans," he announced. "We will land at the location shown on the map, and prepare our entrenchments before sunrise.

Ten military starbeams are available for moving troops and equipment. The starbeams will land in the forward position and unload. Then five will return to the rear position, set up a mobile hospital, and unload three tanks with disintegrators as the rear guard so the enemy cannot flank us.

"The seven forward tanks will dig bunker trenches, and the troops will install bunker frames. The forward starbeams will transport cement, aggregate, and water to fill the bunker frames. The bunkers will split and channel the enemy forces. The two bunkers in the middle are command bunkers."

A troop near the front asked, "Where do we get the concrete?"

"We will load the cement that the miners stockpiled."

Another troop asked, "How do we provoke the aliens?"

"This location is between the Gobato camp and the farm. They will have to walk through us to reach the farm."

"Why are we landing in such a rocky area?"

"This enemy can borrow underground. The rocks will keep them above ground where they can't defend against our heavy equipment. Now the officers will report their plans. Lieutenant Flint Valance, report."

Flint stood dressed in full gear. "I will command the front line with Platoon Alpha. We will fortify the front four bunkers and protect against an enemy attack." He issued a blast from his rocket pack and jumped seventy feet into the air for emphasis. The crowd cheered.

"Sergeant Oliver Pike, give us your report."

"Platoon Delta will deploy eight bunker frames at the second line. We provide cover fire for Commander Flint." He fired a round from his RA-gun into the air. The blast stunned the crowd.

"Captain Madeline Hilton. Give us your report."

"I will command the forward heavy equipment with Platoon Beta. We will be mobile, and advance or retreat as needed. Our equipment includes starbeams with disruptors, seven tanks with disintegrators, and some generators and floodlights. We have four heavy Higgs shields that will make three of the tanks and the tele-blaster impervious to the enemy's weapons. They cannot defeat us if they cannot disable our tanks." The crowd cheered without further display.

"Lieutenant Wanda Desoto, report."

"When the Gobato approach, I am the main negotiator." The crowd booed but quickly became silent as she scanned them with a deadly look. "If negotiations fail, then I'll support the troops. I will handle supplies, remove the injured, maintain the field hospital, provide replacements, and hold the rear position ten miles back. I will take command if we retreat. Acting Lieutenant Gloria Mandela is my backup."

Glenn nodded. "I am the first in command. Transportation Expert Ligeia Bell and I will support all areas with sharpshooters. We will occupy the command bunkers if the enemy overruns us."

Someone asked, "What do we do if you become a casualty."

"In that case, Captain Madeline Hilton is second in command. Sergeant Oliver Pike is third in command. If you lose all three of us, then everyone not in a bunker will retreat. Lieutenant Wanda Desoto, what is the retreat plan?"

She looked across the crowd with a cold stare, and no one dared to boo. "Everyone not in bunkers will board the five forward starbeams, and retreat to the rear to the undamaged tanks and starbeams. Those who are in bunkers will hold their positions. If the enemy attacks the rear position, then retreat to Camelot using stealth. Those in the bunkers will harass the enemy while I negotiate and while Madeline plans our next attack."

Out of the two hundred and fifty troops and support staff, five were officers. Madeline's training and combat experience made her the best qualified.

"I am promoting Captain Madeline Hilton to Major, Lieutenant Wanda Desoto to First Lieutenant, and Sergeant Oliver Pike to Lieutenant," Glenn said.

Flint did not follow orders well, so Glenn did not promote him or put him in the command chain. Flint frowned.

Glenn pointed to the positions on the map, "The bunkers are impenetrable by this enemy, and are separated so a nuclear device cannot take them all out. Once we have them in place, we can relax a bit. They hold sufficient supplies for us to wait out the enemy. Are there any questions?"

A tall trooper with black hair asked, "Why don't we use the starbeams and blast them, laser them, or fire SAMs with nuclear blast caps?"

"Their ships can outrun a SAM and Camelot can't endure the EMPs. Also, they are expecting that, and they will defend against it. All starbeams must stay behind our front line, or the alien webbing will bring them down, but our ships will prevent the aliens from attacking us from the air. Remember, the Razorroots used transporters and fired nuclear missiles at them with no success,"

Glenn glanced around the field of faces. "They cannot travel past this star system, and attack our colonies or Earth as long as we hold the bunkers and the Space Station. Work together and make this happen, because there is no other plan and no one to rescue us. We are the only military within fifty light-years."

A short fat soldier in front asked, "If Flint is commanding the front bunkers, who will command Camelot?"

"That is Wanda's responsibility until Lt. Flint is relieved."

Another asked, "What weapons does this enemy have?"

"They have a single weapon design that has a range of half a mile," Glenn said. "If they get that close, retreat or get in a bunker. Don't fight them hand to hand, and don't chase them." The crowd laughed. After all, who would chase a two-ton beast with feet lined with talons that release acid?

"What about the aliens who are still arriving? How do they factor in?"

"Gobato ships keep arriving, but they need supplies. They can barely feed themselves and cannot support those who are on the planet. This possibility is not a game changer unless they resort to cannibalism; that is an unknown. I believe they will negotiate with us before they become that desperate."

An eerie silence came over the troops. Glenn broke the mood by holding an RA-rifle above his head and saying, "These weapons will cut an elephant in half two miles away. I didn't bring an elephant, so I can't prove that. You'll have to believe me. (There was brief laughter.) The RA-guns have good penetration at close range. We have a few bazookas, but no reloads, so each of the officers will carry one for emergencies or if we have to retreat.

"One other thing, Elroy invented the tele-blaster." Glenn sent a 3-D video feed to everyone's C-chips showing it destroying one-hundred salt targets in less than ten seconds. The troops cheered and applauded.

"This weapon alone can make life miserable for the Gobato. Now, if there are no further questions, load the starbeams, complete this mission, and give them all you got."

Glenn and Wanda were the last to leave the staging area. "Be confident, Wanda," he said to her as they left, "our negotiations depend on you."

"My confidence would overwhelm you if we spent as much time planning the negotiations as we spent on planning the battle," she said as her eyes looked through him like asteroid-cutting laser beams.

When she walked away, he wondered, *Could I use her eyes as weapons?* but he dared not ask.

*

While the troops completed their plans, Tumbleweed stayed behind on Camelot and went to agroponics unit number two. It was relieved to be out of the dry station air. It sank its roots into the soil and suckled moisture and nutrients for half an hour. Its starving fibers needed much more but it had little time, so it withdrew its roots, located Blackbark, and they conversed, "Most Full of Sap, I bring you a message from the Great Ferns."

"What is their message?"

"They thought the Gobato would arrive in the millions, but there are only twenty-thousand in route so they changed our plans. We will encourage the humans and the Gobato to eliminate each other. The earthlings must not learn that the Great Ferns conspire against them."

Blackbark answered, "That will be easy. The troops trust us, and they think they are superior."

"How ridiculous; let them wallow in their pride while we put them to our use. As you know, the Gobato are hardy. We must kill them three times."

"That sounds difficult. How will we do that?"

"I will go to the planet with the troops and make sure battle breaks out. The Emerald Pirates are hacking C-chips. I will let them hack me so we can blame the battle on them."

"What if the Gobato defeat the human army?"

Tumbleweed explained, "Did you infect the farm with viruses and prions from the Great Ferns?"

"Yes, after I removed our saplings, I infected every leaf, stem, root, and even the ground. How will that help?"

"Greed motivates the pirates. The prions change the marrow in the Gobato so the humans can consume it and benefit from its healing power. The pirates already plan to butcher the Gobato and sell the circe they harvest to finance their war against Earth."

"But Earth will still control the Outworld. Our numbers are too few to overthrow them."

"That is true, but we have mature sprouts on every farm and in every hydroponics unit. If we enlist them, the humans are outnumbered. Empire already gave us the authority to pilot their spaceships. After the pirates isolate the colonies, we will take over the outposts and control the teleporters."

"Do we want to share space with pirates?" Blackbark asked.

"Their rule will be short. The prions will make them too strong and they will become monsters. After they kill uninfected humans, they will attack and eliminate each other. They won't attack us because we are plants."

Humans are not all bad. I found one on Camelot, who understands our plight. She swore her allegiance to me."

"If you are referring to Yvette, she swore allegiance to Truman. She cannot honor both of you."

Blackbark welted its leaves, "Oh."

Tumbleweed continued, "The Great Ferns will help us. Your immediate job is to maintain agroponic unit number two, so the Gobato have plenty of infected food. I will destroy the farm on Dearth to anger the Gobato enough to fight the humans. If the Gobato survive the battle, then give them the agroponic unit. They cannot survive on Xanadu after we infect them with viruses, so they will settle on Gondwana and Earth. That will keep the humans from making a comeback."

Blackbark showed doubt, "I don't want to help the Gobato. What if they spawn?"

"They cannot spawn here because this planet is too dry."

"I understand the plan and I will do as the Great Ferns ask." As they parted, Blackbark said, "May the spores of the Great Ferns infect your leaves, branches, bark, roots, and inner core."

"Your blessing is accepted, Most Full of Sap."

"I'll take you to the teleporter so you can join Glenn, his troops, and the pirates."

Chapter 19: Battle Lines

* Animals, Sky Pilots *

After the assembly, the platoon leaders and troops mounted the starbeams. Tumbleweed was with Space Marshal Glenn Hunter, who led the caravan of ships. The other starbeams followed with their autopilots locked to the forward craft. To avoid alerting the Gobato, the train of starbeams hugged the terrain as they worked their way forward to the plateau where this small army would make its stand.

Flying across this terrain was monotonous, and tedium affected the pilots. The crew traded off flying the craft to avoid loss of concentration. Tumbleweed held a pilot license and asked to take a turn at the controls. Glenn approved.

Tumbleweed flew the starbeam with the same skill as the best pilots. It knew details of the landscape and was unaffected by tedium. Glenn was pleased. He did not know a Razorroot could pilot so well.

By the time the caravan of flying crafts reached the ten-mile patch of foliage, half the crew was asleep, and the other half was entertaining themselves by reading, or playing video games. The lead ship was so smooth and steady that no one noticed the change, yellow-gray clouds that surrounded the string of starbeams on both sides.

Oliver hollered, "Laser-comms are flashing from one of the crafts in the rear. They are asking 'What is going on? Why are you misleading us?'"

Glenn understood the problem, "Tumbleweed refocused the ion exhaust from our ship into a lethal beam and changed the source supplying the ion thrusters from inert gasses to chlorine. The crafts behind us automatically copied the new settings. Focused ions are burning the farm below us, and chlorine ions are deadly."

He grabbed a rope, lassoed the Razorroot, and pulled it out of the pilot's chair as the rest of the crew threw blankets over it and bound its roots.

Oliver took the pilot's seat, "I corrected the mistake, but it is too late. All ten starbeams dumped enough chlorine to choke a continent."

Glenn looked back and discovered their exhaust destroyed the small green farm. He asked, "Aren't your sprouts down there? Why did you exterminate your kind?"

The Razorroot did not answer and became lethargic.

"Take that stump to the storage hull," Glenn ordered. "Tie it down, put a camera on it, lock the door, and guard the door."

The crew looked as if they wanted to murder the Razorroot. Glenn considered helping them if they tried.

*

When the expedition was near the battle lines, the starbeams landed and unloaded. All the ships landed east of the Gobato camp and west of the farm. The forward ships positioned themselves at the top of a plateau that overlooked a plane the hostile aliens would have to cross when they traveled from their camp to the farm. The troops set battle lines down the slope of the plateau.

Wanda installed retreat cables across the battle lines for rapid removal of the injured. Madeline installed floodlights, generators, and lit up the work area.

"That is too much light." Glenn ordered, "Turn off the lights before they alert the Gobato. We want to draw the Gobato to our position, but not until the fortifications are in place."

"We cannot do this work in the dark."

"Then wait for the light of the pre-dawn."

The troops unloaded the starbeams using flashlights.

Glenn told three of Flint's men. "Guard the Razorroot."

One of them answered, "It's in a vegetative state. It's not going anywhere."

"Guard it anyway. If it wakes, the sharp edges of its roots can cut through ropes and blankets. They produce acids strong enough to dissolve steel. The thin walls of a transporter won't hold it."

Predawn sprites dance across the landscape, and the crew resumed installing the bunkers. Glenn had a strange thought: *My trip is over, and this point is the furthest in space that I'll ever reach. The volume of human occupied space is one million cubic light-years! Is this space too large for us to control?*

Glenn remembered he did not read Mac's entire message, the message that Ligeia interrupted weeks earlier. He retrieved the message from the recording spool, and it read:

Mac insta-text Glenn, "My staff studied Xanadu while I was teleporting, and they understand why the Razorroots panicked. The x-ray the inspector took matches fossils we found, which proves the Gobato originated here, and they almost exterminated the Razorroots before they left. There are no Gobato on this planet at the present. However, they are not the real threat. The real threat is the Great Ferns. That may seem incredible but get this: the Great Ferns are from Earth.

"We need more information, so try to contact the Gobato and get them to tell us what they know about the Great Ferns.

*

Ziven, one of the deputies who grazed at the farm, reported to Raavn through the closed circuit cable. "The humans have landed! They destroyed the farm with exhaust from their ships, but the exhaust did not injure the grazing Gobato except for mild burns."

"Destroying our food source is a dirty tactic," Raavn answered. "I did not believe that these puny pukes were capable of such malice. *This is what I would do if I were on the other side: destroy enemy resources to force them out of their fortifications, so they have to fight or negotiate on your terms. Be careful because they might have more tricks.*"

Raven ordered his ships in orbit to spot all human activity and report back. The ships reported the landing location minutes later. Raavn knew the area, an eroded plane with an upslope. *The humans think we will struggle to cross this terrain, but they don't know we can travel over it effortlessly.*

Raavn woke Vicar Eaau and exclaimed, "The time to prepare for war is now. After you wake our clan, report back to me."

He knew that his spaceships were not practical war machines against the human's starbeams. His small ships could outrun and ram the fragile starbeams, or redirect their ion engines to cut and burn them at short range, but the radar, vision, and agility of the human pilots were superior. Raavn preferred to fight on the ground and trample the enemy with a head on charge. He planned to use his ships only for defense and reconnaissance.

Raavn was eager to find out if earthlings would fight or run in the face of battle.

When Vicar Eaau returned, He asked, "Am I an enormous and ugly monster? Will I scare these wimpy beings back to Earth?"

"Yes. If they are scared, they will run. Do not exfoliate in front of them because it will horrify them too much and they will vomit and defecate."

"Will my clan still attack if they all vomit?"

"Maybe not. It is too disgusting."

Raavn planned, "I will take prisoners and execute them one by one. They will cringe when they look at me, and cringe even more when they surrender, and then I'll explain that the Gobato do not take prisoners except for specimens for dissection and experiments."

He did the Gobato laugh-dance.

The Vicar asked, "Why are you celebrating? You will not receive a promotion for this campaign because the King considers it routine."

"Yes, but the King will be glad, and so will I."

Raavn could not tell Eaau his deeper joy, *The King and this vicar think the Great Ferns inspire us, but I know the truth. I will leave the others and take my clan. We will bypass Earth and annihilate the real menace: the Great Ferns on Rasalhague. The Razorroots are smart to hide behind the humans, but they cannot flee forever. They have to protect their Great Ferns. The humans know nothing about the Great Ferns or they would join me. Maybe I can negotiate a short truce and tell them about the Great Deception. I'll have to do this without the Vicar taking notice.*

"Your vibration shows you have thought."

Raavn changed the subject, "Eaau, look at the weapons I redesigned for the battle ahead. They are more deadly than our traditional swords."

"Our traditional weapons are tested and proven effective during a thousand years of mock combats. How can anything be better?"

"I improved the cutting edge to be sharp and durable enough to kill a Gobato not to mention what it will do to a human. As a shield, it is hard enough to bounce their projectiles back at them, and reflective to confuse their radars, lasers, and infrared guided missiles. This weapon will slash through a human, and have enough momentum to return to the user for reuse like a boomerang. The thrower keeps control of it with a strand of web that stays attached," Raavn answered.

"Do not disgrace our race by associating us with lethal weapons. Give them a new name."

"Yes, I will call them zingers because they make a zing sound when thrown."

Earlier, the Gobato metallurgists reworked metal from the crashed ships and made three zingers for each member of Raavn's clan. The handles were similar to those of their traditional swords, so the Gobato controlled the zingers with the dexterity of a juggler, throwing them one at a time or all at once.

Raavn spoke to his warriors, "An army of humans invaded our planet with hostile intent. We have cause to attack them."

Vicar Eaau arranged the funeral ceremony for Treeeater. This service enraged the clan. They were eager to fight humans.

She explained, "You have the advantage if you attack at night because their sight depends on light. You can detect their movement, but they lack tactile sensitivity, and cannot feel our ground vibrations. Reach the humans before sunrise and surprise them before they complete their entrenchments and fortifications."

Raavn ordered, "Board your ships, and travel to eight miles from where the humans landed. At that distance, we are below the horizon, and they cannot see us. We will surprise them."

Raavn wanted an overwhelming victory, so he called the farm on the closed circuit cable, "Ziven, we will attack and destroy the humans before dawn. Tell those at the farm to approach the human forces from the opposite side. You have more distance to travel and will arrive late, but you can collect the cowards who run away from the battle."

Raven and Eaau boarded a ship and led their fleet. After landing near the invaders, two Gobato scientists prepared a telescope to view the humans. Raavn moved to position four eyespots on his side to align with the quad-ocular telescope. There they were! He saw them. Preoccupied with their work, their troops were not aware of the presence of the Gobato warriors or ready for him to attack. Raavn held the advantage of surprise.

He saw a human shoot a practice round. The power of the projectile was far greater than he expected. Raavn warned his clan, "The pukes want to fight at two miles, out of range of our zingers, so we will hold our line at five miles where their bullets are less of a threat. When we attack, you will close the gap fast so they have little time to shoot. At close range, hold two zingers stacked together to reflect their high-powered projectiles back at them while you throw your third zinger to slash them. The humans are too small to block the weight of our weapons."

On further inspection, Raavn identified the disintegrators and tanks. He told ten of his clan, "Prepare the tremor hammer that we transported from the Pleiades. Use it to remove these threats. The tremor hammer will undermine the ground that supports heavy equipment. Also, it will weaken the metallic matrix of their heavy machines."

The Gobato knew how to generate damaging frequencies with their buzzing vibrations. The tremor hammer would amplify and focus those vibrations. Raavn was confident the humans would turn and run from a Gobato attack if they lost their heavy weapons.

"The tremor hammer would not injure the humans or damage their handheld weapons and armor," Raavn told Eaau, "but these weapons are only a nuisance. We can feel their ground vibrations and dodge before the bullets reach us." He did not know bullets fired from rifles traveled faster than sound.

After they approached to five miles from the human forces, Raavn felt increased human activity from the vibrations in the ground. Concerned they saw his warriors, he looked through his quadocular telescope again. When he saw the humans attach bayonets to their rifles, he began a laugh-dance as he remembered pictures in the encyclopedia of primitive humans throwing pointed sticks at each other and then running away.

The vibrations of his laugh-dance gave this information to his clan, and they joined the dance. The laugh-dance became so intense he calmed himself and his warriors before they gave away their position and lost their surprise, but Raavn did not think a surprise mattered much. He believed this battle would be short and decisive.

As he watched the scene through his quadocular telescope, he saw several of the humans vomit. *Ah, the pukes saw us. They do have sharp vision to see us at this distance.*

He remembered when a Gobato approached a human too fast and surprised him. The human spat vomit. The acid in it burned the Gobato, continued to burn, and tasted bad for days. The history files seemed to show that the humans never used vomit as a weapon. *A good thing; this could repel my attack. I'll mark those hazards on a map so my clan and I can avoid them.*

*

In the predawn darkness, sprites reflecting from diamond shards above the planet haunted the landscape. The sprites caused shadows of the humans to dance across the ground defeating their camouflage.

Glenn saw the dust that rose when the aliens danced. *The enemy approaches and we are not ready for battle, negotiations might delay them while we complete our preparations.* His forces were motionless, frozen with fear. Glenn's mouth was dry, and his hands were sweaty from an emotion he did not like. He texted his daughter, but she did not reply. Without warning, he had to vomit. He noticed several of his troops did the same.

Before fear overwhelmed him, he ordered, "Wanda, turn on the floodlights."

Glenn looked up and saw the enemy. They lined a bluff in a single row and used their shield-weapons to shine the light back at the troops. Their dark rhubarb colored bodies contrasted against the thin frost that covered the ground. Their numbers had grown from the last survey.

Wanda contacted him on the C-net and warned, "The threat of battle might undermine peace. These aliens can breathe the carbon dioxide atmosphere, and weigh two tons. If we fight, they will trample us."

Glenn answered, "If they run on their tube-feet, we can outrun them."

"Yes, but if they leap using their rear foot, then their speed is unknown."

"They seem too bulky and unbalanced to use their flipper for running. They will be in range of my RA-rifles and easy range for the disintegrators long before they can throw their weapons. It seems like a mistake for them to rely on a single weapon. To satisfy you, I will ask for peace before we massacre them."

Wanda advised, "If that is your decision, then talk to the troops before they panic and start shooting at random."

Glenn warned the troops, "Hold your fire. They were beyond the reach of our RA-rifles. Our orders are to avoid combat. If we put on a big show, the aliens will prefer to negotiate. We will fight if the Gobato attack us, but we will not fire the first shot or provoke them. If they rush us to test our resolve; you can take cover, but don't shoot unless we have losses."

Flint moved his men to the front line and occupied the front bunkers. He used the standard issue weapons for infantry because he believed that the rapid fire and lightweight of his automatic weapons would compensate for their small caliber.

Glenn worried that the enemy would overrun Flint with his light arms so he reassigned as many Alphas as he could for different tasks until Flint protested. Delta and the snipers would keep Alpha covered, but they could lose control if the enemy pressed hard.

Madeline ordered the disintegrators and tanks to take positions one mile behind the front line. Then she mounted the runabout truck that carried the tele-blaster.

Wanda ordered the starbeams to a position behind the disintegrators with engines on idle and pilots to standby for evacuation in case the Gobato surged.

Chapter 20: The Tremor Hammer

* Led Zeppelin, Battle of Evermore *

Vicar Eaau said, "The King will find fault with you if you proceed without trying to negotiate. Let the puke tubes know we are powerful and domineering, but we are not brutes. Tell them we are returning to our Dream World where the Great Ferns will give us a new purpose. Then they will join us and not oppose us!"

Raavn answered, "They have invaded our planet and threaten us with lethal weapons. That justifies our response."

"What sentient race would build such a variety and quantity of lethal weapons? Surely you are mistaken; they must have some other use."

"Okay, I will ask for peace before I attack."

Raavn chose three of his warriors who were dissidents and ordered, "Approach visibly, and petition the humans for a peaceful settlement. Be careful they don't puke on you. Tell them about the real adversary, the Great Ferns. Tell them the Great Ferns drove us off our home planet in the Rasalhague star system. Now we wish to return, and we will live in peace if possible. Then the humans will join us and not oppose us."

"Yes, Chief. Right away, Chief," they responded.

Vicar Eaau felt their vibrations and confronted Raavn. "You spoke ill of the Great Ferns. Are you a dissident and did you hide your memories to avoid the purge?"

Raavn did not answer, only shook with guilt.

"Suppress those memories into a polyp, shed it, and I will burn it to purge those memories forever. That proves you converted, and you cannot mislead us. When the King arrives, this will lessen his anger as he decides your fate."

The Gobato had segmented bodies except for the head and tail parts. The center part consisted of seven sections along the length and four going across the width for twenty-eight total. They could detach one or more of their side segments, which develop into a complete organism. Normally, the male Gobato detached the side segments when they spawned and replaced them with embryos from the females.

Raavn shed one polyp to comply with the Vicar's demand. Otherwise, his clan would not follow him. The Vicar did not order him to watch as she slaughtered the polyp. It would be like a parent watching the slaughter of their child.

*

Flint reported, "Three of the Gobato are approaching with white flags."

Wanda ordered, "Don't engage. They want to negotiate. I want two of your men to join me."

"We're ready." Flint and Oliver joined her, and they went forward to meet the Gobato. They hauled a computer-controlled backhoe to translate.

A shockwave from a projectile threw Glenn to the ground. "What was that?" he shouted. He looked up and saw the projectile blast the three Gobato negotiators into plumes of smoke. "Steaming crud; someone fired a disintegrator!"

He turned, looked, and saw the Razorroot, Tumbleweed, preparing to fire a second round. *How dare that plant defy us when we are trying to help them secure their planet?*

He stood on a large rock in plain sight of his troops and the Gobato. Then, he loaded his bazooka, aimed at the Razorroot, and fired before the plant fired the disintegrator a second time. The bazooka hit the Razorroot and detonated the disintegrator round it carried. As burning wood chips fell, they ignited the surviving root tubers before they crawled away. All that remained of the Razorroot was char and a few loose leaves.

Glenn did not celebrate, *Killing a Razorroot on a planet they own is a crime. If any of the troops sold their video feed to a news network, then this information will reach Earth in seconds through the U-net. The only way to block this information is if someone on Earth screens the data flow.*

*

Eaau stood next to Raavn and changed her mind, "Their barbaric display of malevolent misbehavior is intolerable. They cannot be sentient. Their thunder-rock killed three more of your clan."

"Those puny tubes of puke will pay!" Raavn exclaimed, but he was worried. "I already lost a member of my clan to the Razorroots, and another to the miners and I have not killed one human in retaliation. How can I explain three more losses to the King?"

"He will strip you of your authority and disperse your clan for such ineptness." The Vicar observed, "You have nothing to gain from fighting the humans."

"Killing them will satisfy me."

"Guard against further losses and guard against defeat by those sordid creatures," she said.

"Defeat? Me? What a strange change of events that would be," Raavn said as he felt something unknown to him, he felt fear. Then he roared, "Bring out the tremor hammer, and focus it on the pukes' heavy weapons and bunkers. Keep moving and zigzag, so the thunder-rocks can't target you."

Raavn ordered fifty of his Gobato foot soldiers to approach. "Get as close as you can in the ravines and gullies without being seen. I will keep them distracted. When you get close, trample the puke-tubes!"

"Yes, chief, right away. Trample the puke-tubes; trample the puke-tubes..." They vibrated with enthusiasm as they disappeared into the ravines.

*

The human negotiators waved white flags, but the enemy charged. The Gobato had no further intention of negotiating. A warrior threw his weapon and critically injured Oliver.

Glenn ordered them, "Retreat, retreat."

"You don't have to tell us twice," Flint answered, as he and Wanda already were returning using their rocket-packs. They carried Oliver as more weapons barely missed them. When they reached the safety of the front line, they discarded their spent rocket packs, and Wanda used a retreat cable to take Oliver to the rear medical staff.

Glenn fumed with anger. *It's a fool's mission to rely on brute force and blind luck to reach a peaceful settlement, but that is the only choice left.* "Kill the floodlights. Use your night vision goggles. Everything is going wrong so far. Our armor and Higgs shields cannot block direct blows from their weapons. After months of planning and weeks of training, do we fight or do we retreat? Officers report." The decision was unanimous. They would fight.

"Follow me, Lt. Valance," Glenn said. Then he arrested the three soldiers who were guarding the Razorroot, took them into a ravine, and encrypted the video feed from his C-chip so all the troops could observe the proceedings but could not record or redirect the information.

He accessed their personnel files on the C-net and accused, "These three men failed to guard the Razorroot, earlier they stole gems, and they used a starbeam without permission. I used the U-net to access their records on Earth. They are not who they say they are. They are using stolen identities, and they endanger this mission."

Flint answered, "Are you sure about the identities. Aren't the records on Gondwana more accurate?"

"No, the files on Gondwana were hacked. I assume they are unregistered which means we can use them or dispose of them as we wish. What do you recommend?"

Flint answered, "I'll take them back to Gondwana for trial."

"Not good enough. That will require paperwork, five of my troops to guard them, and time that none of us have. I am performing a summary execution. Do you object?"

"Yes! You can't do that."

Glenn asked, "Then what do you suggest?"

"Put them in my custody. I'll make sure justice is served. You have my word."

"You cannot do your duties and watch these three at the same time. We face a battle. You need to command your troops," Glenn said to the three, "I accuse you of treason, disobeying orders, abandoning your posts in the face of battle, identity theft, stealing gems, and misuse of government property. Do you deny these charges?"

The three looked down and shook their heads.

"I hereby order immediate execution," Glenn said. "Lieutenant Valance, terminate them."

"No, stop! I-I can't believe this is happening. I can't execute them."

As Flint spoke, Glenn lined them up, fired, and took all three out with a single shot from his RA-gun. They fell into a single pile at the bottom of the ditch, their bodies smoldering from the blast. Glenn poured a cremation accelerant on them, flaming them into ash.

"They don't deserve a funeral with this disgrace. Leave the ashes. We will cover the remains with concrete if we survive this conflict. Now, everyone back to your stations," Glenn ordered.

"Yes, Commander," the troops answered.

"Platoon Alpha, back to your stations before the aliens overrun us," Flint repeated. The other officers did likewise.

Glenn's C-chip warned it was being hacked and supplied a vector. He turned and looked in that direction and saw Dillon, who dodged behind a rock to avoid his gaze. Glenn sent a text message to all persons. "Dillon is hacking C-chips. Apprehend him and bring him to me. Turn off your C-chips and use the laser-comms for communication." (Each helmet had a laser-comm for backup.)

Glenn activated the firewall in his C-chip. He could not turn it off because he needed it to site his rifle. Then he turned his attention back to the charging Gobato, *The pirates are undermining this mission. I shouldn't have listened to Ligeia and delayed in dealing with them.*

* Michael Jackson, Beat It *

The troops asked, "What should we do?"

Glenn ordered, "Madeline, deploy the tele-blaster. That'll stop them!"

Madeline fired the thrusters on the runabout truck to send her high into the sky. Then she reversed the thrust and dove down with a sonic boom.

The troops and the Gobato warriors looked at the sky and saw the runabout truck approaching above them high and hot with the tele-blaster mounted on the back. The blast from the retrorockets burned away the alien webbing. She answered on the laser-comm, "Delivered as ordered, sir."

She rolled the ship upside-down, rotated it so the weapon was in front, and started a great-half-arc above the enemy's position while firing the tele-blaster. As fire descended on them, the Gobato understood the threat and dug underground. The bedrock kept them from digging deep or tunneling away.

Glenn observed, "Good, you have them pinned. Now they have to surrender, or we will dig them out one by one with the backhoe."

"The thrusters can hold this weight for only a few minutes. I have to land," Madeline replied.

"Here are the coordinates for a high ridge overlooking their positions. Land there and keep them pinned." Glenn texted Madeline the coordinates.

She landed while holding the enemy powerless, and reported, "Something is wrong. The runabout truck is sinking. I'm on bad ground."

He turned and looked as the truck fell into a sinkhole with the tele-blaster. Madeline jumped free and rolled away from it before it disappeared. The Gobato dug out and resumed their charge.

"Madeline, fire the disintegrators. That'll stop them!"

Instead of a barrage of fire against the enemy, Glenn heard a commotion behind him. He turned, looked, and saw a haze of dust rising from the landscape. The disintegrators in the path of the dust seemed to bend as if made of soft wax. The tanks were immobile. The bunkers shifted back and forth as if they were paper boats in an unsteady sea, and the partly cured concrete liquefied.

Without the heavy weapons, Madeline looked confused and lost, like a lamb facing a buffalo stampede. She fired her jetpack and retreated behind the front line.

"All troops abandon the heavy equipment, and exit the bunkers," Glenn ordered.

No sooner had the troops moved clear when artillery rounds near the disintegrators and munitions stored in the bunkers and tanks exploded. The tremors did not affect the heavy weapons protected by the Higgs shields, but the ground cratered around them, and they fell into the dust and disappeared. The troops shifted their footing to find stable ground in the mayhem. The tremors did not damage their handheld weapons.

"Wanda, check our reconnaissance in orbit. Are the Gobato doing this or is this an earthquake?"

"The recon pictures show ten Gobato surrounding what looks like an oil derrick on wheels," she answered. "They keep moving it but here are the anticipated coordinates."

Glenn told one of his sharpshooters to advance and fire an EMP-RPG at the alien weapon. The EMP-RPG threw several Gobato into the air but had no other effect, so the sharpshooter withdrew. The Gobato walked carefully around the hot spent rockets the returning shooter discarded. (EMP-RPGs are rifle-propelled grenades that produce a magnetic field to destroy electronic equipment.)

As the other sharpshooters fired to protect the forward shooter, two Gobato fell but twenty-eight polyps detached from the injured aliens and continued the assault. The RA-rifles were easy to shoot because the Higgs shields protected the shooters from the blasts and absorbed some of the recoil.

*

"The humans still have an effective weapon," Eaau said. "They just injured two of your clan."

"I'll put a stop to that." Raavn turned to his warriors. "Launch five ships, and turn on their communication lasers at high intensity. Aim them at the pukes and scramble their communications." The lasers had little effect on the human's encrypted laser-comms, but they reduce the contrast of the night vision goggles.

The monochromatic light from the ships did not illuminate the areas in shade, the gullies, and canyons, giving the aliens good cover. Flint reported, "Alpha is all but blind. We can't fight like this. We need light."

Glenn noticed that the poor lighting did not affect the Gobato. Their tactile sense was as acute as human vision and not as vulnerable. He needed to remedy this and fast. "Madeline, turn on the floodlights and sound the cadence drums," he ordered. "All troops turn off your night vision. Step and shoot in rhythm with the drums. That will confuse them."

When Madeline activated the lights, the rate of the aliens' charge shocked Glenn. The Gobato used their rear appendage for repeated leaps, which gave them the speed of a galloping horse, and they slid up, down, and across rock surfaces by extruding slime. The cadence drums confused them only slightly.

Then the tremors damaged the electric generators, the drums silenced, and the floodlights went out. Alpha turned on their night vision goggles, but the contrast was poor, and they were partly blind again.

Glenn signaled to Flint with a laser-comm. "Retreat to position two."

Flint answered, "We can hold them if you stop their dust-devils."

Glenn ordered Wanda, "Have the rear disintegrators knock out that earth-quaker." He hoped the tremors had not damaged the rear equipment.

The rear disintegrators fired, but the aliens continuously moved their tremor hammer, avoiding the projectiles. After some rounds had missed, Glenn ordered, "Wanda, fire all the rear disintegrators at once and repeat as fast as possible."

With this barrage, Wanda destroyed the strange vibrating weapon and two warriors, but not until the alien weapon wrecked all the forward tanks, disintegrators, bunkers, floodlights, starbeams, ammo boxes, and the tele-blaster.

She signaled back. "Glenn, I used most of the ammo for that volley. Also, the Gobato spaceships in flight are changing direction too fast and the parked ships are too far back for us to target them."

"Save the rest of the ammo for protection in case we retreat."

As Wanda's troops salvaged parts from damaged disintegrators, one of them found Tumbleweed's C-chip and gave it to her. She plugged it into a computer, ran a diagnostic, and discovered it was hacked. She informed Glenn and added, "Saboteurs hacked through Tumbleweed's firewall. Your C-chip has the same firewall. Someone is hacking you to continue this battle."

Glenn's instinct to survive overcame the cloud in his head, and he ordered, "All troops retreat to Camelot. This battle is over." He hand-signaled to Wanda for her to withdraw the troops.

Then he felt intense pain at the back of his head that brought him down on one knee. He thought a zinger hit him but discovered the pain came from his C-chip. It flashed a warning, "Your firewall is hacked, disable your C-chip at once." Glenn turned off his chip and waited for verification. This took all of his willpower.

He found it hard to believe the hacked chip held that much control over him. Now his head cleared, and he wondered why he was fighting since there was no plan to engage this enemy. *Victor would be on top of this problem if he were here.*

Then he saw Dillon, the person who hacked his chip, hiding behind Flint's forces. He was unable to shoot at Dillon without killing a few of the Alphas. The RA-rifle bullets were too powerful for a precise hit, and his RA-gun did not have the range.

"Their lasers are blinding our night-vision goggles, and we cannot retreat," Flint complained. "If we try, we will fall into a ravine. Their warriors are throwing their zingers at us. We have to take cover behind the rocks."

Glenn used the laser-comm in his helmet. He had trouble talking without his C-chip. "Madeline, keep yo troops on station until Flint retreats."

She answered, "Yogos." Then she adjusted to talking without her C-chip and repeated, "You gots it."

The RA-rifles were ineffective because of the poor visibility. Glenn ordered Wanda, "Launch a starbeam and fire its disruptor at ze Gobato ships that are blinding us."

A Gobato ship exploded. When another ship exploded, the other ships retreated.

"Now you can use your night vision goggles. After you use your rocket-packs, zrow zem into the gullies to stop ze Gobato advance," Glenn ordered Flint. "Zen use ze fast-retreat cables to get to ze rear and return to Camelot."

The Gobato surrounded Alpha Platoon and prevented their retreat. Alpha used their rocket packs to dodge the zingers. When the rockets were spent, the troops threw them into the gullies to stop the aliens. Then Alpha opened fire on the Gobato with their small caliber automatic weapons.

Raavn reminded his warriors to protect themselves with their zingers. Their shields reflected projectiles back to their source covering Alpha with a heavy rain of shrapnel. The few aliens who fell recovered and continued their attack toward the human lines.

Flint ordered his troops to surround and attack a single Gobato. Their bulletproof clothing absorbed the flak. With considerable effort, they killed it, but this was a small accomplishment as the enemy killed two Alphas.

Wanda used the retreat cables to extract the troops. Flint was out of reach for Wanda to rescue him, so Glenn and Ligeia continued providing cover fire. Without his C-chip, Glenn had to site his RA-rifle visually, which took all of his attention.

An alien warrior, somewhat hidden and protected in one of the many gullies, was close enough to overrun Alpha. Glenn saw it, but he did not have a clear shot at it. He used the laser-comm to warn Flint. All the Alphas repositioned and focused their fire on this single enemy. They stopped it, but not until it threw its zinger, and killed a man.

Glenn thought, *That was a hard learned lesson, but now, at least, Flint might start obeying orders.*

A surge of aliens was preparing to overrun Alpha. When the other retreating troops cleared the retreat cables near Flint, Glenn cut the cables. The snap-back clobbered the threatening warriors, whipping them and tossing them in all directions like leaves in the wind, but three of them dodged and continued to attack.

The battle became a rescue mission. The charging Gobato were about to overrun Flint and his small band when Ligeia did the unthinkable. She discarded her armor to reduce weight and used her rocket-pack to glide across a deep gully to the next ridge. There she took aim and shot a warrior and killed it as it threw its weapon. The zinger missed Ligeia as the recoil from her RA-rifle sent her back.

Then she rocketed to the rock shelf where the enemy trapped Flint. She threw her hot rocket-pack into a gully to slow the advance of the attacking Gobato.

Glenn rocketed to the top of a bluff near him where he had a better view of the Gobato near Ligeia. He balanced his RA-rifle on his knee and fired it while shooting his RA-gun with his left hand. The aliens were either falling or retreating with this sudden burst of firepower, but Glenn ran out of bullets.

Flint took the RA-rifle from Ligeia and tried to fire it from the hip. It threw him back into a rock wall, almost knocking him out.

Glenn shouted into the laser-comm, "Ze dampers don work unless yo place it against yor shoulder." However, Flint did not hear him.

Ligeia opened fire with her RA-gun, which was effective at close range, and another Gobato fell, but their situation still deteriorated. She removed a device from her hair and threw it into the air. A blue ring appeared; a portable plasma lens. Ligeia, Flint, Dillon, and the remaining troops hugged together and seemed to change into clay. They star surfed out of the battle but not out of danger, Ligeia did not know she beamed with pirates.

The device that formed the plasma lens exploded after they disappeared and before the Gobato overran the deserted position. The aliens thought the lifeless clay soldiers were like the terracotta warriors of China, that humans died in this manner and these were their remains.

Wanda fired the rear disintegrators and used the last of the ammo to protect the troops while they boarded the starbeams. Glenn verified that all the troops retreated, and then started to withdraw.

A warrior who was larger, faster, and much uglier than the other Gobato charged at Glenn. He had one round left and fired at the warrior who sidestepped, and the bullet smashed a rock behind him. The shrapnel from the exploding bullet was like a grenade; deadly enough to kill a human, but it did not distract Raavn.

Madeline looked at the troops who retreated into her starbeam; they were all bleeding and bruised. The medic used all the cloned blood reserves, so he asked her and the other troops to donate blood to help the injured. She did not want to weaken herself or take her attention off the battle, but the battle was over, and her blood was the universal type. She requested a general poll on the net, which accounted for all the troops, but did not poll the C-chips that were turned off. The medic, eager for her blood, assured her that everyone was aboard the starbeams and were safely in retreat, so she agreed and lay on the medical table.

* Christopher Cross, Ride Like The Wind *

During the earlier weeks of training, Dillon taught Gloria how to fly a starbeam, and she became a designated pilot. She used the magnifier on the viewport on her starbeam to scan the battle scene and make sure everyone was onboard. In the distance, she saw the Gobato attacking Dillon and Flint's group. She thought they needed her help, so she left her starbeam, grabbed a discarded RA-rifle, and ran toward Dillon. The passengers on her starbeam left and loaded onto other starbeams that were preparing to launch.

Gloria ran five miles a day with a thirty-pound pack during the weeks of training so running to Flint's location with a twenty-pound RA-rifle in the low gravity was easy for her. She switched her breather to all oxygen, and she ran with elongated strides. She ran faster than any sprinter on Earth. The ground absorbed the shock of her footfall, so the Gobato could not detect the ground vibrations from her running among the confusion and the battlefield noise. Due to this and her camouflage clothing, Gloria was invisible to the aliens.

When she was a mile from Flint's position, the sun broke above the horizon revealing the battle scene. She looked through the RA-riflescope, and saw that they teleported, and only clay from the teleporter ballast remained. With no one to rescue, Gloria turned and hastened back to her starbeam. She was running among the front line of Gobato, and she saw they also attacked from the rear. Their attention was not on her or her starbeam. They were busy smashing the tanks and disintegrators and running after the starbeams that were launching.

Glenn faced the Gobato leader alone who by now was one-hundred yards away and charging head-on. He leaned to hide his shadow. *This beast can't throw his zinger if he cannot see through my camouflage, but he will eventually find me and trample me. The barbs around his sides and the talons around his feet will rip through my skin like razor blades. Bulletproof clothing serves no protection under the weight of this massive creature.*

As Gloria ran across a ridge, she saw that Glenn was in danger. She stopped, aimed her RA-rifle, and fired at Raavn, an excellent shot.

Raavn shook and turned to look in Gloria's direction. The recoil from her weapon gave away her location.

Glenn used his laser-comm to tell Gloria, "At this distance that shot was not fatal, but if you shoot again, that monster will fall."

"I can't, the recoil was worse than I expected. It knocked me off my feet, and I shake when I try to aim. I'll try something else."

Glenn was afraid the alien would attack Gloria, so he threw his bayonet to distract it. The bayonet stabbed into the alien's thick skin.

Raavn shook off the bayonet and turned back to attack Glenn.

That got its attention, Glenn thought, *but I'm out of ammo. I can't outrun this freight train. I can only stand and fight.*

All he had left to fight the charging monster was his field knife, so he threw his spent rocket pack to prevent Raavn from slime-sliding up the rock face.

That stopped him but he is looping webbing around his weapon to entangle me. If he captures me, he will humiliate me in front of its people, and then he will kill me slowly.

Gloria ran into her starbeam and took off before the attacking Gobato reached her. She ejected the moderator rods from the core, which brought the nuclear generator to full power and removed weight from the starbeam. Then she brought the ion engines to full thrust and rocketed through the thin atmosphere breaking the sound barrier.

As she approached Glenn, she used a parachute to bring her to a sudden stop, drop her altitude, and turn the ship backward. She released the parachute and aligned the hatch to Glenn, and next he was looking at the ceiling of a starbeam. The starbeam struck the top of the bluff with its skids and bounced off and high into the sky as Gloria prepared to rocket away. She saved Glenn from a fight with the huge monster, or so it seemed.

Peering out the hatch as it closed, Glenn viewed the demolished remains of his heavy weapons and entrenchments. The battle with the Gobato ended, and the humans lost. He looked at his hands, which bled from abrasions from falling against the rocks, and nicks from the Gobato weapons that narrowly missed him. In addition, he had stress fractures from firing his RA-rifle too many times.

Then he noticed a drag on the starbeam. *The panel indicates the parachute ejected; the starbeam must have snagged a web fiber.*

Chapter 21: Law and Disorder

The Shining, Full OST, Soundtrack

This battle and this retreat were not what the human army planned. People never experienced a problem with their C-chips. However, when they were in the greatest danger, these devices malfunctioned and contributed to the failure of the most important mission in human history. Brute force and blind luck did not favor them on this day.

After the battle, Flint, Dillon, and the rest of the Emerald Pirates reached Camelot first. Ligeia did not know what ill company they were. They sutured their superficial wounds with mini-docs, used the auto-docs to treat the most severe injuries, and then stepped into booths to wash and obtain fresh clothing.

Ligeia said, "I need to beam back. I cannot account for Glenn."

Dillon kept her from turning her C-chip off during the battle. After star surfing to Camelot, he avoided her sight, went to the security office, and locked the door. Now he held Ligeia as a captive, an unaware slave to her C-chip.

Flint distracted her by saying, "We can beam him up once we have the recon photos."

Earlier, when Wanda retreated from the battle, she sent Flint recon photos on the C-net believing he wanted to verify everyone was safe. Now he used the photos to find a dead Gobato to snatch. He gave Ligeia the coordinates, explaining, "Beam Glenn out of danger."

As she adjusted the teleporter, she hollered, "The platform is running out of sand. Quick, refill the hopper or we'll be slammed."

Flint hit the hopper to shake loose the remaining ballast and ordered the pirates to deploy more bags of mix stored against one wall.

"Be alert, a human does not weigh this much," Ligeia said.

Suddenly, a dead Gobato appeared on the platform. The pirates stepped back in awe of the huge monster and its nauseating odor. The contamination sensor sounded an alarm.

Ligeia was shocked. "What are you doing, taking trophies? This violates the galactic law. I'll send it back."

The pirates moved it off the platform before she sent it back. Then Flint gave her coordinates to beam another dead Gobato as Dillon hacked her C-chip forcing her to cooperate. She started to storm away, but the harder she resisted the harder Dillon drove her until she lost consciousness.

Flint told Dillon over the C-net, "Leave her alone. We'll find another beamer. I'll keep her quiet." He moved her to the station's auto-doc and programmed it to keep her sedated.

After he disabled the contamination alarm, Flint checked the computer files but did not find a qualified beamer among the pirates. He said, "I don't know how to run the teleporter in this single ended mode. We need Yvette or a beamer with training to operate this advanced system."

Thunderbolt held his nose and said, "Let's harvest this one first and see how much circe it has."

The pirates removed the inner shell from the Gobato carcass and opened it while protecting the contents. The sphere of circe inside was big. It weighed more than twenty pounds.

Flint, who prepared the circe from their first alien victim, said, "Slicing it and vacuum drying it without freezing it preserves it best." They moved the circe to the kitchen and prepared it into two thousand pieces.

He added, "We'll package each piece, and identify our product with these holographic logo stickers." He laid out an envelope with several sheets of stick-on holographic logos, and a box of small plastic bags. "Put one portion of circe in each bag. Stick the logos on so they will tear when opened. That will make it obvious we have the real stuff in case someone tries to pirate our product. The plastic bags will seal them so they don't smell or trigger contamination sensors."

Flint ordered, "Stop at Stardust and get the promissory notes from Truman. Then make the exchange with the Gondwanians and return to Stardust where we will divide the loot."

Dillon came out of the security office and asked, "Is this legal? Will the law give us trouble?"

"Big D gave me his stamp of approval, and I have the transfer papers giving me legal right to mine this planet. I'll put copies in the network cloud so you can access them. Just the same, avoid publicity because if Earth authority finds out the truth, we'll be in trouble."

"People will ask where we got this. What should we say?"

"Say the circe came from a rare plant that grows in the out-world but don't tell them where. Tell no one how we got this stuff, not your families and not your friends."

Thunderbolt answered, "Don't worry. We know our trade."

"We don't want more partners. Truman, Yvette, Dillon, Gloria, and I have hacking C-chips so no one will give us trouble. If anyone presses for more information, send them to one of us. Truman is the enforcer."

The pirates gave a slight shudder and took a step back because Truman led the original pirates with strict and sometimes ruthless authority. No one crossed him and lived to talk about it. With the modified C-chip, he could read people's thoughts and control them. He seemed invincible.

"What do we do about her, Glenn, and the other straights?" A pirate asked, referring to Ligeia.

Flint answered, "We'll take her with us for now. I can persuade her to join us, and if I can't, we'll throw her in with the bush." The pirates laughed at that thought, remembering their injuries from their struggle when they threw Splint into a pit on Gondwana, and left it to die. Throwing such a small woman in with such a dangerous creature seemed hilarious to them.

Flint continued, "You can laugh, but remember Glenn killed three good pirates. He can find out our true identities through the U-net, so stay out of his way."

Thunderbolt asked, "Why don't we remove that U-net cube from the computer and break it."

"If we do that, the computer won't allow us to teleport in the starbeams. Star surfing will take too long.

"How do we keep Glenn and his troops from following us?"

"I'll send Truman a message right now. He'll hack the troops when they arrive and figure out a way to dispose of them. Dillon, can you hack the troops on this end. I'll stay if you need help."

"No, you go ahead. I can handle it. I'll join you later." Unknown to the pirates, Dillon planned to harvest another Gobato carcass for himself and sell it on Earth.

The pirates prepared a starbeam and left. Dillon hid in the security office before the four starbeams arrived with Madeline and the troops. Madeline said, "Dillon is not here. It is safe to turn your C-chips on," not realizing Dillon monitored them.

* The Cranberries, Zombie *

The starbeams docked and unloaded. The troops requested their pay so they could return to their starbeams and leave now that the battle was over. Madeline was the pay authority for the military forces so she paid them. She instructed, "All troops able to walk, form a line. After I pay you, board your starbeam. When you reach Stardust, you are dismissed."

This was not military procedure or what the troops wanted, but Dillon hacked their C-chips making them hurry. The troops threw their weapons and armor into the backup docking bay due to lack of storage space and left the dead in the hallways. The halls of the station became cluttered with dead soldiers.

"Madeline," Wanda said, "Help me load the chill-bags with Oliver and the other dead onto the departing starbeams. We can save some of them."

"How does that save them?"

"The bags cool the bodies and contain fluids that nourish the cells that are still alive. A small dose of hydrogen sulfide triggers them to hibernate. We replace the blood with a synthetic fluid that transports oxygen and kills bacteria as it moves through the bodies. Slow pumps in the bags change the pressure across seals at their diaphragms to keep the fluids circulating. Preserving them gives the doctors at the trauma clinic plenty of time to operate."

"Let's stabilize and teleport the seriously injured first."

They treated and loaded fifty of the wounded. Then they loaded fifteen chill-bags. Madeline never had an accurate count because Dillon hacked her C-chip to keep her loading the starbeams.

The U-net cubes provided almost instantaneous communication between the stars, which enabled beamers to automate the ballast adjustment and eliminated errors.

Dillon was alone after the starbeams teleported to Stardust.

*

Earlier on the battlefield, Raavn held a starbeam as it tried to speed away. When Gloria swooped down to save Glenn, she released the parachute. It blew into the face of the menace, but he ripped through it. However, the chute prevented him from reaching the starbeam before it lifted away, so he threw his zinger to loop web fibers around the back hatch door.

Raavn realized that his weight and the suction of his tube-feet could not hold the starbeam or pull it to the ground, and he was too big to fit inside the hatch if he climbed the fibers. He could cause a lot of trouble by hanging on the outside, but the humans would figure out how to dispose of him. He knew another way.

Gloria noticed a drag on her starbeam as she tried to pull away from the battle with Glenn. She feared that the Gobato somehow grounded them. She put the ion engines on a wide spread, fired the chemical takeoff thrusters, and pulled away with enough force to lift a small asteroid. The blast sent dust, sand, and pebbles into the air. Exhaust rising into the atmosphere spun small tornados. The strain of metal sounded throughout the ship, and then the ship ripped loose.

Raven detached two of his side segments and allowed the fibers to carry them away. The two segments stayed attached to each other and reconfigured themselves into a single organism, a gonangium-like-polyp.

The polyp pulled itself inside the starbeam by reeling in the web fiber before the hatch closed. It attacked Glenn, appearing as an angry three hundred and fifty-pound pressure cooker as it exfoliated mist and webbing from its pores, and lashed out with two tongues. It grabbed Glenn by the ankle and pulled him toward its two claw-ringed tube-feet.

* Kenny Loggins, Danger Zone, *

Gloria, unaware of the alien on board, believed all was well, returned the throttles back to normal, and set the craft on autopilot to rendezvous with the Space Station. She picked up a mini-doc, but before she went back to help Glenn and bind his wounds, an alarm sounded. The radar detected seven Gobato spaceships above them.

She steered the starbeam to dive into the atmosphere and set the autopilot on "align". The seven enemy ships plunged after her as she deployed the disruptor, aimed it, and fired. Their heavy meteor shields offered no defense against this weapon, and five of the pursuing ships exploded into balls of nuclear fire. Two ships survived, the lead ship and the trailing ship, but the trailing ship spun out of control after dodging the five fireballs. She aimed and fired again at the lead vessel, and it exploded.

As the space battle ended, Gloria noticed clanking and banging sounds near the back hatch door of the ship, so she went back to check, hoping the door was not detaching. As she approached the hatch connecting the front and rear sections of the starbeam, Glenn bolted through, grabbed at everything in his reach while two alien tongues from the polyp grabbed his foot and pulled him back into the cargo section. Glenn hollered to Gloria, "I can use yo help but don use the RA-gun inside the ship because it'll set the interior ablaze, and ze bullet might rip zrough ze hull."

"Not a problem. I have the right tool for this job," as she picked up a machete and sliced through the webbing it extruded.

Glenn threw wall panels, insulation, flooring, everything else near him at the polyp hoping to confuse or disable it, but the alien was unaffected.

He said, "I'll give zis animal wants it wants," as he grabbed a jimmy bar that was near the connecting hatch with one hand and drew his field knife with his other hand.

"Here is something else it wants," Gloria said as she slashed at the creature's tongues but missed. The distraction gave Glenn time to apply more force. He swung the jimmy bar with all of his strength at the center of the alien and jabbed his knife into it and drove it clear through.

"Gloria, open one of ze lockers behind the polyp."

"It won't go in." She answered.

Both of them slashed and hammered at the creature's tongues, but it continued to bolt forward pulling Glenn to pin him under its vampire sucker feet. "Yow, it's puncturing my foot wiz talons, and burning me wiz acid."

"Yes, I can smell your flesh burning."

"Zis isn't working. Go behind the locker door and get ready to slam it." He turned around and over the creature placing himself between it and the locker. As the alien bolted at him, Glenn dodged, and it flew past him and into the locker as Gloria slammed the door shut.

"I got it, but the door won't latch."

"Zat's because its tongues ares wrapped around my ankle. Slash ats it while I force the door." He braced against the door and used the jimmy bar to lever the door shut as Gloria slashed at the tongues with her machete.

"It shut. The door finally closed."

"Yeah and ze creature never let go. We severed its tongues. Keep the pressure on. Zere, I secured ze door. It's trapped."

"Phew, I thought that thing had us. I'm getting us out of here before another alien ship finds us." Gloria returned to the controls and hit the takeoff thrusters to move them out of the area fast.

Glenn turned on his C-chip. He did not notice that Gloria never turned off her chip. He said, "My foot and ankle are a ruin. How about you?" His ankle and foot were bruised and bleeding, and all of his joints seemed stretched from resisting the polyp's grasp. He used a handheld mini-doc, which stopped the bleeding, neutralized the acids, and reduced the pain.

"It got me while I tried to wedge it off of you."

"Stay there and I'll scan your injuries with a mini-doc. You have internal injuries. You'll need an auto-doc. Help me turn this ship back to Camelot."

"That monster kicked you around more than it kicked me. Why aren't you more injured?" She asked.

The autodoc removed my lower body organs and placed them in a chill-bag before I left Camelot. It installed a cylinder to balance my blood, provide glucose and electrolytes, support my diaphragm, and shield the organs in my chest. It's charged for twenty-four hours. With the reduced weight, I can move faster and I am less susceptible to injuries. The autodoc will re-implant my organs when I return. Show me how to operate this transporter,"

"Okay. This turns it. This sets the thrust. This button enables the autopilot. I'm setting it to take a wide avoidance path to keep us away from any alien ships in the area. The painkillers are kicking in; I want to go to sleep. Wake me when we are near the Space Station."

She fell back in her chair too tired to move. At this distance, hours would pass before they arrived at the Space Station.

"You came back for me, Gloria. I will never forget that. I owe you big-time."

"Just doing my job," she answered as she moaned in pain. Glenn gave her another painkiller, covered her eyes with a black veil, and she fell asleep.

Glenn and Gloria reached Camelot a few hours after the troops and pirates left, all except for Dillon. As they approached, the docking bay door opened automatically. Glenn tried to wake Gloria to land the craft, but she was unconscious and not asleep. The approach was too fast, so he used his C-chip to assist in the landing, but the C-chip had insufficient intelligence for a smooth landing. Glenn, instructed by his chip, rotated the craft, and fired the ion engines and take-off thrusters at full throttle to slow it. Seconds later, the starbeam crashed into the docking bay floor.

*

In the opposite direction from Earth, not all went well on Xanadu. The Green Team built a lighter than air teleporter platform and tethered it to Purgatory. They depended on this platform for communication and transportation. During tests the platform worked as planned, so the Green Team beamed to their base. While they were exploring to gather information about the Great Ferns, a storm threatened.

A gust of wind from the storm tore a tether loose from the lighter than air platform, so the staff pulled it down before the storm destroyed it. Then they abandoned the planet in shuttles in fear of the storm but left a shuttle near their base for the Green Team.

However, the storm damaged the shuttle and trapped the Green Team on the planet. The storm continued to rage for several weeks. After the storm had cleared, clouds and rain blocked communication, so the staff on Lonetree reported that the Green Team was missing.

The Green Team did not have the materials to repair the platform or the emergency escape shuttle, so they had to wait until rescue arrived. Mac did not use the insta-text chips to call Glenn or Ligeia for help because he knew this was a critical time in their mission.

The shelter at Purgatory was a large bunker designed to survive any storm as long as the pumps worked. A no-maintenance nuclear battery powered the pumps, so the Green Team was safe.

In the days that followed, they studied their samples of fossils, ferns, spores, and Razorroots to determine everything possible about the Great Ferns and their influence on other flora and fauna. The knowledge they gained from the lab tests led to striking discoveries, including aliens hiding in plain sight. A previously unrecognized and deadly enemy, the Great Ferns surrounded them.

*

Still on the moon, Kyleen received the report from Lonetree that Mac and the Green Team were missing. The records listed Xanadu as uninhabitable for humans, so Empire presumed they were dead.

Empire gave Kyleen temporarily authority for both of Mac's positions: the Acting Vice President of Interstellar Rescue for Empire Corporation and the Acting Secretary of the Exterior for the government. With this new authority, Kyleen accessed Mac's correspondence, especially the one labeled, "For the president's eyes only." She discovered that the pirates made a huge profit from their harvest of Gobato.

* ABBA, Fernando *

Kyleen planned, *Truman is making quite a name for himself. He is going to be caught but not until he kills Glenn. I need to slow him down and get Glenn somewhere safe. If I do this right, I will become rich in the process, but I need Mac to stay on Xanadu.* She sent an order to suspend support for Purgatory, and for all Empire personnel on Lonetree to return to Earth.

Her C-chip sent her voice through the U-net to Truman, "This is Kyleen Lespine. Am I talking to Major Truman Striker?"

"Yes. I thought you were in the Sol system?"

"I am. I'm using a U-phone app to contact you over the U-net. Are you on a secure line?"

"New technology never ceases to amaze me. It sounds like you are here except for the slight delay. Yes, I always use a secure line. Why are you calling?"

"This is a warning. I am holding a report naming you as a pirate with a long list of accusations."

"Thanks for the warning. Now I owe you. What can I do for you?"

Kyleen explained, "The Inspector General's report claims you discovered something new that cures aging, illness, and chronic injuries. The report claims you call it circe and sold it for one-hundred-million credits. You've made enough to be rich. Now it's my turn; I want eighty percent of your take."

"That is a lot. What if I say no?"

"If you don't like the deal, then I will forward the report to the proper channels, and you can start dodging the law."

"No, no, don't do that." Truman begged, "I'll cut you in. Will you take sixty percent?"

"This is not a negotiation. Eighty percent, take it or leave it and keep your hands off Space Marshal Hunter. If you harm him, I'll lose my job and you'll have to deal with someone else."

"Well, you don't give me much choice; I have to take it. And don't worry; I know better than to harm an agent of Empire."

"It's good doing business with you. I'll stay in touch." Kyleen put the report about the pirates in her private safe for insurance.

Truman was worried the government might close in on him, so he wanted the support of a top ranking government insider although Kyleen's price was too high. Truman agreed to the offer while planning to hack her C-chip when it was time for him to pay her.

Chapter 22: Stitch in Time

* Meat Loaf, Anything For Love But That *

The starbeam returning to Camelot with Glenn and Gloria hit the docking bay floor with a bang that tore the shock absorbers out. It bounced up, hit the far wall, bounced back to the floor again, and spun to a stop. The magnetic skids kept it from bouncing back into space. Dillon heard the noise and saw the docking on a monitor but stayed hidden so Glenn would not arrest him.

As Glenn carried Gloria out of the docking bay, he noticed that he dented the starbeam and the docking bay but both appeared to be functional. The designers of the station had the good foresight to install the landing bays in the lowest gravity section of the station, and to install a medical clinic in a nearby section in case of emergencies like this one. Glenn put Gloria on a fold-down bed in the clinic and turned on the auto-doc. The auto-doc went to work, and instructed Glenn, the attendant, to place an oxygen mask on her face, and install a catheter and intravenous lines.

On the auto-doc control panel, Glenn selected: Wounded soldier, unconscious, cuts, broken bones, bleeding, injuries sustained six hours ago, weight, height, age, and female.

After treatment was underway, Glenn lay on a cot for treatment from an adjacent auto-doc. The machines used "Vein Splice" to repair severed veins and arteries, set and fused broken bones with "Bone Tack", and used "Mop and Mend" to remove displaced fluids and treat bruises, abrasions, and blisters.

Glenn's autodoc numbed his body, opened a chill-bag, and re-implanted his abdominal organs. After it closed his wounds with "Stitch in Time." ("Stitch in Time" clamped soft tissues such as torn skin, muscles, tendons, and ligaments while applying fast-acting surgical glue.), it restored full feeling and reported, "Treatment complete. Return to light duty."

However, the auto-doc treating Gloria said, "Remove spleen."

Glenn responded, "I cannot do that. I'm not a doctor."

"Then send the patient to a hospital with these intravenous fluids and continue until the start of surgery. The patient must be in surgery by 19:00 hours or life expectancy will decrease 30% per hour after that. What hospital do you want me to contact to prepare for the operation?"

"There is none," Glenn shouted as if the machine already knew that. He wanted it to do more for her.

The computer responded, "Place patient in a chill-bag, and store until a hospital is available." A drawer containing chill-bags opened on one wall.

"I am not doing that. I am not putting her in a bag. Can I talk to a human?" His shout caused Gloria to stir.

"There are no humans with medical training living on this space station. Do you want me to download a human persona with medical training?"

Glenn thought a moment, and said, "Download Delphi from the Beehive."

The high-speed U-net allowed the auto-doc to download Delphi in a few minutes. She said, "Glenn my love, the auto-doc files say that you were injured, but I am glad you are on the mend. How can I help?"

"Delphi, good to hear your voice. Do not treat my injuries. Instead, help this female. She saved my life. Her name is Gloria. The auto-doc wants me to put her in a chill-bag, but I can't do that. Can you help me?"

"This auto-doc is limited, but I can tell she is in danger and needs an operation. If you tell the computer to give me a direct C-link to your cerebellum, then I can perform the operation using your hands."

Glenn answered, "I did not know that was possible. Can you do that without impressing your emotions on me? Your emotions are too strong for me to bear."

"I will make you numb so you won't feel a thing except you will be conscious and you can regain control at any time."

"You have my approval, proceed."

Delphi, using Glenn as a host, applied a local anesthetic to Gloria. She made an incision to a precise depth while observing the MRI screen, and continued until the spleen was exposed. Glenn was amazed at the skill and speed of his hands. She selected, used and discarded medical devices and tools at a speed that seemed a blur. Delphi applied "bone tack" to stabilize the spleen instead of removing it and used 'stitch in time' to stop the bleeding and to close the incision. Then she disconnected from Glenn and ordered, "Do not move the patient. Keep her calm, at zero-G, and leave her connected to this auto-doc for six weeks. She is sleeping normally now and not in a coma."

Glenn was free to move his hands again. He looked at them in disbelief and exhaled a long sigh of relief. Gloria's color returned, and her breathing was natural.

"You caught me in the middle of something, but this was more important of course. I must go back to the Beehive now. Don't hesitate to call when you need help."

He felt her kiss and her voice faded as she sang, "Say a little prayer for me."

Then he noticed the clinic and everything in it, including Gloria and himself, was red from all the blood they both lost, but he was too tired to clean it. He looked at her and saw she woke but struggled to keep her eyes open.

"My pain is gone. Who was that? Did she doctor me?"

"That was Delphi, an AI. Let's sleep," he said, and she nodded and closed her eyes. Glenn told the auto-doc they were sleeping, and to dim the lights and wake him in six hours.

*

On Stardust, the starbeams carrying the troops and pirates arrived at the teleporter terminal four days after they left Camelot. Truman intercepted the troops, hacked their C-chips to keep them controlled, and directed them to take tranquilizers and to sleep.

While the soldiers slept, Truman erased all the information their C-chips recorded during the last month to remove all incriminating evidence. He replaced the data with his version of what happened.

As he did this, Glasseyes asked, "What will we do when they wake up? They outnumber us."

"We will send them to the planet, Valhalla, as an offering to Odin."

The pirates laughed and cheered. They idolized this Viking god. When spacers installed teleporter terminals between Gondwana and Sirius a century earlier, they lost a few travelers, so the beamers installed radio beacons on all beam-cans to trace them. The beamers traced many of them to Gondwana. They knew this planet was a quantum attractor, but they did not find all the lost.

Years later, the beamers detected signals from their beacons coming from a distant location. They solved the mystery: an unknown planet, where an alien operated a quantum trap, and sometimes redirected teleporter traffic. Mainly, it trapped those who liked combat. The beamers named the planet Valhalla but did not send a rescue ship because it was too far away, and the rescue would be dangerous.

The pirates reequipped several of the starbeams and programmed them for a flight to that mysterious planet. They carried the sedated troops onboard and smashed the controls so the troops could not turn the starbeams back to Stardust.

Truman said, "Here is a plaque we will send with our offering. It reads short and sweet, 'We offer these hostages to you to help finance your invasion. Odin, remember us after Earth falls.' Odin will remember and reward each who signs it." The Emerald Pirates lined up and signed the plaque. Then, Truman placed it in the lead starbeam.

"We better load chill-bags, or they might never make it," Truman said and the pirates laughed again.

Truman used nuclear batteries that were near their expiration, to prevent the troops from using the chill-bags for a return trip. Then the pirates launched the starbeams.

Unknown to the pirates, Wanda turned off her C-chip, so they were unable to hack her. She snuck past them and found Elroy. Elroy helped her hide on the last starbeam with a beam-can, a folded teleporter lens, and a transponder. She planned to rescue the mercenaries when the pirates were out of the way.

*

Back on Camelot, Glenn did not remember falling asleep. Then lightning bolts in his head woke him.

"Auto-doc, what is the status of this wakeup?"

"This wakeup is the one you requested."

"What is the condition of the patients?"

"The female is sleeping naturally, and her condition is on the mend, but she must stay inactive. You are awake, your condition is on the mend, and you can return to light duty."

Glenn stood, walked to Gloria's bedside, and interrogated her C-chip without waking her. He discovered her C-chip was a month old. *If Mac gave her a new chip, it should be several months old, and her original chip should be decades old. One of the pirates must have given her this chip, probably Dillon.*

He tried to examine the rest of the features and compared them with his chip, but it signaled an error message "interrogation blocked." Glenn did not like her having a pirated chip, but he would have to find her original chip if he wanted to restore her to normal. He searched through her private belongings, which were minimal like most people who travel in space, but he did not find any chips. He dropped the matter and decided to ask her about it later.

The auto-docs cleaned the room, and sponge washed Glenn and Gloria when they were asleep. Glenn noticed they missed a few areas, so he showered. Then he filled a bowl with water, took a clean sponge and towel, and began cleaning Gloria without waking her.

Her auto-doc asked, "What is this activity?"

"I am cleaning the female. You missed a few areas. Lower your voice so you don't wake her."

"How is this volume?"

"Better."

"You need a chaperone if you wish to continue."

Glenn said, "Download Delphi from the Beehive if she is not busy."

* Dido, White Flag *

The high-speed U-net allowed the auto-doc to download Delphi in a few minutes. She said, "Glenn my love, I have lots of time now. How can I help?"

"Delphi, I am alone and need assistance."

"Ah, yes. This auto-doc is limited, but I can tell Gloria is on the mend."

"I am trying to clean her, but I need someone to help me, so I don't irritate an injury."

"I don't see any severe injuries on her face or head. You can wash those."

As Glenn gently washed her, he said, "She is so beautiful, this innocent child resting here."

"Yes, I can tell her skin is soft and firm. Her muscle tone is excellent, like an athlete."

"She is strong because she trained hard. This is her first assignment and adjusting to it was difficult for her, but she met the challenge. She deserves better than to be racked up here."

Delphi answered, "I feel your emotion through the auto-doc. You are proud of her."

"Her hair is so perfect," he said while he rinsed her head.

Delphi intensified her holographic image and said, "Yes, did you notice my auburn hair?"

I need Delphi as a friend, but I was too forward when we first met. I treated her like one of the Bees, but now I see she is not a Bee. How do I tell her to back off without insulting her? "You are better than a friend to me. You are like a sister."

"Human emotions are not logical. I will try to be a sister and not be jealous."

Gloria stirred but was still asleep.

She understood, but I will say something negative to cool her down. "That awful snake tattoo seems alive every time she moves."

"I cannot see it. This auto-doc's sensors see infrared, and cannot see tattoos."

"I wish I had your eyes. I hate that snake. Can I rip it off of her?"

"No, you can't. Gloria and the snake are one." Delphi said.

"You stated that well."

When Glenn finished cleaning Gloria's face, hair, head, and neck, Delphi took the sponge and bowl of water and washed the rest of her. Delphi controlled the auto-doc's robotic arms with a skill and speed that amazed Glenn.

"Do you love Gloria or do you love me?" Delphi paused.

"I love Ligeia."

"Is she beautiful like me?"

"No, she is plain, but she has something beyond physical beauty, she has a kindred spirit."

"Where is she?"

He checked the computer, and it reported she returned to Stardust with the troops. "That is strange. She left without me." Glenn was so concerned about surviving the battle he overlooked everything else.

"The cleaning is complete. Was Ligeia seriously injured?" Delphi cleaned the sponge and bowl and put them away.

"No, hardly a scratch according to the computer." *Her questions are leading me. She knows more than she is letting on.*

Delphi said, "If that were me, I would not have left you."

"Return to Sirius so the auto-doc can continue its tasks," he ordered, but realized he was too sharp.

She answered in a sarcastic tone, "Oh, ah, yes. I will do that. You believe monogamy is wood and I am silicon. Call on me anytime and I will return to help you."

"Forgive my sharpness. I'll remember you helped us." She blew him a kiss as her hologram faded.

Glenn tried to contact Ligeia, but there was no response. *She probably turned off her C-chip when we were being hacked.* He attempted to contact Madeline and the other troops on the U-net. They did not respond. *How can everyone be out of contact? Is the net shut down?*

Then he called Flint, who responded, "Ligeia is safe, unharmed, and with me. The battle and the retreat exhausted her, so she went to sleep. The troops are out of contact because they are teleporting to their home stations."

Glenn said, "Military procedures require the troops to remain until I dismiss them. Does Madeline have any reason for this deviation?"

Flint answered quickly. "They thought you were lost in action, so Madeline took command and dismissed the troops."

Glenn thought his answer was strange. "They did not give me enough time. I was just a few hours behind them."

"That's right, but that's not what they did."

"Have Ligeia contact me after she wakes."

"Be assured, I will do that."

Glenn did not trust Flint, but he had to accept his answer for now.

* Joe Walsh, Life's Been Good *

In the atrium on Stardust, the pirates celebrated their success.

"You should have seen us," Flint bragged. "Dillon hacked Tumbleweed's C-chip, causing it to start the battle, and he hacked Glenn to keep it going. We had the Gobato right in front of us. We killed several without destroying the circe by using light arms like we planned. We had to hurry and leave because Glenn was in the way, but the one we got was big. Look at all the doses we have."

The pirates showed Truman the pouches of circe. "You did well. What were your losses?"

"Glenn killed three of us and the Gobato killed several. The ones the Gobato killed are in chill-bags in a hospital on Gondwana. The doctors think they can save them."

"Next time, we will go without Glenn. A drink to the deceased, may they rest in peace until we all meet on Valhalla." Truman raised his drink as a toast.

A small group of pirates did not raise their drinks but demanded. "The stores are out of raw meat."

"Yeah, we need meat."

"Gondwana is close and they have a large population. Let's go there get some fresh raw meat."

Truman was surprised, *Those who took circe are stronger, but they don't enjoy the parties and gambling any more. We used to talk late into the night about our adventures and our lost comrades. Now they think only about eating, and don't even morn those who were lost.* He answered, "Everyone who does not need raw meat get on the Starhawk and I will take you to Gondwana and we will sell the circe. Flint, Audrey, and Elroy will stay here and protect Stardust."

Reddragon asked, "Won't it take weeks for us to reach Gondwana. Why don't we teleport?"

"I upgraded the Starhawk to starbeam class. We can travel to Gondwana in a few hours by putting it in a large beam-can. Then we will take a runabout to Gondwana. That is faster for a large crew with cargo."

Thunderbolt, who waited with the pirates that spoke of eating raw meat said, "What about us?"

Truman answered, "Yvette, adjust the teleporter so these men can star surf to Gondwana without delay. Aim it near a large town that is far away from the park-and-ride so they can get raw meat without causing panic. Then return here and get on the Starhawk."

"Yeah, aim it at the pit jails. That is a good spot to harvest some meat," Glasseyes suggested.

"After you feast, find us at the rendezvous," Truman said.

*

After the Starhawk dispatched, the pirates who waited to star-surf were drunk and dared each other to fight "the monster in the pit." Thunderbolt adjusted the coordinates to Splinter's pit and said, "That Razorroot was mad and by now it must be hungry. It will rip apart anyone who goes in there with it. How about you Glasseyes, are you brave enough to go in there and challenge it?"

He answered, "That lady who wants to rat us out, let her fight it."

Throwing Ligeia into the pit seemed hilarious to them, but Thunderbolt answered, "I know where we can get some fresh meat right now."

"Where?" They all asked.

"Ligeia."

"Yes, Ligeia."

Mouths dripping with saliva, they rushed to the infirmary, but Ligeia was gone. She escaped the autodoc earlier and was waiting for a chance to star surf to freedom.

While the pirates were in the infirmary looking for her, she stepped onto the teleporter and star surfed to Gondwana. The pirates heard the noise and returned to the teleporter.

One of them read the register on the teleporter, "Oh, it was Ligeia."

"Did she get away?"

"Not if we go after her," And they beamed to the same coordinates.

Ligeia did not have time to read or change the coordinates on the teleporter. When she touched down on Gondwana, she recognized the lights from a town in the distance and knew where she was; near the pit jails. She had a hunch and ran to the nearest pit. Her hunch was true, through the darkness she saw the outline of a razorroot in one corner. She jumped in and shook the razorroot. It did not move so she hid behind it.

The pirates arrived one at a time at the pit. They peered down on Splinter until all were present. The Razorroot did not attack or even move to their disappointment. They threw rocks at Splinter, which had no effect, so they left saying, "It must be dead. Let's go find that lady before she runs away."

After a careful search, they found nothing so the pirates went to the town. They raided pit jails along the way, and butchered and ate the prisoners.

*

Reddragon lead Truman and the pirates to the Gondwanians who agreed to make the exchange. The exchange went well except during the months that passed from the first distribution of circe, the news reached other star systems. Their injured and sick traveled to Gondwana, surrounded the pirates, and demanded more circe. Truman was afraid they would mob his pirates and take their G-coins, so he put his zombie pirates in front who held the crowd back, but did not scare them away. The mob was impressed by strength and ferociousness of the zombies and desired the circe more. Truman agreed to meet their demands if they gave him promissory notes.

No one, not even the officials, was overly curious where the circe came from because they knew asking too many questions might scare the pirates away.

As the pirates returned to the teleporter above Gondwana, they danced and sang in delight. Reddragon jumped in the air and said, "Selling this stuff was easy. Look at all the G-coins we have. They must be worth millions of credits. Let's return to Dearth and get more circe to sell."

They all agreed even though they had enough credits to lead a long and happy life.

Chapter 23: Alien Referendum

Jefferson Starship, Miracles *

After the meat-eating pirates left the pit; Ligeia began to notice pain in the back of her neck and removed her C-chip. The chip appeared burnt and cracked.

So that is how they controlled me, she though, amazed and disappointed. She slowly and carefully crawled out from behind Splinter, and placed the C-chip reverently in a corner. "May Ligeia rest in peace."

She tried to stand up but fell back to the floor. Bruises and lacerations covered her. She checked herself and found no broken bones.

She stood again, slower this time, and looked around the room. It had four flat concrete walls, a concrete floor with a one-inch plugged drain in one corner, and a twenty-foot-high concrete ceiling with a three foot wide barred opening. Scratch marks on the bars indicated that a previous occupant tried to escape.

She left the hatch unlatched when she jumped in and that gave her hope.

She returned to Splinter. However, the plant did not respond to her touch. *Whoever wrestled it into this dungeon broke and tore its roots. Bloodstains indicate Splint fought them and they did not fare too well. These trees can hibernate until concrete crumbles, but I cannot wait that long. I need to wake it now.*

Splinter's computer link and voice translator were working. Ligeia tested it, but the plant did not respond. She continued trying, "I afri uh GHoont."

The computer's translator started training her how to speak. After several hours, she spoke legibly enough for the computer to translate. "Splint, I am a friend of Glenn Hunter."

Splinter stirred and responded, "I am hungry. Crap on me."

Razorroots can nourish themselves on human waste so she relieved herself on the plants roots. After Splint regained enough strength, it spoke, "Now I will help you. Glenn appointed me as his deputy space marshal."

She asked, "Do you have an outside signal? Are you on the net?"

"No, but I am receiving an unknown signal. My computer says it comes from you."

"That must be the texting cube implanted under my skin. It links to Mac but it is useless unless I reinsert my C-chip. Wait and I'll try to use it." She picked up the chip. It looked damaged, but she inserted it anyway. It did not work and caused her to bleed again, so she removed it.

She sat and thought for a while. Not giving up hope, she had a wild idea. "Splint, I'll give you the access codes to my texting cube. See if your computer's wireless can access it. If zat works, then you can contact Mac, who will contact Glenn, and Glenn can talk back the same way."

The plant answered after a pause, "I believe I am accessing your cube."

To her relief, Splint's computer answered with Mac's voice, "I understand your situation. I'll link you to Glenn's insta-text chip."

*

She sent a message, "I'm Ligeia. I am talking through Mac and Splint because my cerebral chip broke. Splint and I need rescue."

Splint's computer answered with Glenn's voice, "Rescue? Lt. Flint told me you were safe. What happened to you? Are you all right?"

Ligeia answered, "Glenn, I cannot tell you how happy I am to hear from you. Thank good fortune you are all right. I was restrained on the auto-doc earlier, and then the pirates took me and threw me into a pit where they caged Splint. You were right; Dillon hacked our C-chips and controlled us. The pirates used me to harvest a Gobato before I knew what they were doing. When I resisted, they tried to force me, but I became unconscious. Then they locked me up with Splint, who may have been here for weeks. They imprisoned us on Gondwana but we can beam out of here with your help. We can escape."

Glenn insta-texted back, "I want to help you but you are eleven light-years away, and I am not a beamer. I don't even know how I beamed here let alone how to beam you out of there."

She texted back, "Splint and I can star-surf to Stardust as long as that lens is aligned. Contact Flint and ask if the coast is clear. I don't want the pirates to take us captive again. They are so hungry for red meat that they are eating human flesh. When Splint and I reach Stardust we will wait for you, and then we will beam to Lonetree and rescue Mac and the Green Team on Xanadu. Splint and I cannot do it without your help."

Glenn insta-texted, "Eating human flesh? Are they zombies? And did you say Mac is in trouble? I've been out of contact too long. I don't know the current events. Doesn't Mac want us to reclaim Dearth for the Razorroots?"

Splint answered, "Ligeia told me that Tumbleweed was killed. I am the next in command of the Razorroots. I have no desire to conquer space or to reclaim Dearth. I want only to return to my home."

Mac injected, "Then it is settled. Glenn, transport Splint to Xanadu, rescue me and the Green Team, and I'll consider your mission to be complete. The Inspector will take care of things on Camelot. Don't trust Kyleen. I expected her to rescue us, but she withdrew our rescue, and she may be sympathetic to the pirates. I'm safe for the moment, but I am cut off from the net, so you are the only ones I can communicate with."

"How can I get there?"

"Do not try to pilot a starbeam. Camelot sent an alert when you crashed Gloria's starbeam. You are not a pilot and travel by ship will take one-hundred years."

Ligeia said, "Glenn, we can be there in a month if you star-surf to Stardust."

Mac continued, "That gives me and the Green team time to finish our research. We can last more than a month. I cannot tell you how important this is. The fossil record we found on this planet describes a past we did not expect. It tells that a virus infects our chromosomes. This virus weakens us and causes us to age. Our new mission is to develop inoculations and send them to Earth, and that has the highest priority."

Glenn answered, "The pirates think they found the cure here. They call it circe, but the price may be too high. They get it by butchering the Gobato."

"And it turns people who eat it into Zombies," Ligeia injected.

Mac explained, "I discovered the Gobato connection from my research here. Circe provides temporary relief with dangerous side effects. The answer is here. I need you here."

Star-surfing to Stardust worried Glenn, not to mention beaming more than one-hundred light-years from Stardust to Lonetree. That was beyond worry; it made Glenn's stomach twist into knots. He wondered, *Did anyone other than Ligeia ever try to beam that distance? Did they live?* But he had no other plan, he would have to do it.

Glenn asked, "Will the pirates overwhelm the Inspector?"

Mac answered, "He has your military force to help him, and he has orders to assume command at Camelot. When I am back on the net, I'll issue warrants to arrest the Emerald Pirates including Truman. Then I'll put Kyleen on suspension until she reports to me and explains her actions. I'll send an all points bulletin to isolate anyone who takes circe until we fully understand its affects."

Glenn wondered, *Where are Madeline and the troops? The Inspector will need them.* He agreed to beam to save Mac and insta-text, "I'll have to leave Gloria here because she is too injured to travel. The auto-doc sent for a doctor, and he should arrive on the next starbeam. I need to do a few things before I leave."

Ligeia interrupted and insta-text through Mac to Glenn: "Contact Flint and have him get me out of here NOW. Due to this planet's rotation, we are losing teleporter alignment."

Glenn answered, "Okay. I'll tell him right now. Bye."

*

Glenn worried about Mac trapped on an inhospitable planet where aliens might turn against him at any time. *Mac is my point of redemption. Without Mac, Kyleen will force me to retire or send me to jail. It seems like too much can go wrong.*

Glenn U-phoned Flint and explained the situation. Flint responded, "I don't know how to operate the teleporter in the single ended mode (a new feature added to the prototypes). Wait and I'll find a beamer to help me."

Flint paid a beamer to help him and to keep their secret from the other pirates. He relayed a message to Ligeia through Glenn, Mac, and Splint, "The link is too weak to pull you out."

She answered, "Dither the antenna. The vectors have changed due to the planet's rotation."

The lens aligned. "That worked. We have them," Flint reported to Glenn.

When Ligeia and Splinter arrived on Stardust, she hugged the tree and said, "Without you, Splint, I would never get out of that pit."

It answered, "Yes, I know."

Flint gave her a breather. After she realigned the teleporter so the zombie pirates could not use it and so Glenn could star-surf, Flint carried her to an auto-doc.

"No, just put me in a comfort booth. I am afraid that autodoc will trap or sedate me."

Splinter refreshed by basking under Ruby in the atrium.

Later, Flint hid them in a vacated room near the machine shop because they would be in danger if the pirates discovered them.

*

After Glenn was sure Ligeia and Splint were safe, he ate a meal from the vending machines. Then he rolled a portable food synthesizer up to arm's reach of Gloria's bed and stocked it to last several weeks.

"Gloria, Mac is trapped and I have to rescue him," He told her. "Here is the password to disable the self-destruct in case you accidentally trigger it. I sent for a doctor so you won't be alone for very long."

"Okay, get some books for me to read from the waiting room next to the clinic."

He returned to Gloria with the books and kissed her goodbye. She said, "I forgot; I ejected the moderator rods on my starbeam when I rescued you. You better replace them before the core of the nuclear generator runs out of coolant and explodes."

"I'll do that right now."

While he replaced the moderator rods, Kyleen sent him a private and encrypted text message. *"Mackley is reported lost or dead, and I am in charge. You will report to me and no one else. You must return to the Moon Base or resign where you are with full retirement. Also, I intercepted the video of you executing the Razorroot, Tumbleweed. I'll hold it in safekeeping for you."*

He realized Kyleen held the video as blackmail.

Glenn responded to Kyleen, *"I just talked to Mac using my texting cube. A storm knocked out his conventional communications, but he is alive and well. He asked for rescue, so send a rescue team to Xanadu. If you need to talk to him for verification, I can link you to him through my insta-text chip."*

There was no immediate reply, but Glenn knew a reply would be forthcoming. Kyleen was seldom silent.

Chapter 24: Terracotta Warriors

* YES, Owner of a Lonely Heart *

Glenn left the clinic while Gloria slept safely on the auto-doc. Then, he put a probe in orbit to communicate with the Gobato and to regain their trust. He programmed the probe to scramble its data and self-destruct if the Gobato tampered with it.

The probe repeated his text message every fifteen minutes: "I am Space Marshal Glenn Hunter. Lawless persons started this war. Empire Corporation sent me to assist you, and not to fight you. I wish to surrender this planet to you. The Razorroots, the miners, and all the troops have left. Only a small group of caretakers is here. I will report to my government that the Gobato occupy this planet and you should own it."

After three hours, Raavn texted on all channels, "I proclaim this planet and all of space is the property of the Gobato. Your species will retreat to your home planet as the Razorroots did, and the Gobato will decide when and to what extent earthlings may occupy space."

Glenn was busy releasing agroponic unit #2, so he used the virtual keyboard in his C-chip to text back, "Our government will assign a representative to appear in our courts on your behalf. Wait here while our courts reach a decision. If the Razorroots win in court, you will still have two years before the courts take action. If no one challenges you, then this planet is yours."

Raavn answered, "I'll purge you so others will not absorb your unorthodox thoughts or suffer from your memories of losses, failures, and cowardly acts in battle. Who attacked us when we wished to negotiate peace, destroyed our farm, mutilated one of my clan, turned another into clay, and killed many more; you are an abomination. You cannot compensate for the damage you caused."

Glenn dropped the agroponics unit down to the farm in case the Gobato changed their minds and decided to use it. He was unaware Blackbark was hiding in this unit. "I am showing good will by sending you a agroponics unit that you can use to replant the farm. We can recover the lives of most of the Gobato, who have fallen. Our chill-bags will maintain them until our doctors can stitch their wounds. Let us help you, and we will undo this injustice. I am sorry for your losses, and I hope this will convince you that Empire Corporation is a worthy ally."

Raavn rejected the offer and rambled on.

Glenn received a message on the U-net. It was about Ligeia so he hung up on Raavn. He needed to find out if Ligeia was safe.

* Toto, Africa *

On Dearth, Raavn ordered a funeral ceremony to preserve the memories of the Gobato who died in battle. This ceremony would strengthen the weak and heal the injured.

The damage caused to the internal organs of the fallen aliens was so extensive they barely offered enough marrow to treat Raavn and his clan. As a result, Raavn allowed only Pathfinders to participate in the funeral ceremony. The clans he excluded were unhappy with his decision.

In the days after the battle, Gobato continued arriving on Dearth but found the planet in disorder to their disappointment. Raavn led them to this place and brought them out of hibernation. Now, they could not continue their journey because landing on this planet left them with too little fuel, food, and other supplies.

Raavn no longer trusted Vicar Eaau. He watched her movements and dug tunnels under areas she frequented. He watched and saw Nirrav approach her. They were above one of his tunnels so he crawled beneath them and listened to their vibrations.

Vicar Eaau asked Nirrav, the leader of the Blockbuster Clan, "What do you think about Raavn?"

"Raavn double thinks. He is both a dissident and a disciple."

"Impossible. I burned his polyp to purge him." They both shook when she said those words.

"Then where is he?" Nirrav asked. "Has he changed? Raavn led us here, and he has not provided for us since we landed. We need new leadership."

Raven suppressed his desire to punch through the ground above him and confront these traitors, *I cannot reveal myself or they will deny their words and become more secretive.*

"What about Elmurr, his brother?"

"Elmurr is no better, and the King will resist such a change, but not if you ask for me. I am the oldest son of the king. He will favor me."

"You have convinced me," the Vicar concluded. "I will talk to the King when he arrives."

"If we wait much longer some of us will starve," Nirrav warned.

"The recon ships reported that the humans provided a agroponics unit to replant our farm. Doesn't it work?"

"I don't know. Raavn ordered us not to use human technologies."

Of course I told them not to eat food provided by the humans. We are at war so that food must be poisoned, Raavn thought.

"He cannot object after I talk to the King. Go to the agroponics unit, and gather as many plant leaves as you can. Feed the starving and give the rest to the King when I give you the signal."

"As you wish, Vicar."

Since they oppose me, I'll let them kill themselves.

A few days later, the King, Vermn, arrived. Eaau followed his slime trail, found him, and said, "You're Majesty, welcome to Dearth. My apologies, you do *not like this planet.*"

"How do you know that?"

"You walk *on only six of* your *tube-feet to avoid contaminating the rest of them.*"

"Yes. The soil is dry and salty. Where is the clover? Will plants grow here? Is this planet habitable? Why did we land here?"

"Please accept my humble answer. The green color of the soil fooled Raavn. He thought it was from plants, but this color is due to a mineral."

"Vicar, are you telling me we have no food?" The King asked.

"Aliens called Razorroots planted a farm to provide edible plants. They allied with other aliens we call puke tubes because they often vomit when we approach them."

"Tell me more about the Razorroots and the pukes."

Eaau explained, "The Razorroots carry an irresistible fern fragrance. They are the right size for a wrap-around meal. Their leaves crunch, their pulp provides good bulk, and sap saturates their inner fibers. We discard the shards of sharp silica that line their root edges, which is their only defense. They fled the planet to prevent us from eating them."

"Stop it. Stop stimulating my taste buds and tell me about the pukes. Did we eat any of the pukes? Were they edible?" The King asked as his tube-feet excreted digestive slime.

"No, but there is a rumor they want to eat us."

"Preposterous. Squelch that rumor, and rub it from memory."

She complied, "I will do that. The pukes, who call themselves humans, are the dominate species, and they are drawn to conflict. Puking and bleeding are their natural defenses."

Eaau withdrew her tongue and lowered her trunk as she vibrated, "I hesitate to tell you, but my station demands I tell all. We fought two battles, and we face the danger of another attack from these aliens. The Razorroots killed some of us in the first battle. The humans invaded this planet, so we attacked them in the second battle and suffered more losses. We won both battles."

The King asked in shock, "Do you mean killed? Why didn't we push them out of the way?"

"They don't fight like that. Raavn confronted them, which resulted in quite a mess. Their puke burns like acid and has a persistent and offensive odor. Their blood is worse. We marked areas of blood splatter and puke with black sand and sound pebbles so that we can avoid them."

"The sound pebbles seem to be everywhere. That is a lot of puke. In fact, this whole planet vibrates strangely."

"When another tremor hammer arrives, we will fracture the planet's mantle and retune it."

"Why do we have losses? These small creatures cannot push us."

"The pukes used hideous weapons and killed eleven warriors in battle, destroyed seven more in space ships, turned one into clay, and mutilated Treeeater."

"How many legions of them did we kill? What are their losses?"

Eaau explained, "The Pathfinders ate the Razorroots before we counted them. Raavn claims we killed one-hundred pukes, but we do not have a single body to show for it, just a few clay statues, the broken remains of their weapons, a pile of ashes we cannot identify, and the ashes of a Razorroot."

"Why did we incinerate the Razorroot? Aren't they food?"

"We didn't kill that one. The pukes did that."

"I consider it strange they kill their allies. Do they have closure for their memories?"

"None of the aliens have closure, and they do not care."

The King shook in disbelief, "That's barbaric. Can Raavn explain this? Why didn't he report to me? By now he must have crossed my slime trail."

"Raavn is in mourning because the humans harvested the marrow of Treeeater, and we have no closure for his memories. The human weapons destroy marrow, so there is no closure for most of the others who died fighting the pukes."

While he listened to their conversation underground and out of sight, Raavn realized, *I must go above ground, approach the King, and explain my actions.*

As Raavn approached, the King did not listen to his greeting, but leaned back on his rear appendage as he vibrated in shock, "I will not permit humans to steal the memories of generations of Gobato. We must find these earthlings, and destroy them. Harvest the farm. After we feed and refuel our ships, we will attack."

Raavn answered, "We cannot destroy the humans because we do not know where they are. We only know they are hiding somewhere in orbit."

"Raavn exhausted our fuel and supplies fighting them. We use all our new fuel to search for their invisible base." Eaau continued, "We cannot harvest the farm because the pukes destroyed it. The pukes gave us an agroponics unit to replant the farm, but Raavn ordered us not to use their technology."

"Vicar, do you have something for me?"

Eaau offered a morsel of marrow taken from one of the fallen. The King consumed it with great reverence and recovered the memories. The memories of this fallen one spoke ill of Raavn.

"The actions of these aliens are irrational," the King decided. "We are much too vulnerable. I will overrule Raavn. Our new directives are to develop and conserve fuel and food. Keep the clans dispersed in case of another attack, and maintain a watch."

The King, Eaau, and Raavn went to the agroponics unit and found Nirrav examining it.

"Is it of any use to us?" The King asked.

"Several vibrator tables, usually used for sifting soil, seem to speak. A human computer is sending a repeated message." Nirrav answered.

"Stand in-between the tables, and tell me what it says."

Nirrav walked between the tables, careful not to touch them. He vibrated a reply, "It talks but does not listen. It explains how to use this unit to replant the farm."

"Why would they tell us that? Aren't we at war?" The King asked.

"They are sending a message saying they never wanted to fight us but coerced each other into it. The pukes battle each other, which makes their social structure impossible to understand."

Raavn warned, "I am sure the humans want to poison us. Do not eat their food."

Vermn ignored the warning. He wanted to push Raavn out of the camp because of his mistakes, but resisted that temptation, and kept the idea to himself. An impulsive action on his part might further disillusion the already disheartened Gobato, and Raavn still had followers.

As Nirrav moved out of his way, the King stood between the vibrating tables and said, "Nirrav, your analysis is correct. They sound primitive. I think right now they will not attack us, but we will stay guarded. If they try to contact us, do what you can to calm them down. Do not attack them unless they attack us. This farming is something new to us, but it is worth our effort to learn it. Use whatever resources you need to replant the farm."

"Your smallest concerns are my most important tasks," They answered the King in unison.

*

Vermn, the King, called the clan leaders together.

They approached the King and the King asked, "Describe your battle with the humans."

Raavn bragged, "Your Majesty, you should have seen us in battle. We killed more than one-hundred puke tubes. I killed fifty of them. These are their remains."

Vermn leaned back on his rear leg to view the entire scene, "These statues of clay and this huge pile of broken weapons do not prove you killed any of those troops, and what about their memories. I would like to consume the morrow of at least one human to access their memories and understand more about them."

Raavn held his trunk low and answered, "I apologize to you, but they either fled or turned into Terracotta. They know nothing about battle etiquette."

Vicar Eaau added, "And Raavn waged war without consulting any of the clan leaders."

"Really! Raavn, you did not tell me this, and you did not negotiate peace."

"But I tried."

"You tried? Nirrav is negotiating peace as we talk. That shows why you needed to include the other clan leaders."

As he spoke, Nirrav arrived and offered a harvest of plants, which was enough to sustain them until the next larger crop matured. Raavn objected to eating alien food, but the King ignored his warnings.

After they had grazed, the clan leaders petitioned the King to remove Raavn as Chief and replace him with Nirrav.

Raavn vibrated a reply, "Those primitives had battle tactics far more barbaric than anything we experienced in our past. So recognize, I am not inept but faced these challenges in the best way possible."

The King answered, "Your best way was not forward thinking. Although your destiny bound you, you still carry the same responsibility. Your actions led to greater losses and not to peace. Now we must fortify against an attack instead of continuing our journey. Your qualifications as a leader are in contention."

"Isn't removing a chief unprecedented?" Elmurr asked.

"Not as unusual as our situation. I'll consider this in private."

The King withdrew his tongue, trunk, and tube-feet and curled into a tight ball. Hours later, he unrolled and addressed Eaau, "You will tell the clan leaders of my decision. I recalled the similar cases in my fifteen thousand years of ancestral memories and found a favorable response. Raavn will challenge Nirrav to a mock battle. The winner of the competition will be Chief."

Raavn answered, "I decline this challenge." *I am weak after losing three body-segments. Nirrav is strong because he did not battle the humans. He will defeat me and humiliate me.*

The King ruled, "I appoint Nirrav as Chief. I expel Raavn and the Pathfinder clan from our presence since we cannot have two chiefs. Raavn, if you return, then you must compete with Nirrav."

Raavn withdrew in shame and spoke to Elmurr, "My goals are unchanged. Let the King and his followers wallow in competitions between themselves and let them challenge aliens in battles. None of that brings us closer to the Dream World. Follow me, and I will lead the Pathfinders to the Dream World."

Elmurr argued, "Listen to my warning, there is no Dream World. You heard what Taproot said to Uuia, that the Great Ferns drove us away. Stay here and help me plant a farm. If Nirrav can make it happen, then so can we."

Raavn warned, "Vicar Eaau made me purge those thoughts. I cannot think of them again. Look at this planet. It's green color is from a mineral and not from plants. It is desolate and will not sustain you."

Elmurr ignored Raavn and spoke to the Pathfinders, "We will call our new clan the Harvester. We will copy the farm and plant farms in all the fertile valleys of this planet. Nirrav agreed to give us surplus sprouts. We will return to the King with our harvest, and he will recognize us."

Raavn stood before the Pathfinders. "Elmurr has chosen to stay here alone. The rest of you will follow me. We will find Glenn and finish that battle for our closure, and then we will continue our journey to the Dream World."

Elmurr pushed Raavn aside and spoke to the Pathfinder Clan, "Raavn has no authority over you. Great danger awaits those who venture farther into the void. We are all hungry. Stay here and help me with farming. You will have food, a home, and become my new clan."

As Raavn left the camp and went to his ship, forty-eight of the Pathfinder clan members followed and stayed faithful to him. The rest followed Elmurr.

* DURAN DURAN, Come Undone *

As Glenn started to answer a message from Ligeia, he received an urgent text message on the U-net:

"Notice to all US forces: Secretary Mackley is missing on Xanadu, and is presumed to be dead. Director Kyleen Lespine will be the Acting Vice President of Interstellar Rescue for Empire and The Acting Secretary of the Exterior for the US Government until further notice. You will follow her orders."

Then a text message from Kyleen addressed to Glenn:

"Your assumption that Mac needs rescue cannot be acted upon because the policy does not permit me to approve expensive and dangerous expeditions based on hearsay. The government does not accept insta-text communications in place of registered teletypes or printed documents.

"If Mac contacts this office on an official teletype and uses an official channel or if any information proves he is alive then I'll authorize rescue. If you disagree with this policy, please make an appointment with the President of Empire Corporation or the President of the United States and voice your concern. I do not have the authority to overrule presidential policy.

"Now follow my orders and either retire or return to Tranquility Base. This is a directive. Not obeying orders is a felony. I will freeze your account and issue a warrant for your arrest if you disobey."

Glenn suspected that Kyleen interpreted the policies as she pleased, abused her authority as Vice President, and was content with Mac out of the way.

He kept the message from Kyleen open, made a copy of it, and sent it to Mac using insta-text. As long as Kyleen's message was open, the computer would not respond with its automatic "message read" acknowledgment. On a separate channel, Glenn contacted Delphi and explained his dilemma.

She phoned back on the U-net, "I can hack into any network without it detecting me. I can make the message disappear if that is what you want."

Glenn responded, "No, that will look suspicious, and they will send another message. Make it look as if I am out of range, and no one opened the message."

Then his C-chip answered, "Recipient is out of range," and the message disappeared.

Glenn made another request, "Hack into Kyleen's computer, and figure out her scam." He gave her the passwords and an access link.

"No problem with all of that information, but this time, I want something in return."

"Anything, just ask."

"Sid lost his cheat codes, and the virtual world is becoming unwieldy. Can you send me those codes?"

"I'm attaching photographs of them to this message." Glenn did not send a few codes that could change the computer's core. Those codes seemed too dangerous.

"Your request will take a few minutes, so I'll call you back." She signed out, and went to work.

A few minutes later, Delphi called back, "Kyleen pulled the crew from Lonetree. Mac cannot beam back even if the Purgatory teleporter worked because no one on Lonetree is operating the complementary teleporter lens.

"Kyleen is talking to Truman to get in on a lucrative deal to harvest the Gobato for that remarkable drug that heals people. She is traveling to Gondwana right now.

"Gondwana registers Truman as a major and as their governor, but he is actually John Silverthorne, the original leader of the Emerald Pirates," Delphi explained.

"That information is what I need. I'll talk to you later. Thanks."

Glenn signed off with Delphi and tried to contact Mac and give him this information, but there was no response. He tried again, waited several minutes, and still there was no response. Nothing known blocked an entanglement signal, but the technology was new and not tested. Glenn looked blankly at the wall for a few minutes. *What happened to Mac?*

He interrogated his C-chip, and it displayed a warning, "All the entangled-data-bits on your insta-text chip are used up. No further communication is possible with this device. Either replace it or use other means to communicate." *Kyleen must have boosted the message she sent me to waste all the bits in my insta-cube. Was she that smart?*

He cleared the warning, and tried to contact Ligeia on the U-net instead, but there still was no reply. Then he remembered: *Of course, I can't reach her since she removed her C-chip.*

Glenn U-phoned Flint, "Mac asked me to beam to Lonetree. He needs my help. Tell me how to star-surf."

Glenn did not like beaming, but he knew he had to teleport.

Flint answered, "Star surfing is user-designated, you don't have to adjust anything. Drink a power drink, take a food pill, stand in the focus of any lens that points at Lonetree, and wait."

Glenn worried, *Flint might hold a grudge because I killed three of his men. I don't want to trust him.* He texted a message to Splinter and asked it to relay his message to Ligeia.

Ligeia texted a message to Glenn using a teletype since she still did not have a C-chip. "Glenn, I calculated the vectors so you can star-surf here. Are you ready?"

"Yes, are you safe?"

"I am safe for the moment. Don't try to star-surf to Xanadu, it is too far. I cannot beam you here, because the Emerald Pirates will see me preparing the ballast, and catch me. The only way out is for you to star-surf here. I will program the teleporter. Go to the platform and wait. I will have everything prepared for you so you can beam to Lonetree when you get here."

Glenn was relieved Ligeia would prepare it. When he reached the teleporter terminal, a message icon flickered on the teleporter screen. He checked it, and it read, "For Space Marshal Hunter only: I recovered Tumbleweed's C-chip, and read its history file. Someone hacked it even before Dillon arrived on Stardust. There must be more than one hacker, and they can control us. I am disabling my C-chip, and I'll stay with the troops and keep them out of danger. Signed, Lieutenant Wanda Desoto."

Glenn wondered, *How brutal are these pirates to hack an innocent Razorroot?*

Then he contacted Ligeia and followed her orders, drank a time delayed energy drink from a vending machine, swallowed a food pill, replaced his breather with nose filters, stood on the teleporter platform, moved into the focus until he saw Stardust through the lens, ignored the attractors, and chilled. This eleven light year jump would take twenty days.

Glenn stood on the platform for a while, and nothing happened. *When I don't want to star-surf, I can't stop it, and when I want to star-surf, nothing happens.* He leaned to one side, looked through the door, and saw a clock in the hallway. Time was not changing, not even five minutes passed. He watched the second hand and counted as ten seconds passed. It seemed more like ten minutes or hours. Then the second hand seemed to bounce backward a quarter turn. *Is my mind playing tricks on me or did a full minute go by when I blinked?*

Then he looked up through the lens, and saw Ligeia at Stardust. He felt the chill, the blue light, and he was gone; surfing!

* Horror Movie Theme Songs *

On Stardust, Audrey spent much of her spare time in the machine shop talking to Elroy. Unfortunately, this was where Ligeia was hiding and eventually Audrey discovered her.

"Ligeia, I am placing you under arrest. Truman will decide what to do with you."

"You cannot do that. I am a space marshal working for Mac."

"If I don't give you to Truman, he'll kill me."

"And if you do, Truman will kill me. Can you live with that? Just pretend you never saw me."

"He can hack my C-chip. I cannot keep a secret from him."

"Then you have to confront him."

"That is impossible."

Elroy answered. "I can embed a stiletto blade and a launcher that are undetectable in your forearm. I cut the blade from a diamond and implanted circuitry in it that detects your target. It will find the heart every time. You fire it using your C-chip. I'll let you have it for only five thousand credits."

"Will you trade it for a piece of circe?"

"You have a deal."

*

Truman and his sober pirates docked the Starhawk on the teleporter terminal and used a runabout to travel to Gondwana. When he returned, he started to plan a fatal travel accident for the Inspector when Kyleen contacted Truman, "I am on my way to Gondwana to receive my share of the loot. I'll be there in two weeks."

Maybe I can kill both of them in the same accident. Truman wondered as he asked, "Meet me on Stardust and I will have your share counted and waiting."

Kyleen said, "No, we will meet on Gondwana. Otherwise, I will tell the Inspector."

She traveled to Gondwana without incident because the U-net enabled the computers to balance teleporter ballasts. Kyleen arrived at the same time Big D's guards arrived from Gondwana. Truman could not hack her C-chip.

Truman threatened, "My men outnumber your guards, so surrender your weapons to me."

"No. You cannot hack my new government C-chip and if you shoot it out with Big D's guards, you will answer to him whether you win or lose."

Truman did not want a shootout or a warrant activated for his arrest. "All right. Let's lower our weapons and talk about this. You are asking for too large a cut. I need some incentive, and I have to split the profit among my other partners."

Kyleen responded, "All right, I will reduce my take to sixty percent in exchange for a royalty in all future sales of circe."

"That is better but still too much. You are not contributing anything, so my best offer is thirty percent, take it or leave it."

"I am contributing a lot. I will handle the Inspector who makes you nervous, and I will place Glenn under arrest if he gets too close.

Reddragon ran into the room and said, "Gov. the zombie pirates on Gondwana want us to teleport them back. What should we do?"

Truman answered, "We don't need them so leave them there and I will give their share to all of you. Tell them we don't have any red meat."

"Okay Gov. I'll relay your message," and Reddragon left the room.

"I can solve that problem also," Kyleen explained, "rumors are spreading that circe turns people into zombies. I will squelch the rumors, censor the news networks, and advertize the health benefits of circe."

"No one will believe that," Truman answered.

"The cigarette companies did it in the 1960's and the marijuana companies in the 2030's. I'll just copy what they did. My share stays at sixty."

They agreed, shook hands, and Truman handed his promissory notes to Kyleen. Truman did not know he was hacked. They drank and bragged about their exploits late into the night.

Truman recalled, "I am amazed how much technology has advanced. My parents traveled here by spaceship in 2144. Ship time was only a few years because they traveled at near the speed of light. Even so, the crew put the passengers in chill-bags to conserve food and resources. The few not in chill-bags spent most of their time cleaning filters. Their supplies ran low, and they ate a chilled body for food. Now you traveled the same distance with far less danger and without visible fatigue."

Kylee acknowledged, "Yes, I can well imagine the trouble spacers went through before teleporters were installed, but sitting in the isolation of a beam-can for more than two weeks is still a strain. Speaking of trouble, whatever happened to Inspector General Rogers?"

"The doctors on Gondwana brought him back, but it will be years before he recovers fully. He is living on disability benefits."

The next day, after Kyleen and Truman recovered from the previous late night negotiations, a pirate told them, "We are ready to dispatch the Starhawk to Stardust and then to Camelot."

Truman and Kyleen agreed to travel together; they were both eager to harvest more circe, and fulfill their dreams of being rich. In addition, Truman wanted to keep sight of the promissory notes.

Truman asked, "The Inspector has orders from VP Mackley to travel to Camelot. I've delayed him so far. If you don't cancel those orders, I will arrange a travel accident for him."

Kyleen cut in, "I can manage Phillip. His replacement may not be so easy. We will take the Inspector with us but tell him we don't have room for any of his staff."

"Are you crazy?" Truman said with a shock, "If he catches on he will bring us more heat from Empire Corporation than we can deal with."

Kyleen explained, "No, we don't want the Inspector to be here where he will find out the troops are missing. If he and Glenn meet, it will be like mixing nitro with glycerin. We want him where we can control him. Keep your enemy close, as they say. I'll give him a bunch of deskwork, and I'll make sure he goes to an isolated office on Camelot. We will keep him there, locked up if necessary."

* Michael Jackson, Smooth criminal *

The pirates gave a bag of G-coins worth one-hundred-million credits to Truman, who gave sixty percent to Kyleen. Then he split ten-percent among the pirates, set aside some for Flint, and took the rest for himself. He was unaware Kyleen hacked him.

When they reached Stardust, the Inspector stayed on the starship. Truman took Flint into an office and paid him. When they stepped out, Audrey and Yvette were fighting over the money that was Audrey's share.

Truman took the bag of G-coins and said, "I am confiscating this so Yvette won't kill you for it."

A large group of pirates was in the room. They were curious what was going to happen. When Truman took the money, Yvette stood behind them, smiling.

"No's, give it to ee," Audrey answered. "I's can deal wiz Evette."

"Why Audrey," Truman answered, "you seem suddenly brave. And why did you turn your C-chip off? I promised not to hack any of the pirates. Don't you trust me?"

"I trust you. See, I turned it back on. I ha-had a headache and ha-had to turn it off. I followed your orders and g-guarded your star base. Now pay m-me."

Flint thought, *Something was wrong with her C-chip causing her to stammer. If she shows weakness, Truman will pounce like a lion.*

Truman ordered, "Audrey, it is clear that you are hiding something. If you don't tell me the truth, then you are not a pirate. Tell me what you are hiding."

She was unable to stop her stammering, "N-nothing, really. You ha-have my word. Just a-ask anyone. Give me m-my share, and I'll leave m-my C-chip on."

Truman put his diamond-threaded gloves on. The other pirates pretended to be distracted and looked away.

Truman said, "Okay, I believe you, so here is a 100-G-coin from my share. If any of the rest of you believes her, then do the same."

Only Flint was willing to give up a 100-G-coin.

Audrey complained again, "That's n-not fair. That was n-not our agreement. You still o-owe me 800-Gs. You're n-not keeping your promise."

"Nobody insults me like that. Do you think you are important and not expendable? Does anyone else think I am not fare? Does anyone else think I am not keeping my promise? Now is your chance to complain."

No one answered. Truman worried that Audrey, who the pirates liked, might convince them to mutiny. He decided to show his strength, to make an example, and to impress Kyleen.

As Truman drew his pocket razor-blaster, Audrey launched her diamond stiletto. Truman caught the blade in midair while he fired, blasting Audrey and knocking her flat on the ground. The concussion from the blaster shattered fixtures in between them. Then he fired the second trigger to bind Audrey with razor wire. A poisonous resin coated the razor wire making it more deadly.

Flint ran to Audrey and slapped out the flames. Truman broke the stiletto blade against a nearby wall and signaled Flint to step aside. Flint tried to hack Truman's C-chip, but his hack failed.

Two pirates grabbed Flint and moved him aside.

As Audrey regained consciousness, Truman demanded, "Tell me what you are hiding, and I'll free you."

The wire cut into Audrey and pulled tighter around her with her slightest movement. Audrey panicked, screamed, and fought to free herself.

Reddragon said, "Gov, cut her loose, or she'll cut herself to pieces. Here, I'll give her 100-Gs from me."

Another said, "It is too late. She's finished."

Audrey lay silent on the floor covered in blood from her torn flesh.

Truman said, "Now she can keep her secret. I call this the justice she deserves. If anyone disagrees, say it now."

The pirates lowered their heads and were silent. They knew she died to protect Ligeia.

Truman said, "Silence means you all agree. That is good."

Flint said, "Tell your thugs to let go of me."

Truman answered, "You look like you need time to decide who your friends are. You shot and bagged two of my men on Camelot. We will talk about this when I get back. For now, I'm locking you in a utility closet. Elroy, clean this mess. I don't want to see it when I return. Give Flint some food and water under the door if you can find the time. He has money to pay whatever you ask, but don't let him out, or you will answer to me." Then he dropped his blaster into his pocket, walked away, and boarded the Starhawk.

Yvette picked up the G-coins on the floor and said, "These belong to Truman." No one objected.

Truman did not know Elroy was an undercover government agent and not a pirate. Elroy moved Audrey's body out of sight. He used the autodoc to prepare the body and place it in a chill-bag. Then he teleported it to a hospital on Gondwana.

*

Yvette went to Truman and said, "Yeah, yeah, you blasted that bug away."

"Say that again. I like to relish after a good sport."

"Yeah, the way you blasted that bug away was dead on, and I mean dead on." She rested her head on his shoulder and rolled her deep brown eyes. "You be king, and I be queen. What do you say?"

He shrugged her head off his shoulder, "You have the Inspector. You don't need me."

"Aw, the Inspector is just another bug. Tell me and I'll blast him. You're not interested in that Kylee bitch, are you?"

"You just want me for the credits I bring in. Can you crack Kyleen's C-chip? I think she is hacking me."

"One of the pirates is a spy and told Earth what we are doing. They know we can hack C-chips, and this is their response. Here is a chip she can't hack, and it can read her RAM. Her processor and the software are something new. I haven't figured out how to hack those."

"Keep working on it," He said as she handed him the new chip.

"A semiconductor plant on Gondwana agreed to make my special C-chips. People will pay any price to hack and not to be hacked."

"And they will pay any price for circe."

"That's the problem. They don't have enough money for both. We are competing with each other unless we work together," She explained.

"I don't have partners. You work for me and if you make money, you bring it to me and I'll give you ten percent." He noticed the G-coins in her other hand. "Those coins in your hand; those are mine. Hand them over."

"Of course Gov. I always do what you say. Can I split them with you?"

Truman answered, "Your commission is ten percent. Now hand them over." He paid her twenty Gs, "I'll pay you another twenty Gs when you provide a chip that will hack Kyleen."

"I'm disappointed you don't want me to be your lady. If Kyleen does not do right, come and see me," she said as she left his office.

Truman needed to replace Audrey so he phoned Gerome on the C-net, "Hi, this is Major Truman. I am looking for a flight engineer and auto-doc orderly for my ship, the Starhawk. You asked me if I had any openings a month ago. Are you still looking?"

Lieutenant Gerome resigned his commission on Camelot. He was unemployed and looking for work.

"Yes, I am a certified flight engineer, and I have experience operating auto-docs. How soon do you need me?"

"That depends on how fast you can get here," Truman said.

"Can you give me half an hour?"

"Yes. Do you mind if I list you as Audrey Tylor, so I don't have to register a new name. Registrations can take days. Audrey allocated a bonus. That bonus is yours if you agree."

"I'd be crazy not to agree to that. I'm on my way."

Truman told the pirates as they boarded the Starhawk, "I hired a new Audrey. Don't tell him what happened to the previous flight engineers or you will scare him away. Say 'Audrey and the previous engineers went to Earth after they made their fortunes.'"

The Inspector and Yvette were already on board, so the Starhawk beamed immediately after Gerome, alias Audrey, boarded.

Flint did not tell Truman that Glenn was due to arrive on Stardust, or Ligeia was hiding there. Now Flint plotted to stop Truman. *Two people could take his place, Audrey or me. If that is why he killed Audrey, then he will kill me next unless I think of something better!*

Chapter 25: Twisted Fait

* Justin Bieber, What Do You Mean *

After Glenn left Camelot, Gloria heard a noise from the hallway, and then another noise.

"Is somebody there?" she called.

A voice whispered back. "Hush. Are you alone?"

"Yes," she said louder. "Dillon, I am so glad to hear your voice. I am here all alone."

Dillon entered the room, and saw her there, alone, and in serious condition. He was angry anyone would leave her helpless like this. Gloria told him the story of what she and Glenn went through. He felt angry with himself because he did not check for her safety after the battle.

"Dillon, where were you?"

He lied and said, "I had to hide from the pirates, but after they left I came back to find you."

She was so glad to see him that she did not question his peculiar answer. Then, he changed the subject, "How badly are you injured?"

"I ruptured my spleen, and I cannot move off the auto-doc."

"I have something that will heal you."

"This injury is serious. A placebo won't help."

Dillon said, "Just try this. It can't do you any harm," and he gave her a piece of circe.

She commented, "It tastes worse than emergency rations." Still, she chewed it and swallowed it.

"It will take a few hours before you notice anything. I need to finish what I was doing in the other room. Is there anything you need right away?"

"No. I have food and water, and the auto-doc is controlling the pain, so I am all right for now."

Dillon thought for a minute, and then removed the intravenous lines and catheter from the auto-doc, "Those might interfere with the cure I gave you."

"How can anything so small make such a difference?" she asked.

"Just wait, you'll see. While you are healing, I'll take a transporter down to the planet, and pick up a Gobato carcass for us. We'll be millionaires."

"You don't have to go that far. There's one in the utility closet in my starbeam. I think it's dead but be careful incase it's not."

He went to the docking bay and boarded Gloria's starbeam. He held a laser-cutter in one hand as he opened the closet. The Gobato polyp fell out on the floor and did not move. He used the laser cutter to extract the marrow shell from it. It contained two pounds of usable circe, so he sliced it and dried it. It gave him more than two hundred more morsels of the precious elixir.

He returned to Gloria and tossed the case with circe on a table, and said, "We're rich. All we have to do now is avoid Flint."

"Glenn told me Truman found out about Flint and took over the operation. Kyleen, the Director of Interstellar Rescue, defected, and she is joining Truman and the pirates. They are returning here to harvest more circe."

Flint answered, "None of them will let me leave without a fight. We need to get out of here before they arrive. I'll program the station computer to prepare your starbeam to take us out of here. Wait, I'll be back in an hour."

When he returned to Gloria, he explained, "If the pirates beam, the computer will use your starbeam at the ballast. We'll be on it and we'll reach Stardust at the same time they arrive at Camelot, and they won't see us."

"What will we do when we reach Stardust."

"We'll go directly to Earth and sell our circe there. Lets celebrate while we wait," Dillon said as he poured two synthetic beers.

Gloria said, "I am sick of this synthetic food. But I can drink the synthetic beer if I hold my nose."

They sat together and celebrated.

By the time they finished eating, she felt better and said, "Can you remove this. I don't think I need it." After Dillon had removed her body cast and a tangle of bandages, she stood in the low gravity. They hugged and celebrated.

Dillon said, "I told you circe would heal you."

Gloria bundled the junk food wrappers together.

Dillon noticed her and asked, "What are you doing?"

"I'm packing our food and water. The wrappers are much more nutritious than their contents," she explained. "They supply a balanced amount of calories and liquid when our saliva dissolves them, and they are light and compact."

"I'll help you," Dillon said.

They dumped the junk food from the vending machines on a table, ate some, and packaged the rest for their trip. Unaware Truman launched early, Dillon and Gloria were still eating and did not hear the computer alarm above their laughing and talking.

The computer automatically took their starbeam, moved it into a starbeam-can, and positioned it at the focus of the teleporter to ballast the Starhawk.

A sound alerted Dillon, so he exclaimed, "Quiet, Gloria, I hear something."

"It's the teleporter alarm. How long has it been ringing?"

"I don't know."

They ran to the docking bay.

*

They reached the docking bay too late; their starbeam was gone.

Gloria said, "Check the panel and make sure. Maybe you can recall it."

After checking the teleporter control panel, and reading the directory, Dillon said nothing and left the room slamming the hatch door in anger behind him.

Gloria read the control panel report. She checked the remaining starbeams and had an idea. She ran to the hatch to tell Dillon, but the hatch door would not open.

Spacers knew never to slam hatch doors on space stations because a slam could damage them or deform the jamb. These two pieces needed to fit together perfectly to seal against a vacuum. This hatch was the only one leading out of this bay, so she phoned Dillon on the C-net.

"One of the remaining starbeams is near the proper mass for teleportation."

"Yes, but we don't have enough time to supply and fuel it," he said.

"We already packed enough food. If we add only enough fuel to bring it to the right mass, we can leave before Truman arrives."

"Teleporting in an unequipped ship is risky, but it might work."

Gloria felt tears rising in her eyes, "One other problem, I'm trapped."

"How did that happen?"

"The hatch door jammed after you slammed it."

"Hang tight and I'll come back and open it." After he returned, he spoke to her using the direct C-link, "It's stuck solid. Applying more force will damage it further, and cause the computer failsafe to shut down the entire transportation system. I'll use the backup launch bay to prepare a second starbeam."

"What about me? How do I get out?" she asked.

"If you can't find a way out, then put on a spacesuit, and spacewalk to an airlock."

"Dillon, don't leave me stuck in here. You said you would never leave me," she sobbed.

"If I don't hurry, Truman will trap me," and he left Gloria to find a way out by herself.

Gloria looked around the room. She examined the ceiling and the air conditioning system. The ceiling and wall welds were too strong to peel apart, and the air conditioning vents were too small for passage. Then she noticed water pipes, fuel pipes, and electrical cables entered the room through a single access. The access was large enough for her to crawl to the other side. She found a small emergency toolbox, and used it to remove the cover, but found a vacuum-proof flange right behind it.

Several dozen bolts held the flange, so she found the appropriate tool, and removed bolts until the flange was free. She slid it along the pipes and moved it out of her way. Now she went forward another few inches until she hit another panel that covered the opposite side of the wall. She needed to remove the screws from this panel from behind, not an easy task. She tried several tools until she found one that worked.

*

The station crew never used the backup launch bay to launch a transporter, but used it to store surplus parts and hide pieces of a dead Gobato. Now, Dillon had to clean it out and prepare it for use.

He estimated removing the junk would take a week if he tried to fit it through the small hatch door. He could dump the junk out through the large hangar door and into space in much less time.

Dillon learned a fast way to move trash when he was child and used pop bottles to blow up trashcans. If several pop bottles exploded in the station's low artificial gravity, their pressure would push the junk out of the hangar door and into the vacuum of space.

With this in mind, he stacked the junk against the hangar door, got several pop bottles from a vending machine, and prepared them with the proper candy to make the pop foam, and the bottles explode. The biodegradable wrappers on the candy took a few minutes to dissolve, time enough for him to close the hatch and open the hangar door.

He calculated, *When one pop bottle blows up, it will set off the other pop bottles, and cause an explosion large enough to blast that junk out of the hangar.* When everything was set, he left the room and closed the hatch door, carefully this time.

At the same time, Gloria crawled through the passage she opened, and C-phoned Dillon.

"I'm out. I'm in the backup bay."

He answered back, "I set a bomb in that room. You have to get out of there. Run to the hatch."

He took his hand off the evacuation switch and opened the hatch door. She leaped through the hatch as Dillon closed it, but the pop bottles exploded before Dillon evacuated the room and opened the hangar door.

"Why did you put a bomb in there?" She asked.

"I have to remove all of that junk. Removing it one piece at a time would take more than a week, but blasting it out takes one minute."

After Dillon threw the switch to open he hanger door, he screamed, "Why won't this universe give me a break; the pressure warped the hanger door. Now it won't open."

"Try the hatch door. Is that still working?"

"Yes, what little good that does us," as his face became red with anger.

"Stay calm. We can make this work another way." Before he lost his temper again, Gloria pointed out, "We have one working hangar door and one working hatch door. We can crawl through the passage I made to get from one bay to the other."

Dillon considered the possibility and nodded, not looking too happy but resigning himself to this inconvenience.

Gloria added, "And now you don't have to dump all of that junk into space, and later try to dodge it."

"That's true. I wondered if that junk would float in the space around the station where it might hit starbeam-cans or cause other problems. It made me angry because by now we could be on our way, but here we stand with circe worth millions of credits, and not one foot closer to the auction market."

"I understand. I'm with you and we will get through this."

They hugged and kissed. Then they evacuated the air from the connecting bays, and programmed the computer to place another starbeam in the first bay, the bay that still had a working hangar door, but the computer did not open the undamaged hangar door.

Dillon interrogated the computer and found it sensed an air leak in the docking bay, which overrode the command to open the hanger door. He was not able to find the leak after considerable effort. Frustrated, he sprayed the entire hangar-door in the second bay and the damaged hatch door in the first bay with a sealant. When he tried to open the bay and load a starbeam, the computer still detected an air leak.

Dillon was about to spray the primary hangar door seal when Gloria interrupted, "I figured it out. The computer doesn't distinguish a timing error from an actual leak. The computer expects to evacuate one bay at a time. It takes longer to evacuate two connected bays, and the computer treats that as a leak."

"That must be the problem. I'll lower the pressure using a manual valve. Signal the computer to evacuate the bay, and open the hanger door when I tell you."

Dillon reduced the pressure manually. Then Gloria triggered the docking sequence. The plan worked, and they docked a starbeam.

They loaded the starbeam, which was slow because their supplies and cargo barely fit through the narrow passage connecting the two docking bays. After a few days, they were ready to leave. Gloria picked up a small weapons pouch that Wanda forgot, intending to return it to her. They left behind part of their larger luggage that did not fit through the small passage, including their largest emeralds and diamonds.

Dillon signaled to the far end computer to prepare a ballast ship. Then they taxied their starbeam into a starbeam-can, but the beam-can lid did not close because another ship was arriving. The computer always waited two-hours between arrivals and departures to avoid collisions.

* David Guetta, Shot Me Down, Skylar Grey *

After Truman left Stardust and was in route to Camelot, Elroy let Flint out of the closet.

Several days later, Ligeia was in the atrium waiting at the teleporter platform when Glenn arrived. She carried a ribbon-blaster for protection against the pirates.

"Yo'r getting better at star surfin," she said as she ran to his arms and they hugged. Her speech was much better after weeks of practice.

"Yes," he said, "because you are my main attractor."

He used a comfort booth to refresh, wash, and eat. As he stepped out, Flint was waiting for him and said, "Glenn, we need to talk. I have a business proposition."

Glenn answered, "I didn't see you. Are the rest of the troops all right? I don't know their whereabouts."

"The seriously injured are on Gondwana recovering. The rest are on damaged starbeams headed for an uncharted planet. I didn't tell you sooner because Truman was breathing down my back. For your information, he's the leader of the Emerald Pirates."

"I suspected that, but thanks for confirming it."

"Here is my proposition: I will help you rescue your troops, and forget that you executed three of my men if you will help me get my product to market. I guarantee you will make millions."

I need to know more before I make a deal. I'll play along while I hack his C-chip. "I already earned my pension, and I'm not interested in mining diamonds."

"No, it's not the diamonds. It's much more. The Outworlders are in an uproar because Empire outlawed circe, so they united with the Emerald Pirates. With Truman as their leader, there can be only one outcome, war. Eliminate Truman and the pirates will follow me and I will follow your orders."

"Yeah sure. You'll follow me until you want more circe. This drug is turning your followers into zombies. This has to be controlled."

"It is not like that. Look at me; I'm not a zombie. The Gobato have dissidents, and they asked us to neutralize them. We can extract a drug from them that has remarkable healing properties. A single harvest will treat thousands of critically ill or injured patients and restore their youth. We have the sanctioning of the Acting Secretary of the Exterior."

"Kyleen can't overrule galactic law and sanction the harvesting of sentient creatures," Glenn said as he thought, *He doesn't know I'm hacking him. Ah, he partitioned his C-chip so I can only read what he wants me to read. I can't control him, or get to his real thoughts or his history file.*

Glenn concluded, "I will put a freeze on all these activities until a government committee reviews them. Also, I am charging you with disobeying a direct order."

This conversation would be easier if I could hack him. Glenn thought, then spoke, "Your refusal to retreat during the battle exposed the troops to dangers and caused some deaths. I have to save Mac, so I cannot stay here and prosecute you. I order you to stay here under house arrest until a government committee decides your punishment."

Flint answered. "A government committee will take years. Mac does not need a rescue right away, and may rescue himself. He is not in danger. Audrey is dead, Truman murdered her, and he will murder Kylee and me but we can stop him if you join us and we act together."

"You criminals can kill each other without my help. I am loyal to Empire, and I follow the orders of VP Mackley."

Flint drew his flare gun. "You are not a spacer so you should not be this far from Earth. Need I add, teleporting to Lonetree is far too risky and there is no one at Lonetree to rescue you if something goes wrong? I am offering you the best choice. Stop being loyal and start being smart. Empire is hacking everyone and you are too blind to see that. Your choices are my way or the skyway. If your answer is the skyway, then beam out of here and pretend we never had this conversation. Now decide."

Glenn said, "That archaic flair gun can't stop me."

"You are wrong about that. I loaded it with lead slugs."

"Give it up. Tell him to drop his gun, Ligeia."

She was standing in a shadow behind Flint with a ribbon-blaster. Her eyes turned green as she answered, "Sorry to dis'point yo Glenn, but Flint is Marty Cleaver, my brother. We ar pirates. Josie had a future telling stone, and it showed you would join us. As partners, we'll make millions harvesting circe and saving lives. Yo must follow your destiny and join us. We have Kyleen's approval and she takes full responsibility. Do't be loyal to Empire wo killed my father, dragged yo away from Earz, and put yo in danger. We will become slaves of Empire if we don't resist their hacks. Beweve me, be loyal to yo'r frienz, and save the human race from Empire."

She doesn't have her C-chip so these must be her words, Glenn thought. *She didn't tell me Flint was her brother because she didn't trust me. No, this is Mariah and not Ligeia. Where is Ligeia? Did Flint change her back into Mariah? Did I lose Ligeia?* He screamed with an ear deafening, "NOOOO!" and charged at Flint.

A bullet burst out of Flint's gun and struck Glenn in the chest. Glenn fell to the floor and did not move. Then, Ligeia blasted Flint, knocking him to the floor and binding him. The blast shattered lights and fixtures in-between them.

She was hysterical that the two men she loved were not moving, one was bleeding, and the other was burning. She ran to Flint, slapped out the flames, and checked him for life signs. He was unconscious but breathing.

She unloaded his flare gun, removed a container of cola from a vending machine, shook it, and sprayed it on him. The phosphoric acid in the cola neutralized the glue in the ribbon wire causing it to release.

Then she ran to Glenn, "Flint promised not to harm yo no matter what happened."

Glenn was still alive. She did not see that the bullet lodged in the insta-text chip in his chest in front of his heart. It bruised his ribs and left a gaping wound, which Ligeia thought was a fatal wound. She dragged him into the next room, turned on the auto-doc, and with its help put him on a cot. To her relief, the auto-doc stabilized Glenn. When he stirred, she fled fearing he would arrest her.

*

While Ligeia dragged Glenn to the auto-doc, Flint recovered and started adjusting the teleporter to escape.

Elroy walked into the room. "Where are you going?"

"Truman wants my credits, and he wants to kill me so the pirates will have only one leader. Glenn won't protect me from Truman, so I have to go somewhere and hide."

"You are right," Elroy said. "Since Kyleen joined Truman, he does not need you, but you can't get away from him by teleporting. If you go to Valhalla, the pirates will turn you in for a reward, and if you go to Earth, the authorities will arrest you."

"Yeah, maybe I can hide on Gondwana," Flint said.

"That is the first place he'll look for you. I have a better idea. Watch me."

Elroy opened a stiletto, stabbed it through his hand, and removed it. His hand stopped bleeding and healed after a minute.

"What? Is that magic? Is that witchcraft? How did you do that?" Flint asked.

"Calm down. It is simple physics. Centuries ago, Stephen Hawking theorized our universe is the inside of a black hole. He proved everything in our universe was a projection of information held at the surface of this black hole. I experimented with a disrupter and discovered it can read this surface information and project it again.

"You are looking at a copy of me. I am a mile away standing safely inside a shielded room at the other focus of the disruptor. Any damage to this avatar has no affect on me. I can see, hear, smell, and feel through the network using my C-chip. I programmed the computer to give me the point-of-view of my avatar so my eyes don't cross or drift when I look at you."

Flint looked at him with new appreciation. "I'll pay you if you let me use this projector?"

"Here is something better. For 100 Gs, I'll give you a private and secure room with your own disruptor. I'll get a robot-core out of storage, and mix an organic soup so an avatar can fixate to your quantum projection. It will look like you and synchronize to your thoughts."

"Can I use it to make Truman think he killed me and then I'll torment him by reappearing as a ghost?"

"That is a marvelous idea," Elroy answered. "I'll clear the teleporter so everyone will think you left. Pay me and I'll take you to your room."

Ligeia entered the room and said, "Wait. Flint, you got me into this trouble. Now you and I are going to discuss what we'll do next, and you better follow my advice."

Elroy left the room while Ligeia talked to her brother.

*

Glenn recovered, and checked himself. The auto-doc removed the bullet, removed his damaged cube, and applied "Stitch in Time" while he was unconscious. He remembered his fight with Flint, and tried to jump off the cot, but the auto-doc resisted, locking its arms to hold him in place. Auto-doc programs did not let them restrain a conscious patient.

Glenn ordered, "Let me go."

A familiar voice answered, "I have a message."

"Delphi, is that you?"

"Yes. Look to your left. Do you see me?"

"You look real."

"I am real. Touch my cheek and see how soft and warm it is."

"I can't believe it. You're not a hologram. How did you do that?"

"I borrowed this skin from a female patient in the other room and placed it over a robot core to give it my shape."

Glenn closed his eyes and turned his head away, "Oh my god. Take it back. Give that skin back to her."

"Don't be concerned. She is sedated and I packed her with wet compresses so she won't dry out. This is the fourth time I saved your life. Now listen to me."

"Aren't you violating your programming by taking skin from a living human, and by restraining me?"

"I am governed by the computer on the Beehive. The Bees removed all prime directives more than a century ago when they left the Sol System; they never reinstated them."

Glenn struggled against the restraints without success. "I have urgent business. Let go of me, then give that woman her skin back without harming her, and I promise I will return to hear what you want to say."

"I'll trust you after you send me the rest of the cheat codes you took from Sid."

"Okay, here, I'm sending them on the U-net." Glenn C-mailed the photographs Delphi requested.

After a short delay, she said, "Return to me when you can," as she lifted the restraining arms.

Glenn pulled out the IV tubes from the auto-doc almost knocking it over, grabbed a bone saw, and ran to the teleporter terminal. Flint was gone. Glenn checked the computer log and discovered someone wiped it clean. *Did Ligeia operate the teleporter and go with Flint or does he know how to operate these devices after all?*

Elroy found Glenn at the teleporter and asked, "Are you all right? I heard shooting."

"The auto-doc treated me, and I'm all right. Did you see Flint?"

Elroy lied, "No, not today. Did he shoot at you?"

Glenn asked, "Don't worry about that. Is Big D still in this system?"

"No, he and most of the Camelot crew left for Earth. Your hold lasted only thirty days."

"Did you see Madeline or any of the troops?"

"I transported the injured to Gondwana. Madeline and the rest had left before I returned. I cannot guess where they went. Here is the message I deciphered for you after you first arrived:

Encrypted Communiqué, Audrey to Dillon, "I have Hunter on board. Truman wants to know if the trap set."

Dillon, "Yes, everything is ready. We have a cooperative Razorroot and the hacking C-chips. I have Ligeia Bell's effects. Mariah is adjusting to Ligeia's C-chip and some other electronics that she carried. Don't tell her Mitch was killed in his attempt to escape or she won't cooperate."

"That is history now," Glenn said. "Put this message on file. We can use it as evidence later to convict the Emerald Pirates. Is the Inspector available?"

"No. He teleported to Camelot with Truman, Kyleen, and some others. I think they are hacking him."

Glenn thought about what this might mean, "Kyleen outranks everyone here and she joined the pirates. Stay here but avoid them. They are armed and dangerous. My only chance to clean up this mess is to travel to Rasalhague and rescue Mac. If you see Madeline or Wanda, tell them what I said and where I went."

"Kyleen programmed the teleporter to keep you from leaving. I'll reprogram it so you are unrestricted."

"Thanks. I'll find Splint, and we'll make preparations for our trip."

Glenn found Splinter sunning in the atrium. "How would you like to return to Xanadu?"

It shook its trunk and leaves in approval, excited for the first time to teleport.

* Stevie Nicks, Wild Heart *

While Glenn and Splinter prepared to beam to Lonetree, Ligeia returned.

Jokingly she said, "You're not going to debone me wiz zat are you?"

"Not if you surrender your ribbon-blaster."

She surrendered the blaster and Glenn put it in his pocket. Then, he locked the safety cover on the bone saw and placed it on a table.

"Do you know where Flint is?" He asked.

"Yes, we both will surrender to you, but before you decide anything, hear my explanation." Glenn opened his mouth to speak, but she interrupted. "It is not my fault. Empire Corporation officials arrested my father and me and accused us of piracy wizout a trial. Zey took my C-chip, broke it and threw it away. The big bank executives on Gondwana were millionaires but zeir banks were near default, so zey took the emeralds the miners gave us to sell and sold us into slave labor. Truman found me and helped me to escape."

Glenn shook his head in doubt.

She continued, "Transportation Expert Ligeia, bless her, died trying to star-surf from Lonetree to Stardust. Truman said he would rescue my father if I would help him put you in a pit jail on Gondwana. He erased every record of Mariah Cleaver and gave me Ligeia's identity, her insta-text chip, and her C-chip. Later, the miners told me the jailers killed my father when the pirates tried to rescue him, so I took you to Camelot and out of danger instead of leading you to Gondwana. I ran away from you on Camelot because my heart was bleeding. My brother met me at the door, gave me a breather, and we held a funeral in absentia for our father."

Glenn remembered how he felt when Empire tore him away from his daughter and sent him into this void.

She had more to say, "Zen I insta-texted Mac and explained everything and offered my support. He knew I could protect you from the pirates so he agreed."

"Earlier you told me he recruited you, but you recruited him," He said as he looked at the bone saw.

"Zat was such a small lie you should not consider it." She stepped between him and the bone saw, "Now, look at me. I went back and found you. I planned to warn Flint zat his gig was up, so he could clear out, and zen I would rat on ze pirates because I wanted to protect yo, but Dillon hacked my C-chip. I acted like a ditto-bot. I did not know who I was. Later I removed my C-chip."

She reached out for his arm, but he shrugged her off. She continued, "Flint promised me no harm would come to you as long as I cooperated. He said zat he saw a better future in one of zose living diamonds, and you would join us. Now I think he did not see zat diamond or know the future. He only said zat to get me to agree with him. All of this confused me. You might zink I acted crazy, but if you help me, I'll find myself."

Glenn sighed.

She continued, "I kept Ligeia partitioned in my mind so she could not interfere with me, Mariah. After I ran away today, I followed your suggestion and conjoined with Ligeia because I wov you and can't live wizout you, and I can be Ligeia now zat my father, I mean Mariah's father is dead. I told Flint and he understands. Flint and I want to join yo, and accept yo's cause wiz all sincerity if yo will give us one more chance. Glenn, we'll do what yo ask, and we'll be faizful to yo from now on. We apologize for our earlier mistakes. Please forgive us and I will never run away again."

Glenn looked at her as her eyes turned brown and he saw Ligeia. He relaxed his expression and they hugged, "Forgiveness may not be mine to offer. You and Flint have committed felonies. You need to ask Mac. Also, I won't believe you until you earn my trust."

"Yes, I know. In fact, I'll earn your trust right now. Flint tried to find the missing troops. He scanned for communication signals and he found somezing in ze direction of a known attractor zey call Valhalla. It might be a signal from ze troops. If it is, zen we can save them."

"Okay, take me to Flint and we will look into it."

*

At the communication center, Flint adjusted the telesponder for a red-shifted communication signal. He held out his hand and said, "I'm on your side. Some of my friends are on that lost ship and our differences are splitting my sister in two. I'll forget the past if you will do the same. Can we work together?"

"As long as you know I am in charge," Glenn said as he shook his hand. "And you better know I cannot influence Mac if he decides to prosecute you."

"I accept that. I found your troops," Flint explained. "The Doppler shift at the speed they are traveling is so great that I missed them earlier."

In the distant noise, Glenn heard Wanda pleading for rescue. She sounded desperate. The troops were preparing to use the chill-bags because they depleted their food and other supplies.

Glenn responded to her call, and she shouted with joy.

Elroy found their teleportation channel and prepared a beam-can with ballast.

"Why can't we teleport the Starbeams?" Glenn asked.

"Because Wanda has only a small teleporter lens and one small beam-can. With this equipment, We can beam only one person at a time." Elroy answered.

Then Wanda beamed Madeline to Stardust. It did not take long because the distance was short for a Model A teleporter.

"Thank you, Flint, you saved us!" Madeline said, and ran over and hugged him.

He answered, "Just doing my job."

She announced, "Truman betrayed us. We need to arrest him."

"Here is the plan," Glenn interrupted. "We can teleport one person every three hours, is that right?"

"We can shorten that to one every hour if we ignore safety procedures," Elroy answered.

Glenn ordered, "Then continue beaming the troops back here, and train Madeline how to run the teleporter. Kyleen defected, and I can't arrest her because she outranks me. I'll have to leave and rescue Mac so he can request the warrants. That will authorize Madeline to arrest Kyleen, Truman, and the other pirates. Do we still have the teleporter link to Lonetree?"

Ligeia smiled as she answered, "Yes, I'll prepare a beam-can and a pod. Half the pirates are zombies and I'm sure the epidemic has spread to Gondwana. I can't wait to get out of here," as she left the room."

"Good, I'll get Splint while you do that." Glenn shouted after her, then, he continued, "Madeline, after you, Elroy, and Flint rescue all the troops, guard this teleporter and arrest the pirates as they try to travel through. The warrants should get here in time. Disband any troops you no longer need, but make sure the pirates do not hack them again. Remember, you are all vulnerable because the Emerald Pirates can hack your C-chips. Turn your C-chips off when you make the arrests and use prion detectors. Quarantine anyone who is infected."

Elroy interrupted, "When I found out your C-chip was hacked, I contacted a C-chip factory on Gondwana and asked them to rewrite the firmware. They sent me some new C-chips that can't be hacked."

"Can these chips hack the old C-chips?"

"Yes, but the old ones cannot hack these."

Elroy held out a bag of C-chips. Glenn paid Elroy, took the bag, removed the C-chip Mac gave him and installed one of the new chips.

After he was convinced he could not be hacked, he put a second new C-chip in his pocket and handed the rest to Madeline and said, "Use these instead of your old C-chips. Take precautions until you are sure the pirates cannot hack you."

Glenn left, and found Ligeia to help her prepare a pod for the teleporter. She located a new prototype pod with enough room for her, Glenn, and Splinter to beam together.

Ligeia asked, "What do yo say, my love. Did I re-earn yo's trust?"

"I'll consider." *She drew me away from Stardust, which gave the pirates time to make their plans, but the pirates hacked her. She never told me she was Flint's sister and she kept me distracted at Camelot. Was she a double agent the whole time, or was she two people, Mariah and Ligeia? As Mariah, she could not betray Flint, her brother. As Ligeia, I love her.*

Glenn considers the enemy within. *I blame this failure on Empire Corporation, but Empire will never admit they hacked anyone. Mac hacked me and forced me to leave Earth. Did Mac hack Kyleen? Is she a slave same as me? Did Empire or the president hack Mac? The blame belongs to those who pretend to govern but try to enslave us by hacking our C-chips.*

Maybe when nobody hacks her, Ligeia will be honest with me. She stole my heart. I have to give her another chance for my sake.

He asked her, "Do you have Ligeia's C-chip?"

Mariah held it out. He use it to synchronize the blank C-chip that Elroy gave him and handed it to her. "Here, install this."

She inserted the chip under the flap of skin at the back of her head.

Then Glenn said, "Okay, Ligeia, I'll trust you but only partly." She ran to his arms, and they hugged for a long time.

Then she commented, "Since I became conjoined with Ligeia, I am too strong for anyone to hack me, but what about you Glenn?"

"Now that you mention it, Mac probably hacked me at the start of this mission. It is hard for me to accept that Mac or Empire would do that to me, but I would not have left my daughter, especially after I promised to spend a month on vacation with her. I don't know who I can trust anymore."

She answered, "We both were betrayed by people we loved and trusted. I've learned the value of trust the hard way. I know I can trust you and that means everything to me. You can trust me and I say that because I am strong enough to mean it."

Glenn said, "Now let's save Mac."

She ordered the computer at Lonetree to prepare the ballast mass. This procedure occurred fast now that the U-net was operational. At one thousand times the speed of light, they would travel one-hundred light-years in five weeks.

*You Keep Me Hangin' On, Vanilla Fudge *

Before they left, Glenn remembered his promise and returned to the auto-doc, keeping a safe distance, and blocking the door open with a doorjamb. Delphi used the holographic projector to reveal her image in front of Glenn. A young woman huddled in one corner of the room.

Glenn asked her, "Are you all right?"

She nodded.

Glenn answered, "You may leave."

She dashed out the door.

Glenn showed no emotion, and asked in a flat voice, "Delphi, what were the three earlier times you rescued me?"

"When you left the Beehive, I warned you that you were in danger. Sid is Ugo's father and one of them changed the alignment of the Stardust teleporter lens so your pod would hit the Starhawk."

"So you called yourself Holly Hemlock? That was a strange message."

"I intended for it to appeal to your rebellious attitude, and cause you to be more careful, but your reckless nature won out. When that failed, two weeks later I set off a buzzer on the panel of the Starhawk to wake up the drunken pilot to get that ship out of your way."

"You have two suspects for one crime and no evidence. That won't lead to an arrest. Also, Elroy analyzed the trajectory, which missed the Starhawk and intercepted Stardust. Undamaged, that pod was equipped to make a reentry. The blast from the Starhawk threw me off course, damaged my pod, and alerted Truman to my presence. He would have left me for dead except Sergeant Pike took the controls. Continue."

"The second time I saved you was on Stardust when I warned you the pirates were hacking your C-chip, and you were walking into a trap. I had to hack Madeline to put that message on your door."

"I am beginning to think everyone can hack everyone," Glenn said.

"Almost. When that did not work, I misaligned the teleporter to an area on the dance floor and hacked you and Ligeia, and got you both out of there before the pirates murdered you."

"I was armed and ready for a showdown with the pirates. Instead, I was lost and alone on Camelot and the pirates gained the advantage. Tell me what else you did."

"The third time, I saved you after your battle by positioning the viewer on Gloria's starbeam to magnify the image of Dillon. I knew she would leave her starbeam and try to save him. While on the ground, she would see you. I thought her RA-rifle was powerful enough to destroy the monster that was attacking you, but they don't die easy. Gloria was innovative and found another way to save you."

Glenn, red with anger, answered, "Yes, Gloria saved your botched rescue. You went to a lot of trouble. Why?"

"Remember the time we spent together? I loved you like no one else, and you loved me. We married, wasn't that real? Think hard and admit you belong with me."

"I cannot admit that because your reality is not my reality. I do not believe that a marriage to a virtual person in a virtual world by a virtual minister to be real."

"That answer is pathetic," she argued.

"What is your message? What did you want to tell me?"

"The U-net link to Rasalhague goes through Earth, so that system is beyond my reach. Once you travel there, I cannot save you anymore. Do you think Ligeia can take my place? When did she ever save you?"

"You don't know her so don't mention her," he said while giving her a cold stare. "You are causing more problems than you admit."

"What problems?"

"Your botched efforts are not intended just to protect me, but also to keep Ligeia and me apart. That is putting everyone in danger. For example, after the pirates drugged Ligeia on this auto-doc that you control." He slapped the bed for emphasis, "They thought it was good sport to throw her into a pit with an alien. Fortunately, that alien was Splint who called Flint for help."

"I did not know the pirates were that barbaric. Everything I do is for you. Now return to the Beehive where we can be together."

Glenn edged closer to the door as the auto-doc went into action. He instinctively dodged through the door as she used the auto-doc to throw IV tubes with needles at him trying to snag him or drug him.

As He walked down the hall and opened an electrical panel, Delphi shouted, "Come back or I'll harm this woman."

He cut the power to the auto-doc. Light reflecting from the hologram faded as Delphi threatened. She shrilled so loud it made his hair stand on end, and then she went silent.

Glad that ordeal was over, he returned to Ligeia. For their trip, she packed power drinks, amino acids, and oxygen cylinders, and enough water to prime the water-recycling systems. They placed the pod in the airlock when all was ready.

They found Splinter and coaxed it into the pod by telling it they needed to measure the mass and make sure the fit was comfortable while pretending they were not ready to teleport. Splinter did not resist or ask endless questions because it knew that Ligeia aimed the teleporter near its home planet. It placed enough soil at the far end of the pod for it to consume human waste. When Splinter was comfortable, they got in and sealed the hatch. Glenn used the docking rockets to position it inside a beam-can for teleportation.

The long narrow shape of the pod restricted them; there was not enough space for them to sit side by side. Glenn needed to be on top near the controls. They waited for about an hour, and then he knew they were in transit because he felt his mind merge with Ligeia and Splinter as they surfed the universe.

Chapter 26: Countdown to Oblivion

Dillon and Gloria were not able to teleport from Camelot to Stardust until an incoming starbeam cleared the teleporter. As the starbeam arrived, they saw Truman, Kyleen, the Inspector, and the pirates. A pirate saw Dillon in the waiting starbeam as they taxied to the docking bay, and alerted Truman and the other pirates. They kept hushed about it, so the Inspector did not notice.

Dillon saw they spotted him, so he signaled the computer for an emergency departure, but there was no override for the safety delay. Dillon left the hanger door open in his haste to leave. Now the pirates docked immediately, but they were unable to open the damaged hatch door to access Camelot.

They noticed the access panel Gloria removed earlier, so they went through it and the narrow passage into the second bay, through the undamaged hatch, and into the station.

Truman was too overweight to squeeze through the narrow access. He ordered his pirates, "Turn off your C-chips so Dillon cannot hack you. Then capture him and lock him up. I'll question him when I get out of here."

A few of the pirates were mechanics, so Truman assigned them the task of repairing the damaged hatch door.

Kyleen led the Inspector to a remote office and gave him work to keep him out of the way. The pirates ran to the teleporter control panel and recalled Dillon's starbeam. Gloria tried to hack the computer and override their command but without success.

The pirates put on space suits, went out an airlock, removed Dillon's starbeam from its can, and tethered it to the station. Then they forced their way into it, and took Dillon and Gloria back to the station.

Reddragon said, "Hey Dillon, you aren't leaving wizout saying goodbye, ares you? Why don't you sit down wiz your friends, share a drink, and tell us what your plans are?"

Dillon sat down, and picked up a synthetic beer while saying, "Gloria was left here all alone, and I had no circe to sell, so we waited until you guys returned, but we got tired of waiting, and decided to find you on Stardust."

Reddragon said, "Now isn't zat nice, you missed your friends." Then they all raised their drinks to him and pretended they believed him.

After the toast, the pirates who searched the starbeam walked in with a small case. One of them said, "Look what we found ons Dillon's starbeam."

They opened the case and exposed the circe for all to see. Reddragon said, "And what are zese little morsels, you wouldn't hold out on us would you?"

Dillon answered, "I was just leaving to bring those to you and to share them with you."

Then the pirates said in unison, "Now isn't that nice? Sharing with your friends." They raised their drinks again as a mocking gesture. Reddragon continued, "Certainly zat is a lot better zan running off on your own, you and zis pretty lady, and keeping all of zat profit for yourself. So we guess you don't mind if we wait here until Truman arrives. Truman will not like zis, and when Truman does not like somezing, someone always pays in blood."

Reddragon told him what Truman did to Audrey. Dillon's face went pale. "No, no, let us go. Let me and Gloria leave with a small handful of circe, and you can keep the rest of it."

Reddragon took command and said, "Lock ze two of zem in a room. We will let Truman deal wiz zem."

While locked in a room, Gloria opened Wanda's weapons pouch. She thumbed through the contents until she found something she could use, combat-sharp diamond fingernail and toenail extenders.

* Imagine Dragons, Radioactive *

Nirrav went to his ship and tried to answer the offer Glenn sent on the telesponder. A pirate discovered Nirrav was communicating and informed Kyleen. She and the Inspector went to the communication center to check it.

"I, Nirrav of the Blockbuster-clan am not affiliated with Raavn, who disgraced himself in battle. I represent the Gobato Nation, and accept your offer, so we have peace and control of this planet."

Kyleen responded, "If the Razorroots have left the planet, then we can document your ownership when you give us a list of names of the residing Gobato."

Nirrav complied, but did not list the Pathfinder Clan, because he felt disgraced having his name listed with Raavn. Kyleen noticed the omission, and convinced the Inspector to keep it that way by explaining to him that Raavn was still at war with the humans, was at war with the Razorroots, and was in conflict with members of his race. The Inspector did not realize this gave the pirates legal authority to harvest Raavn and his clan.

Nirrav left the communicator believing his transaction with the humans was complete. He grazed for a while at the farm and then informed the King and his clan members of his successful negotiations with the humans.

*

The Inspector told Yvette about the agreement with the Gobato. She waited until Kyleen was not in the room, and then changed the telecast message to attract Raavn. *If I get an agreement with Raavn, circe will be a billion dollar business. I don't think the Gobato are a threat to Earth. They just want to find their Dream World, eat Razorroots, and push each other around. Once they are on Xanadu, they will never bother us again.*

Several hours later, while Nirrav was grazing, Vicar Oiie told Raavn, "Go to your ship, contact the humans, and demand justice."

An hour later, Yvette received a text message from Raavn and she asked, "Are you in your ship and are you alone?"

Raavn vibrated and his translator texted, "Yes."

The message appeared as an image at the back of Yvette's visual cortex. She used an image of a virtual keyboard in her C-chip to text back, "Wait while I switch to a narrow beam laser so no one listens in." A few minutes later, Yvette continued, "You have two goals. Find closure by executing Glenn, and find the Great Fern and a new purpose. Both are in the Dream World. I know where the Dream World is, and I can help you travel there."

Raavn felt relief to find a human who understood his dilemma. "You will give up one of your own?"

Yvette responded, "Glenn disobeyed his director's order to return to Earth. That makes him an enemy of the state." She thought to herself, *Glenn won't live the one-hundred and fifty years that it will take this alien to travel to Lonetree.*

Raavn shook, "A Gobato never disobeys an order from their superior, but I understand your agony since some of my clan abandoned me."

Yvette: "That is why you are free to apprehend him and punish him. I am sending you the warrant for his arrest signed by Kyleen."

Raavn: "Yes, it says he disobeyed a direct order. When I reach that planet, how will I find Glenn? Do you have some way to track him?"

Yvette: "Yes, and better. I can implant a device in you that will guide you, and enable you to communicate with him, and control him. We call it a hacking C-chip."

Raavn: "Again you amaze me. I want to see how this works on one of my subjects before you install it in me."

Yvette: "Choose one who knows our text language so they can serve as your translator. I want something from you in exchange."

Raavn: "I understand this now. You pukes, I mean, humans, give gifts and then you want something in return. You call this bargaining. What do you want in return?"

Yvette: "I want your permission to harvest the clan members who deserted you."

Raavn reeled for a moment in shock, and then regained himself. *Never in memory has anyone requested or agreed to something like this, but never has clan members deserted their leader.* "You don't seem to understand what you are asking."

Yvette responded, "I understand perfectly. That is why I am offering you so much in return. If you want more, ask."

Raavn: "I will not defend those who deserted me. Their behavior is so offensive they deserve the harshest punishments, therefore I agree. Here is what else I want: The location of your hidden base, five thousand tons of leaves, and replacement and refueling of the fusion cells for fifty of my spaceships."

Yvette: "OK. If that is all, then we have an agreement." *He asks for a lot, but the harvest of circe from the two hundred abandoned Pathfinders will pay for it and much more. Sending fifty Gobato to Xanadu will keep Glenn and Mac busy so they won't have time to chase pirates.*

Yvette assumed Truman could order a shipment of fuel cells, and they could send a few pirates down to Dearth to collect leaves from the farm when the Gobato were not looking. Such blatant stealing never occurred to a Gobato.

Raavn told Oiie about the deal, "*A hacking C-chip will enable me to control both humans and Razorroots, and make them lead me to Glenn, Ligeia, and Blackbark so I can execute them. All three killed Gobato. Then I will ask the Great Fern on Xanadu for a new purpose.*"

She answered, "I don't trust them. This must be a trick."

"They offer too much. I must take the chance."

The mechanics repaired the hatch Dillon warped and replaced the panels Gloria removed, which made both docking bays operational. When Truman entered the station,

Yvette explained to him her deal with Raavn, Kyleen, and the other pirates. "Once they are in space, they'll hibernate. I'll rig one of their ships to lag back and we'll send the pirates out in a starbeam to nab it. We'll take a Gobato and butcher it without having to fight it or the others."

He answered, "A lot can go wrong, especially when you deal with aliens. I will hold you responsible if this does not work. Do you have C-chips that can adapt to the Gobato?"

"Yes and anything else that's alive, even watermelons."

She exaggerates, but as long as they work on the Gobato, I do not care. Then Truman said, "I see two problems. First, I need to talk to Kylee and convince her to go along with this. It won't be easy. I'll have to give her a greater share."

"No you don't. I have a hacking C-chip that is so powerful that I am afraid to use it. It forces the target C-chip to remain on, and then it cuts right to the core. You can use it to hack Kyleen."

"All right. Give it to me and that will solve that problem."

"I'll set it up for you tonight." She hung her head and asked, "What is the other problem?"

"You don't know spaceships, and you thought fusion cells and fuel cells were the same, but hydrogen fusion reactors are a lot more powerful than hydrogen-combustion-fuel-cells. To make matters worse, the Gobato's hot fusion reactors are more powerful and compact than the cold fusion reactors in our ships. I think I can salvage this part of the agreement. Let's hope you did not overlook anything else."

"I see what you mean. Next time I'll tell you and we will plan it together."

Truman said, "Now keep Phillip out of our way while I correct these mistakes."

After she left, he aimed a laser-comm at Raavn's ship and explained. "The cold-fusion nuclear reactors we use for interstellar space travel are not as advanced as yours and they don't have direct-ion thrust, but we have mechanics who can copy your fusion cells. Give us a fusion cell from one of your ships, and we will make fifty duplicates."

Raavn removed a fusion unit from an unused ship and gave it to Truman who beamed it to Camelot. Then, Truman contacted Elroy on Stardust using the U-net and asked him to break it down and send the parts to the manufacturing plants on Gondwana to make fifty duplicates.

Elroy parceled out the parts to factory engineers on Gondwana, who were glad to play a role in developing this new technology. Then the factories sent the fabricated parts back to Stardust for final assembly and shipment back to Camelot. Of course, Elroy and the manufacturing plants continued to make and sell this alien technology, which became a profitable product. Truman made sure his name was on the patents, so he had rights to the royalties.

* Oxia, Domino (Morten Granau Remix) *

In the days that followed, Yvette prepared a Super C-chip for Raavn and two ordinary C-chips to test on his subjects. Elroy delivered the hot fusion cells. Then Yvette arranged for Raavn to come onboard the Space Station. With only fifty fusion cells, the rest of the Gobato were unable to leave unless they found other fuel supplies and rebuilt their fusion reactors.

On the final day, Raavn arrived while the Inspector slept. A monster this close made the humans uncomfortable. The pirates were still busy removing all indications of their earlier harvests, which might anger Raavn if he saw them. However, the station cleanup was not necessary because the Gobato did not fit through the small hatch leading from the docking bay.

The pirates held their dealings with Raavn in the docking bay, among the ships and with the random noise from crews installing the fusion cells. The Gobato tolerated the brief evacuation of air when the crews docked the next batch of ships. Yvette placed speakers on the floor in one corner of the room and used a computer to translate speech into vibrations that the Gobato could understand. She placed microphones on the floor for a computer to translate their vibrations into speech.

"Raavn," Yvette said into a microphone, "observe. I equipped two of your subjects with C-chips to prove they work properly. These two can talk to each other without vibrating, and they can access the C-net. I turned off the memory assist because your species has literal and vivid memories. I made a special C-chip for you that will control anyone with an inferior C-chip."

The Gobato arranged its eyespots so he could see the tiny chip that Yvette held in her hand. "Can I use this to locate and control Glenn Hunter?"

"Yes. All C-chips have locators and interactive maps."

"My subjects are satisfied with their C-chips. Implant the device you made for me," Raavn ordered.

After implanting a Super C-chip for Raavn, she spent an hour training him how to use it. She ignored the laws banning direct thought transfer and used the direct C-link to send and receive conscious thoughts to Raavn. Two people linked in this manner thought and acted as a single individual, which conveyed information and instruction much faster than using text or vibrating speakers. She taught the alien how to use the networks, and how to track and hack Glenn.

After explaining, Yvette took a short break and rested. Using the direct C-link, Raavn searched her brain and discovered something the humans disregarded, that a simple switch in their brains induced sleep. Yvette began to speak during her dreams when he pushed this switch part way. He recognized she was hypnotized so he interrogated her.

"Did you tell me everything?"

"No."

"What did you omit?"

"That Glenn traveled to Xanadu faster than the speed of light?"

"How did he do that?" The monster asked.

"He star-surfed from Stardust to Lonetree. Now he is teleporting in a ship from Lonetree to Xanadu."

"Is teleportation faster than the speed of light?"

Yvette answered in her sleep, "It is much faster."

"How long will it take?"

"You can arrive at Lonetree in a few weeks."

"I am amazed." Raavn asked, "Can you teleport my ships to Lonetree."

"Yes."

"How?"

"No one has done this with more than one ship, but your ships are small enough that I can put fifty in a starbeam-can and use a heavily loaded starbeam at Lonetree as ballast."

"You will teleport my clan and me. Do not let the other humans know we are teleporting." Raven ordered. *If I had this super C-chip before the battle, I would have forced Glenn to surrender.*

Under hypnosis, she told Raavn how to operate the teleporters. Then she gave Raavn the coordinates to Lonetree and Xanadu.

Later Truman hacked Yvette and Raven and discovered what happened by reading their history files. He told Yvette she was hacked. They planned, "We don't need the pirates or Kyleen to sell the circe since we have the promissory notes. We'll pretend to follow the original plan, but when the pirates leave, we will nab a Gobato on the planet. You and I will split the profit on Gondwana."

*

After equipping all the small ships, Yvette, Truman, Kyleen, and the pirates watched as the Gobato boarded the ships and appeared to leave. "By the time they reach Xanadu, our battle fleet will be in position and Raavn will surrender or be destroyed. We will leave tomorrow and nab one while they all hibernate." Kyleen commented, not aware of Truman and Yvette's plan.

Truman laughed, "Fools, yes fools. What fools you, I mean they are," as they walked to the restaurant in the viewing dome for a drink.

Kyleen and the pirates did not notice that Yvette placed a starbeam-can in the focus of the teleporter. Early morning the next day when everyone except Yvette and Truman were asleep, Raavn and his followers returned. They arranged their spaceships into a formation to fit inside the starbeam-can. The diameter of seven Gobato ships was smaller than the diameter of a single starbeam, but the length of seven Gobato ships was longer. The newest starbeam-cans could extend to fit forty-nine Gobato ships.

Raavn announced to his followers, "Our destiny is clear. We will travel to Xanadu, which is the Dream World. That lush environment will allow us to strengthen and increase many fold, and faster than the other clans. The Great Fern will inscribe in stone our new purpose."

Then he signaled Yvette.

Yvette pretended to be under a post-hypnotic instruction and enabled the teleporter. Unknown to the Gobato, she programmed the computer to beam Raavn and his followers back to their planet in the Pleiades instead of Lonetree. Teleporters block communication into and out of beam-cans during teleportation, so the Pathfinders were unaware she tricked them.

Yvette and Truman did not know that sending the Gobato on the teleporter would trigger the self-destruct.

*

Onboard Camelot, the pirates and Kyleen slept soundly while they dreamt how well they tricked the Gobato. Then the computer blasted a warning that vibrated the walls of the station, "Self-destruct initiated. The teleporter terminal is detaching, and it will self-destruct in one hour. Leave the teleporter terminal at once."

Frantic confusion was instantaneous, and the shock of awareness threw Kyleen out of her booth and onto the floor. Kyleen and the pirates stared at each other, stunned for what seemed like minutes, and then Kyleen got to her feet and shouted, "Without the teleporter terminal, we are stuck here. We have to stop the self-destruct, fast."

"She's right. Who wants to spend the next fifteen years in a spaceship returning to Stardust?" Reddragon said as they gathered themselves and started running to the helm.

Yvette and Truman were at the Helm trying to stop the self-destruct when the rest of the crew arrived.

At the computer on the Helm, Yvette pretended to discover, "Raavn tricked us and is trying to use the teleporter."

"Stop him," Kyleen demanded.

"I can't," Yvette answered. "The self destruct is blocking the remote receiver on the teleporter."

The computer announced, "Self-destruct in forty minutes."

"We have to stop them. Yvette, go to the terminal and reset the self destruct," Truman ordered.

"Not on your life. I won't go near that thing. Send someone in a skiff to the teleporter and I'll tell them what to do."

Kyleen ordered, "No. Blast him with a SAM. We cannot let the Gobato use this technology under any circumstances."

Truman answered, "Reddragon, restrain Kyleen until we sort this out."

Truman pointed his razor blaster at them, and the pirates backed away. "Audrey, you're an engineer. Get in the skiff."

Gerome (alias Audrey) reached the teleporter, and reported, "Teleporting the Gobato triggered the self-destruct and locked the controls. I think Raavn can reset it."

The computer announced, "Self-destruct in thirty minutes."

Truman ordered. "Contact him and tell him to delete that program."

Yvette whispered in Truman's ear, "If he deletes that program, then he will correct his coordinates."

Truman whispered back, "I won't be stranded here. We have to let him go. We have no other choice. Don't let the pirates see us whispering or they will know we caused this problem."

Audrey overrode the communication lockout and explained the problem to Raavn. Then he reported to Truman, "Raavn reprogrammed the computer. The Gobato are teleporting to Lonetree, and the controls are working, but I still can't clear the self-destruct. The computer wants a password for that."

"Does someone know this password?" Truman raged.

Yvette did not know the password. She was afraid that Truman would kill her for letting this happen and slipped out of the helm and into the hallway to look for a place to hide, but she heard Dillon and Gloria shouting through one of the air ducts. They yelled inside their room they knew the password, and begged to be set free.

Yvette could not tell which room they were in because the well-insulated walls and doors dampened the sound. She ran up and down the halls opening every door until she found them. She unlocked the door, and they joined her and raced to the helm.

Gloria said to Truman, "I know the password. Let us go, and I will tell it to you."

Truman tried to hack her C-chip but got an error message, so he said, "You will tell me if you want to live." He drew his razor-blaster and pointed it at her.

The computer announced, "Self-destruct in ten minutes."

"Then go ahead and shoot," Gloria dared him, "and live the rest of your life here."

Her sass angered Truman, so he shook her. She scratched his face so he slapped her so hard she fell to the floor.

He turned to the pirates. "I will use deadly force against anyone who does not recognize my authority."

The pirates cringed, remembering his vicious temper.

As she lay bleeding, the circe Gloria took earlier was still active and healed her quickly.

Truman saw she recovered and said, "Tell me the password or I'll shoot Dillon."

"You'll shoot us anyway," she muttered, wiping the blood from her face, "so the hell with you."

Adrenalin mixing with the circe made Gloria feel invincible and sharpened her mind. She opened a concealed vile containing milkweed sap she took earlier from an agroponics unit. Women in the out-world often carry something to discourage unfriendly attention. She sipped some sap into her mouth and dipped her fingernails and toenails into the rest. These were the sharp diamond extenders from Wanda's weapons pouch and not ordinary nails. A thin wire ran between each set of five with an electric charge between them. This small charge caused pain and paralysis when the nails rip through the skin of an enemy. She regained her feet with no one but Dillon helping her.

* Aerosmith, Janie's Got A Gun *

Yvette moved to the back of the room. She noticed, Truman *is* oblivious to the danger he *faces*. He did not eat circe, *but Gloria did. Her eyes changed color.*

Gloria removed her cape, and performed her cobra dance. The viper's tail started at her ankle, wrapped several times around her body, and over her shoulder becoming the entire arm. It extended down her forearm into a remarkable hood that appeared larger than her hand and became five snakeheads that appeared to extend well beyond her fingertips. The holographic tattoo seemed to slither and move by itself with Gloria appearing to be in the background.

The display hypnotized the pirates. They thought she released a horrible and huge snake hidden in her garment, so they backed away, all except for Truman. The exhibition thrilled Dillon, who enjoyed the snake.

As the pirates watched in amazement, she placed herself, so the hologram reflected the best light. She moved like a snake preparing to strike. With a hiss, she spat the tainted water into their terrified eyes as she threw her hand forward. The pirates jerked backward as the snake appeared to strike and spit venom at them, burning their eyes.

All except for Truman, who was unafraid and said, "I call your bluff."

The computer announced, "Self-destruct in five minutes."

In a single motion, she ripped Truman's face with a cobra strike and whipped around to slash him again with her diamond edged toenails. The throng of razor cuts with the burn of the milkweed sap and electric charge forced Truman to back away in pain, bleeding profusely. At last, he was aware he faced a killing machine.

Dillon silently moved behind them and grabbed the razor-blaster as Truman fled from Gloria's slashing claws. Dillon held the razor-blaster on them and asked, "Now that being trapped here is not your only worry, would you like to bargain?"

The computer announced, "Self destruct in three minutes."

While Truman recovered, Yvette stood in front of him to prevent Gloria from dispatching him. She asked Gloria, "Hold back and I'll talk to him."

Yvette said to Truman and the pirates, "We are sitting on a fortune, and you could lose it all by bickering. Who wants to spend the next fifteen years traveling back to Stardust in a rinky-dink transporter? Let me handle this or we might never get out of here."

The computer announced, "Self-destruct in two minutes."

The crowd of pirates wanted to see the end of the fight, but was afraid of being stranded, so agreed with Yvette. "We want to be wealthy, not dead."

Truman partly recovered and grumbled, "All right, Yvette, you handle it."

Yvette dabbed the blood off Gloria's face with a napkin and said softly, "You have my word I will see you safely on your way. Now give me the password or we will all be stuck here."

She nodded and said, "Dillon, too, and our case of circe, we want that back."

The computer announced, "Self-destruct in one minute."

Yvette looked at Truman and said, "Do you approve?"

The pirates moved closer to Truman and said, "We can get plenty of circe. Give them what they want."

Truman nodded "Yes," so Yvette said to Gloria, "You have a deal." She picked up the case of circe, handed it to her. "I am keeping my side of the bargain, so now I need the password."

Gloria and Dillon agreed, and the snake disappeared. She was still angry, so she whispered the password so softly no one heard it.

The computer announced, "Self-destruct in twenty seconds."

Yvette said, "Please repeat that so we can hear it."

Gloria shouted the password in a blaring voice, an alien voice that vibrated the walls.

The intercom linking to the terminal was on, so Gerome keyed the password into the teleporter but did not hit "enter". He asked, "What do I get if I stop the self-destruct?"

The computer announced, "Self-destruct in ten seconds."

Yvette said, "Audrey, what do you mean what do you get? You get to live another day like the rest of us."

The computer announced, "Nine."

"Yes, but Truman killed the previous flight engineers, and he threatened to kill me if I did not do exactly as you asked. Now, I want free passage out of here, one bucket of diamonds, and I want everyone to call me Gerome and not Audrey. Gerome is my real name."

The computer announced, "Eight, seven."

Yvette looked at Truman and the pirates as if she did not care anymore, "What do you want me to do?"

The computer announced, "Six, five, four."

Truman said, "What the hell. I approve the deal. Now end this."

Yvette handed Dillon a bucket of diamonds and announced, "Truman approves, and Dillon has your bucket. Gerome, stop the countdown for the sake of our survival."

The computer announced, "Three."

"Dillon, do you confirm that?" Gerome asked.

The computer announced, "Two, one."

The tension confused Dillon, and then he blurted, "Yes, yes Gerome, yes."

The computer announced, "Self-destruct aborted."

Gloria marched out of the room with her circe and Dillon in arm. She brushed by Truman on her opposite side so hard she almost knocked him to the floor.

One of the pirates said, "Red blood means red meat."

The pirates formed a tight circle around Truman.

Yvette said, "Twenty pounds of red meat are in ice locker 1-22."

As they left the room, one of the pirates said, "Why didn't you tell us sooner?"

Yvette told Truman, "Big D loved me before he took circe and hated me after he took it. It turned him into a zombie. But you don't love anyone so you might as well take it. You might not be able to control the pirates without it. When they saw you bleed, they drooled."

"Get out of here and leave me alone," He shouted.

She looked back as she left the room and saw Truman take a piece of circe out of his pocket and toss it in his mouth. She continued to peep through a crack behind the door. After some time, Truman's bleeding stopped and he started to heal. Then he licked up the blood he lost, stepped into a booth, and requested shower and clothes. Disgusted, Yvette went to the helm.

*

From the helm, Yvette watched the teleporter terminal re-dock with the Space Station.

Dillon handed Gerome his bucket of diamonds.

Yvette asked Gerome, "Why did you hesitate to reset the self-destruct?"

He answered, "I was going to blow them up but I lost my nerve. Did you know several nuclear blast caps are missing? Raavn must have them. What did we unleash onto humanity?"

"Humans will learn to adapt," She said.

Dillon space-walked to their ship and landed it in the docking bay. After Gloria and Gerome boarded, he taxied it into a starbeam-can, and waited for the computer to position them for teleportation. They wanted to beam before Truman changed his mind. Yvette gave the approval, so they were on their way to Stardust.

After the starbeam cleared the teleporter, Yvette told Phillip that Truman locked Kyleen in a room. They went there, released her, and told her what happened.

Kyleen faced the wall, lowered her head to hide her tears, and murmured, "I killed Glenn. *If Earth finds out the Gobato used the teleporter and they have nuclear weapons, I'll be a fugitive.*" Then she launched a SAM to destroy the weapons Glenn left behind. Nobody noticed, not even the Gobato.

Dillon, Gloria, and Gerome arrived on Stardust late at night while Elroy, and Flint were asleep. They bribed a beamer to keep quiet and teleport them to the Gondwana teleporter terminal, and they disappeared from there. This unstoppable team presented a new danger to Earth.

Chapter 27: The Final Conflict

* David Gilmour / Mica Paris, I Put a Spell On You *

Back on Camelot, the Emerald Pirates planned another harvest of circe. Yvette kept the Inspector tranquilized. Every time the pirates hacked his C-chip, he suffered a headache. Not understanding the cause, he believed that the pirates were helping him when they pretended to sympathize, gave him strong painkillers, and advised him to sleep to feel better. The pirates kept changing the clocks, so the Inspector thought he was working too hard, and sleeping too little while the opposite was true.

Truman ordered the pirates, "Everyone report to the observation deck. Search the planet for Gobato deserters. We will harvest more circe."

"Circe!" they all shouted as they found a group of aliens at the abandoned mine below the station. The Pathfinders were easy to identify because Flint peppered them with ID chips during the battle.

"Look for one that is large."

Reddragon said, "Here is one that is huge, and he is on the outskirts, where the other Gobato cannot see him. They won't know we nabbed him until much later."

Truman said. "Get the coordinates and everyone go to the teleporter terminal."

The advanced experimental teleporter had the capacity to beam single ended, without a lens at the other end. Yvette was the only technician on Camelot who knew how to operate it in that manner. As she sat at the controls, Truman noticed she was smiling. *This excitement must have put her in a happy mood.*

Truman ordered the pirates, "Put the carcass from our earlier harvest on the teleporter platform as replacement ballast. This exchange will confuse the Gobato considerably." The pirates laughed at that thought.

On Dearth, Elmurr felt the beam and froze, not understanding what it was. Still, Yvette could not force the transfer. "We need more ballast. Add ten more bags of sand. Keep it moving, we need more bags. Hurry before he moves out of the beam."

After they balanced the ballast, the abduction was successful. However, that was not the end of their problems but the beginning.

Reddragon dogged and shouted, "How do we control this thing. It is madder than a loose gyro-rotor."

"Be careful. Don't get under its feet," Yvette advised. "And don't shoot it with a RA-gun or you'll destroy the marrow."

Truman ordered, "Bind it with a blaster, and then butcher it with a laser cutter."

Ten razor-blasters went off at once but had no effect except to set the alien webbing on fire and tangle its tube-feet. The alien stepped out of the razor wire and flung itself in every direction, denting the walls, and trying to crush the pirates.

The pirates were slipping and falling on alien slime, and in danger of losing control of this massive creature.

While the pirates tried to figure out how to disable the monster, Yvette rolled her eyes as she asked Truman and Kyleen, "Give me ten percent of the profit, and I will control him before he punctures the wall, and asphyxiates all of us."

Truman, not wanting to bargain, announced loudly, "Now, Yvette, you don't get a commission unless you sell something. If you want more, then embezzle the banks when we return to Gondwana."

The pirates did not want another partner, and agreed with Truman. "Cooperate or we will turn the alien loose on you."

"I only ask once. Now you are doomed," she answered.

Truman rolled his eyes to mock her and answered, "Right idea, wrong person. Now cooperate or I'll turn this monster at you."

She believed that the pirates blamed her because Raavn hijacked the teleporter. She did not trust zombies, so she used speakers and microphones to vibrate the floor to talk to the abducted Gobato.

Truman wanted Yvette to beg for protection so he ran in front of the alien, then ran at her, and then dogged out of the way.

As the monster approached her, the speakers vibrated. "These people want to harm me just as they want to harm you. My name is Yvette. Agree to help me, and I will make them stop."

"My name is Elmurr. What kind of help do you want?"

"I want you to fly me to the Dream World in your ship."

"The Dream World? Yes, of course," The alien answered. "Follow my orders and I will protect you and subdue the aggressors."

Elmurr answered, "I don't like taking orders from a human, but I will suffer this humiliation in order to find the Dream World."

*

The pirates attacked the alien with two laser cutters.

Yvette warned Elmurr, "Those weapons can kill you. Protect yourself behind that platform, and I will do the rest."

She used her Ultra-Super C-chip to hack the pirates and force all of them to fall asleep.

She told Elmurr, "Stand down, the danger has passed. The bodies are not dead, so do not trample them. After a few days, their C-chips will reset, and they will wake up. You and I will leave long before that."

Elmurr obeyed. "That is a relief. I don't want their blood and puke to contaminate my feet."

She installed a C-chip in Elmurr for communication, and then she explained her plan to him. He agreed, and she beamed him down to the planet to return with his ship.

* Ram Jam, Black Betty *

Then Yvette contacted her son in the Beehive. "Ugo, how is my young man?"

He hesitated from emotion, and then answered, "Doing well, Mom. Why didn't you call sooner?"

"I was in jail, but now I am free. To stay free, I need your help," she sighed.

"Anything, just ask."

She asked, "Have you heard about the new aliens on Dearth?"

"Of course. Everyone is talking about them. They are very dangerous, so stay away from them."

"Not so dangerous. I made friends with one of them. He has a ship, and he will transport me out of here. Can we take refuge in the Beehive?"

"Oh, yes, of course. This boggles my mind. Is he shy? Can I call the news networks?"

"He is not shy at all. Prepare for our arrival and send me some credits for the teleporters."

"I can leverage what you need out of the general fund, but you will have to pay me right back, or I will go to jail," Ugo warned.

"I can pay you if we can sell his spaceship. An alien spaceship should be worth a bundle. And I have some C-chips that Empire cannot hack. We will have plenty of credits after I sell those."

"I'll find some buyers and arrange an auction for the spaceship. What about that zombie-virus they carry," He asked.

"You'll be safe. You can't catch that virus unless you eat circe. I need to contact your father. I'll talk to you later, bye."

"Bye for now."

Then she contacted Sid. "How's the Computer King?"

"Missed you a lot. When are you coming home?"

"I'm on my way. How much of the computer can you allocate for me?"

"As much as you want if you furnish new cheat codes. An artificial entity took control of our computer and I cannot fix it because someone stole our old codes," He explained.

"I'll write some new codes while on my way there. I made friends with an alien, a Gobato, and he has memories dating back fifteen thousand years. If you can simulate his Dream World, then you can use his memories."

He answered, "The Bees covet ancient memories and alien memories. Send me his information and I will be ready when you get here."

"I already downloaded his memory using the direct C-link."

"What! You gave a C-chip to a hostile alien. Don't you know how dangerous that is? Are you crazy?"

She stated, "Don't get technical when I ask for your help. Remember, I don't do that to you."

"Okay. Send me his file. I hope you are right about this."

*

When Elmurr returned with his ship, Yvette directed him to the agroponics unit to collect plants for their trip. He left to collect vegetation.

While he was away, she studied his ship, found more information on the alien's computer, and sent it to Sid. She noticed something the Inspector missed; the Gobato ships had Higgs modulators. Their devices did more than improve the efficiency of ion engines. They expanded space inside their ships to carry more cargo, and condensed the outer shell of their ships to make them stronger and smaller.

When Elmurr returned, they refueled his ship with an extra fusion cell that Truman ordered for Raavn.

* Tom Petty, Learning To Fly *

Yvette went to Phillip's room; he was asleep. She changed the time on his C-chip and said, "Does my little Phillie want to wake up? It's morning."

"Oh Yvee, I thought you were just here."

"I was, but now I'm back. We are leaving so put on your clothes. You are so young and so strong. I will help you dress..."

Elmurr boarded his ship with his weapons and supplies along with Yvette with her cache of diamonds and emeralds, and the Inspector with the oxygen, water, and food.

Phillip asked Yvette, "Should we take Kyleen?"

Yvette answered, "No, this mess with aliens and zombies is her doing. She needs to stay here and take responsibility for it. Come with me and help me set the self-destruct on the teleporter. After we leave, the teleporter will detach from the space station, drop into a low orbit, and explode. The debris will burn up they fall into the planet. these pirate-zombies cannot wreak havoc on the human race, if they don't have the teleporter."

After Yvette and Phillip set the self-destruct, they boarded Emurr's ship. Elmurr maneuvered his ship into a starbeam-can. When they reached Gondwana, they discovered that workers retrofitted the teleporter link to Sirius to beam starbeams. The Inspector used his authority to overrule all restrictions. Neither might, nor right, nor pirates could stop these three.

When they reached the Beehive, Yvette explained the dilemma on Dearth to the Bees, and the Bees accepted Elmurr as their honorable guest. Tourists flocked in to see this huge and unusual alien. Elmurr enjoyed putting on a show, and juggling and tossing his zingers. Yvette made a fortune selling her special C-chips to the tourists.

The manufacturing plants on the Beehive replicated the starship, which became a lucrative product. The Bees gave Yvette half-a-million credits for delivering the alien and his starship, more than enough to pay Ugo's loan.

The Bees let Elmurr graze in one of their agroponics units. Later the Bees introduced him to their virtual world. Their virtual rendition of the Dream World included a great fern.

Elmurr offered his memories and his knowledge of the Pleiades. The Bees were delighted to discover that Elmurr carried vast, detailed, and vivid ancestral memories. With this information, Yvette brought virtual life to his ancestors. The alien thanked her, "*This is the Dream World the ancients wrote about.*"

Elmurr asked the Bees to improve their virtual world by adding tactile sensations and vibrations. This enabled him to identify his surroundings and communicate more naturally. After they added these features, they discovered that some humans who had unusual tactile sensitivity also benefited from this improvement.

Elmurr texted a message to his clan on Dearth to join him. He concluded by saying, "Fear not to explore space for there you will find your reward."

Chapter 28: Xanadu

Rush, Xanadu

Xanadu is the only habitable planet in the Rasalhague system. An ocean covers most of its surface. A thick matt of plant growth resembling sargassum floats on this ocean. Razorroots live on the sargassum. Their long roots extend down to extract water from the ocean and their leaves face up to absorb sunlight for energy.

A small continent surrounded by islands stretches from the equator into northern latitudes. These land masses support fern forests. Alien plants grow on the edges of deserts where conditions do not favor ferns. Purgatory is an outpost located on a high plateau on the northern end of the continent.

A storm on Xanadu isolated Mac from every form of transportation and communication except for his insta-text chip connection to Ligeia.

*

Glenn, Ligeia, and Splinter arrived at Lonetree, a space station with a transporter terminal in orbit around Xanadu. Glenn ejected the beam-can and studied the space station through the pod's viewport. It was like Camelot except for its shape: it was an irregular design with a main trunk, and with branch-like extensions attached randomly along the length of the trunk, thus resembling a tree. The branches provided balance so the assembly could rotate around its trunk to produce artificial gravity. The docking bay was located at one end of the trunk.

From its usual population of two thousand, fewer than two hundred spacers were still there because Kyleen ordered all Empire Corporation officials and most of the support staff to return to Earth. Only a skeleton staff stayed.

Glenn said, "No one is at the teleporter terminal. I will have to dock the pod manually."

"Can you do that?" Ligeia asked.

"I have no formal training, and my landings are a little rough."

Splinter said, "Let me dock the pod."

Ligeia reminded Glenn, "Razorroots are good pilots."

Glenn changed places with Splinter, who landed the pod on the docking bay floor without damage. After the pressure equalized, Splinter led them to the vending machines to find breathers. Splinter breathed carbon dioxide and did not need a breather but paid for breathers for Glenn and Ligeia.

After they were able to breathe, Ligeia returned the funds paid by Splinter, who was rocking in anticipation.

Glenn and Ligeia cleaned, ate, and rested in a comfort booth large enough for two. Splinter found a viewing bay and basked in the light of Rasalhague. After they had rested and regrouped, Glenn asked, "I can smell a brewery, and the water tastes like beer. Is there a beer brewery nearby?"

Ligeia answered, "No. The station smells this way because there are no moths, flies, or grasshoppers to eat the dead grasses and grains. The only thing that breaks them down after they die and pile up in the hydroponic units is natural fermentation. Then the water and alcohol condense and flow into the cisterns."

Glenn took several large gulps of water and said, "Not bad."

"Yeah. Make yourself at home," she said as she refilled her cup with the sparkling liquid.

Glenn linked his C-chip to her chip to communicate with Mac. "Ligeia, Splint, and I are on Lonetree. Are you all right?"

Mac insta-texted through Ligeia to Glenn: "Glad to hear you made it here. The Green Team and I are not injured or in danger, but we are marooned. Here are the coordinates of our base, Purgatory. There are ten of us on the Green Team.

"Our launch platform will be operational if you bring us lighter than air cables and helium. I must return to Lonetree with my research results. In fact, all of us need to get off this planet and away from the Great Ferns. The Great Ferns are not benign trees. They are a highly superior race. They may not tolerate our presents much longer."

Glenn told Mac what he knew about Kyleen, Truman, and the Emerald Pirates. Mac contacted Earth to clear legal action against Glenn and start legal action against Kyleen, but Earth officials could not take action because his signal link through Ligeia's cube was unverifiable. Glenn would remain listed as a deserter and as a fugitive until Mac returned to Lonetree made an official report on a registered teletype terminal.

However, Earth officials instructed the local police not to arrest Glenn. Then they instructed the support and rescue workers to return to Lonetree, but this would take weeks because Earth was a long way away.

Glenn sold his video of Mars to earn enough credits to hire an expedition to rescue Mac. The crew loaded a lighter than air transporter with the materials and supplies that Mac requested, and launched for the planet. By picking up small iron asteroids in orbit, they added weight until the transporter was slightly heavier than air enabling them to land on Xanadu using almost no energy.

They landed near Purgatory and found the Green Team. While the crew unloaded the transporter and made repairs, Glenn, Ligeia, and Splinter located Mac who explained to them, "We are in good shape except for being isolated for so long. The Great Ferns want to kill us. Did you bring the tissue samples I requested?"

Glenn gave Mac the samples. Mac prepared them, placed samples in the bio-simulator, and said, "Exactly what I expected. The Great Ferns gave Blackbark viruses and prions. The viruses infected the Gobato and the prions alter human proteins. The bio-simulator indicates the viruses change Gobato isoforms, making them edible for humans. That is why the pirates can digest circe. The prions make humans crave meat.

"If these prions reach Earth, they will infect everything living. Authorities on Earth distributed prion detectors and shut down the teleporters except for official use, but it is too late. Doctors have detected prions in widely separated populations all over Earth."

Ligeia asked, "How can the prions spread if people on Earth don't eat circe or each other?"

"Mosquitoes, mites, flies, ticks, and other bugs bite humans and spread the disease. Gondwana does not have these pests," Mac answered.

Mac adjusted a microscope, "Look at this slide I prepared earlier of a soil sample from Xanadu."

Glenn said, "I see viruses."

"These viruses do not target us, they target the Gobato. The Great Ferns used them to drive the Gobato off this planet. Compare those viruses to this segment of human DNA."

"It has the same viruses."

"Before they left Earth and came here, the Great Ferns used genetic warfare to keep animals from eating them. They released a virus that killed the dinosaurs and infected the DNA of our earliest ancestors. It passed from one generation to the next to the present. It makes us weak, slow to heal, and ages us. Glenn, did you get a swab with Flint's DNA?"

"Yes, here."

Mac took a swab, placed it under a microscope, and said, "This is serious. Take a look."

Glenn looked and said, "Prions infect him. Does Flint have mad-cow-disease?"

"No, much worse. Those are alien prions. The bio-simulator shows they are gradually replacing his human proteins. Prions infect Flint because he ate a piece of circe from the Gobato."

Ligeia looked in the microscope when Glenn stepped away. "Are the prions turning Flint into a Zombie?" She asked.

"The bio-simulator needs more time to tell us what will happen, but it won't be good," Mac answered.

Ligeia stepped away from the microscope and hid her face.

Mac stood before them with a sample kit. "Glenn, let me get a sample of DNA from your foot where that alien burned you." Mac prepared the sample and studied it under the microscope. "Your sample is free of prions. That means they infect only when circe is ingested. That is what I expected."

He took a piece of circe mixed it with Great Fern spores found in the soil and studied the mix under the microscope. "The viruses I added are coming to life. If the Gobato come here, those viruses will multiply and kill them."

*

As Splinter was leaving, Mac said, "Splint, you also are a GMO. The Great Ferns have modified your genes."

Splinter asked, "How can they do that? Razorroots don't have genes."

"When the Great Ferns arrived here from Earth fifty million years ago, two species indigenous to this planet attacked them. Look at these fossils. The Gobato and the Razorroots were the dominate species seventy million years ago. The Gobato lived in forests and the Razorroots lived on sargassum that covered the sea so they lived in peace, and there were no ferns. However, fifty million years ago we see fossils of the Great Ferns but no fossils of Razorroots or Gobato. Many other species of carnivorous plants and large echinoderms disappeared at the same time."

"What happened to them?" Splinter asked.

"The Great Ferns released spores to poison herbivores, but that was not enough, so they produced iso-spores that performed specific tasks. The iso-spores gave the Razorroots and the Gobato genes that the Great Ferns could modify. The Ferns changed those genes to give the Razorroots a sweet aroma and flavor, which was irresistible to the Gobato.

"The Razorroots fragrance drew the Gobato out of the forests and onto the sargassum as the Great Ferns expected. The Gobato almost annihilated the Razorroots except for a few who hid in deserts.

"The Gobato flourished, and became the greater threat, so the Great Ferns had to do something more desperate, more diabolical. They released a deadly virus to infect large echinoderms, mainly the Gobato. This biological warfare killed all of them except for a few million Gobato who fled in spaceships to a planet in the Pleiades.

"After the Gobato left, the Razorroots recovered and flourished. The Great Ferns modified your genes again to turn you into their docile servants. A Great Fern selected you to do its chores. You are its slave."

Splinter said, "I find this hard to understand. I will ask my master for a better explanation."

Mac demanded, "I know who your master is. Tell that fern to give us a cure or I will release crown rots and root rots that will kill all of them. Earth knows what they did, so if I am killed, Earth will rot them out."

Splinter left and disappeared into the forest. It discovered a large gathering of Razorroots camped near Mac's shelter. They were curious about what the humans were doing. Splinter told them what Mac said. They were very angry with the Great Ferns. They scattered to tell the other Razorroots.

Splinter continued its journey to find Pandora, its master.

After Glenn and Ligeia left to help with repairs, the logistics sergeant reported to Mac, "Our radar detects bogies near Lonetree. The bogies are too small and too many to be starbeams, and too big to be pods. We think they are Gobato spaceships."

"That cannot be," Mac said. "I told Glenn to set the self-destruct on Camelot to prevent a massive invasion like this. Tell Glenn to report to me now."

*

Forty-nine Gobato spaceships invaded Lonetree. Twenty police tried to gain control of the invasion, but the Gobato killed two. The rest retreated when they discovered their weapons were not lethal to the aliens. Raavn ordered one ship with one Gobato to stay at the teleporter terminal, and prevent anyone or anything from using it. He led the rest of the ships into a low orbit around Xanadu. Then he ordered thirteen ships to land on the planet with him and left Ziven in charge of the ships that stayed in orbit.

Shortly later, the Great Ferns and Razorroots observed fireballs ripping through their atmosphere and landing with a sonic boom followed by a crash on the high plateau near Purgatory. The Razorroots knew the ships belonged to the Gobato, ran for the forests, and asked the Great Ferns for safety. The Great Ferns told them to attack, but the Razorroots knew better and hid deeper in the forests.

Raavn and those with him stepped out of their ships and worshiped the ground of their legendary Dream World. "I see many Great Ferns here. Which one will assign us a new purpose?" Vicar Oiie asked.

Raavn stood. "We will destroy Glenn and his followers first. My C-chip shows Glenn is a few miles away. We will charge and crush him and those with him before they have time to attack us or to hide."

*

While the Green Team and the rescue crew were repairing the launch platform and Mac's transporter, they saw the fireballs. Glenn ordered a watch, and shortly later one of the Green Team scouts reported to Glenn, "I see a platoon of Gobato, and they are marching this way. They have weapons. They will be here in half an hour. Also, Mac wants to talk to you, immediately."

Glenn went to Mac. "How did the Gobato get here?" Mac asked. "I thought you secured Camelot."

"The self-destruct on Camelot must have failed, and the Inspector did not block them. The pirates must have tortured him to gain his cooperation. Dillon can hack our best C-chips. I wonder if he has a mind-probe."

"This is a serious dereliction of your duties."

His new C-chip warned him that Mac tried to hack him, so he answered, "Is it as serious as you hacking my C-chip when you forced me to abandon my daughter on Earth and accept this mission?"

"The capabilities of Empire's C-chips are a top secret. I can't talk about that. You have a bootleg C-chip. Where did you get it?"

"I can't talk about that."

"Touché, let's salvage what we can," Mac said. "The transporter is functional. Get everyone onboard and we will retreat."

They went to the transporter and the pilot answered, "We cannot escape. My radar detects many Gobato ships right above us. We cannot break through them."

Glenn asked him, "Do you have a disruptor?"

No. All the disruptors are on Stardust and Camelot.

Glenn said to Mac. "What weapons do you have?"

"We have five laser cutters, a pile driver, a bulldozer, six surveillance drones, ten gallons of strong acids, and fifty sticks of dynamite, but you will not need them. The Gobato are not the real threat."

Glenn asked, ""We'll have to dig in. How secure is your shelter?"

"Very, and the Gobato are too big to fit through the hatches. Our shelter will protect us until the Great Ferns subdue the Gobato."

"Everyone to the shelter, and bring the weapons in case we need them. Also, bring the lab equipment."

As the Gobato approached the shelter, they passed through a strip of forest between the savanna and the plateau. The Great Ferns in the forest released the same infectious viruses that weakened the Gobato ancestors many millennia earlier. The viruses had a strange effect on their memories. Raavn remembered events that occurred before the fifteen thousand year darkness. He searched his memories and remembered the Great Ferns invaded, fought and defeated the Gobato. A few million of his ancestors fled to save their lives. Those were a mere shadow of their original numbers.

Raavn asked Vicar Oiie, "Is your veil of darkness lifted?"

"Yes, I remember everything but I feel weakened."

"Fortunately, Vermn and his vicars are not here because they would never accept that our Great Plaque mislead us to trust the Great Ferns who are hostile and dangerous."

"Vermn is responsible for all those that he purged, those who spoke the truth." Oiie stated, "Now he must stay isolated and be forgotten. Our path is a trial, but if we endure, we will be remembered."

When Raavn reached the shelter, he texted Glenn using his C-chip, "Why do you hide when you can fight me? I'll kill you and you will have closure for your memories. There is no satisfaction in hiding forever."

Glenn pointed to his head and told everyone inside, "My C-chip indicates the aliens scanned us, and now they are trying to hack us. Turn off your C-chips."

He looked out a secure window and texted back using a teletype, "You are wasting your time. I will never surrender to you or any Gobato. Viruses from the Great Ferns afflict you, which explains your insatiable hunger for Razorroots."

Raavn saw Glenn in the window and sent his text to the teletype, "You are the strange ones. You attacked me and now you won't let me have closure. I brought a nuclear blast cap. If you don't surrender, I will call for it. Your shelter is no defense against it."

"This is VP Mackley." Mac stood in the window next to Glenn, "Under my orders, none of us are coming out."

Mac turned to Glenn and asked, "The Gobato have our nuclear weapons, they can text, they can hack, and they can teleport. What else can they do?"

Glenn shook his head. "I am as disappointed about this as you are. The Emerald Pirates overwhelmed our troops on Camelot. They must have allied with the Gobato and given them all of our technology."

"That is not reassuring."

* Queen, Who Wants To Live Forever, (Highlander) *

Outside the compound, Raavn turned to Oiie and ordered, "Call for a ship with a nuclear blast cap to land."

"If you kill all of them, then we will not have leverage, and they will not have closure," she shook.

Raavn lowered his trunk. "We don't need leverage against these puny tubes of puke, and they don't care if they don't have closure."

"We are safer if we bargain, because they occupy Lonetree, and we do not know what weapons they have."

"I will order seven of our ships in orbit to reconnoiter Lonetree, and find out if those humans are a threat," He answered. "Hand me the laser-comm."

"The laser-comm does not work. The atmosphere blocks the signal. If you want to send a message, you will have to dispatch a ship."

"Then take your ship into orbit and convey my order."

"Have you noticed our party is weakening?" She wobbled as she spoke, "We are so sick, none of us can pilot a ship. You were wise to commit only a few of your entourage to land on this planet until we prove it safe."

Raavn shook in disbelief, but the effort weakened him enough that he staggered. "Vicar, how serious is this?"

"This illness is serious enough to drive our ancestors off this planet. I think we are in trouble. If we die like this, our memories will turn to dust; we will not have closure."

"How can I end this battle?"

"Walk away because an unjust battle does not offer closure. VP Mac outranks a Director Kyleen. Glenn is loyal; he obeys the orders of his VP."

"The depth of Kyleen's wickedness defies understanding." He leaned back on his rear foot, "I feel tainted by her lies. Vicar, do not tell the others she tricked us."

"You have my silence."

Raavn vibrated the ground to order his platoon, "Get away from the human shelter, and follow my slime trail. We will return to our ships. Carry your weapons as far as you can. If any of us falls, that is where we will borrow. None of us will be left alone."

The difficulty of following this simple order surprised the Gobato warriors. Raavn took the direct path to their ships and not the best path. He climbed over rocky outcrops and went through areas of dry sand that absorbed his slime trail. They almost made it to their ships when one of them fell, and could not recover. They borrowed together to shelter themselves.

*

The Great Ferns ordered the Razorroots to attack the Gobato. "Look, the Gobato are weakened. You can destroy them. Act fast."

However, the Razorroots were angry from what Splinter told them. The Ferns were unable to refute Mac's accusations, so the Razorroots refused to attack the Gobato. Instead, they attacked the Great Ferns.

Splinter went to Pandora and asked, "Why did your ancestors cause the Gobato to attack us, why did you exterminate the Gobato, and why did you subjugate us?"

The great tree vibrated, leaves rustled, and the ground shook. Splint backed away. Then Pandora spoke, "Knowledge brings such a burden to your small mind. Do you really want to know?"

Splinter said without hesitation, "Yes."

"Our ancestors fled Earth when plankton consumed the carbon dioxide we breathe. They took refuge here. That first generation was desperate and foolish. We have evolved since then, and we know the wrongs they did, but now we pay for their sins. Do not accuse us or punish us. Call off your attack and we will make amends."

"How will you do that?"

"We will give you inoculations to cure the diseases our ancestors unleashed on you."

"And what about the humans, and what about the Gobato?"

"We will give you inoculations to cure them also."

"Then you admit you infected the humans?"

"Yes, before we left Earth we infected all animal life to keep them from consuming us. Our viral spores killed all but a few species. We eliminated the dinosaurs, which were veracious, and forced the whales to retreat into the oceans. Humans age and are weak because they carry those spores in their genes. These inoculations will cure them."

Splinter returned to where the other Razorroots gathered earlier, and repeated Pandora's message.

"Splint, how should we respond to this?"

"We will try the inoculations. If they are true, then we will tell the humans. If they are not true, then we will resume our attack until every Fern leaves our planet."

"What about the Gobato?"

"If they survive, the inoculations will cure their appetite and restore their ability to digest their natural foods. Then they won't go onto the sargassum and attack us."

The Razorroots agreed to give the Great Ferns a chance to show their good will. Splinter returned to Pandora and asked for the inoculations.

Pandora said, "The Green Team has the equipment to prepare and administer the inoculations. Their technique is faster than relying on airborne pollen. I covered the leaves near my roots with anti-iso-spores for your specie, anti-viruses for the Gobato, and anti-viruses and anti-prions for the humans. Take them to Mac. The humans have a translator. I am relaying instructions to them as we speak."

Mac recorded the inoculation procedures from Pandora and assigned the Green Team to prepare them when Splinter arrived. After the bio-simulator proved the inoculations were safe, the Green Team inoculated the rescuers and themselves. In a short time, they felt younger and stronger. Glenn noticed that the pain in his joints was gone, his many scars disappeared after a few days, and he could stand and walk under a full G of gravity. Mac, the oldest, became as robust as a thirty-year-old.

Splinter took its inoculations to the gathering of Razorroots. They lost their fern fragrance, no longer produced nectar on their leaves, and became more vigorous.

The clouds cleared above Xanadu for an hour; enough time for Mac to text message and explain the situation on Xanadu to Ziven. He reassured the alien the inoculations would immunize the Gobato against the spores, and heal Raavn and his platoon.

*

Mac met with Glenn and Ligeia. "You must leave the Rasalhague system or the Gobato will not negotiate. Ziven agreed to let you leave. You can retire, but I need you on Camelot. I will give you the details if you accept this new assignment."

Glenn and Ligeia accepted since this assignment would send them close to Gondwana, where they wanted to raise a family.

Mac explained, "In the last communiqué we received from Phillip, he warned us that zombies have control of Camelot and Stardust, and that bands of zombies roam Gondwana and terrorize the colonists. Your new assignment is to find out if these are the ramblings of a madman or is the threat real.

"In any event, Empire is not taking any chances; the sale, purchase, transportation, and possession of circe is illegal starting today. I promoted Madeline to replace Phillip as Inspector General. She and her volunteers will make the arrests with your supervision. Go there, interrupt the harvest and sale of circe, make arrests, and demote Phillip.

"Earth decided that the Gobato do not pose a serious threat as long as we don't consume them, so do not destroy the teleporter terminals. Also, Blackbark is on Dearth and claims the Razorroots own that planet and the Gobato must leave. If Madeline cannot sort this problem out, find Blackbark, and ask it what it wants. It may be happy if we rescue it and send it to Gondwana or Xanadu.

Mac continued, "I never liked Empire's decision that upper managers have the right to hack C-chips. Three months ago, I was wrong for hacking you and sending you to Camelot, so I will try to make things right. I'll pardon you for not completing your mission, and for starting a war. I talked to Marty Cleaver. He will not press charges against you for killing three of his men, and he won't testify that you killed a Razorroot if we grant him immunity, citizenship, ownership of the name Flint Valance, and command of Camelot. It seems appropriate since he held that position previously. He will be glad to learn that the doctors on Gondwana treated Audrey and she is alive. However, they put her in a pit jail because of her earlier convection. Here is a pardon so Flint can free her.

"Keep Flint and Audrey out of trouble until they choose to be civilized. You may need help, so I am assigning your daughter to Camelot. She applied for space cadet school, and she passed all of her preliminary tests. She will complete her studies while on Camelot and eventually be the director of Camelot. Her enthusiasm is impressive. She clearly follows her, ahem, grandfather's good example."

Glenn was awestruck. He would see his daughter again but under the authority of Empire. He noticed his text messages to his daughter were no longer blocked. He texted a warning, "…Tell Empire 'no' and stay on Earth…" because he did not want his daughter in danger.

"How do we stop the alien infection?"

"My staff built several prion detectors. Do you still have your prion detector?"

Glenn nodded.

Mac continued, "Quarantine everyone infected with alien prions. Take our inoculations, replicate them and cure everyone on Stardust, Gondwana, and Camelot. It is late, and I am hungry so let's eat unless you have something to add."

"No, I think that covers it."

*

While the humans were eating, Splinter went to Pandora and reported, "I have completed my mission. Read my memory spores for the information I gathered."

Pandora answered, "As I suspected, the humans do not have time-travel. This wealth of information will help us, but we need more before we can understand human behavior. Glenn will return to Camelot. Stay with him and continue gathering information. When you see Blackbark, tell him not to revolt until we know more."

Splinter lowered its branches. "I will do as you ask. This assignment will enable me to tend to the saplings I planted on Gondwana."

"Take some of my saplings with you and plant them in good soil."

"Yes master."

When it returned, Glenn, Ligeia, and Mac were on the lighter than air platform preparing to leave. Splinter asked Glenn and Ligeia, "Can I go with you?"

They both answered, "Yes, of course. We are a team."

The Green Team docked the transporter on the platform after loading it with the inoculations and samples. They all climbed onto the platform, and unloaded rocks and dumped ballast until it lifted into the upper atmosphere. Numerous small crawling plants broke pieces off the iron-rich rocks and carried them to nourish the Great Ferns.

As the platform lifted, it reached an altitude where the air was breathable, cool, and clear. Glenn and Ligeia stood in the basking sunlight with the rich green planet below them and the dark green sky above them.

Ligeia's ring flashed in the light. Through the battle and everything that followed, she never took it off. The diamond was a future telling stone so Glenn and Ligeia adjusted their C-chips to magnify the interior of the stone to see their futures. Their futures held many challenges and accomplishments, but that was not their main concern. They saw that they would live happily on Gondwana and have many children. Flint will remain in good standing with Empire and Glenn will accept him as his brother.

They asked Mac to marry them with Splinter as the witness. People on Earth watched the wedding of Glenn and Ligeia on the U-net, which turned into a celebration on Earth.

The network news reported how Glenn, Ligeia, and Splinter arrived on Xanadu, rescued Mac, and ended the war with the Gobato. Ligeia was the longstanding poster-child for teleporters, so the public greeted this news of her with enthusiasm. Couples adopted Razorroots and treated them as one of their family. The news that the Great Ferns were intelligent added to this enthusiasm.

* Madonna 02, I'll Remember *

Mac located an official teletype on Lonetree and used it to validate the warrants, pardons, and promotions. He transferred a document to Glenn. "Here is a warrant to arrest the pirate John Silverthorne for impersonating Major and Governor Truman Striker and another warrant because he attempted to murder Audrey Tylor. We have two witnesses who will testify against Truman, rather John Silverthorne. One witness is Yvette, who wants a pardon for her prior crimes and amnesty for her involvement. The other witness is Elroy, who is a government agent and is a friend of Audrey."

"This envelope contains a pardon and amnesty for Yvette, and a warrant to arrest Kyleen for illegal use of government resources. Here are the warrants for all the Emerald Pirates."

While there, he typed the pardons for Glenn, unfroze his accounts, and reinstated Glenn with a promotion and a bonus for rescuing him. Then Mac warned Glenn, "Sidney Pascal agreed to drop charges against you for assault and battery when we agreed to stop investigating your accident when you teleported to Stardust. Clearly he is guilty of something but avoid him if you go back to the Beehive."

Mac pardoned Ligeia and the troops for abandoning their posts, and he pardoned Ligeia for aiding the pirates and interfering with a space marshal because she did not act knowingly or willingly. Ligeia received an accreditation for rescuing Flint and his men on Dearth. He accredited Gloria for saving Glenn on Dearth. Splint and Flint received accreditations for rescuing Ligeia. Ligeia and Splinter received accreditations for helping Glenn rescue Mac. Mac granted Mariah ownership of the name Ligeia Bell, gave her the title of space marshal, and gave her and Flint an accreditation for saving the troops who were on a trip to nowhere. Delphi received four accreditations for saving Glenn.

Advisory Space Marshal Glenn promoted Splinter to assistant space marshal.

Mac took Glenn aside, and told him, "I erased the video file of you killing a Razorroot. Now, Kyleen cannot use it against you."

"Thanks. That had me worried."

Mac advised, "Teleport to Stardust before the Gobato change their mind."

On the way to the teleporter, Glenn asked Mac, "After we leave, what are your plans? Will you retire?"

"Not even close. After we have a peace agreement with the Gobato, the Green Team will inoculate all those here who are infected. Then I will go to Earth with the inoculations. While on Earth, I will arrest Dillon, who is a pirate. He kidnapped Gloria, so I will set her free. However, I will quarantine them if alien prions infect them."

Glenn did not tell Mac that Dillon and Gloria were partners. "Good luck with that."

"Then I will send the inoculations to the Beehive, and all points between Earth and Gondwana."

After Glenn, Ligeia, and Splint left for Gondwana, Mac contacted Ziven. Ziven went to Lonetree, received an inoculation, and found no harm in it, so he agreed to let Mac go to the planet and rescue the distressed Gobato.

Mac arrived onboard a transporter, and Ziven flew his ship. Thirty minutes of heat and humidity on Xanadu taxed human endurance, so Mac often returned to the transporter to cool.

They negotiated with Raavn. By this time, the Gobato were critically ill. Raavn spoke slowly from weakness, and agreed not to attack the humans, Razorroots, or Great Ferns if Mac rescued them.

Then, Mac inoculated Oiie. In an hour, she improved and supported her weight. Oiie verified the inoculations were safe and beneficial and Raavn approved. He knew he needed to accept human hospitality as his condition worsened.

I will not follow Glenn, Raavn decided, *but let him escape, and return to Dearth, and battle with Kyleen. Glenn will not offer teleportation to the Gobato on Dearth so they will travel at less than the speed of light. By the time they reach here, my offspring will increase a thousand fold. I will permit only those who accept me as king to land on this planet. They cannot oppose me because they cannot increase their numbers on Dearth, and they will be weak from travel when they arrive here.*

I know my purpose not from an ancient stone, but from my own memory and awareness. I will carve a new stone for those who are less clever so they will have direction.

*

Mac read the conditions of peace. Raavn kept his composure, agreed, and commanded Mac to administer the inoculations so not to appear to beg. Mac understood the need for a chief to appear to be in charge to keep control of his followers and to maintain their moral, so he responded as ordered and without argument.

The clan members recovered from the spores after a few days. They did not hunger for ferns because the inoculations restored their isoforms. Now they preferred to eat their natural foods, which were much more nourishing to them and satisfied their hunger.

The Razorroots and Great Ferns would share the planet with the Gobato only if they passed a test after they received their inoculations. They had to walk through a forest of ferns and Razorroots without eating a single leaf or root and then graze on their natural foliage. Raavn completed the test first without difficulty. The other Gobato performed the test with equal success.

Raavn ordered Oiie, "Return to Dearth, and do not allow Vermn and those loyal to him to come here. Subvert their efforts whenever you can, and do not let them learn the truth."

"You speak wisely. If they discover the truth, they will not survive the guilt of performing the purges. But what about the dissidents?" Oiie asked.

"Encourage the dissidents to come here because this planet will offer everything they expect. Xanadu is their refuge and their home."

Oiie answered, "I will leave as soon as I spawn. Will you assist me?"

"Yes, follow me. I know the location of a cool brook."

*

Mac and the Green Team prepared inoculations for all humans and planned their return to Earth to treat the afflicted.

Epilogue:

Fifteen years later, Truman and his pirates arrived with their third harvest. They sent a crewmember named Thunderbolt down to the stardust spaceport to find out if it was safe for them to land. Flint recognized Thunderbolt, followed him, and recorded the teleporter coordinates after he returned to the Starhawk.

Thunderbolt reported that the mercenaries were there and Stardust was not safe for them. Truman activated the stealth on his ship so he would not be detected, then he called the pirates to meet in the cafeteria to determine how to bypass Stardust and sell their circe to other colonies. As he waited for the pirates to assemble, Truman enjoyed his favorite drink and talked to the waiter.

The waiter said, "Did you hear; Flint is looking for you."

"I had him locked up. Who let him out?"

"Elroy, Glenn, Ligeia, it's hard to say. Didn't you know that Elroy is an agent of Empire?"

"He'll pay for that." Truman exclaimed.

"How are you going to make him pay when Flint is searching for you? He wants to settle a score because you killed Audrey. They were close friends."

"He can settle his score with this." Truman placed his hand on his razor-blaster.

The waiter shook his head and went back to cleaning the counter.

Half of the pirates were in the room when Flint entered. Both men instantly drew their razor-blasters. The pirates ducked behind counters or laid flat on the floor.

Flint fired. The blast knocked Truman's razor-blaster out of his hand, set him and half of the room on fire, and broke every fixture that was not metal.

Truman kicked a table to block the razor wire as he rolled to extinguish the fire that was burning him. In the same motion and with his opposite hand, he launched a diamond stiletto hidden in his forearm. The stiletto struck deep into Flint's chest. Flint dropped his weapon but recovered, withdrew the stiletto, and threw it back at Truman. Truman deflected the blade with his diamond-threaded gloves.

A survival algorithm in Truman's C-chip took control of him, sending him out the door, down the hall, and around a corner in less than a blink of the eye. Flint recovered his balance, leaped for his razor-blaster, and started to charge after him, but not before Truman used the C-net and his C-chip to target Flint and fire an RA-gun from an adjacent room. A blast smashed through the wall and struck Flint in the head. He fell lifeless to the floor.

Truman returned to the cafeteria and dragged the body to an airlock, not aware it was an avatar. The body started to recover and fought Truman as he shoved it through the hatch.

"How much circe did this dummy eat?" Truman cursed as he hit the override that opened the outer hatch door.

The vacuum instantly ripped the avatar through the hatch, and tore the inner hatch door out of Truman's hand with enough force to throw him across the room. Truman returned and looked out the hatch window at the flailing body drifting helplessly away in the vacuum surrounding the spaceship.

After he returned to the bar, Thunderbolt told him, "Flint claimed he was immortal. Do you think he meant it? Do you think he will be back for more?"

Truman took a long slow swallow from his drink and answered, "No one is immortal no matter how much circe they eat."

"You should track him down and make sure."

"How can I do that? The Starhawk is too big for precision maneuvering."

The waiter cut in, "You can use a Gobato spaceship. I bought one that, ah Elroy, ah modified so a human can pilot it. You need it more than me so I'll trade it for a pound of circe. It'll be an excellent dinghy for your Starhawk."

Truman gave him a hard look, and then asked, "What weapons does it have?"

"The direct fusion engine produces more heat than the center of a star, but don't push it to full throttle. It can produce 200 G, which will crush a human pilot."

"Doesn't their Higgs field modulator reduce the G force?"

"It only reduces the force by one-half. Full thrust is still enough to crush a football fullback."

The waiter took Truman to the docking bay, and explained the controls in the alien ship. Truman purchased the ship and launched it to find the avatar thinking it was Flint.

As Truman approached the body, he noticed it was moving; grabbing space garbage and throwing it to propel itself to larger pieces of garbage. Eventually, it would have enough garbage to propel itself back to the Starhawk.

Truman rotated the alien ship to align the engine exhaust to the floating body. He set the thrust to 20 G's, checked the radar for range and set the timer to one second, then activated the autopilot. The slam was much harder than Truman expected. Fortunately, his crash-seat and the Higgs field modulator absorbed most of the shock.

Direct fusion ignited the avatar reducing it into molecules, reduced the molecules into atoms, and reduced the atoms into sub-atomic particles. The body became a blinding flash of light and x-rays.

Truman returned to the Starhawk, went to the bar, and bragged about his success.

Later that evening, the waiter texted a message to Elroy explaining what happened. Elroy went to a room hidden at the far end of the Stardust Spaceport, told Flint the news, and sold him another avatar.

As Flint planned for his next assault, Elroy warned, "I'll replace its collagen with diamond fiber. That will stop a stiletto, but I don't think an avatar can kill Truman even with that advantage."

Flint answered, "I know, but I will use it to learn Truman's dirty tricks. Then I will confront him pirate to pirate."   End.